When a Heart Finds WOW!

Brenda Hill

iUniverse, Inc.
Bloomington

WHEN A HEART FINDS WOW!

iUniverse books may be ordered through booksellers or by contacting:

iUniverse
1663 Liberty Drive
Bloomington, IN 47403
www.iuniverse.com
1-800-Authors (1-800-288-4677)

ISBN: 978-1-4759-2932-4 (sc)
ISBN: 978-1-4759-2934-8 (hc)
ISBN: 978-1-4759-2933-1 (ebk)

Printed in the United States of America

iUniverse rev. date: 06/19/2012

Dedication

I would like to dedicate this book to my late sister, Janice (Jane) Smith. I know she is in Heaven, looking down and saying, "I told you so."

Thank You

First of all, I thank God for my gift of writing. I thank Rich for delivering me the message to write my first novel and I thank Donald for his point of view. A very special thanks to my Mom, Shirley Taylor; my children, Donnell, Nicole and Justine; my brothers, Charles and Michael; my close friend, Deborah, and others who have always supported me.

1

Janice

Janice proudly said to the receptionist, "Hello, I'm here to see Mr. Perry. My name is Mrs. Perry." The young woman sitting behind the oversized glass receptionist desk showed no sense of urgency to assist Janice and continued to read *American Lawyer*.

Again, Janice proudly said, "I'm here to see Mr. Perry. My name is Mrs. Perry."

Without looking up from her magazine, the young woman boldly responded, "The only Mrs. Perry I knew was Marvin's mother."

Immediately, Janice said, "Excuse me, what did you just say?"

The young woman soon sat up straight and redirected her attention from the magazine to Janice, the Mrs. Perry who undoubtedly was not Marvin's mother. She looked at Janice from head to toe and took in her shoulder length hair, down to her five-inch aqua-blue Stilettos. Jokingly, the young woman answered, "Uh, I didn't know Marvin was married."

Janice placed her left hand on the desk, leaned over until she was eye level with the woman. "I don't see anything funny and I definitely don't feel like playing games with a woman who obviously didn't look in the mirror before she left the house this morning."

The young woman uncrossed her long legs and tugged at her tiny blue skirt. She popped her gum twice and slowly asked, "What do you want?"

"Now that you know Marvin has a wife, will you please page my husband?"

Before the woman picked up the phone to begin her page, she rolled her eyes at Janice and mumbled, "Yes ma'am right away ma'am." Loudly, she paged, "Mr. Perry, please come to the front desk. Your *wife* is here to see you."

The woman slammed down the phone and pointed her finger in the direction of the reception area. Janice didn't move. The woman stood up and put one hand on her left hip. "Have a seat. Your *husband* will be right out."

Janice replied, with a curt "Thank you," and sat down on the white leather sofa.

As she looked around the law office, she wrinkled up her nose at the three armless chairs with different colored stripes along the side of the wall. A large sign above the chairs read, *Franklin and Franklin. In any case, your new start is near.*

Janice turned towards the receptionist desk and stared at the woman's nameplate, "Paula Morgan." Under her breath she said, "Here we go again. Judging by Miss Paula's performance, she has fallen into one of Marvin's presentations of life."

Janice stood up and walked over to the receptionist desk. "So Paula, how long have you been working here as a receptionist?"

"Oh girl, please, I ain't no Paula and I absolutely ain't no receptionist. I'm just sitting here while Paula is copying my case files for an important client of mine. My *name* is Linda Franklin, Attorney-at-Law, thank you very much."

Janice held back a laugh and thought who does she defend, all of the non-talking people of America? "Oh, I'm sorry Linda. I just assumed since . . ."

"Now, Mrs. Perry, you know what happens when you assume."

Before Janice could respond, Paula, the real receptionist, appeared nervously holding several sheets of paper. Linda snatched her case files out of Paula's hands and yelled, "It's about time!"

Paula looked as if she was about to cry. She looked at Janice and asked, "Can I help you?"

"Yes, will you please page my husband, Mr. Perry?"

"Who do you want to page?"

"Marvin Perry."

Linda threw her case files on the desk. A few sheets fell to the floor. She looked directly at Janice and shouted, "I'll go get him before you have a baby."

As she turned the corner in her six-inch canary yellow platform pumps, Linda swung her long light brown hair.

It was Janice's turn to take in Linda from head to toe as she left to find Marvin. Janice thought they must have loose dress codes for attorneys or just loose attorneys. Under her breath she said, "Marvin is definitely messing around with that woman. I can tell by her funky attitude."

Janice dialed Marvin's number, but the call went straight to his voicemail. She couldn't believe how Marvin kept her waiting. She was furious that he forced her into a cat fight with who she believed to be his latest conquest.

Five minutes later, Linda returned. She stood in front of Janice with her arms folded across her chest. "Marvin wanted me to tell you he's running late and will meet you downstairs in 10 minutes."

Through clinched teeth, Janice said, "Thank you and have a nice day." Janice took the elevator down to the lobby and pushed her way through the revolving doors that led out to Wilson Boulevard. The sweat wasted no time before it made its way down the sides of Janice's face. She didn't know if it was because of the June mid-day heat or she was just overheated from recent events. Once Janice reached her jet black BMW X3 that was parked a block away in front of the Arlington Mall, she smiled and said, "TGIF."

Determined to only give Marvin the 10 minutes he stated and not a minute more, she counted down the minutes. When she glanced in her side mirror, she noticed a tall slim woman on the side of the 4203 building. Janice was certain it was Linda because of the bright yellow blouse and short blue skirt.

She stretched her neck to see what Linda was doing, but only caught glimpses of her arms wildly flapping in the air. Seconds later, Janice saw Marvin dart out from the building and bend down as if he picked up something. "What the hell?"

Janice stretched her neck even further with her eyes intently on Marvin. She could see the back of his curly head and his hands shoved into the pockets of his tan tailor made jacket. It almost killed her to watch the two of them together and not hear what was said.

Several minutes later, Linda walked back into Janice's full view. She held out her hand. Marvin moved to the right, out of Janice's sight and pulled Linda with him. Janice hit the stirring wheel. "I can't see a damn thing."

Janice started her engine and put her truck in reverse. With her new parking spot, she could clearly see both of them. Marvin walked away from Linda and began to cross the street. Linda ran after him. When

Marvin ran to the other side of Wilson Boulevard, she stopped in front of the building.

Janice continued to watch how Linda kept her eyes on Marvin even after he got into her SUV. She couldn't help but think that there was something going on between Linda and her husband.

Marvin reached over to give Janice a kiss on the cheek. Angrily, she pulled away from him. Marvin let out a huge sigh and leaned back in his seat.

"Sweetheart, don't act like that. I'm sorry I kept you waiting so long."

"Marvin!"

"Janice, let's go. I'm starving."

Janice didn't say another word. In her rear view mirror, she could see Linda still standing in front of the building. *She is watching this truck like a lovesick teenager.* When Linda went back into the building, Janice said, "Finally."

At the stop light, Janice turned to look at Marvin. "Who is Linda Franklin?"

Marvin looked straight ahead and ignored Janice's question.

Janice asked again, but this time, she raised her voice, "Who is Linda Franklin?" The more Janice said the name, the more she asked herself where she had heard that name before.

Marvin looked out the window and replied, "I don't know. Who is she?"

"Marvin, don't play stupid with me. She's the young attorney, light complexion, long light brown hair with nails so long she looks like she has trouble wiping her ass."

"That's not Linda, that's uh, I don't even remember her name, but I know it's not Linda." Marvin laughed.

Janice gave Marvin a disapproving look. Marvin cleared his throat. "Her name is Beverly Frank."

"Whatever Marvin. What were you and Beverly Frank doing on the side of the building?"

"Janice, I don't know what you're talking about. I left my meeting and came directly out the front of 4203 Wilson Boulevard to meet my beautiful wife for lunch."

"I saw you Marvin. Why are you lying?"

"I don't know who you saw sweetheart, but it wasn't me."

Janice learned a long time ago to pick and choose her battles, especially with Marvin. From experience, she knew it was just too exhausting to fight him on every lie that came out of his mouth.

"Marvin, one of these days, all of your lies will catch up with your lying ass."

"Janice, I don't want to hear your bitching today. Let's go eat and get it over with. I have another meeting in two hours."

"You know what Marvin, let's not eat. I seem to have lost my appetite."

"Come on sweetheart, stop acting like that. I'm sorry I was late. You know you are the only one for me. Besides, I'm hungry and I left my wallet in the office."

"What else is new Marvin?"

2

Paul

Desiree screamed into Paul's ear, "I can't believe you haven't left yet and what's taking you so damn long? Rehearsal was supposed to start at six o'clock sharp. Everyone is waiting for you."

"Hello darling."

"Don't you darling me. Get your late ass over to the church right now."

"I'll see you later Desiree," Paul said to the dial tone that hummed in his ear.

Paul jumped to his feet. His black leather chair spun around a number of times before it knocked several sheets of his Schaefer Contract onto the floor and nicked the corner of his mahogany credenza. "After 17 years of marriage, that got damn woman still don't know how to talk to me."

Paul raised his chair over his head and looked 10 stories down. He slammed the chair on the mixed gray carpet and slid it over to his desk. "Shit, with my luck, I might end of killing some damn body. That's all Desiree want is for me to go to jail so she can spend all my damn money. If it wasn't for Cynthia, she would see my ass much later."

Paul took out his frustration on the burgundy and gray wall. Desiree and Cynthia's pictures fell to the floor. "Vivian!"

With her note pad held tightly in her masculine hands, Paul's assistant ran into his executive office. "Yes, Mr. Davis."

"Vivian, I'm leaving now. On your way out, make sure you drop off this Fed Ex package."

"Off to rehearsal Mr. Davis?"

"Yes, my little Cynthia is getting married tomorrow. Sometimes, I can't believe my baby girl is even old enough to get married."

Paul touched the gray hairs around his chin. He leaned his six-foot frame up against the wall next to his confidential file cabinet.

Vivian laughed, touched Paul on his shoulder and looked into his grayish eyes. "Oh, Mr. Davis, you're only 49 and if I say so myself, you are most definitely still a babe magnet."

Paul kept his back to the wall. He thought, "She has got to get in at least one flirt a day. Standing in my face smelling like she just ate a whole onion dipped in sour milk. On my drunkest night, I wouldn't tap that."

Paul put on his poker face and conducted himself as the shrewd businessman and stickler for rules he was and politely said, "Thank you Vivian. Will I see you tomorrow?"

"I wouldn't miss it for the world Mr. Davis."

Paul looked at his Cartier. He knew at any moment, his phone will ring and Desiree will scream her head off again about the time. Like clockwork, Desiree called.

When Paul turned onto Watkins Park Drive, he saw two Rolls Royce Limousines parked in front of the mega church. He parked his glacier white Bentley behind a red Ford F-150 Pickup Truck. Paul reached into his glove compartment and pulled out a silver flask filled to the top with Grey Goose Vodka. He took two big gulps and placed the flask back into its hiding place.

Paul popped a few Altoids into his mouth. He swiftly walked across the parking lot and up the stairs to the side entrance of the church. Immediately, he spotted Desiree hunched over in a corner.

Seconds later, Paul's phone vibrated in his pocket. He deliberately ignored Desiree's call and looked at the bridesmaids carry multiple bags of silk white bows to the center of the aisle. Paul frowned at the never ending fresh white roses, white calla lilies, white tulips, and baby's breaths arranged in small bouquets. He shook his head at the white tulle swags that connected them to the left sides of the numerous rows of theatre seats.

Paul looked around at his family members and others he didn't know until he found Cynthia. "There you are Baby Girl. I'm sorry I'm late. You know how work can be."

Cynthia hugged her father. "Oh Daddy, you're always late. Promise me you won't be late tomorrow."

"I promise."

When Desiree turned around, she saw Paul hug their daughter. She yelled across the pulpit, "Rehearsal is over," and gave Paul the evil eye. Everyone but Paul stopped what they were doing and stared at Desiree.

Paul disregarded Desiree's angry outburst and continued to greet his family. "Hey Chester, what's been going on?"

"Just adding up all of your money Little Brother. I see Desiree spared no expense."

"Did you expect anything less?"

"Nope." Chester laughed. "Hey Paul, who's the Popeye looking guy over there hugging your wife?"

Paul turned around. "I don't know. It's the first time I've seen him. Maybe he's one of Cynthia's future in-laws."

"Mighty chummy I see."

"I'll be right back Chester."

Just as Paul made his way over to Desiree, the mystery man left Desiree's side. "Desiree, who was that Popeye looking MF?"

Desiree smiled and brought her voice down to a whisper. "Paul, don't start your shit in church. He's nobody."

"Well, does nobody have a name?"

"I'm sure he does, but I don't know it. Ask somebody else."

"So, you just let nobody and anybody feel up on you?"

"Paul, don't start with me. You're the one that was late. If you had brought your ass here when I told you to, you would know who he is."

After a few moments of silence, Desiree finally answered, "His name is uh, Frank Beverly, one of Brian's family members. Are you happy now?"

"Why didn't you just say that at first?"

"Because, when you come off with that jealous, accusatory tone of yours, I don't like it. Now, if you will excuse me, the rehearsal dinner is behind schedule. I have to get these people over to the Gaylord."

Paul covered his face with his large left hand. "One of these days Desiree."

Chester put his hand on Paul's shoulder. "Little Brother, don't even sweat that. You know Desiree is a huge flirt."

"Yeah, I know that Chester. I also know she's done a lot more than flirt. I just haven't been able to prove it yet."

"So, did you find out who Popeye was?"

"Frank Beverly. He's Brian's cousin or something."

Chester looked at Paul and started to laugh. "You mean Maze Frankie Beverly?"

Paul had a puzzled look on his face. "No, I said Frank Beverly."

"Little Brother, I think Desiree just pulled a fast one on you."

"That lying bitch!"

"Calm down Paul. We're still in church. I'm sorry. I was just messing with you. Maybe his name is Frank Beverly, but I doubt it."

Chester continued to laugh as he sang the words, "*Before I let go.*"

Paul smiled at Chester and showed him his balled up fist. "Let's go eat. I'll meet you at the hotel."

"I'm right behind you Little Brother."

Paul saw his future son-in-law at the altar.

Brian waved. "Hey Mr. Davis."

"Hello Brian. You better be good to my baby girl or you'll have me to deal with."

"Yes sir. Mr. Davis, I want to thank you for paying for all of this."

"Well Son, you should be thanking Mrs. Davis. By the way, have you seen her?"

"Yeah, she's with Cynthia. I believe they're on their way to the hotel."

"Hmm. Brian, do you have a family member here by the name of Frank Beverly?"

Brian looked up into the high cathedral ceiling. After a couple of minutes, he smiled and asked, "Like Maze Frankie Beverly?"

Paul thought if it wasn't for Brian marrying his daughter tomorrow, he would wipe that silly grin right off of his face.

As if Brian read Paul's mind, he removed his smile. "Mr. Davis, what does Frank Beverly look like?"

"Dark complexion, real buff and has a bald head. He was wearing a too small gray shirt and black trousers."

"Sorry sir. Don't sound like any family member of mine, but I did see a guy that looked just like that get into the limo with Cynthia and her Mom."

Paul took his keys out of his pocket. "Brian, we better get over to the hotel. Do you have a ride?"

"Yes sir. Me and the guys have a limo too."

"Okay Brian. See you at the hotel."

As Paul walked away, he said, "Shit, this wedding is costing me a fortune. Where is my damn limo? As usual, nobody thinks about me except when it involves spending my damn money. Desiree, one of these days, all of your lies will catch up with your lying ass."

3

Janice

Janice hid behind the P.F. Chang menu. Marvin's phone rang three times, but he did not answer. Under her breath, she said, "If that damn phone rings one more time."

Janice put down her menu. "Marvin, are you going to answer that damn phone?"

"For what? It's just business and I'm on my lunch break. Besides, this is my time with my favorite lady."

Janice looked at Marvin repeatedly check his Rolex and look behind his back. "Marvin, is everything okay?"

"Yeah, why do you ask?"

"You just seem a little antsy, that's all."

"No, I'm just hungry and I'm looking for the server. I told you, I need to get back. I have another meeting."

"Yes, you told me. It's in two hours."

"Janice, you don't have to keep repeating every damn thing I tell you. Do you think I'm lying or something?"

"Are you?"

"Am I what?"

"Lying?"

"Here we go. What do you think I'm lying about now?"

"Oh, everything and nothing," Janice mumbled.

"Janice, if you have something to say, just say it."

Janice looked down in her lap. When she looked up, Marvin was looking at the door. Janice followed Marvin's gaze. "Well, what do you know? There's Beverly Frank."

Marvin asked, a weak "Who?"

"You know, Beverly Frank from your office."

"Yeah."

"Marvin, we should ask her to join us."

Marvin drank his water. "Janice, I don't have time for your shit. As a matter of fact, I need to get this food to go. I just remembered I have to tighten up my presentation before my meeting."

Janice stood up and started to walk towards Linda.

"Janice, where are you going?"

"I'm going to invite Beverly Frank to join us."

"Janice, wait. I have to tell you something."

Janice sat down and gave Marvin her full attention. Out the corner of her eye, she could see Linda watching them. Marvin reached for Janice's hand. "I lied about Beverly, I mean Linda."

"Is that right?"

"Her name is not Beverly Frank, it's Linda Franklin."

"Go on Marvin."

"I didn't want to put a damper on things so I lied about her name. Lately, we've been getting along so good. Linda is my buddy's friend. Before you and me got back together, she hooked me up with this job. Janice, I gotta be nice to her. I'm sorry I lied to you. Will you forgive me?"

"Okay Marvin, tell me this. If that's the case, what's up with her funky attitude? When I came to your office, she had the *nerve* to tell me there was only one Mrs. Perry and that was your mother."

"Janice, Linda always has a funky attitude. That's why my boy has so many problems with her. I promise you Janice, there is nothing going on between us. I am a happily married man."

Marvin waved his one and a half-carat platinum wedding band in front of Janice's face. "There is no one for me, but you. I love you sweetheart and only you."

Janice looked at Marvin drink his Heineken and thought he is as handsome as he is intelligent. He can charm his way into any woman's heart, underwear, and bank account. Everything he said could be true. Janice hated when Marvin gave her plausible answers. He wasn't always honest with her, but she hoped this wasn't one of his infamous presentations of life.

Janice could never stay mad at Marvin for long. "I love you too baby." She kissed Marvin on the lips and all was good again.

4

Paul

Just as Paul pulled up to the luxurious Gaylord Hotel, he saw Cynthia and the bridesmaids get out of the limo. The valet attendant waited for Paul to get out of his Bentley, but with his eyes firmly on the limo in front of him, he remained behind the wheel.

After a few moments, the driver closed the door to the limo. "I guess Brian didn't know what he was talking about after all." Paul reached in his glove compartment. He was about to take another drink when Chester tapped on his window. "Hey, what are you doing in there? The party is inside."

"Chester, stop smudging my damn window and get in. You know what I'm doing."

Chester laughed, went around to the passenger side and got in. "What are you doing out here? Like I said, the party is inside. Let's go eat and drink up all your money."

"Ha, Ha, very funny. I'm drinking now."

"Yeah, I can see that. You really need to cut back on that stuff Little Brother."

"I will, tomorrow."

Chester chuckled. "Did you ask Brian about Frank Beverly?"

Paul took a sip out of his flask. "You know I did. Brian said he's not a family member, but he did see him get into the limo with Desiree and Cynthia."

Paul saw Cynthia walk towards the limo. She tapped on the limo window. The window came down and after a few moments, the window went back up. Seconds later, the driver opened the door and Desiree stepped out. Paul threw the flask up to his head. He looked at Chester, but said nothing.

"Man, put that down and let's go inside."

"All right Chester, I'm going to take one more drink. What the hell?" Paul's flask almost fell out of his hand when he saw Frank Beverly get out of the limo and walk into the hotel.

Paul and Chester looked at one another. Paul shouted, "I'm going to kill the bitch!"

Chester threw up his hands. "Don't you do anything stupid. When Desiree is out of your sight, she is as wild as a tiger with a toothache and as phony as a three dollar bill. All Desiree wants is to spend your money and live like the rich and famous. For the life of me, I can't understand why you can't see it."

Paul shook his head and again, said nothing.

"She is a master at pushing your buttons. She does it every chance she gets and tonight is no different. This is Cynthia's night. Whatever is going on, you can deal with it after the wedding."

Paul drank the last of his vodka. "Chester, I'm cool. Let's go inside."

"Look at me. You're not cool. Remember what I told you Little Brother. Don't do anything stupid."

Paul and Chester went inside the Gaylord. The guests were busy mingling and eating lobster bisque, shrimp and crab imperial. Desiree was telling the event manager what to do, when to do it and how to do it. Cynthia and Brian were looking into each other's eyes oblivious to anyone else or anything that was about to transpire around them. Paul and Chester searched, but saw no signs of Frank Beverly.

Reluctantly, Paul sat down next to Desiree. She pretended not to see him and continued her conversation. Paul whispered into her ear, "Desiree, I need to speak to you right now."

"Not now Paul."

Paul squeezed Desiree's knee under the table. For a second time, Desiree gave Paul the evil eye. She got up from the table, walked to the center of the room and grabbed the microphone. "Attention please, may I have everyone's attention? Thank you. I have a special treat for my precious Cynthia and her groom to be."

Desiree turned towards her daughter. "Cynthia Darling, I hope you will be as happy as your father and I have been for the last 17 years." Desiree smiled and looked at Paul. "I take that back." She turned back to Cynthia and said, "I hope you will be even happier as you and Brian start your new lives together. To set the tone for this evening, I'd like to introduce to you all a very, very special guest, the fabulous Mr. B.F. Beverly."

The muscular mystery man Paul was so eager to find was now in front of him singing Anthony Hamilton's "Because I Love You." Paul caught Chester's eye from across the room. He nodded and raised his glass. Chester also nodded and raised his glass.

Desiree came back to the table and sat down next to Paul. "How do you like me now?"

"I'm sorry." Paul gave Desiree a gentle squeeze on her knee.

"You should be. Enjoy the food and the music. After all darling, it's all on you."

"Don't I know it?" Paul leaned over and kissed Desiree on her cheek.

Desiree sipped her Champaign and gave Paul a mischievous smirk.

"I told Cynthia I would stay here at the hotel tonight and tie up some loose ends. I will see *you* tomorrow at one o'clock sharp."

"Yes darling, I will see you tomorrow at one o'clock sharp."

As Desiree walked towards Cynthia and Brian's table, Paul admired his wife's voluptuous rear-end. He smiled and under his breath said, "It's all good."

5

Marvin

"Sweetheart, thanks for lunch," Marvin said after he ate the last bit of his shrimp fried rice.

"You're welcome baby."

Marvin wiped his mouth, leaned back in his chair and tilted his head to one side. "Who loves you?"

Janice looked straight ahead and replied, "You do."

"Sweetheart, we need to leave. My presentation is in 30 minutes."

"Okay," Janice said and tossed her VISA card on the table.

On the drive back to Marvin's office, Janice was quiet. When she stopped in front of the 4203 building, Marvin put both of his large hands around Janice's face and kissed her passionately on the lips. Marvin wanted Janice to feel a warm tingle that radiated from her highlights in her hair down to her ruby red toenails.

Marvin's hands were still around Janice's face. He looked into her medium brown eyes. "Who loves you?"

Janice enthusiastically replied, "You do."

"That's right and don't you ever forget it."

"I won't."

"Remember, I'll be late tonight."

"How late Marvin?"

"I should be home around 10 o'clock. You just make sure you have on something sexy for me. I mean the whole gear, shoes and all. If my presentation goes as well as I think, I will be in a *celebratory* mood."

"Good luck on your presentation baby."

Marvin got out of the truck with a spring in his step. He took three strides and slowly turned around, blew Janice a kiss, and waved goodbye. Janice waved back and gradually pulled off. Marvin looked around a second time. "Finally, that damn Janice is going to get me killed. Now, I gotta deal with Linda and her shit."

With no signs of either Janice or Linda, Marvin picked up his pace and headed straight to his glacier white Bentley parked on the side street adjacent to the 4203 building. Before he could get his key out of his pocket, Linda came from behind a white commercial van. "Marvin! When the hell did you get married?"

Marvin asked a dumb-founded "What?"

"Don't what me. You heard me loud and clear. When the hell did you get married and how in the hell did she find out where I worked?"

"Sweetheart, I'm not married to anybody. Who are you going to believe, me or some crazy woman that walked in off the street?"

"She sounded pretty convincing to me."

"Linda, you know you are the only one for me."

"Marvin, you had to tell her something for her to come down here and say she's your *wife*. Coming up in my place of business acting like she owns the damn place. Got the nerve to ask me for her *husband*. Why would she do that Marvin if she wasn't married to you?"

"I don't know Linda. Maybe she wants to be."

"If she's not your wife, who in the hell is she?"

"Sweetheart, she's just somebody I used to deal with off and on. I saw her at a fundraiser and now, I can't seem to get rid of the bitch. What can I say? You know everybody loves Marvin, including you."

Marvin pulled Linda close to him. He held her tightly around the waist. One by one, he planted soft kisses on her forehead, her left cheek, her right cheek, and on her lips. Marvin whispered into her ear, "Now stop acting like that sweetheart."

Linda said nothing. She looked down at the envelope in her hand and waited for Marvin to speak again. "Linda, think about it for a minute. You treat me so good. You buy me this car, give me money, and give me all the good loving I need. If I was gonna marry somebody, don't you think it would be you?"

Linda pushed herself free from Marvin and held up the envelope. "Don't know, but the court says you did."

"The court must be wrong. I'm *not* married, never been married and never will get married . . . unless of course it is to you. They have the wrong Marvin Perry I tell you. You need to do a little more research Linda.

My name is Marvin *D.L.* Perry. If the DL isn't in the middle, then it's not me."

"Marvin, you 50-year old no good lying cowboy boot wearing curly head bastard. All I did for you."

"I want the keys to my Bentley right now Marvin." Linda held out her hand.

"Linda, this isn't your car. Remember, I make the payments."

"Oh yeah, but it's in my name and if memory serves me correctly, the last payment you made was six months ago."

"Sweetheart, you're blowing this all out of proportion."

"Out of proportion my ass. You may have your little *wifey* fooled, but I aint no fool."

"Linda, I tell you it's not true. It's not what you think."

"Marvin, you really don't wanna know what I think."

"Come on sweetheart. Let's get out of this alley. Let me take you to dinner so we can talk about everything that's bothering you in that pretty head of yours."

"Marvin, we just had lunch."

"Oh yeah, I guess we did." Marvin laughed and threw his jacket in the back seat. He made a mental note to make damn sure Linda wasn't following him when he was with Janice.

Linda put her hands on her hip and said, "Marvin, I don't see a damn thing funny."

"Sweetheart, come on. Let's get a drink and I'll straighten this whole thing out. Can you leave now?"

"No, I can't leave now. I have a job." Linda wrote the word job with her long curly nails.

Again, Marvin pulled Linda close to him. He kissed her on the lips and placed his hand underneath her short skirt in between her legs. Linda moaned. "Stop Marvin, I have an important client I need to see."

"Sweetheart, you know you like it. You go handle your client and I'll go to my meeting. Meet me over at the lounge in about two hours. We'll talk about all of this while I cool you off."

Marvin thought, "I know you all too well Linda. You love Dick Sr., Dick Jr., Dick the first, second, and the third. It don't matter whether you're mad as hell, because I know you will never refuse any member of the Dick family."

He looked around to see if anyone else was in the alley. He opened his car door on the passenger side and told Linda to get his bag from the seat. When Linda bent over, Marvin came from behind and gave her the explanation he knew she wanted and one she would gladly accept. Linda cried out Marvin's name until he was done. Marvin shook his head behind Linda's back. "I'll see you in two hours Linda."

"Okay Marvin, I'll be there."

"That's more like it. You know you are the only one for me."

Linda smoothed down her skirt and started to walk towards the building. "I'm sure your wife thinks so too."

Marvin ignored Linda's comment and got into his Bentley. Just as he was about to pull out of the parking space, a young woman half his age energetically walked in front of his car. Marvin immediately honked his horn and eagerly watched as the young woman stopped at the corner. She smiled at Marvin and stuck out her thumb. Marvin smiled back. "Women will be the reason I die."

6

Desiree

Desiree looked at her Cartier. "Are you two lovebirds ready to call it a night?"

"Not yet Mrs. Davis. Do we really have to spend the night apart?"

"Oh, Brian, it's only one damn night. By this time next year, you'll be half way to Hell somewhere and Cynthia will be trying to find your ass."

After Cynthia laughed at her mother lay down the law to Brian, she hugged and kissed him. Brian protested, "Not me Mrs. Davis. Me and Cynthia will be together forever."

"Yeah, yeah, well tonight, you won't. You two have until midnight. I'm staying here too, so don't think I won't know if you're together."

Cynthia smiled and asked, "Is Daddy staying too?"

"No, he went home. He'll be at the church tomorrow at one o'clock sharp."

"Mother, why one o'clock?"

"That will guarantee that his late ass will be there on time."

"Daddy is always late. I should call him before he goes to sleep."

"You do that honey. Tell him goodnight for me too. By the time I finish up here, I'll be damned if I want to listen to him talk about how much money I've spent."

"Mother!"

"Mother nothing. You know how your father can get. By now, he's probably deep into the vodka. In about 30 minutes, he'll be calling all kinds of hogs, dogs, sheep and whatever else. Oh, another thing, don't bother calling me tonight. Once I finish tying up some loose ends, I'm going to hit that bed like a ton of bricks."

Cynthia looked at Brian and smiled. "I won't call you Mother."

Desiree shook her finger at Brian and then pointed to her watch. "I mean it Brian. Midnight is your cut off time."

"Yes Mrs. Davis."

Desiree walked out of the ballroom and went directly to the front desk. The young man behind the desk smiled and asked, "How may I…?"

"Ring B.F. Beverly's room."

The desk clerk hesitated and fumbled with the phone.

"Didn't you hear me? What's wrong with you? Ring the damn room already."

Nervously, the desk clerk said, "We don't have a B.F. Beverly."

Desiree rolled her eyes. Slowly, she said, "Ring Brent Foster's room."

"I'm sorry Ma'am, there's no answer. Would you like to leave a message?"

"No, I don't want to leave a damn message. Ring it again."

While the desk clerk continued to make contact with Brent, Desiree reached into her purse for her phone. Under her breath, she said, "Where in the hell is he?"

"Right behind you my dear," Brent whispered into her ear. Do you have to make a scene everywhere you go?"

"No, just everywhere I am." Desiree smiled.

"You got that right. Let's go to the bar and have a nightcap."

"Brent Darling, I have a better idea. Let's go to your room and have it there."

"Why my room? Does hubby have a Lojack on your ass?"

"No, but I'm sure if there was such a thing, he would be the first one to buy it."

"Well, I may not like the man, but I can see why he wants to keep you near. A woman like you can't be trusted any further than you can spit."

"If that's the case, than why are you with me?"

"Because I trust no one and I don't spit."

"Well, you can trust this." Desiree pointed to her rear-end.

"Yes, I can."

Brent displayed a devilish smile and opened the door to his suite. Desiree smiled as she slowly walked across the marble foyer and looked around at the rich décor and floor to ceiling windows. She threw her purse on the sofa and said, "Be a dear Brent and pour me a glass of Champaign while I use the little girl's room."

Desiree closed the bathroom door behind her. She took her phone out of her bra and dialed home. On the fifth ring, Paul answered, "Hello."

Desiree couldn't figure out if Paul was half asleep or half drunk. "Paul Darling, I just called to say goodnight."

"I was already asleep."

Desiree rolled her eyes and fixed her hair in the large mirror. Brent knocked on the bathroom door. "What are you doing in there? Come on out. Your drink is ready and I need a hug."

Desiree covered the phone with her free hand. *I hope Paul didn't hear that.*

"Who is that?" Paul asked.

"Ah, that's just the TV darling."

Again, Brent knocked on the door. "Desiree, come on out."

Paul abruptly hung up the phone. Desiree looked at the door and then looked at her phone. "Oh well, let me get this over with before Paul gets here."

Desiree swung open the door. "Brent, are you crazy? You knew I was talking to Paul. Why did you do that?"

"Rule #1, if you're going to play the game Ms. Desiree Diva, you need to know how to control your players. I thought you knew that."

"I do, I just thought I could trust you."

"Rule #2, trust no one."

"Give me the damn drink." Desiree snatched her Champaign from Brent's hand. "That wasn't funny. Now, I'll have to deal with Paul's shit tomorrow. Because of you, he may even bring his drunken ass here tonight. Brent, you're going to get me killed."

"No Diva, by not following the rules, you're going to get yourself killed. Enough about that nonsense grasshopper, Hubby will get over it. Now, bring your fine fat ass over here."

7

Janice

On the drive back to Janice's office, all kinds of thoughts about Linda and Marvin raced through her mind. "He pissed me off with those could be true or could not be true answers. I still don't know a damn thing for sure."

Janice turned her truck around and headed south on Interstate 495. The last thing Janice wanted to do was spy on the man she loves, but she just couldn't shake her strong desire to find out the truth.

When Janice got to the corner of Wilson Boulevard, she remembered her mother telling her if she looked hard enough, she would always find what she was looking for, but when she found it, would she really know what it was? Stop looking. If there was something shady going on, it would surface on its own and when it does, there would be no doubt in your mind what was really true.

"You're right Ma. I was getting ready to go down that long and dark road to Spyville."

Janice drove past Marvin's job and took the exit heading north on Interstate 495 towards her house. Janice smiled as she thought about all of the naughty and nice things she was going to do to and for Marvin when he got home.

Janice turned right on Brown Station Road and made a left on Berry Court into the driveway of her two-story colonial. "My mind must be playing tricks on me. That looks just like Marvin walking down the street. No, that can't be Marvin. He's at work in an important meeting. This man is dressed in jeans and a white shirt. I'm sure Marvin had on a tan suit at lunch."

Although Janice was 99% positive that the man walking down the street was not her husband, she continued to look at him. When the man got to the end of Berry Court, he looked to the left, then to the right before he crossed the street. "That is him."

Marvin stopped in front of a glacier white Bentley that was parked on the corner of Berry Court and North Berry Court. Marvin got in and drove off.

Janice pulled out of her driveway and followed Marvin. One unanswered question after another plagued Janice's mind, "What the hell is going on? When did he get a damn Bentley? How can he afford it? Why didn't he tell me? Why isn't he at work?"

Janice picked up her phone and then put it back down. With her heart beating faster and faster, Janice continued to follow Marvin down Route 214. Deep down, Janice knew if she kept following Marvin that she was about to discover something that would rock her so hard that even she doubted she could bounce back from.

Janice slowed down. She wanted to turn back and pretend she never saw Marvin leave their house and get into a Bentley she knew nothing about.

All of a sudden, Janice didn't want to know where Marvin was going and who he was going to see. She just wanted things to go back to the way they were eight months ago when they said, "I do."

Janice pulled out a Virginia Slims Menthol. "I need to calm my nerves." Before she lit her cigarette, she looked at it. "These things are going to kill me, but if I continue to live a lie, I'll end up dying of unhappiness anyway. I just have to trust I'm strong enough to handle whatever I find out."

Janice resumed her speed and continued on her pursuit of truthfulness. She followed Marvin into Mount Oaks Estates. "Who lives here? Wow! Look at these houses. Does he have some rich uncle I don't know anything about?"

Marvin pulled his Bentley into the driveway of an all brick and stone two-story home that sat on two acres of land. Janice stopped a block away on the opposite side of Westbrook Lane. She saw Marvin's Kawasaki in front of the three-car garage and a red tri-cycle lying upside down on the lawn.

Marvin got out of his Bentley and walked down the wide sidewalk and up five stairs to the two-story marble entry way. He opened the door and walked inside. Janice couldn't make sense as to why Marvin had a key to this beautiful mansion. "Who lives here? Who would trust Marvin with a key to their home, especially this one?"

Janice stared at the magnificent home. She wondered what Marvin was doing on the inside. She saw the mail courier go up to the door. When he got closer to Janice, she rolled down her window. "Excuse me. I'm looking for my friends, Marvin and Linda . . ."

"Yeah, Marvin and Linda Franklin, a nice looking couple, live right over there. Marvin is home. I just took him a package."

"Are you sure Marvin and Linda Franklin live there?"

"Lady, they've been there ever since I started this route five years ago."

Janice's eyes grew bigger and began to water. Her heart pounded in her chest and she had trouble breathing.

The mailman walked closer to Janice's truck. "Are you all right Miss? Should I go get Marvin?"

"No! "I'm sorry sir. I knew they were doing well, but Wow."

"Yeah, these houses are really something. I guess I better get back to work. Have a good day Ma'am."

Janice was glad the mailman left. She could no longer fake a smile and hold back her tears. With both of her hands covering her face, she rocked back and forth in her seat and cried her eyes out. Through her wet fingers, she screamed, "Marvin, how could you do this to me, to us? I thought things were going to be different this time. You don't love me. I gave you my heart and you just threw it away like it was nothing. How could I have been so stupid? What am I going to do now?"

After 20 minutes, Janice wiped her tear stained face. She wondered what Marvin would do if he knew she was practically at his door.

When her phone rang, Janice jumped. She looked at her caller ID, threw the phone on her seat, and let the call go to her voicemail. Seconds later, Janice listened to her message—"Hey sweetheart. Where are you? I called you at work and left you a message an hour ago. My presentation was good, but I have to go to another meeting right after work. It could go on for hours. I miss you. Call me back as soon as you get this message."

"You lying bastard." Janice wiped away her tears. She didn't want to talk to Marvin, but she didn't want him to know that she too was not at work.

She put on her cheery voice and called Marvin. "Hey baby, I was in a meeting. I'm glad your presentation went well."

"Thank you sweetheart. I'm glad you called me back. I just wanted to hear your voice and remind you, I'll be late again tonight."

"I got your voicemail. I'll be working late too."

"Janice, is everything all right? You sound strange."

"I'm just tired Marvin, that's all."

Marvin paused and said, "I love you sweetheart."

It took everything out of Janice to say, "I love you too. Have a great meeting."

"All right sweetheart. Tonight, I want you to run a bath, light some candles, drink a glass of wine, and relax. I'll come home and dry you off."

"I'll be waiting Marvin."

"You better. See you later sweetheart."

Janice hung up the phone and looked at her watch. "It's already four o'clock. I should go to the door and confront him. No, I'll wait until Linda comes home and confront them both. I know, I'll go home, get my gun and then come back and confront them. Better yet, I'll go home, wait for Marvin to come through the door and as soon as one word comes out of his lying mouth, I'll shoot him in it."

Janice looked at the luxurious home. "No man or woman is worth me giving up my freedom. I'll be in jail and his ass will still be on Westbrook Lane living the life while I'm selling my booty for Virginia Slims. No thank you."

A claret metallic red Jaguar pulled into the driveway and blew the horn. Marvin opened the door and stood in the entry way. Janice looked at Linda step out of the XK. Linda walked over to the passenger's door and out jumped a little toddler. Marvin ran down the five stairs and met the little boy midway of the sidewalk.

Marvin wrapped his arms around the little boy and kissed him on the cheek before he swung him around in circles. Marvin lowered the little boy and again, kissed him on the cheek. Marvin put his arm around Linda's waist and kissed her on the lips.

Tears streamed down Janice's cheeks. "They look like the perfect little family." Janice put both of her hands up and said, "I'm done."

She started up her engine. Marvin looked her way. For a brief moment, their eyes locked. Janice made an illegal U-turn in the middle of Westbrook Lane and sped away.

8

Paul

Paul took one gigantic leap out of bed, threw his cell phone clear across his huge master bedroom suite and hit the six-foot gold framed mirror. Glass shattered everywhere. Paul surveyed the damage to one of Desiree's small, but very precious possessions, and said, "I was sick of that damn thing anyway."

With both of his hands balled up in tight fists, Paul threw punches in mid air. He yelled at the broken pieces of mirror lying all over the floor, "I'm sick to death of your lying, cheating, scheming, selfish, ungrateful fucked up ways. I don't know why I keep putting myself through the same bullshit year after year. All that I do for you and you're still never satisfied. The more I give you, the more you want. The more money I make, the more money you spend. The more I try to believe in your lying ass, the more you give me reasons why I shouldn't. I knew you were up to something. I knew it."

Paul stood in the middle of the floor sweaty and out of breath. "I'll be damned if she's going to drive me crazy too. Get a grip man."

Paul walked over to his mini bar and poured himself a large drink of Grey Goose Vodka and cranberry juice. With glass in hand, Paul went into his dual walk-in closet and pulled out a gray case. He threw it on the bed and walked back over to the mini bar.

For the next three hours, Paul sat in his chair and drank one vodka and cranberry juice after another. He stared at the gray case and tried to remember if Desiree had ever told him the truth about anything.

"What the hell is that buzzing sound?" Paul got up, but fell back down into his chair. "Damn, I must be drunk." Paul laughed.

Paul had been drinking as hard as he had been thinking. He made another attempt to get out of his chair. The second time, he made it and stumbled over to the dresser. Paul grabbed his phone and looked at the caller ID. "What the hell is she calling me for? What lie you going to tell me this time?" Paul yelled into the phone, "What?"

"Hello darling. Did I wake you?"

"Yes, you did."

"I'm sorry, you hung up on me earlier. I just wanted to see if you were feeling okay."

"Is that right? You were so worried that you called me back three hours later.

"No, I didn't mean anything bad happened. I just thought you probably went to the bathroom and just forgot all about me and fell back to sleep."

"Yeah, that food went right through me and I was in the bathroom for hours. You know me all too well darling. After that, I went right back to bed."

"Well darling, tomorrow is the big day. I will let you go back to sleep. I'm going to sleep too so I can look just as beautiful as the bride tomorrow."

"You do that darling and I will see you all tomorrow." Paul looked at the gray case.

"Don't forget Paul. Be at the church at one o'clock sharp."

"Oh, I'll be there. Goodnight Desiree."

"Goodnight Paul Darling."

Paul hung up the phone and threw it on the bed beside the case. He took out his .357 Magnum and aimed it at one of Desiree's pictures. "I'll be there darling sooner than you think. Tonight is the night that I'm finally going to find out just how much of a liar and cheater you really are."

Paul put his revolver back into the case. "Frank Popeye Beverly likes to sing, does he? Let's see if he can sing to the tune of this."

9

Paul

"Hello Mr. Davis. Did you forget something?" the desk clerk asked.

"No, I just decided to stay the night after all. Can I have the key to my wife's room, please?"

For several minutes, the desk clerk stared at the computer screen. Paul looked at the desk clerk and asked, "Is there a problem? I've spent a lot damn money in this place. Where's the manager?"

"Mr. Davis, there is no need to speak to my manager. Sir, I apologize. I'm just not feeling very well tonight."

Paul calmed down and extended his opened hand.

The desk clerk smiled and gave Paul the key to the room. "Here you are Mr. Davis. I hope you *enjoy* your stay."

"Thank you, I will."

Looking around for Desiree and any signs of a male companion, Paul opened the door to her suite. He followed the trail of clothing that led to the bathroom. Paul picked up Desiree's bra with his gun and dropped it next to a man's pair of black boxer shorts. He heard the shower running in the bathroom, along with a man singing and a woman moaning.

Paul walked towards the bathroom. He turned the doorknob, opened the door to a small crack, and listened to the noises in the shower. After a few seconds, he closed the door.

Paul took three steps away from the door and dialed his brother. "Chester, walk my baby girl down the aisle tomorrow."

"Little Brother, why are you whispering and where are you going?"

"I'm going to jail right after I make a motherfucker sing and a lying bitch dance."

"Paul, what's going on? Where are you?"

Paul didn't answer. After he heard Chester say, "Don't do anything stupid," he disconnected the call and turned off his ringer.

With gun still in hand, Paul walked back towards the bathroom door. When he got half way down the hall, the water in the shower stopped. Paul also stopped. He sat down in a chair in the corner.

Paul laid his gun across his lap with his finger tightly gripped around the trigger. When the bathroom door opened, Paul carefully stood up, stepped closer into the corner and made sure he was totally out of sight. What seemed to be hours for Paul was just a few minutes before Desiree and Brent emerged from the bathroom with matching hotel bathrobes.

Brent held Desiree around her waist from behind. They walked in unison and sang the words, "If loving you is wrong, I don't want to be right." Desiree laughed and said, "That's right baby, if loving you is wrong I damn sure ain't gonna do right. You hear that Paul?"

"Yeah, I hear you loud and clear," Paul said as he stepped out of the corner and pointed his gun right at Desiree's heart.

Desiree screamed and jerked away from Brent's arms. Paul stuck his feet out and Desiree fell flat on her face. She squirmed and screamed, "Paul, please don't hit me, please don't kill me. Please, it's not what you think!"

"Bitch, shut the hell up. I haven't even touched you yet."

Brent stood as straight as an arrow with his hands in his robe pockets. He looked at Paul and asked, "How did you get into my room?"

"I'll ask the questions. How long have you been screwing my wife?"

The gun was an inch away from Brent's head. Before Brent could answer Paul's question, Desiree jumped to her feet. "Darling, don't do this. It's not what you think. I came to pay Frank for tonight and I spilled something on my silk dress. That's why I have on this robe."

"Woman, do you honestly think I'm that stupid?" With his free left hand, Paul backhanded Desiree. He watched her half naked body land on the king-size bed and then fall to the other side, just missing the marble dresser.

Brent grabbed for the gun. Paul tightened his grip and the two wrestled. They knocked over the beige chair, the ice bucket and the two glasses of Champaign that sat on the glass table. A shot was fired. The lamp fell over next to Desiree. She jumped up and screamed, "Paul stop, stop!"

While Paul and Brent continued to fight, Desiree crawled on ice and broken glass to get the phone. She dialed 911 and screamed, "Please, please, somebody help me. Please help me. My husband has gone crazy. He has a gun and is trying to kill me!"

Paul turned to look at Desiree. Brent stepped in front of Paul and knocked the gun to the other side of the room. "Davis, it's time for you to go nigh tie night."

Paul fell to the floor and did not move.

10

Marvin

With a half dozen of roses in one hand and a bottle of Sutter Home White Zinfandel under his arm, Marvin was all set to put his plan into motion. On his way home, he even thought of the perfect explanation to tell Janice.

Marvin opened the front door and sang, "Janice, I'm home." He closed the door with his left knee and placed the roses and wine on the kitchen table.

"Let me call my sweetheart. By now, she should have cooled down." Marvin's call went straight to Janice's voicemail. On his fifth call, he left a message, "Janice, I'm worried about you. I've called you five times now. Pick up the damn phone so we can talk about this."

Marvin hung up and called right back. Again, his call went to her voicemail. Marvin grabbed his keys. "To hell with Janice," and slammed the door behind him.

Thirty minutes later, Marvin turned off of Route 714 onto the parking lot of The Colossal Lounge. He went straight for the bar and ordered, "Heineken, no glass." Marvin pulled down his sunglasses. "Now there's a backside that even a blind man can see and one that I personally know."

Before Marvin headed across the dim lit Jazz and old R&B lounge, he took the top of his Heineken and touched his forehead, his stomach, his left shoulder and his right shoulder. He walked over to the corner next to the stage where the woman stood laughing and drinking with two men. For several seconds, Marvin stood behind her. One man looked at Marvin and frowned. Marvin put his index finger over his mouth. He pressed up against the woman's back and whispered into her ear, "Karen Stewart, do I know you sweetheart?"

Karen's smile widened as she turned around, flung her arms around Marvin's neck, and pushed him against the high top table. "When did you get here Marvin?"

"I just got here a few minutes ago. I was getting ready to call you when I spotted your uh . . . assets."

"Why were you going to call me?"

"Do I need a reason?"

For a moment, Karen was quiet. "Don't be silly. I was just curious, that's all. I'm really glad to see you, so shake off the cobwebs and let's dance."

Cajmere's "Percolator" blared from the big speakers. Karen took Marvin by the hand and pulled him onto the dance floor.

Marvin danced the night away. He completely lost track of time.

"Karen, it's midnight. I gotta go."

"Where do you have to run off to? If you weren't such a great dancer, I would have kicked you to the curb at 10 o'clock. Will you walk me to my car?"

"Anything for you sweetheart. I would take care of the bill, but I left my wallet outside in my Bentley. If you'll wait, I'll run out and get it."

"Sweetie, you know I got big bucks."

"That's not all you got big. Damn girl, what you been eating since I last saw you? Don't get me wrong, you still look good and all." Marvin slapped Karen on her behind.

Karen smiled and paid the $83.05 check. Marvin held her around the waist until they got to the double-glass doors that led out to the parking lot. Marvin scratched his head and looked from side to side.

"Marvin, is everything all right?"

"Yeah, I just remembered, I didn't drive. The Bentley was getting detailed and I came over here to kill some time. I guess the guy couldn't reach me and locked it up in his shop."

"Good, that means you have to come home with me."

Marvin looked at Karen and gently kissed her on her blackberry colored lips. He sat back in the white Chrysler 300M Stretch Limo and said, "Driver, we're in a hurry, so put the pedal to the medal." Again, Marvin kissed Karen on her lips. "I got plans for you."

"Not as many as I have for you."

Marvin laughed and sat back on the soft silver leather seat. He thought about where his Bentley might be. He couldn't report it stolen in front of

Karen because he already told her it was at the detail shop. Marvin decided he would call the police later that morning. Meanwhile, he still needed transportation to find Janice. Marvin smiled when he remembered Karen lived two streets over from Linda. "Sweetheart, do you think chunky up there can drive this thing any faster?"

"Don't call him that. He's really sensitive."

"He should be, "Chunky," Marvin whispered."

"Jackson, can you please drive a little faster? We're in a hurry," Karen said and laughed when Marvin kissed her on her breast.

When Jackson drove up the long paved driveway and stopped in front of Karen's two-story brick home, Marvin was eager to get out. He put his hand on Jackson's shoulder. "Don't bother getting out chunky, I'll take it from here."

Marvin gazed at the crystal chandelier that hung in the enormous foyer and nodded at the stone fireplace. He leaned against the marble column and asked, "Hey Sweetheart, do you have anything to drink?"

Karen went into the gourmet kitchen and brought back a bottle of Moet.

"Here, drink on this while I put on something a little more comfortable."

"Don't be too long sweetheart," Marvin said.

As soon as Karen reached the top of her black swirl staircase, Marvin tiptoed to the front door and opened it. Before he closed the door, he whispered, "Sorry Karen, I got more important things to do than bone."

Marvin jogged the two blocks to Linda's house. When he hit the corner of Westbrook Lane, the first thing he noticed was his Bentley parked in the driveway. As he got closer, he saw three of his Armani suits, a pair of Sean John Jeans, and a Calvin Klein shirt thrown over his motorcycle seat. One black cowboy boot was stuck on his handlebar and the other boot was near his kickstand. Pieces of cut up pictures of Linda and Marvin encircled the five boxes that were sitting on the lawn next to the Evergreen Boxwood Shrub.

Marvin ran to the door, jammed his key into the keyhole, and turned the key back and forth—it didn't move. Marvin banged on the door and yelled, "Linda, why did you change the damn locks? Open up this fucking door!"

Linda didn't respond. Marvin continued to bang. "Linda, if you don't open up this fucking door, I'm gonna break every fucking window in this house!"

Linda flung open the door and spit on Marvin. "You don't live here no damn more." Linda held up Janice and Marvin's marriage license in one hand and a glass of Merlot in the other.

Marvin stormed past Linda and stepped on her long red silk robe. "Why did you change the damn locks on me?"

Linda waved the license in Marvin's face. "I told you, if I found out that you got married to that crazy bitch, I was going to take the Bentley, MJ and . . ."

Marvin snatched the paper out of Linda's hand and slammed the front door shut. With contempt in his eyes, he looked at Linda and said, "Like your shit don't stink."

Marvin knew this day would come, but he was not prepared for that day to be today. The thoughts of losing everything he held dear to his heart and pocket rapidly flashed before him. Without hesitation, Marvin landed one hard punch across Linda's right jaw, which sent her to the floor and the wine glass against the living room wall.

Marvin jumped on top of Linda and straddled her slim body. He saw the terror in her eyes and how her legs trembled with fear. "Oh, you ain't so bad now, huh?"

Linda's long nails dug into Marvin's skin. He tightened his grip around her neck and yelled, "All the shit I've put up with and you do me like this!"

Linda tried to pry Marvin's hands from around her neck. She squirmed, kicked, and struggled for breath, but Marvin continued in a rage. When his phone vibrated in his jeans pocket, Linda knocked Marvin to the floor and gasped for air. "Please, don't."

She attempted to crawl away, but Marvin, practically on her back, grabbed Linda from behind and choked her. Linda thrust her body forward while Marvin pulled her backwards by her neck.

Minutes later, Linda fell to the floor with Marvin's hands still around her neck.

11

Desiree

Desiree looked at Paul lying unconscious on the floor. She stood up and stumbled over the broken glass table. Brent caught her by the arm. "Bitch, are you stupid?"

"Bitch? Who are you calling a bitch?"

"You, in fact, you're a stupid bitch at that. I told you time and time again that you're going to get your ass killed messing with hot head hubby, but you won't listen. I'll be damned if you're going to get me killed too. Ain't no woman, especially one like you worth dying for."

Desiree stared at Brent as if that was the first time she ever saw him. When Brent put on his shoes, she asked, "Where the hell are you going?"

"You're not only stupid, you're crazy too. I'm leaving. I've had enough action for one night. I'm not staying here for the police to question me. As far as they're concerned, it was a domestic dispute involving just you and hot head hubby here."

Desiree couldn't believe how cruel Brent was being towards her. "We both created this mess and now you're just going to walk out and leave me here to deal with this shit."

"Yep."

Desiree removed a piece of glass out of her chin. "I thought you loved me."

"I do love you Diva. I love all women, but as I told you before, I trust no one. The next time you need a singer or hot fun in the summertime, use the yellow pages."

Brent walked towards the door. With tears streaming down her face, Desiree ran in front of Brent and stretched her arms across the length of the door. "Brent, please don't leave. You can't leave me, I love you."

"Desiree, I'm going to tell you one more time to move your ass away from the door."

"Please, please don't do this." Desiree grabbed Brent's arms. "I'll go with you."

Brent clapped his hands. "Bravo. Diva, I'm not going to tell your ass again, move. I need to get out of here before the cops show up."

Brent shoved Desiree to the floor and opened the door. He looked back at Paul still unconscious lying on the floor and Desiree next to him sobbing. "Damn shame, a 10 million dollar drunk and a two dollar Ho, both too damn stupid to know when it's time to let go." Brent saluted Desiree goodbye and closed the door behind him.

Desiree dragged herself up from the floor. She kicked Paul in his side and said, "Damn you Paul." When she heard a knock on the door, Desiree smiled. "Brent, you've come back." She wiped her face, smoothed down her hair and swung open the door. "I knew you'd come back."

A muscular police officer rushed in. "Ma'am, are you all right?" Desiree rolled her eyes. "Yes, he's out cold now." Desiree pointed to Paul lying on the floor.

In less than a minute, the hotel room was filled with police officers. One of the officers took Desiree's statement while another put smelling salts underneath Paul's nose. Instantly, he came to and asked, "What happened?"

"That's what we want to know," one of the officers said.

Before Paul could answer, Desiree yelled, "He tried to kill me, that's what the hell happened! The gun is over there."

One officer picked up the .357 Magnum while the other officer dragged Paul to his feet and immediately cuffed him. "Sir, you're under arrest."

Paul yanked away from the tight grip of the officer. "She's lying. I never touched her. Someone assaulted me. I'm the victim. That bitch had another man here. You have to believe me."

The officers paid no attention to Paul's plea and forced him out the door. "Desiree, tell them the damn truth. Tell them."

Desiree ignored Paul's angry plea and continued to give her account of what happened.

12

Marvin

Marvin yelled, "Linda, Linda!" He turned Linda's lifeless body over onto her back and smacked both of her cheeks. When she didn't respond, he checked to see if she was breathing and cried out, "Oh God, what have I done?"

Marvin positioned Linda's arms above her head and administered what he could remember of CPR. After a few minutes, Linda slowly came to.

Marvin wiped the sweat from his forehead and thanked God he didn't kill her, and let out a huge sigh of relief.

Linda tried to get up, but Marvin gently pushed her back down. "Stay there for a moment."

Linda felt her head. "My head hurts. What happened?"

Marvin was still on his knees. He felt guilty and full of remorse for what he'd done to her. He looked up the stairs to where he knew MJ was sleeping. Chills went down his spine when he thought about the pain he would have caused his son if he had killed his mother. A tear slowly fell down Marvin's cheek. He looked at Linda lying on the floor with her eyes closed and said, "I'm sorry, I never meant for this to happen."

Linda opened her eyes and said nothing. She looked at Marvin with eyes as cold as ice. Marvin wasn't sure that Linda heard his apology. "Linda, did you hear me? Please say something. I don't know what happened. I just lost it. I'm sorry. I really didn't mean for any of this to happen."

Again, Linda said nothing. She allowed her finger to do the talking for her and pointed to the door.

Marvin closed his eyes. "All right, I'll go." He stood up and took one last look at his home for the last five years. "Linda, I really am sorry. Please tell MJ I love him." Marvin hoped Linda would have said something before he walked out the door, but she still said nothing.

Once Marvin was outside, he stood in the driveway and looked at the multi-million dollar house that was once his home and the glacier white Bentley that was once his luxury ride. He cursed at the five boxes of his belongings and the torn up pictures on the lawn. He cursed each piece of clothing that he threw off his motorcycle and cursed again when he pulled the boot off of his handlebar. Marvin was totally disgusted about leaving behind the luxuries he had grown accustomed to having. He thought about how, in one night, his entire world came crashing down around him and if that wasn't bad enough, he almost killed the mother of his son.

Marvin felt his phone vibrate in his pocket. "Now you call. If it weren't for you following me today, none of this shit would have happened tonight."

Marvin looked at his caller ID and expected to see Janice's number, but it was Karen. At that moment, Marvin realized he didn't have any place to go to but Karen's place. After what happened with Linda, Marvin didn't have the energy to face Janice nor did he trust himself around her.

Reluctantly, he dialed Karen's number. "Karen."

"Marvin, where did you go?"

"I . . ."

"Marvin, are you still there?"

Marvin's attention was instantly drawn towards the sirens and the red and blue lights flashing from the three police cars that sped down Westbrook Lane. *Linda called the cops.*

"Marvin, what's going on? Are you coming back over?"

"Yes, I'll be right there."

Marvin quickly put on his helmet and sped out of the driveway. Two police cars stopped in front of the house and the third car followed the speeding motorcycle.

Marvin went to the left and took a sharp right, another left and down the hill. He could still hear the sirens, but he could no longer see the flashing red and blue lights behind him. Karen's house was two streets over and up the hill past the stop sign. Marvin was confident his driving skills had paid off. He accelerated his speed even more as he got to the corner that would lead him up the hill to Karen s house.

Marvin barreled up the hill, not bothering to stop at the stop sign. Out of nowhere, an SUV slammed into Marvin and knocked his bike one way and him another. When all the screeching of tires, banging and noise stopped, Marvin's body landed on the sidewalk just 20 feet away from Karen's house.

13

Janice

Janice stood on Dee's roof top terrace and grabbed the railing as she looked out over the Chesapeake Bay. "Dee, I'm not ready to face Marvin just yet. Can I stay here tonight?"

"Girl, you know you don't have to ask. Stay as long as you need to."

"Thanks."

Dee poured Janice a glass of Chardonnay and asked, "Are you okay?" Janice sipped her wine. "I knew something wasn't right, but never in a million years did I ever think Marvin lived a double life right underneath my nose. I just can't believe it."

Dee put her wine glass up to her mouth. "I can."

"What did you say Dee?"

"I said I can believe it. Janice, you just never wanted to see it. For one thing, Marvin was always gone and when he was away, he called you 50 times a day. If he missed you that damn much, he should have brought his ass home to you. Plus, he always had a ready-made excuse for *every* damn thing. That curly head pretty boy did the same shit he's done for the last 10 years. He never changed. Hell, men don't change. They just change the way they do dumb shit so it takes us longer to catch on. Yeah, I can believe his lying two timing ass did it. Men ain't shit."

To stop the tears from freely streaming down her cheeks, Janice squeezed her eyes shut and took another sip of her wine. "Dee, I just gave Marvin the benefit of the doubt, that's all. Unlike you, I do believe people can change if they want to. I really believed this time, things would be different and Marvin had changed."

"Girl, I told you, men don't change and none of them are worth shit."

"Dee, if you really believe that then why do you want a man?"

Dee looked puzzled. She poured more wine into both of their glasses and yelled out, "Because I just do! Now drink your damn wine with your making sense, broken heart ass."

Both women put their glasses in the air and burst into loud laughter.

"Dee, none of this is funny."

"I know, but at least you're laughing now instead of the way you looked eight hours ago."

"What did I look like?"

"Like you were about to jump off my roof into the six o'clock rush hour traffic."

Janice sighed deeply and asked, "Dee, how could I have been so stupid? All the problems we had before we got married with the women calling, fancy cars turning up that I knew he couldn't afford, the frequent disappearing, the lying and scheming never really left. He hadn't changed. He just condensed the multitude into one lavish package."

"No, you're not stupid Janice. You loved Marvin and gave the bastard a second chance. I wouldn't of, but you did. I know I talk a lot of stuff, but if there are problems before you get married, there will be problems after you get married. Just because he put a ring on your finger, it doesn't magically make the problems disappear. Girl, don't be so hard on you. You're not the first woman to believe something that wasn't true for the sake of love and marriage and I guarantee you won't be the last."

Janice smiled. "Who's making sense now?"

"What do you mean now?"

Janice turned her head to the side and scooted to the edge of her seat. She put both elbows on her knees, covered her face with her small hands and cried out, "Dee, it really hurts. Again and again, I gave Marvin my heart. He just took it and threw it away like it was nothing. I was so in love with that man. Despite my doubts, I was good to him and I believed I was good for him."

Dee tried to comfort her friend by offering her more wine, but Janice stood up with her glass in her hand. "You know . . . people say all the time they want a good woman or a good man. Hell, there are plenty of good women and men in the world. If that's all people wanted, we could just have two lines of good women and good men, pair them up, send them home together and everybody should be happy, right?"

Dee hunched her shoulders. "I guess."

"Do you know what I think?"

"What do you think Janice?"

"I think people just want that specific man they want or that specific woman they want to be good. I know now Marvin was never in love with me. I was just somebody he cared for that made him feel good until the woman he really wanted became good."

Tears flowed down Janice's cheeks. Dee shook her head and filled Janice's glass up for the third time. "Janice, are you going to leave Marvin?"

Janice looked into her glass as if the answer to Dee's question was in it. "Yes, I am. Wouldn't you?"

"Hell yeah! I would leave him right after I drive the truck over her, him and the baby."

Janice laughed at Dee. "See, you know you're wrong."

"No, I'm not. Marvin was wrong and stupid. I bet you he's somewhere right now thinking about just how stupid he was, not for lying and leading a double life, but for getting caught with his dumb ass."

Janice's phone rang. "I know Marvin is not calling me at three o'clock in the morning. *It's not him.* "Hello."

A woman on the other end of phone asked, "Is this Mrs. Perry?"

Janice nervously said, "Yes, this is Mrs. Perry."

"I'm calling from the Southern Maryland Hospital Emergency Room. We have your husband, Marvin Perry, here. He was in a bad motorcycle accident."

"Oh, my God! Is he . . . ?"

"Ma'am, they just took him into surgery."

"I'll be right there."

14

Paul

In a low voice, Paul said, "Chester."

"Man, where are you? I've been all over town looking for you."

Before Paul answered his big brother, he took a deep breath. "I'm in jail."

"I told you . . . !"

"Look Chester, the last thing I need right now is to listen to you tell me I told you so."

"You're right, you're right." Are you all right Little Brother?"

"Yeah, I'm all right."

"Paul, tell me what happened."

"I caught that lying, cheating ass wife of mine red handed."

"What do you mean?"

"Come on Chester, do I have to spell the shit out for you? I caught Popeye screwing my wife."

"Whoa! How . . . I mean before I left, I thought everything was fine between you two."

"So did I. After the rehearsal, I went home and Desiree stayed behind at the hotel. She said she was spending the night to tie up some loose ends. Around midnight, she called me to say goodnight. In the middle of the conversation, I hear a damn man in the background."

"So you rushed over to the hotel to drag her back home?"

"No, I hung up on her."

"Then what happened?"

Paul didn't want to tell Chester the truth of how he first reacted when he heard the man's voice. He also didn't want his brother to know he had been heavily drinking while he planned his attack on Desiree and her lover.

Paul said, "An hour later, she called me again. That's when I knew something was up. She wasn't sure if I heard the guy or not because I didn't rush over there. So, I played along with her and let her think I didn't hear him. I waited for a few hours and then I went to the hotel packing."

"Premeditated," Chester said.

"The guy at the front desk gave me the key to what I thought was Desiree's room, but come to find out, it was Popeye's room. I let myself in and heard the two of them in the shower going for it like dogs in heat."

"Is that when you called me?"

"Yeah, that's when I knew I was going to jail. I stayed out of sight until the both of them came out of the shower. They were wrapped up in each other's arms singing and shit. When I stepped into sight and pointed the gun at Popeye's head, Desiree looked like she peed on herself."

Chester chuckled. "I'm sure she did and then some."

"Popeye just stood there like he was Billy Bad Ass."

"Little Brother, please tell me you didn't shoot anybody."

"No, Chester, I didn't shoot anybody."

"Thank God."

"Oh, believe me, I wanted to shoot both of them and I would have too."

"Well, I for one am glad you didn't, but I'm curious, what stopped you?"

Paul hesitated before he said, "Desiree kept telling me it's not what I think. She stood in front of me in a bathrobe and lied her ass off. I never hit her before, but something in me snapped. As soon as the words left her mouth, I turned and knocked the shit out of her and that's when Popeye and I started tussling over the gun. I remember the gun going off and Desiree screaming on the phone telling somebody I was trying to kill her. Everything else is a blur. The next thing I remember is the police picking me up off the floor and hauling my ass off to jail."

"I'm sorry you went through that. Now what?"

"Well, the judge won't see me until Monday morning.

"Let me make a call. I know a judge that owes me a favor and just happens to be a good friend of mine. Sit tight. I'll have you out in plenty of time to walk your own daughter down the aisle."

"Don't worry about it Chester. You can walk Cynthia down the aisle tomorrow. I can't face Desiree right now."

"Man, to hell with Desiree! You are one selfish S.O.B. Tomorrow, your daughter is expecting her daddy to walk her down the aisle and all you can think about is your no good, lying, cheating ass wife. Throughout your entire marriage, that woman has been nothing but trouble for you. When it comes to her, I swear the more money you make the more stupid you get."

"Wait a minute Chester."

"No, you wait a minute. For years, I've been Brother Hubbard and worried about you. All because of that damn no good wife of yours, I've gotten you out of one jam after another. I've tried to protect you, but no more—I'm tired."

Paul was shocked and mad all over again. "Chester, I'm a grown ass man. I never asked you to worry about me or protect me. My wife is good people. She just has some fucked up ways."

"After what Desiree did to you and you're still defending her? I tell you one thing Little Brother, Desiree is not the only one that has some fucked up ways."

Paul was silent and so was Chester. Paul was used to Chester being his voice of reason and a calming rock in his life. To hear the harsh words about Desiree and the harsh criticism of his life, it really hit him hard.

After several minutes, Paul was the first to speak. "Chester, I just love the woman. I've been married for 17 years. How do I walk away from someone I've spent nearly half of my life with? I'm almost 50 years old. At this age, I don't want to start over again."

"I know man, but are you going to spend 17 plus more years running behind her, worrying about what she's doing and who she's doing it with? All I see you do is work around the clock making millions. As fast as you make it, she spends it. When you're not working, you're drinking yourself to death. You have cut yourself off from all of the people who really care about you. Believe it or not, your family consists of more than Desiree. Paul, you're a good man. You deserve a good woman that loves you for you and not for what you can do for her. You deserve to be happy. What do I have to do, knock you out in order to pour some sense into that stubborn, hot head of yours?" Chester laughed.

"Hey, don't get carried away. If I were out of here, I would have dropped you to your knees for talking to me like that."

"Yeah, right. Popeye dropped you to your knees like a bad can of spinach and that's why you can't remember a damn thing."

Both Chester and Paul laughed. Paul said, "Chester, I would have taken him if I hadn't been drinking."

"Yeah, but you didn't. Seriously, messing with that damn Desiree, you could have been the one that got shot or worst, killed with your own gun."

"You're right."

"Enough about that. Are you ready to walk your baby girl down the aisle tomorrow?"

"Yeah, get me out of here."

"That's what I want to hear."

"Thank you and I . . ."

"I know Little Brother, I know. Give me about an hour."

15

Janice

Janice brushed passed the long line of patients that were waiting to be seen by the stern looking woman behind the desk. "Excuse me, excuse me, my husband, Marvin Perry, was just brought in. Can you please tell me where I can find him?"

"Ma'am, have a seat. Someone will be with you shortly."

"Please, I need to find out what's going on with my husband."

"Ma'am, I said someone will be with you shortly."

"No, I need to find out what's going on with him right now!"

The woman stood up and pointed towards the waiting area. "Right now, you need to have a seat."

Janice wanted to press for more information, but the already irritated look on the woman's face, along with the crowd that gave her the evil eye, told her she better sit down before someone yoked her from behind.

At four o'clock in the morning, after the day she had, the last thing Janice wanted to do was sit in a crowded, cold emergency room filled with babies crying and people yelling.

There was only one available seat next to a man that held a cup in his hand that looked as if he was about to hurl at any moment. Assuming that would be the safest place for her, Janice opted to stand near the doorway. As she stood in her four-inch heels, she looked around the emergency room at all of the people. She could tell the ones who had obviously been there for a while because they were snuggled up on one another and tried to make themselves as comfortable as possible. The newcomers, like her, stood around with their faces twisted into knots as they waited for their turn to be seen by anyone that would help them.

Janice's gaze stopped at a woman who also stood in high heels. From a side ways view, Janice thought the woman resembled Linda. She stared at the woman and thought about Marvin when he held his son and kissed Linda in front of their multi-million dollar home. The more Janice thought about it, the angrier she got. It didn't matter if it just so happen to be in a crowded emergency room, Janice made up her mind that she was going to confront Linda.

Janice made her way to the other side of the crowded emergency room. When she realized it wasn't Linda, she stopped dead in her tracks. Janice smiled at the woman and made a bee line to the bathroom. Under her breath, she said, "Damn, there are two of them. I sure hope she doesn't talk like her too."

In the bathroom, Janice looked in the mirror at the image staring back. She looked like she felt, tired, mad, hurt and a little intoxicated from the four glasses of wine she drank with Dee.

Janice turned on the faucet and threw cold water over her face. "What am I doing? After what he did to me, why am I even here?"

Janice grabbed a paper towel, held it over her face and silently cried into it. Regardless of what happened earlier, she knew she still loved Marvin and the thought of him dying or already dead sent chills down her spine.

After several minutes, Janice reached for the faucet and wished she could turn off her feelings as easily as she turned off the water. She dried her face, combed her hair and put on a new coat of lipstick.

Janice walked back into the waiting room. She was ready to take her spot next to the door, but someone else had taken it. The little time Janice spent in the bathroom, the waiting room had accumulated even more people. Luckily for her, a man offered her his seat. Janice graciously accepted it and was thankful she no longer had to stand in her heels.

For any reason, Janice hated to go to hospitals. The longer she stayed in them, the more likely she would have a panic attack. *I can do this.* Janice felt light-headed, her heart raced and she had trouble breathing. She walked outside and immediately took a deep breath. A few feet away from the door, Janice lit a cigarette to calm her nerves and wished she had a drink to go along with it. She thought about calling Dee, but didn't want to wake her friend until she had more information.

After 20 minutes, Janice was calm and determined to find someone to give her an update on Marvin's condition. As soon as the emergency room doors opened, Janice heard the woman call, "Family for Marvin Perry, please come to the information desk."

Janice ran to the desk and literally bumped into AJ. "I thought that was you."

"Are you just getting here Janice?"

"No, I've been here for about an hour or so. AJ, have you heard anything?"

"Yeah, I was just talking to the doctor. He asked if you were here. I told him no and that I was Marvin's brother, so he told me."

"Told you what?"

Janice prepared herself for the worst. AJ hugged Janice and said, "He's all right Janice, pretty banged up though. He has a couple of broken ribs, a punctured kidney and he broke his leg in five different places. They had to put pins and stuff in them."

Janice covered her face with her hands. She was relieved that Marvin was alive, but scared of the injuries AJ described. She looked up and asked, "Do you think they will let me see him?"

AJ shrugged his shoulders. "Marvin is in the intensive care unit right now. Because of the pain, the doctor said he's heavily sedated. He wouldn't know if you were there anyway. It would probably be best if you came back tomorrow."

In some strange way, Janice was relieved that she didn't have to face Marvin. "AJ, do you know what happened?"

"Janice, all I know is he was driving his bike and a truck ran into him.

AJ looked at his watch. "I have to leave now. Are you going to be okay?"

"Yeah, I'll be fine."

"Well, you take care. If you need anything, give me a call."

"Thanks AJ."

After AJ left, Janice found the doctor and convinced him to let her see Marvin. She cringed when she saw the left side of Marvin's badly bruised face. Although he was sedated, one eye was open and his other eye was swollen shut. There was a tube down Marvin's throat and he was hooked up to all kinds of machines. His right leg was badly swollen and there were traces of dried blood around the 14 pins in his leg.

Again, Janice felt light-headed and could hardly catch her breath. She ran out of the ICU, down the hall and out the hospital doors to her truck. All of her held back tears came out like a water hose turned on full force.

For an hour, Janice sat in her truck, cried her eyes out and smoked one cigarette after another. When the sun began to rise, she decided it was time to go home.

As soon as Janice pulled into her driveway, she noticed there was a pile of what looked like junk and huge boxes all on her front lawn and sidewalk that led to her front door. "What the hell."

Janice jumped out of her truck. She snatched off the envelope that was addressed to Mrs. Perry and pulled out a few pieces of clothing. She recognized the clothes all belonged to Marvin. "Whatever Linda. I guess you found out the truth today too."

Janice was too tired to think about anything else or do anything else. She left the boxes in the yard as is and went into her house. She climbed the 13 stairs to her bedroom and threw the envelope on her mahogany dresser. Fully dressed, she laid across her king-size bed and was asleep before her head hit the pillow.

16

Desiree

"Ma'am, I think we're done here. Are you sure you don't need to go to the hospital?"

"No, I don't need to go to any damn hospital. What I need is some sleep so I can be fresh for my daughter's wedding tomorrow."

The officer didn't respond—he looked at the other officer and said, "Yes Ma'am, have a good night."

Desiree held the suite door open for the officers to leave. She closed it but opened it back up to ask how long Paul would be in jail when she heard one of the officers say, "Man, can you believe that? I wouldn't have blamed him if he had shot her. After an hour with her, I wanted to shoot her myself."

Desiree slammed the door and said, "Bastards." She stood in front of the oval shaped mirror and felt her swollen jaw. "I can't believe this shit. I hope that drunken ass Paul rot in jail for spoiling my night and messing up my beautiful face."

Desiree turned from side to side to make sure there were no visible bruises. "I guess it's nothing a little makeup can't cover up. How in the hell he knew I was in Brent's room is beyond me. He's lucky Brent didn't kill his ass and make me a very, very rich widow."

Desiree closed her eyes and thought about how Brent left her high and dry. "One day, I'll make your ass pay too Brent, but right now, I have to get the hell out of this room and figure out who is going to walk Cynthia down the aisle tomorrow."

Desiree opened her eyes and threw her hands up in the air as she remembered that she also had to find another singer to replace Brent. She slammed the door behind her and continued her ranting and raving down the hallway until she stepped onto the elevator. The young man on the elevator smiled at Desiree and asked, "Are you enjoying your stay here Ma'am?"

"Hell no, this hotel needs better security."

The young man coughed. "Ma'am, did something happen?"

"Oh, shut up." Desiree pushed the elevator button to the lobby.

The elevator stopped. With a huge smile on his face, the young man got out on the third floor and said, "Have a nice morning Mrs. Davis."

Before the elevator completely closed, Desiree pried the door open. "You, it was you! That's how Paul found me. You were at the front desk and it was you who gave my husband that key."

Desiree stood in the elevator doorway and watched the young man fall to his knees and laugh hysterically. "I'm going to have your damn job for this, you little bastard. You just wait and see!"

The young man yelled back, "If I do, it'll be well worth it," and laughed until he was out of Desiree's sight.

17

Paul

Paul silently said, "Thank you God," when he saw Chester at his cell with a police officer ready to set him free. "Man, what took you so long?"

"You should be thanking your lucky stars that your big brother is your lawyer and a damn good one at that. Oh yeah, and having a friend that's a judge didn't hurt either."

Paul agreed and gave Chester a tight hug that was full of love and gratitude. Chester held on to Paul longer than normal and said, "Let's go and just so I don't have to get out of my bed again in the wee hours of the morning, I'm taking you home with me."

Paul started to protest, but Chester said, "Say what you want Little Brother, but I'm not taking my eyes off of you until tomorrow night. Just so you know, I'm driving you to the wedding myself. Just think of me as Mr. Chester, your personal chauffeur."

"All right Chester, whatever you say."

Paul was thankful that he only had to spend a few hours in jail and didn't have to miss walking his daughter down the aisle.

Chester stopped his magnetic gray metallic Camry in front of his three-story brick colonial home. "Here we are sir. It's not as elaborate as the Davis monster across town, but I'm sure you will be quite comfortable here."

Paul gave Chester a half-hearted smile and asked, "Do I pay you enough?"

"Why do you ask that? Is it because my house is not as big as yours or is it that I don't drive a Bentley or have somebody driving me around like you do? You pay me plenty, but if you want to give your big brother a raise, believe me, I won't turn it down."

Paul was silent and looked straight ahead.

"Little Brother, let me tell you something. I'm happy that you're doing extremely well financially, but money can't buy you happiness. You see that right there?"

Paul looked at Chester's house.

"That's a home. In it, is a beautiful woman waiting for me and we are happy in it together. We're not trying to hide from one another. When I'm in my home, I want to say baby and she will hear me and come a running. I don't want to have to call her on the intercom or phone and we're in the same place."

Again, Paul was silent.

"Hey, I'm not saying it's anything wrong with a luxurious home, I'm just saying I don't need it to be happy. In my home, there is a tremendous amount of love, happiness, trust, respect, laughter, and peace—no amount of money can buy what we have."

Paul shook his head in agreement and the two of them got out of the car. As they walked down the asphalt driveway to the front door, Chester put his arm around Paul's shoulder. "Cheer up. I tell you what, if it'll make you feel better, you can give me a raise. Besides, it will help me out when I pay for our other five houses."

Paul turned his head to look at Chester in astonishment and asked, "What five houses?"

Chester gave Paul a mischievous grin and said, "We have one in Florida, one in Italy, New York, Las Vegas, South Carolina and the Bahamas. Oh, that's six."

"Hell, seven houses, I think I'm paying you too much." Paul laughed.

"No, not too much, but I am very well compensated Little Brother. Let's get some sleep."

18

Janice

"Janice, are you all right?"

"Dee," Janice said groggily.

"Yeah, what are you still doing asleep?"

"What time is it?"

"It's 2:15 in the afternoon."

Janice popped right out of bed. "Oh my God, I can't believe I slept that long. I have to get back to the hospital."

"Janice, what happened last night? You left so fast, I didn't know what was going on."

"I'm sorry Dee. Marvin was in a terrible motorcycle accident. I was at the hospital until 5:30 this morning."

Dee offered an insincere reply, "I'm sorry to hear that. How is he?"

Janice didn't like Dee's uncaring tone and gave her the short version of Marvin's condition, "He's pretty banged up. Dee, I have to go. I'll call you back."

"Ooookay, I'll talk to you later then."

Janice hung up the phone and sat on the side of her bed. She looked down at her slept in wrinkled clothes and looked over her shoulder at Marvin's untouched pillow. Slowly, she got up, walked over to the window and saw the boxes of clothes that Linda placed on her lawn last night. Janice thought about the previous horrific day and night and was in no hurry to rush back to the hospital.

On her way to the bathroom, Janice shed her wrinkled clothes. When she came out, she stopped in front of the dresser and picked up Linda's letter.

"Before I can digest anymore bad news, I definitely need something to eat"

Janice threw the letter back on her dresser and went downstairs. As soon as she reached the bottom step, her phone rang.

"Janice, I'm in the hospital," Marvin said.

"I know Marvin. I was there all night, but you were out of it. How do you feel?"

"I feel like a truck ran over me."

"From what I was told, a truck did run over you."

"I guess the feeling is accurate. Janice, I love you. I need to explain things. "Please don't leave me. I need to see you and . . ."

Janice yelled, "Marvin, Marvin!" She tried to call him back, but the line was busy. She redialed the number, but it was still busy. On her sixth attempt, the phone rang several times, but Marvin didn't answer.

Janice ran upstairs to her bedroom. Thirty minutes later, she was fully dressed and ready to go. She put the letter from Linda in her purse and headed to the hospital.

Once there, Janice stopped at the information desk to get Marvin's room number. When she got to the room, the bed was empty. Janice's heart began to race. Immediately, she thought while they were on the phone, Marvin died. She ran out of the room to find a nurse. "Where is he?"

"Oh, honey, he's all right. They just took him down to x-ray. He should be back in about 15 minutes."

Janice let out a huge sigh of relief and repeatedly thanked the nurse. She thought about waiting the 15 minutes outside so she could minimize her time in the hospital, but something inside her told her to stay.

Janice went back to Marvin's room to wait. There was an older gentleman that occupied the other bed. He looked at Janice and said, "Hello Miss."

Janice smiled and sat down in the chair next to the empty bed that was assigned to Marvin.

Twenty minutes went by and Marvin still hadn't returned. Janice reached into her purse for her phone and saw the letter Linda wrote. Under her breath, she said, "I guess I might as well get this over with."

Dear Mrs. Perry,

    I know now that you were telling the truth when you came to my office and Marvin is the one that is crazy and has been lying. According to your marriage license, you married Marvin on June 18th of last year. Since you are legally his wife, I thought I would be woman enough to tell you some things about your husband that I'm sure you don't know.

    Marvin and I lived together for 5 years until tonight when he tried to kill me. Believe me. The police will catch up with him.

    We have a four-year old son named Marvin, Jr., which after tonight, he will never see again. For your review, I have included a copy of his birth certificate.

    Marvin don't work at the law firm you visited and never has. That is my Daddy's and my law firm. By the way, please refrain from coming there again.

    Marvin charmed me out of hundreds of thousands of dollars and I'm sure he has stolen even more from me, but I can't prove it yet. Do not trust him with your checkbook.

    Marvin is a broke ass liar, cheater, and thief. The Bentley is mine and the house is mine. Again, please refrain from coming to my house ever again.

    Marvin don't love nobody but him. He will use you and when you got nothing, he will move to his next victim all in the same day. Girl, watch your back.

    By now, I'm sure you found his belongings that I placed at your little home. I'm through with him. He's all yours Mrs. Perry.

Linda Franklin,
Attorney-at-Law

Janice thought the letter sounded more like a Cease and Desist Order that warned her to stay away, but was shocked at the things Linda wrote. *Marvin tried to kill her?"*

When she thought about Marvin living with Linda before and during their eight-month marriage, she was angry all over again. *He has a son.* Janice shook her head in belief and disbelief.

Marvin's hospital phone rang. "It's probably AJ checking on Marvin. Hello."

The woman on the other end of the phone quickly asked, "Who is this?"

"This is Mrs. Perry, who is this?"

"The only Mrs. Perry I knew was Marvin's mother."

"Linda, what do you want?"

The woman said, "No, this is not Linda. This is Marvin's fiancée, Karen. He was at my house last night when he had the accident. Is he all right?"

Janice was past angry and done with all of Marvin's fiancées coming out of the woodwork. Her sympathies for Marvin quickly changed to contempt.

Janice shouted, "I'll tell you what, if you're his fiancée, then you bring your ass down here and find out if he's all right. Then, you take him home with you and you be the one to take care of his broken up ass."

Janice slammed the phone down so hard that it fell to the floor. She saw the man in the other bed peek through his curtain.

A few minutes later, the orderly brought Marvin back to his room and transferred him onto his bed. He was awake, tube free, but still banged up and bruised.

The man in the other bed tried to get Marvin's attention, but Janice blocked his view.

Marvin was still groggy and in a low voice said, "Janice, I'm so glad you came. I've missed you. I love you." He reached out for Janice's hand, but Janice didn't move. She stood there and looked at Marvin as if she could finish the job the truck started last night.

Through tight lips, Janice asked, "How are you Marvin?"

"I'm hanging in there. You see my leg."

"Yep."

"Janice, sit down. I need to explain."

"I'll stand, go ahead."

"I know you're upset about what you thought you saw yesterday. Sweetheart, Linda is my client. A few months ago, one of her high profile clients threatened her life. The firm hired me to be her bodyguard.

Everyday, I let myself in and made sure the place was safe before she and her son got home. Linda always had a thing for me. She tried, but I don't have anything to do with her and that's the truth."

"So, you never lived with Linda?"

"Hell no, I'm sure she wanted me to. The only woman I've ever lived with is you."

"Is that your son Marvin?

"No way. Just because he sees me everyday, the little guy has attached himself to me. You know I love kids. I can't wait until we have kids."

Janice continued to stare at Marvin with a look that could kill. "Who is Karen?"

Marvin reached for his water pitcher and said, "Sweetheart, I'm tired. I don't know any Karen."

Something inside Janice snapped. "You don't know, huh?" Janice took her fist and punched Marvin in his good eye and knocked the water pitcher clear across the room. "Your fiancée, that's who she is. I'm tired of all your damn lies. How could you do this to me?"

The whole time Janice yelled, she hit Marvin in his face. Marvin put up his hands and tried to protect himself.

The nurse heard all of the yelling and rushed into the room. "What is going on in here?" The nurse's eyes flew wide open when she saw Janice hitting Marvin. She ran back out of the room into the hallway and yelled, "Security, security!"

When Janice heard the nurse call security, she stopped and looked over at the man moaning and practically falling out of his bed. Marvin laid flat on his back, tired from his accident and all of the blows Janice landed on his already bruised face.

Janice grabbed her purse. "Marvin, don't you ever bring your lying ass back home. Tell your fiancée to take care of you, because I'm done."

Janice walked out of Marvin's hospital room, pushed the elevator button and vowed never again to return to Southern Maryland Hospital.

19

Desiree

The next morning, Desiree was immaculately dressed in an off-white linen pants suit and sashayed into Cynthia's room humming the wedding march. From the looks of her, no one would ever guess that less than six hours ago, her husband caught her with her lover, her lover deserted her and underneath all of that singing and heavy makeup, she was hiding a swollen jaw and a bruised ego.

"Cynthia, chop, chop. Today is the big day. Let's get a move on. We have so much to do. First, we have to get you something to eat. We don't want you passing out at the altar. Then, we have to get your hair done, your nails, makeup . . . . Where are the girls?"

"Good morning to you too Mother."

"Cynthia, get out of that bed. What's wrong with you? Today is supposed to be the happiest day of your life."

"I am happy. I'm just trying to wake up. What time is it anyway?"

"It's nine o'clock."

Cynthia still didn't get up. Desiree threw the covers to the bottom of the bed. "Girl, you better get your ass out of that bed."

"Mother, I just have a feeling that something is wrong."

Desiree looked away and opened the drapes. She looked out the window at the Potomac River and asked, "Why would you say that? It's a beautiful day and the wedding will be perfect."

"I don't know. It's just a feeling I have."

Desiree continued to look out the window. She thought about telling Cynthia that her father wouldn't be the one to walk her down the aisle. She felt if she told Cynthia the news too early that she would want to know why and be upset throughout the day. Desiree decided not to tell her daughter anything until two minutes before it was time for her to walk down the aisle. That way, Cynthia would have no time to worry and she would just walk down the aisle on the arm of her half brother and get married. Desiree smiled with satisfaction as she completed her perfect plan.

When Desiree turned around to look at Cynthia, she noticed Cynthia was staring at her. Desiree walked to the bed and asked, "Now what?"

"I have to call Daddy to make sure he'll be on time."

"No! I mean, you don't have to do that sweetie. He'll be there on time—I promise."

Cynthia's phone rang. "Good morning to you too." Desiree tried to see who Cynthia was talking to, but she jumped out of bed and ran into the bathroom. Five minutes later, Cynthia pushed open the bathroom door. "Okay Mother, I feel better now. I'm getting married today."

"Good, now get your ass back in there and put on some clothes. Hurry, we need to go."

Once Cynthia was out of sight, Desiree turned around and threw her hands up in the air. "Damn you Brent. At this late date, where am I going to find another singer?"

Desiree's phone rang. Not appreciating whomever it was that interrupted her thought process, Desiree yelled into the phone, "What is it?"

"Desiree Darling."

"You have some damn nerve calling me after the mess you left me in. What the hell do you want?"

"That's not what you said last night, I love you, please don't leave me."

"I said what do you want Brent?"

"Chill, Diva. I'm sorry. I told you I wasn't going to stay around and be questioned by the police and I meant it. I'm calling because I didn't want to leave you in a jam."

"Oh, besides the one you left me in last night."

"That's why I'm sending you a replacement singer."

"What kind of replacement?"

"Simmer down Diva. You'll get your money's worth. It's a woman though. I thought a woman wouldn't make that hot head hubby of yours jealous."

Brent laughed. "By the way, is he still seeing stars?"

Before Desiree answered Brent's question, she put her hand over her mouth and whispered, "He's in jail."

"Didn't see that one coming and you're still purring? That's interesting, interesting in deed. I thought you would have sweet talked him into believing you by now and all was good. Well, in that case, maybe I don't need to send you a replacement after all, unless of course you want one."

"Do whatever you want to Brent. I don't have time to play games with you right now. Just make sure I have a damn singer here."

Desiree hung up on Brent and a gigantic smile formed across her lips. As she thought about the day ahead, she too felt better. "I have a singer and Brent is mine again. He still loves me. I'll spring Paul later when he's had time to cool off. A week or two will do it. All is good again in D's world."

Desiree grabbed her purse and yelled, "Cynthia, let's go!"

The day zoomed by and it was almost time for the wedding to begin. The temperature was a perfect 75 degrees and not a cloud in sight. The church was beautifully decorated and most of the 350 guests had already arrived except for a few that were still making their way to their seats.

The five bridesmaids and maid of honor were all dressed in garnet chiffon dresses, each made a little differently than the other, but flowed just the same with each step they took in their four-inch matching silk pumps. Their faces were impeccably made up and complimented their up hairdos. Desiree was adamant about each of them wearing their hair up. She thought it not only looked classy, but a perfect way to make sure everyone saw the single strand of diamond earrings she bought for them. Each bridesmaid and maid of honor was as pretty as a picture.

The five groomsmen and best man were all dressed in black tuxedos with a garnet tie and black shirts held together at the wrist with diamond cufflinks, also compliments of Desiree. To distinguish the best man from the groomsmen, he wore a crisp white shirt. The groom wore a black long tail tuxedo with a crisp white tie and shirt held together with one-carat diamond cufflinks. All of the guys smelled good, looked good and were as handsome as the bridesmaids were pretty.

The flower girl resembled a miniature bride. She wore a no sleeve white sequined ball dress with a garnet sash tied around her tiny waist and baby's breaths placed throughout her curls. The ring bearer looked like a mini groomsman that had too much sugar, but still was cute as a button.

Desiree looked back at the wedding party and couldn't be any prouder at the way everyone looked. She beamed with joy when she saw Brian's short haircut. "Look at you—I almost didn't recognize you without your long hair. I love it."

Brian shook like a leaf on a tree. "I wanted to surprise Cynthia."

"She'll be surprised all right."

Desiree was dressed in a one arm snug fitting pale fuchsia silk gown with feathers lightly dangling off one shoulder and diamonds on her ears, fingers, around her neck, her wrist and on the tops of her shoes to let everyone know she had money and lots of it.

When the wedding planner signaled the wedding party to follow her, Desiree stepped into the room where Cynthia waited. She looked at her daughter and tears instantly streamed down her face. "Cynthia, you are breathtaking."

Cynthia smiled at her mother as she stood in her $10,000 custom made white ball gown with sequins everywhere and diamonds on her ears and around her neck that her mother insisted she wear. Cynthia looked like a princess out of a fairytale minus the wand. As Desiree stood eyeing her daughter, she thought about how much Cynthia loved Paul and how important it was to her that he walked her down the aisle. *It's time to tell her the truth.*

Desiree held Cynthia tightly in her arms and whispered in Cynthia's ear, "I need to tell you something."

"What is it Mother? Is it Brian? What happened?"

"No sweetie, it's not Brian. I'm so sorry. Your father won't be here. He's had an unfortunate delay so I've asked Dante to take his place and walk you down the aisle."

Desiree waited for Cynthia to throw a fit.

"Oh, is that all."

Desiree was shocked and let go of Cynthia so she could look her in the face. "Did you hear me?"

"Yes Mother, I heard you. Now go on, the wedding planner is calling you."

Desiree was relieved that Cynthia took the news better than she expected, but she still couldn't help but to feel guilty. Before Desiree left, she kissed Cynthia on her cheek. "I'm really sorry sweetie."

Desiree saw Cynthia step into the hallway of the church. She looked back at her daughter and read her lips, "Where are you Daddy?" Desiree shook her head and walked down the aisle towards her seat in the front row.

She looked at the bridal party and smiled as each of them made their way down the aisle and took their places on the huge pulpit. The pianist began to play again and the doors opened wide. All 350 guests stood up. Desiree heard a man say, "Excuse me." She quickly turned her head to see who had the audacity to arrive late at her daughter's wedding. She was shocked to see it was Dante and Chester taking a seat one row behind her. Desiree was outraged that Dante ignored her instruction and gave him the evil eye. Dante hunched his shoulders.

Desiree turned back around and wondered who was walking Cynthia down the aisle. She knew she checked on Paul's release last night and was told he would remain in jail until his arraignment on Monday. *It couldn't be Paul, could it?"*

As she waited to see who was walking her daughter down the aisle, Desiree's heart beat faster and faster. She braced herself and turned to the left. Desiree bit her lip when she saw the answer to her question right in front of her.

Paul purposefully stopped at Desiree's row, gave her a devilish wink and blew her a kiss. Desiree's eyes got huge. Her mouth dropped to the floor and sweat formed beneath all of her diamonds. Paul resumed his steps until he was right in front of Brian, the best man and the Pastor.

"Who gives this woman away, the Pastor asked."

"I do," Paul proudly said to the Pastor and kissed Cynthia on the cheek before he gently guided her towards Brian. Paul then took his rightful place on the front row next to Desiree. "Hello darling, are you surprised to see me?"

Desiree didn't answer Paul and continued to look straight ahead. When the Pastor instructed everyone to sit down, Desiree flopped down in the seat as if her legs gave way. Paul smiled and sat down.

Too close for comfort, Desiree discreetly moved her leg. Paul pressed his leg tightly against the silk fabric and took her right hand and placed it next to his upper thigh. Desiree felt something hard in Paul's pants pocket. She cleared her throat and nervously pulled back her hand. She put on her million dollar smile, looked straight ahead and silently prayed, "Pastor, would you pronounce Cynthia and Brian husband and wife already?"

Paul leaned over and whispered into her ear, "You didn't think I would actually miss walking my baby girl down the aisle, did you? Besides, I brought a special gift just for you."

Desiree broke out into a coughing fit. Paul smiled and heavily patted Desiree on the back.

Desiree looked at the Pastor and tried to send him a subliminal message to end the ceremony.

The Pastor said, "I now pronounce you husband and wife. You may kiss the bride."

Desiree said, "Finally," and bounced to her feet. Paul grabbed Desiree by the arm and hurriedly walked down the aisle behind the last groomsman and bridesmaid. Desiree waved at her guests and thought she better get away from Paul before he really kills her."

20

Janice

Two weeks had passed since Janice left Marvin in the hospital beat up, banged up and no doubt feeling worst than the pain he felt from the truck that hit him. Surprisingly, neither Janice nor Marvin contacted one another. Marvin spent most of his time drugged and when he thought about the mess he gotten himself into, he wished he was drugged.

Janice spent her days at work and most of her nights, she constantly replayed in her mind the day she followed Marvin, the letter from Linda, the phone call from yet another unknown fiancée and all of the lies she believed Marvin has told her.

Not hearing from Marvin or anyone from the hospital, Janice assumed Karen was taking care of him or Linda forgave him, replaced his wardrobe and hired someone to care for him. "Whoever he's with, good riddance. As far as I'm concerned, either one of them can have him. I'm through with him, his lies and our marriage."

Janice threw the chicken breast on the cutting board and stabbed it with her knife. "I could run him over myself for taking away my choice and lying to me day in and day out. I don't care how much I loved him. If I knew then what I knew now, I damn sure wouldn't have chosen to be in a marriage based on lies, fiancées, a baby, a baby mama and too much damn drama. The only thing left to do is to tell him the marriage is over."

The hurt, the betrayal and the ultimate taking away her choice had hardened Janice's heart and at the same time, gave her an odd sense of relief.

Janice danced to her favorite Jazz music while she cooked dinner for one, something else she had to get used to. When she heard a knock at her door, she stopped. "That's strange, I'm not expecting anyone. Who is it?"

"It's AJ."

Before Janice opened the door, she said, "If AJ drove all the way from Silver Spring, something bad must have happened to Marvin." She opened the door and asked, "Hey AJ, what's going on?"

AJ didn't say a word and walked past her with two hospital bags. When she saw Marvin with crutches under his arm standing in the doorway, Janice's attitude instantly changed from concern to anger. "What are you doing here?"

"I live here," Marvin said and hobbled past Janice and dropped down onto the brown micro-suede sofa.

Janice slammed the door behind him. "No, you used to live here. I believe you live with one of your fiancées and your son. I don't know why you came here, because I'm not going to take care of your broken up ass. You have fiancées coming out of the woodwork—go live with one of them. After all you've done, you really have some damn nerve showing up here. I don't feel sorry for you. You just got what you deserved."

Marvin never responded to anything Janice blurted out. He was on the sofa with his hands covering his face.

AJ interrupted Janice before she went into another flurry of Marvin's indiscretions. "Janice, please, I need to speak to you in private."

"AJ, I don't know why you brought him here. We are through. You need to get his stuff and get him out of here"

"Janice, you don't understand."

"Understand what AJ? Understand that he has been lying to me way before we got married and hasn't stop lying since or he has a fiancée while married to me or a baby by another fiancée that he lived with while he lived with me as my damn husband. So AJ, you tell me what the hell I don't understand!"

AJ frowned and looked over at Marvin. "Janice, I don't know what's going on, but Marvin is really sick."

"It serves him right. God don't like ugly."

AJ took a deep breath and said, "Besides breaking his leg in five different places, Marvin's kidneys are all messed up. The doctors said they're in pretty bad shape. If his kidneys don't get any better within the next few months, there's a possibility he may have to go on dialysis or need a kidney transplant."

"I don't care AJ. Take him home to his people and let them take care of him. I'm not doing it."

"Janice, please, there is no one else.

"Well, try one of his fiancées then."

"I know you're upset and I can't blame you, but no one will take care of him.

"AJ, do you really expect me to take care of him after what he's done to me?"

"Janice, I'll help you."

Janice looked at AJ as if he was crazy.

"I mean, I'll take care of him—just please let him stay. I promise you, I'll come here everyday, feed him, take him to his doctor's appointments and if you need me in between, call me. Please say yes."

Janice didn't say yes and she didn't say no. She just threw her hands up in the air and stomped upstairs.

A half hour later, Janice heard the front door closed. She ran downstairs. By the time she got to the last step, AJ had already pulled out of the driveway.

Janice looked around and didn't see Marvin or his bags and happily yelled out, "Yes!"

"Sweetheart, I'm glad you're excited I'm still here."

Janice turned around and walked towards the guestroom. When she saw Marvin with a wide smile on his face and his good leg hanging off the side of the bed, she said, "Give me a damn break."

Disgusted with the sight of Marvin and the entire chain of events, Janice grabbed her purse, said a few obscenities and stormed out the house.

21

Marvin

Marvin heard Janice squeal tires out of the driveway. "Thank goodness she's gone. I did not want to hear that shit today."

Marvin dragged himself to his feet and hobbled out to the kitchen on his new found wheels—metal crutches. With each step he took, the more tired he got and the more his metal crutches squeaked. When Marvin reached the refrigerator, he was almost out of breath. He leaned in and looked to see what kind of meal he could quickly throw together. He saw Janice was in the middle of preparing chicken breast and potatoes. He placed the dish into the already warmed oven. "That was easy enough."

Marvin sat down on the edge of the gray leather stool, rested his elbows on the black granite countertop and tried to catch his breath. He propped his crutches on the side of the counter and one fell on the floor. He struggled to reach it, but as he bent over, he felt light-headed and a sharp pain traveled down his side. Marvin banged his fist onto the counter. A tear slid down his cheek. For the first time in his life, Marvin felt powerless. He was weak as a kitten, all of the women in his life hated him and on top of all of that, he was literally immobile.

To Marvin, his love of cars took precedence over his love of women. He looked through his mail and said, "If I had a car, at least I could drive until I figured a way out of this mess. Damn, I can't let MJ grow up without me. Poor guy would talk crazy just like his non-talking mother."

Marvin opened up the refrigerator and saw two Heinekens. "Hell, I'm already in pain, a beer won't matter." He took a big gulp and rubbed his forehead. "How in the hell am I going to stay in this damn house 24 hours a day with her feeling the way she do?"

Marvin knew Janice was still angry at him and doubted that she would listen to anything he had to say. He took another drink of his beer. "At least I don't have to worry about going to jail. Ole girl felt sorry for me and retracted her statement and all charges against me were dropped. I still can't let her keep MJ from me. She said she didn't want me back though, but I can get her back, the Bentley, and my son, but right now, I want something to eat that don't taste like cardboard."

Marvin smiled. "I can't trust Janice to cook for me anymore—she might put something in my food to make me sicker than I am. No, she wouldn't do that, but just in case, I'll cook my own meals."

With things the way they were, Marvin knew it was going to be rough from here on out. The best thing he could do for himself and Janice was to stay out of her way until she came around. In time, he was confident that Janice would come around. The only question was when.

Marvin ate his food, left his mess behind on the kitchen counter, and hobbled back into the guestroom. Unable to remove his clothes, Marvin laid across the bed, fully dressed and thankful that he had enough strength to accomplish the things he did.

Marvin felt the effects of the pain pills. Moments later, he was fast asleep.

22

Desiree

As soon as they turned the corner, Desiree unlocked arms with Paul and headed towards the ladies room, a place she knew or at least hoped Paul wouldn't go. To make sure she was alone and before she emptied the contents of her purse onto the counter, Desiree looked underneath each stall. "Good."

Desiree dialed Brent's number and jumped up and down as if she needed to go to the bathroom. "Brent, please answer, you have to answer. If you show up, I'm good as dead and so are you."

Brent's phone went directly to his voicemail. "No, I don't want to leave a damn message." Desiree redialed the number. She heard some of the bridesmaids outside the door and quickly left Brent a message—"Don't come to the reception. Paul is out of jail and has a gun. Call me as soon as you get this message."

Just before the giggling bridesmaids burst through the door, Desiree placed her phone and contents back into her purse and pretended to re-do her lipstick.

"Hello Mrs. Davis, it was a beautiful ceremony," one of the bridesmaids said.

"And so are you two. In fact, the entire wedding party looked spectacular. You girls hurry up. We will be taking pictures soon."

Desiree rushed out of the bathroom in search of a safe place far away from Paul so she could continue her efforts to warn Brent.

The one person she tried to avoid happened to be the first person she ran into. Paul stood at the end of the hall. Out of nervousness, Desiree stopped dead in her tracks. Paul looked at her and patted his right pocket. Desiree moved towards the front door.

Cynthia called, "Mother, where are you going?"

"Oh, Cynthia, I was just going to get something out of the limo."

"Never mind that, come over here. I want you and Daddy in this picture."

Shit. "Coming darling."

Desiree and Paul walked towards the bride and groom. Desiree stood next to Brian and Paul stood next to Cynthia. Neither of them said a word. The photographer took several pictures before he called the rest of the bridal party.

Desiree quickly went to a corner and checked her phone messages. When she didn't receive a message from Brent, Desiree let out a deep breath. *I have got to get out of here.*

Desiree saw Paul talking to Chester and decided to take that opportunity to slip out the door. Once she was outside, Desiree realized she rode in the limo with Cynthia and the bridesmaids. "Damn, I can't take the limo. Hell, I'll just send it back."

Desiree jumped into the limo. "Bernard, take me to the hotel. Bernard didn't move. He turned around and asked, "Where are the others?"

Desiree sucked her teeth. "They're not coming. I need to get out of here now."

Bernard still didn't move. "Won't they be late?"

Desiree let out an impatient sigh. "Not if you come back to get them, they won't. Now, just go."

"Does Mr. Davis know you're hijacking the limo?"

Desiree yelled, "Yes! Now stop asking me all these damn questions. Just get me to the hotel."

Bernard shook his head. "Okay, if you say so."

"Yes, I do say so."

The reception was due to start in one hour. During the entire 40-minute ride to the hotel, Desiree repeatedly dialed Brent and filled up his message box. When Desiree got to the hotel, she jumped out of the limo. "Now, go back and get the others."

"Yes Ma'am."

Desiree ran into the hotel, went straight to the ballroom and looked around for Brent. She went to the front desk and the clerk from the night before was there. As soon as she saw him, she rolled her eyes. "You again."

The desk clerk smiled, but said nothing.

"Wipe that sheepish grin off of your face or I'll wipe it off for you. Have you seen Mr. Foster?"

"No Ma'am."

"I'll deal with your smart ass later."

"Ma'am, whatever you say."

Desiree left the desk and walked over to the bar. She realized time was not on her side. There was 15 minutes left before the reception started. Desiree drank her double Martini. "No sense running down the heels off my Prada. I'll just wait it out and if Brent shows, I'll cut him off at the path.

23

Paul

Paul noticed the bridesmaids were still at the church, the limo was gone and Desiree was nowhere to be found. He rubbed his temples and thought about how he must have put the fear into Desiree because she only stayed around to take a few pictures. Paul shook his head and continued to rub his temples.

Chester walked over to Paul. "Are you all right Little Brother?"

"Yeah man, I'm okay."

"I saw Desiree running out of here looking like the ghost that stole Tiffany's. What did you say to her?"

Paul laughed and patted his right pocket. "I just told her I had a special gift just for her."

"I don't care what Desiree does today. Promise me you won't do anything stupid at the reception."

Paul briefly looked away. "Chester, I can't make you any promises, but I will do my best."

"You better, because I've already used up all of my favors. If you don't, you'll be spending the rest of this weekend with Big Booty Bubba." Chester took his two fingers and pointed to his eyes and back out to Paul. "You know I got my eyes on you."

"Chester, didn't I tell you I'm a grown ass man? When are you going to stop treating me like your little brother?"

Chester put his arm around Paul and said, "The day I die."

"Let's go Chester."

The bridesmaids arrived at the hotel thirty minutes behind schedule. The wedding planner snapped her fingers and rolled her eyes at everyone. The mother of the bride was still missing in action and the 350 guests showed signs of impatience and hunger. With an obvious attitude, the wedding planner circled the ballroom and yelled out her name. Still,

Desiree was a no show. Paul instructed the wedding planner to go on without her instead of holding up the bridal party's entrance.

Unaware that there was a delay, Cynthia and Brian were in their own little world at the back of the line. Everyone except Desiree was in place and ready to make their grand entrance into the beautifully decorated ballroom that was draped in diamond like crystals and pearls. Six huge ice sculptures and cascades of flowers and candelabras were strategically placed throughout the ballroom with waterfall flower centerpieces placed on top of the 35 tables that were all covered in silk silver tablecloths with garnet colored napkins, monogram plates and crystal glassware. On one side of the ballroom in a corner, was a comfortable lounge area lit by candlelight and a six-person band that played Smooth Jazz on the stage in front of the dance floor.

With a loud and jovial voice, the disc jockey announced, "Please put your hands together and welcome for the very first time, Mr. and Mrs. Brian Anderson."

The 350 guests clapped, whistled and watched Brian carried his bride into the room where he gently placed her down on her three-inch white silk and diamond strapped sandals in the middle of the dance floor.

Paul looked at his now married daughter and his new son-in-law gaze into each other's eyes as they danced. He admired how much in love they were and wondered if he would ever feel that way for anyone. He knew he and Desiree hadn't been happy for years, but never thought things would be so out of control. He felt his pocket and briefly closed his eyes. *I have to do this.*

Chester and Dante sat at the table adjacent to Paul's with Chester's wife, Victoria, Dante's girlfriend and four other family members. Paul saw Chester raise his eyebrow at him. *I wish he stop worrying about me.*

Chester leaned over in his chair. "Hey, are you okay?"

"Yeah, I'm fine. Talk to your wife and stop babying me."

Chester repeated his gesture with his fingers.

Paul decided to allay Chester's concerns by starting a conversation with the family members at his table. He told a joke that got the entire table to laugh uncontrollably. Paul saw Chester turn around and resume his conversation with his wife and others at his table.

Twenty five servers made their way around the room and brought out the six course meal of shrimp, salmon, chicken, asparagus, salad, and what looked like an entire store of food. The reserved tables had finished their meal and there was still no sign of Desiree.

Cynthia and Brian mingled and stopped at Paul's table. "Hey Daddy, are you having fun?"

"I sure am. I'm full now and sick of how much of my money all of these freeloaders just guzzled down."

"Ah, Daddy." Cynthia kissed her father on the cheek, placed her arms around his neck and said, "I love you for it."

Paul patted her on the arm. "I know. Have you seen your mother?"

"Yeah, she's over there."

Paul turned around in his seat and saw Desiree standing in the corner by the band and talking to a man he didn't recognize.

The disc jockey announced that it was time for the father and daughter dance. "I guess we're up Baby Girl."

As Paul recognized the Stylistics' "You're a Big Girl Now," he smiled at Cynthia and took her out to the middle of the dance floor. When the man in the band began to sing, Paul looked to the ceiling and tried to remember where he heard that voice before. Cynthia talked about Brian and how many babies they were going to have. Paul smiled at Cynthia, but paid no attention to what she said.

Slowly, Paul danced Cynthia around in a circle so he could face the band. Paul's entire body stiffened.

"Are you okay Daddy?"

"Yeah Baby Girl, I'm fine."

Paul was no where near fine. When he saw the man who had an affair with his wife, who knocked him out cold, and caused him to spend time in jail, it sent fire through his veins. It took every bone in his body not to stop dancing and throw Brent off the stage or worst.

While Brent sang, he took his index finger and pointed to the side of his head. A few seconds later, he pointed his finger at Paul and made a cut throat gesture. The motions of Brent's hands were smooth and appeared that it went along with the song, but Paul knew differently. He looked at Chester and saw the worried look on his face.

When the song ended, Paul kissed Cynthia and handed her back to Brian. Brent walked off the stage and stood next to Desiree in the corner. Paul made his way towards them and put one hand in his pocket. He looked back and saw Chester had gotten out of his seat, but didn't see him. When Paul reached Desiree and Brent, he saw Brent with a gun aimed directly at him and Desiree's hand on his arm. Before Paul could react, a shot was fired, Chester pushed him to the side and they both fell to the floor.

The music was so loud that no one even heard the shot that went off. On the other side of the room, people still danced, but the people closest to Paul and Chester screamed and ran for cover. Brent shoved Desiree in the corner and ran out the side door. Desiree screamed out, "Oh my God," while Paul yelled out, "Someone call 911, my brother has been shot."

Paul held Chester in his arms while he rocked him back and forth. "Hold on Chester, I got you, hold on. You're going to make it Chester. I told you I was a grown man, why did you jump in front of me? You didn't have to do that. Chester! Chester! Open your eyes man."

Paul continued to rock his brother. "Did somebody call 911?" Tears streamed down his cheeks. Paul pressed down on Chester's wound and tried to stop the blood that gushed out of his chest. "Come on Chester, hold on. Help is on the way, just hold on."

Paul looked up at the short, rounded woman with long, mixed gray hair and hazel colored eyes that screamed to the top of her lungs when she saw her husband lying in a pool of blood. "No, not my Chester. Please, God no, don't take my Chester away. Chester, get up baby, get up!"

Victoria fell to her knees beside Paul, buried her head into Chester's bloody chest and continued to scream and cry. In an attempt to wake Chester, Victoria grabbed him and shook him, but he didn't move. Paul held Chester in one arm and with his other arm, patted Victoria on her back.

With tears in her eyes, Desiree kneeled down a few inches away from Paul, Chester and Victoria and asked, "Paul, why did you have to bring your gun?"

Paul didn't answer Desiree. He continued to rock his brother and pat his sister-in-law.

The paramedics arrived and pulled Victoria up and moved Paul to the side so they could work on Chester. Paul stooped down and looked at the paramedics insert tubes and put an oxygen mask on Chester. More paramedics arrived with a stretcher which blocked Paul's view.

Desiree walked over and stood beside Paul. He looked up at her with tears in his eyes and asked, "What do you want? Haven't you caused enough trouble?

"Paul, I'm sorry. This wasn't supposed to happen. Why did you have to bring your gun?

"Desiree, what the hell are you talking about? I don't have a gun."

"I felt it and you said you had a gift especially for me."

"You no good, selfish bitch. Can't you see my brother is dying and you're asking me about a fucking gun? Are you crazy?

Paul reached into his pocket. "Here's your gun," and threw his uniquely shaped flask with a long slim neck onto the floor. He pulled out an envelope and threw it at Desiree. It almost hit her in the face before it dropped on the floor beneath her feet.

Desiree reached down, picked up the envelope and through tears, read the heading, *Petition for Divorce*.

24

Janice

With no particular destination in mind, Janice headed out of her driveway quick, fast, and in a hurry to put as much distance between her and Marvin as the freeway would allow. For hours, she drove around Interstate 495 and rambled on to the empty seat next to her and listened to Al Green's "How Can You Mend a Broken Heart."

By the time the song started to replay for its umpteenth time, Janice broke into tears and shouted, "God, this isn't fair. Why is this happening to me? I'm a good person. I don't deserve this. How could Marvin do this to me? He comes back to me all broken up and after what he did, how can he expect me to take care of him? I will never take care of him and I will never forgive him for ruining my life!"

Janice turned off of the highway onto a nearby exit and tried to regain her composure. Tired of driving and tired of thinking, she turned off her music and lit a cigarette. In an attempt to find some form of relief from the heaviness deep within, Janice leaned her head back onto her headrest and closed her eyes.

After she calmed down, Janice apologized to God and asked for His strength and guidance. For a while, she just sat in silence, puffed her cigarette and looked out at the lights ahead. An extremely large sign read, "Gaylord, next exit," caught Janice's attention and finally, she had a destination.

Janice sat up straight, got back onto 495 south and drove one more exit to the Gaylord. As she got closer to the entrance, Janice noticed in front of the hotel, there were three limos, six police cars, two ambulances, a fire truck, and a mob of people, including a bride in a beautiful wedding gown crying and the groom standing next to her with his arm around her shoulders. Janice's first instinct was to drive away, but she couldn't take her eyes off of what appeared to be a wedding gone bad. Curiosity got the best of her. Janice slowly parked her truck at an angle where she could still see the crowd.

Minutes later, three paramedics rushed out someone on a stretcher and quickly placed the injured person into the ambulance. A man ran behind them. Once the ambulance doors closed, the man stopped dead in his tracks. His arms fell to his side as if whatever was holding them up was no longer there. The man's head hung low as he shook it from side to side. For a brief moment, the man looked around as if he was looking for someone. Janice caught a glimpse of his face and noticed he was a handsome middle-aged man, but looked like she felt, hurt, tired and very sad. For some reason, Janice's heart went out to this unknown man. She felt from him that he had just gone through something horrible that was far worst than what she dealt with.

After the ambulance left, the man hugged the bride and quickly walked over to a glacier white Bentley identical to the one she saw Marvin get into weeks ago. Instantly, Janice's attitude changed and her focus quickly drifted away from the unknown man in pain back to her man, who she had no intentions on going home to anytime soon.

Janice gave her face a quick touchup and hopped out of her truck. She walked past the crowd into the hotel in search of a bar. When she got to the bar, there were more people from the wedding. Janice found a seat at the end of the bar and ordered a vodka and cranberry juice, something stronger than the normal Chardonnay she usually drank. As she sat there and sipped her drink, she couldn't help but to overhear some of the wedding guests share their stories about what they thought happened. She heard one lady say, "The bride's dad shot his wife's lover and his brother got in the way."

A man said, "The wife's lover shot at the husband and ended up shooting the wife."

An older couple said, "The mother of the bride was the one who shot her brother-in-law, because he was always in their business."

Janice thought by the different stories the guests told, she would have never guessed they were all at the same wedding. What a shame it was to spend months planning the perfect wedding, buying the most beautiful dress and all of the other intricacies that go along with ensuring the perfect day and the only thing people remembered was that someone got shot. Her problems seemed minuscule compared to what the unknown newlyweds were going through.

Before Janice's lips touched her glass, she felt someone tap her on the shoulder. "Excuse me Miss."

Janice turned around. Surprised to see the handsome man in front of her, she smiled. "Davey, I can't believe it's you."

"Janice, I thought that was you. Girl, you're looking good. You haven't changed a bit. If I may say so, you look even better than you did 15 years ago."

"Well, you don't look so bad yourself Davey."

"You are the only one that calls me that. What are you doing here all alone on a Saturday night?"

Janice didn't answer. She just smiled and took another sip of her vodka.

Davey pointed to the bar stool next to her. "May I join you?"

"Sure."

Davey sat down and smiled as if he just hit the lottery.

"Davey, what are you doing here?"

"I was just at a wedding a buddy of mine invited me to. After all of the ruckus, I couldn't find him, so I decided to follow the crowd down here."

"I saw all of the police cars and ambulances out front. What happened?"

"Janice, I'm going to tell you like I told the police, I don't know. I was on the dance floor getting my groove on. Out of the blue, people started running and screaming. I heard somebody say, "He has a gun," and I dove right to the floor."

Janice laughed at Davey's illustration of his dive. "I did hear someone got shot up pretty badly though. That's too bad."

"Enough about that. You still haven't told me why you're here, looking as great as ever, and drinking by yourself on a Saturday night?"

"I'm just having a drink. Is that a crime?"

"Yes, it's definitely a crime for a man to let his beautiful woman spend the night alone in a bar. Who knows what could happen?"

Janice began to feel warm and tingly. She didn't know if it was from the vodka, from Davey or the rated R thoughts about Davey that swam around in her head. Janice laughed out loud.

Davey smiled at Janice. "I bet I know what you're laughing at." He then whispered into her ear, "The house is on fire."

Janice laughed even louder.

Davey took a sip of his Courvoisier. "Girl, back in the day, I was so in love with you."

Janice was surprised at Davey's statement and seriously doubted its validity. "Davey, if my memory serves me correctly, you were living with someone."

"Yeah, but I spent all of my time making love to you. She was on her way out."

Janice shook her head and took another sip of her vodka. "Before I respond to your "stuck on booty" rationalization, yes, you were with me a lot, but every night, you went home to someone else. If you were so in love with me back then, why wasn't it just me, especially once your relationship ended?"

Davey ignored Janice's question and took another sip of his drink.

Janice smiled. "Oh, it's all coming back to me now. You told me your weakness was that you loved *all* women."

"I never said that." Davey laughed.

"Oh, yes you did and you proved it time and time again. Seriously, Davey, I may not have liked it, but I always respected you for being honest with me and not taking away my choice."

"Hey, I'm an honest kind of guy."

Janice half-heartedly agreed with Davey and took another sip of her vodka. "Davey, tell me something."

"Yes, Miss Janice."

"You have been calling me for 10 years asking for booty and for 10 years, I've been saying no. Have you ever wondered why?"

"No, I just thought you were hung up on some loser."

Janice didn't particularly care for Davey's nonchalant answer and got a little hot under the collar. Going down memory lane only reminded her of why they went their separate ways.

Janice took a deep breath, looked Davey straight in the eyes and calmly said, "Davey, years ago, whenever you called, I used to hope this would be the time you finally told me you loved me and just wanted me, but each time, I was disappointed. You didn't give a damn about me, how I felt, what I wanted or what was going on with me. You just wanted familiar booty, an add-on sex partner to what you already had at home. Whether you care or not, that my dear was the reason I've been saying no to you for 10 years."

Davey drank his Courvoisier down in one gulp and ordered another.

"Janice, we could have been together, but noooo, you weren't ready to be loved. You kept hanging out with that big mouth, man hating girlfriend of yours. She didn't want to see us happy so she kept fixing you up with that Pretty Boy Floyd. You know the one that drove the red sports car."

"You're right Davey. Blame it on me."

"Whatever happened to that pretty boy?"

"I married him."

Davey took his drink and tapped Janice's glass. "See, that's exactly why you're out here all by yourself on a Saturday night. He's probably out with another woman. Hell, he probably got two women—out there trying to scam his way into somebody's panties."

Although Davey's timing was off, his statement about Marvin was sadly true. Janice briefly looked away. She felt like Davey just stabbed her with a knife.

Janice ordered another vodka and cranberry juice. For a few minutes, neither Janice nor Davey said a word. Both pretended to look around the bar at the other patrons. Janice was the first one to break the silence. "Davey, are you still married?"

"Yes, I am, but if you want to continue this conversation upstairs, I won't stop you. My boy got a room here for the weekend, but he's not coming back. It would be a shame to waste it."

"Davey, I don't swing with married men. Besides, I'm married too."

"I won't tell, if you won't."

"Davey, you're the same as you were 15 years ago. The only thing different about you is that you have less hair."

Davey rubbed his bald head. "That's a good thing, isn't it?"

"Yeah, it is. I can always depend on you to be you."

Janice was on her third drink, which was two too many. She laughed at everything and talked her head off. Memory lane was back where it belonged and Janice was having fun. She totally forgot about what initially brought her to the hotel.

Davey was back to his charming self. He told jokes and gave Janice compliment after compliment. The wedding party was gone and the bar was almost empty. Davey looked into Janice's eyes, leaned over and kissed her on the lips. "It's so good to see you."

Janice kissed Davey back and felt that same weird chemistry between them that against her better judgment, led her back to his arms years ago. For a brief moment, she wished it was Marvin that kissed her and all of the problems between them never existed. Again, Davey kissed Janice. This time, the kiss was more passionate and last a little longer. Without a word, they both put down their drinks. Janice followed Davey upstairs to his buddy's room.

On the way upstairs, in Janice's mind, she tried to justify that she wasn't technically cheating because she and Marvin were through. Deep down, she knew what she was about to do was as wrong as the day was long, but she continued to walk to the room. Janice thought it was just like that R. Kelley song, her mind was telling her no, but her body was telling her yes. She was about to do something she had never done before and the very thing she said she would never do.

The moment they got to the room, Davey stripped down to his birthday suit and leaped onto the bed. Janice slowly took off her printed dress and eventually joined him. A part of her had second thoughts and the other part of her wanted to go through with it. Davey had no problem coming to attention, had already suited up and was ready to go. Janice thought Davey planned the whole thing, but how could he? Knowing Davey, he was always prepared for whatever could happen."

"Janice, stop thinking so much and help me put out this fire."

Janice closed her eyes and allowed Davey to work his magic.

An hour later, Janice watched Davey get dressed as fast as he undressed. She remembered how she used to hate that about him, but now she was rather thankful for his speedy exit.

Davey smiled from ear to ear. Janice thought Davey felt extremely proud of himself for finally conquering his 10-year Janice drought.

"I never planned for this to happen, but I'm sure glad it did. Janice, you can stay here if you want. My buddy won't be back tonight.

"Thanks, I just may do that."

"I'll see you later. We'll have to do this again real soon."

After Davey closed the door, Janice immediately sat up on the side of the bed and yelled out, "What the hell did I just do?"

Janice brushed down her hair and rubbed her temples. She tried hard to discern the mixed up feelings she had about what just happened. She glanced around the immaculate suite—half admired its décor until her eyes fixed on the empty condom package that lay on the pillow. A devilish smile formed across her face as she thought about Davey's skills in the bedroom. "Davey was as good as he was 15 years ago, but there was not a bit of magic, at least not for me."

Janice hadn't planned to have sex with Davey and it never occurred to her to pay Marvin back. She knew what she did was wrong, but was surprised by her lack of guilt. She thought about the way she felt after the many times she and Marvin made love and wondered if she would ever feel that way again with someone else. Janice felt empty and alone. She could tell by her actions that her heart was no longer with Marvin and definitely not with Davey. The magic she and Davey shared 15 years ago disappeared when the love disappeared.

Again, Janice smiled. "I wonder if Davey wanted to feel that powerful magic again and that's why he kept calling me all those years. He must have thought I had some kind of magical booty."

Janice looked around the room. "Sad, if Davey only realized that it's the love between two people that make the magic—he would have stopped obsessing over mine." Janice laughed and said, "I doubt it. Magic or not, Davey don't care. He was happy as a lark when he left. I guess men are just different. For most men, sex is a pleasurable exercise of the body. For most women, sex is a pleasurable exercise of the heart and body. I guess when there's no love, sex is just sex. Oh, well."

Janice stood up, let out a huge sigh and shook her head at her moment of temporary insanity of looking for magic at Davey's place. She glanced around the beautifully decorated suite and said, "This is the second place I don't want to stay."

Minutes later, Janice came from the bathroom showered, dressed and again, going no place in particular. On the outside, she looked as if nothing ever happened, but on the inside she felt sad, empty and an overwhelming craving for hot wings. Janice's stomach growled and she laughed.

It was 11 o'clock and she hadn't eaten since noon. Janice left the room and once again, she had a destination.

25

Paul

Paul made every effort to keep up with the ambulance a few hundred feet ahead. He weaved in and out of traffic and drove 80 mph. Out of his window, Paul yelled, "Drive man," and relentlessly honked his horn at a man who refused to drive one mile over the 40 mph speed limit.

When Paul finally reached the hospital, he parked in front of the emergency room exit in a "no parking zone." The hospital security guard yelled at Paul, "Hey buddy, you can't park there," but Paul ignored the guard's command and hurried inside the emergency room.

"Ma'am, can you tell me anything about my brother, Chester Davis? The ambulance just brought him in about 15 minutes ago."

The young lady behind the information desk wrinkled up her nose at Paul, handed him a clip board and said, "Sir, you need to sit down and fill out these papers before the doctor sees you."

Paul was taken aback by both the young lady's facial expression and what he thought was her inability to comprehend the plain English language.

"Didn't you understand me? I said I'm here for my brother, Chester Davis."

"Sir, don't you need to be seen?"

Reluctantly, Paul looked down and saw Chester's blood on his shirt and hands. Growing more and more agitated with each minute that went by without an answer about Chester, Paul banged on the counter with his half bloody fist. "No, I don't need to see a damn doctor. I told you, I'm here to find out what's going on with my brother, Chester Davis. As a matter of fact, get me a doctor. I'm tired of wasting my damn time. Get me a doctor now!"

The people in the waiting room stopped what they were doing and all eyes were intently on Paul. The young lady picked up the phone and turned her back to Paul. Dante, Victoria, and Paul's two sisters, Marie and Janice, could hear Paul yelling before they entered the hospital and quickened their steps.

"Dad, Dad, try to calm down," Dante said.

Paul turned his head and waited for the young woman to get off the phone. Dante found seats for his aunts and walked back to Paul. "How's Uncle Chester?"

"I don't know son. I'm trying to get some damn answers from these incompetent people!"

A stocky security guard stood in front of Paul with his hand on his stick.

"Look buddy, you need to calm down right now. I know you may think you own the place and you can do what you want, but if you don't start respecting this hospital and its rules, I'll be forced to remove you from the premises. Now, you have five minutes to move that pretty white Bentley of yours or I'll move it for you."

Under his breath, Paul said, "Here we go again." Paul got right up in the guard's face. "Look Barney Fife, I'm not going anywhere until somebody in this hospital tells me what's going on with my brother."

The security guard didn't budge. He looked Paul directly in his eyes. "I got your Barney Fife, all right," and grabbed Paul by his shoulder. Paul lost his temper and was about to hit the guard when Dante stood in between them and blocked his dad's would be, knock out punch.

The security guard was visibly shaken by Paul's actions. That's r . . . ight, you bet . . . ter get him."

"All . . . right Bar . . . ney Fife."

Dante yelled at his father, "Dad, please! You're making matters worst." Dante turned around to face the guard. "Sir, I'll move the car."

Paul threw Dante his keys. While Dante spoke to the guard, Paul looked at the young lady behind the desk. "Somebody better tell me something real fast."

Victoria, an otherwise quiet woman, said, "Paul, stop acting like a hot headed sixteen-year old and cut out all of your foolishness."

Paul said nothing.

Victoria hugged her brother-in-law and in her soft voice said, "Chester is going to be all right, you'll see."

"You're right Big Sis, on both counts. Let's sit over here."

Paul kissed Victoria on the top of her head and guided her and his two sisters to a seating area away from the crowded emergency room. When Victoria wasn't looking, Paul stared at her and wondered if Chester didn't make it, God forbid, how would she handle it? "I wonder what's taking Dante so long. I'll be right back."

Paul went outside to look for Dante. Across the parking lot, he saw Cynthia and Brian pull up in the limo and next to his car stood Desiree talking to Dante. Paul ran to his car. "Desiree, get the hell away from here. If it wasn't for you, none of us would be here, especially Chester. Haven't you caused enough trouble?"

"Paul, I'm sorry. Please let me help you." Desiree touched Paul on the arm.

"Help me? You know how you can help me? Find that Popeye looking motherfucker and turn him in for shooting Chester. I tell you one thing, if Chester doesn't make it, you better hope the police find him before I do and your ass better hide too."

Cynthia ran up to Paul. "Daddy, what's going on? How's Uncle Chester?"

"Ah, Baby Girl, what are you doing here? Go on, this is no place for you on your wedding day."

"Yeah, some wedding day."

Paul hugged Cynthia. "I know Baby Girl. Go on your honeymoon. Once I hear something about Chester's condition, I'll let you know. Brian, take Cynthia and go now."

"Yes, sir."

Paul looked at Desiree. "You need to get the hell away from here too unless you want to join Chester."

Once Paul was back inside, he noticed his sisters were not in the waiting room where he left them. He didn't dare go up to the young lady at the desk again. Instead, he went to the bathroom. Paul looked in the mirror at the dried up blood on his chin and his white shirt that was saturated with Chester's blood. He washed his face, his hands and buttoned his jacket.

For what seemed like forever, Paul stood in front of the mirror and blamed himself for Chester getting shot. Chester always protected him and this was no different. As he thought about the possibility of Chester not making it, a tear slid down one of Paul's cheeks. He didn't know what he would do without him, but he did know if Chester died, so would Popeye.

Paul went back to his seat. Dante was there waiting for him. Paul asked, "Dante, have you seen your aunts?"

"Nope."

Fifteen minutes went by and there was still no word about Chester and his sisters and Victoria were still missing in action. Paul had a bad feeling. Unaware of the two young doctors approaching them, Paul looked down and said a silent prayer.

"Dad, look."

Paul looked up and sprung to his feet.

"Are you Paul Davis?" the doctor asked.

"Yes, I am."

"Can we please see some ID?"

Paul thought the doctor's request was strange, but he didn't protest. He gave the doctor his driver's license. The doctor looked at it, nodded to the other doctor and returned Paul his ID. Paul said, "This is my son, Dante Davis."

One of the doctors shook Dante's hand and said "Follow me please."

Paul and Dante looked at each other. In silence, they followed the doctors down a long, dark, narrow hallway that led to a small waiting room with four empty chairs. *This can't be good.*

Once they were inside the room, one of the doctors closed the door behind them and said, "Please sit down."

Paul said, "Look, I don't want to sit down. What's going on with Chester?"

One of the doctors put his hand on Paul's shoulder. "I'm sorry to inform you that your brother didn't make it. When they brought him in, he was already gone. We still tried to revive him, but it was nothing else any of us could do. I'm very sorry for your loss."

The other doctor patted Paul on his shoulder and looked at Dante. "I'm very sorry for your loss.

Paul clinched his teeth together, raised his balled up fist into the air and yelled, "Fuck!"

With tears in his eyes, Dante yelled, "Dad, Dad!"

Paul just looked at his son and hugged him tightly. They heard a scream coming from the hallway. As soon as they opened the door, Paul saw the security guard that he had a run in with earlier. For a moment, their eyes met. The security guard walked away. In another small room, Paul saw Victoria slumped over and cried out, "My Chester is gone. Oh no, this can't be. Please bring my Chester back, please. His two sisters tried to console Victoria the best they could. Paul wanted to go to Victoria and tell her how sorry he was, but his legs wouldn't move. He tried to speak, but no words would come out.

Victoria turned around and slowly walked towards Paul until she stood directly in front of him. For minutes, through swollen tear filled eyes, Victoria just stared at Paul. All of a sudden, Victoria slapped Paul across his face as hard as she could. Paul briefly closed his eyes and felt the sting from her heavy hand. "Victoria, I'm so sorry."

"Shut up! This is all your fault. If it hadn't been for you and that evil wife of yours, my poor Chester would still be here. For years, Chester begged you to leave that woman alone before something tragic happened, but you wouldn't listen. He worried about you and your happiness more than you did about yourself. I told him you were a grown man, but that never stopped him. Every time your hot head got you into a mess, my Chester broke his neck and bailed you out. He worried about your drinking too much, he worried about your million dollar company and he worked for you day and night and made sure you were always taken care of and all you did was take, take, take. You being the selfish, arrogant, self centered S.O.B that you are never stopped to think what it was doing to him and the people who really loved you. He tried to protect you from any and everyone that even looked like they were going to hurt you and today he took a bullet for you and now he's gone! You did this to him, you did this to us and I will never forgive you. I will never forgive you!"

Again, Victoria cried out, "Chester, oh Chester."

Paul's sister, Janice, went over to hug Victoria. Paul shook his head and felt every bit of the shame and blame for Chester's untimely death. He knew Victoria was in shock, but he felt everything she said to him was true and it hurt him worst than any hurt he'd ever felt before.

Dante went up to his father and put his hand on his shoulder. "Are you all right?"

"No, take care of your aunts and make sure they get home safely. I need to get out of here."

With sympathetic eyes, Janice looked at Paul and nodded as he turned around and left the hospital.

As soon as Paul got in his car, he automatically opened his glove compartment to get his flask. When he remembered he left it at the hotel, he hit his steering wheel, grabbed it tightly, and yelled, "Dammit!" Paul put his head back against his headrest and sat there in the parking lot. He thought about Chester and all of things Victoria cried out. The last place he wanted to go back to was home. It was 11 o'clock and he needed a drink like a fish needed water to live.

Paul sat in his car and tried to think of where he could go to release some of his pain. After a few minutes, he started up his engine and drove with no particular destination in mind. "I paid $8,000 for liquor and only had one damn drink. I know exactly where I can get plenty to drink."

Paul arrived back at the hotel and went directly to the ballroom. He stepped under the police tape and stood in the spot where he last held Chester. Paul felt like his head was going to spin off his shoulders. He couldn't stand it anymore. He left the ballroom and walked down the hall to the bar. The bar was empty except for one woman that sat at the far corner. Paul told the bartender, "All of the leftover booze I paid for, sit it right in front of me."

The bartender nodded and poured Paul a vodka and cranberry juice before sitting the bottle of vodka in front of him. "Sir, I'm sorry to hear about your brother. Is he going to be all right?"

"No."

"I'm very sorry Mr. Davis. Nothing like that has ever happened here. I get off at one o'clock, but for you, the bar will be open for as long as you need it to be. I'll be in the back if you need anything else."

Paul nodded a thank you and finished his drink with one big gulp. He was about to pour another drink when the woman at the far end of the bar said, "I'm sorry too."

Paul continued to pour his drink. Not wanting to engage in a conversation with anyone, let alone some strange woman, he decided to ignore her and hoped she got the message.

Again, the woman said, "I'm sorry too."

Paul thought the woman was beginning to sound like a parrot. Before she repeats I'm sorry all night, he better respond and get rid of her. Without looking up from his drink, Paul said, "Thank you. What are you sorry for?"

"I'm sorry that you went through something horrible at your daughter's wedding and I'm sorry that you lost someone very close to you."

This time, Paul looked at the woman. "You are either psychic or just nosey as hell and enjoy eavesdropping on my conversation."

"Neither, I saw you earlier when you ran behind the ambulance. When the doors closed, I saw your arms fall to your side as if whatever was holding them up was no longer there. I saw you hang your head low and shake it from side to side as if you couldn't believe what just happened. When you looked around for your daughter, I caught a glimpse of your face. You looked like you do now, hurt, tired and very sad. From that glimpse, I could feel you had just gone through something horrific and for some unknown reason, my heart just went out to you."

Paul stared at the woman. He couldn't believe she got all of that just by a moment's glance at him. He also couldn't remember anyone ever paying that much attention to him and then getting everything right about his feelings. Paul thought if it was anyone else, he would have told them to mind their own damn business, but with this woman, it was something different about her. There was a sense of peace and calming to each word she spoke. He could truly feel that what she said to him came from her heart. Paul wanted to hear more of what she had to say. "May I offer you a vodka and cranberry juice?"

"Why not, I'm in no hurry to go home."

The woman walked over and sat next to Paul. For the first time in four hours, Paul slightly smiled. He extended his hand and said, "My name is Paul."

"Hello Paul, my name is Janice."

"I have a sister name Janice. "It's very nice to meet you Janice."

"I would say the same, but I met you earlier."

26

Desiree

Just making Desiree's 15-minute deadline, the security guard ran towards the limo and yelled, "He's dead!"

Desiree peered over the top of her dark shades at the man. "Are you sure he's dead?"

The guard tried to catch his breath. "Yes, the man in the bloody shirt, his son and three other women were in the back room. I heard the doctors break the news to them. They all cried."

"Very well done officer." Desiree smiled and handed the security guard $300.

He shoved the three crisp $100 bills into his pocket and repeatedly thanked Desiree for his small fortune.

"Driver, take me to the Hilton."

In his rear view mirror, Bernard frowned at Desiree, but said nothing.

"Is there a problem?"

"No Ma'am, no problem."

"Just keep your eyes and your judgment to yourself and get me to the damn hotel."

"Yes, Ma'am."

Once Bernard pulled out of the hospital's parking lot, Desiree said, "I can't believe this shit is happening."

Bernard looked back in his rear view mirror. "Did you say something Ma'am?"

"I'm not talking to you. Stop being so damn nosey and drive."

"Oh, I'll drive you all right," Bernard said under his breath.

"What was that?"

"I said oh, it's a nice driving night."

When Bernard came to the next corner, he purposely increased his speed and made Desiree sway to the left and drop her phone. She gave Bernard a cold look and dialed Brent's number. "Please pick up, please pick up. I have to warn you."

"Hello," Brent answered.

"Brent, the police are looking for you and Chester is dead."

"Slow down Diva. What did you just say?"

Bernard made a sharp right and made Desiree sway again.

"I said the police are looking for you."

"Diva, why are the police looking for me?" Brent asked.

"They want to question you because you killed Chester."

"Man, I swear you must have 666 on your ass. Every time I'm with you, I get closer and closer to Hell. You better hope they don't find me. If I go down, you go down."

"Are you threatening me Brent?"

"No Diva, I'm just simply stating facts."

"Keep your facts to yourself and get over to the Hilton. I'll meet you there in 30 minutes." Desiree hung up on Brent.

Bernard pulled up to the Hilton and slammed on breaks. Desiree almost fell out of her seat. "Bernard, are you crazy? You made me break my damn nail driving like a maniac."

"You told me to hurry."

"You're just being a smart ass. You can hurry yourself right on down to the unemployment line."

Bernard got out and opened Desiree's door. "Does this mean I'm fired?"

"Are you dumb or just stupid? What do you think?"

"I think it's a good day after all."

Bernard gave Desiree a salute, got into the limo and drove off.

Desiree ran to the hotel bar and looked for Brent. "Bartender, give me a double Martini now!"

"Yes, Ma'am."

Desiree was just about to call Brent again when he walked up. "Brent, what took you so long?"

"Diva, I'm here now. Hurry up and tell me what you want to tell me because I'm not taking any more chances hanging out with you."

"Paul didn't have a gun. It felt like a gun, but it was a damn flask. He kept telling me he had something special for me and I thought he was going to shoot me. You know what it was?"

"What"

"Divorce papers."

Brent held back a laugh when the server brought Desiree's drink. Desiree took a huge drink of her Martini.

"Divorce papers? Well, what do you know? I was wrong about hot head hubby after all. The $10 million dollar drunk does know when to let go. How about you Sweet Cheeks, do you?" Brent laughed.

Desiree rolled her eyes. "Hell no. For 17 years I've put up with his jealousy, his drinking and the rest of his shit and I'll be damned if I leave without getting what's rightfully mine."

"What's that, a million dollar ass whipping?"

"No, half."

"Diva, you are what they call . . . an adulterer. Do you really think you're going to get half? Come on now Diva. He may be a drunk, but he's not a stupid drunk. By the time that man gets through with you, you'll be lucky if you have enough to get your nails done and your hair did." Brent laughed even louder.

"Brent, this isn't funny. You have to get out of town for awhile."

"No, I have businesses to run. I just can't pick up and leave because you tell me to. Besides, I didn't kill anybody. If you hadn't pulled my arm, you would be a grieving widow right now instead of an almost broke ex-wife."

"That wasn't the plan and you know it."

"Plans, whatever happened to your spontaneity?"

"Because of your spontaneity, my brother-in-law is dead."

"Yeah, I can tell you're all broken up about it."

"Brent, I didn't want him to die."

Brent didn't respond. Desiree took a sip of her Martini. "Hell, he never liked me anyway, but that's not the point."

"What the hell is the point Diva?"

"I told you. You have to get out of town for awhile."

"I should have shot your Diva ass. I told you—I can't go. The police are looking for a bald head man in great physical condition that sings. Do you know how many men fit that description? They won't find me. They will be looking for Frank Beverly."

Desiree thought about Brent's logic and said, "Okay, just keep a low profile then, but I'm leaving for a couple of weeks until things settle down."

"Suit yourself Diva."

"You know that cheap bastard had the nerve to give me two weeks to get my things. That's my damn house. I'm the one who picked it out, decorated it, cleaned, it and took care of it."

"Yeah, with his money."

"*Our* money Brent."

"Well, it ain't gonna be our money for long. Hey Diva, have you been to the bank yet?"

Desiree's mouth flew open and struggled to form the words, "No, not yet. I didn't know he was going to serve me divorce papers at my daughter's wedding. Actually, I didn't think he had the guts to divorce me."

"Diva, sometimes you think too damn highly of yourself. Every man and every woman has a limit as to how much crap they'll take. Some are short and some are long, but never doubt there's always a limit. He just took too damn long reaching his. I would have divorced your ass in a year. Then again, I wouldn't have married you, because I know what kind of woman you are."

"What kind of woman am I Brent?"

"The kind that if she doesn't beat her grieving hubby to the bank Monday morning, she'll be shit out of luck. You may be already too late. If that's the case, don't even think about looking my way. I have bills like normal people. One more thing, just because you may be having a cash flow problem in the very near future that will not negate your financial obligations, if you know what I mean. Okay Desiree Sweetie?"

Desiree rolled her eyes at Brent. "I should have left your ass alone years ago."

"Should of, could of, would of, but you didn't."

Desiree briefly closed her eyes, and pinched the top of her nose. The last two days of wedding preparations, scheming and literally dodging bullets had finally taken its toll on Desiree's vigor. She was tired and wanted to go home but shook her head when she realized she couldn't possibly go back home tonight or any other night.

When Desiree opened her eyes, she saw Brent staring at her with a wide smile on his face.

"Why so gloomy? Are you missing hubby dearest?"

96

"No, I just realized I can't go home. I guess I'll just have to stay here for the night. Care to join me?"

Brent shook his head and leaned across the table. "Diva, you're a glutton for punishment. No, I'm not staying with you tonight or any other night."

Desiree yelled, "Then leave," and threw her Martini in Brent's face.

Brent slowly licked the remnants of her Martini from the side of his face and stood up. He bent down and kissed Desiree on her cheek. "Bye Diva. Stay rich."

"Oh, shut up!"

27

Janice

Janice heard her phone ring, but decided not to answer. Paul poured her a vodka and cranberry juice. He picked up his glass and asked, "What shall we toast to?"

"To happiness."

Paul tapped Janice's glass. He took his other hand and covered his face.

Janice sensed that Paul's pain ran much deeper than she imagined. At that moment, all she wanted to do was ease his pain. "I'm sorry. If you'd like, we can toast to something else."

"You didn't do anything to be sorry for. Everything was entirely my fault. I'm the one that's sorry."

Janice could tell Paul wasn't talking about the toast. "Would you like to talk about it?"

"No."

"Okay, if you change your mind, I'm a pretty good listener."

"I'll keep that in mind."

Paul gazed into Janice's eyes.

Janice smiled. *He must be trying to look into my soul.*

"You're pretty and you have pretty eyes too."

"Thank you."

Paul picked up his drink and nodded. "I can tell you're a good person."

Janice didn't respond. She felt Paul wanted to talk, but wasn't quite ready. She discreetly checked her caller ID. Her eyes widened when she saw the last call was from Marvin. Janice quickly closed her purse and took a generous sip of her drink.

When she looked up, she was surprised to see Paul had been watching her the entire time.

"Is something wrong Janice?"

"No, why do you ask?"

"When you looked at your phone, your expression changed."

"Just someone I never expected to call, that's all."

"I never expected my brother would die at my daughter's wedding either, but it happened. Chester was a good person too."

"Who is Chester?"

Paul took a sip of his drink before he answered, "My brother."

In a soft voice, Janice said, "I have a brother name Chester."

"He didn't deserve any of this. If I could, I would trade places with him in a heartbeat."

While Paul talked, Janice noticed his full curly eyelashes and his eyes were also pretty—only now, they were glossy and filled with sadness.

"Today, I gave my Baby Girl away, served my wife of 17 years divorce papers and right in that room, I held my big brother in my arms and watched him die. That's why I have all this blood on my shirt."

Janice nodded and did everything she could to hold back her tears.

"That bullet was meant for me. I should be the one dead, not Chester. You toast to happiness, I don't see happiness in my future."

Again, Paul covered his face with his hand.

"Paul, I'm really sorry about your brother. I know it doesn't seem like it now, but one day, true happiness will find you when you least expect it. I can tell you too are a good person and you deserve to be happy. Although you look like the meanest person in the world on the outside, I can tell you're a softie at heart."

Paul uncovered his face. "You can tell that about me?"

"Sure, when you smile, your entire face lights up—you should do it more often."

"Janice, are you happy?"

"Not as happy as I could be."

"Are you married?"

For a few seconds, Janice fidgeted in her seat. "Yes, I mean no."

Paul raised his eyebrow at Janice's response and asked, "Well, which is it?"

"In my heart, no, I'm not married.

"I'm sorry to hear that. You know the heart always wins."

Janice looked at Paul and smiled. She liked the way he talked. She could tell he was a man full of passion and didn't have a problem expressing his good or bad feelings.

"I'm not trying to be nosey, but what happened?"

"Yes you are. Let's just say my husband found happiness in too many other places than home."

"Sometimes, we men are stupid like that. When we have a good woman at home, we're in the street looking for someone else. When we have a bad woman, we're at home while she's in the street with someone else. Tell me something Janice. Do you see true happiness in your future?"

"I sure do. One day, I know that all of my dreams will come true and I will be a happy, happy, camper."

Paul continued to smile at the stranger he just met. "Tell me your dreams?"

"Okay, my dream is to make a difference in how we treat each other by teaching the key to delivering extraordinary customer service, consistently and effortlessly all over the world. I plan to have my own network and consulting business with five consultants, including myself teach through seminars and workshops based on the concepts in my book, *Remember What Your Mamas Taught You, a unique way of looking at customer service.* I also plan to own an event hall where that would be the home for my seminars and when I'm not using it—I can rent space to people for all of their happy occasions. Think about it, no one ever rents a hall for a sad occasion. That way, I will be happy and I can also share in other people's happiness."

Paul was still smiling. "You should see how your face lights up when you talk about your dream. It's good that you know exactly what you want. So, you wrote a book huh? How is it doing?"

"It's getting there."

"Well, the second one you write will be a best seller."

Janice felt a strange, but exciting feeling in her gut that caused her to quickly turn her head towards Paul. She stared at him as if she saw a ghost. "A second one? You know, I was thinking about writing a novel."

"You should write about your experiences, something people can relate to."

"Maybe I will."

Janice looked down in her lap and smiled. She tried to make sense of the strange feeling she just experienced. When she looked up, Paul looked directly in her eyes. "I could help you with your dreams. I have many connections, but then again, you'll become famous and forget all about me."

"I wouldn't do that. Success is nothing without someone you love to share it with." Janice smiled after she quoted Paul a line from the movie, *Mahogany*. Janice knew Paul didn't get it, but it was funny to her and she continued to laugh. "Paul, can I ask you something?

"Sure."

"Why are you here and not with your family?"

Paul was quiet and held his head down.

Janice touched his hand. "You don't have to answer if you don't want to."

"Before I came here, I was with my family, part of it anyway. After the doctors told us Chester died, I saw his wife slumped over and she was crying. Victoria was in so much pain. When I walked into the room, she stood in front of me and just stared at me. Then, she slapped the taste out of my mouth and blamed me for Chester's death. She told me for years, my brother begged me to leave my wife before something tragic happened. You see, it was my wife's lover that shot my brother. It was intended for me."

Janice covered her face.

"She told me I did this to Chester, I was selfish, and all I did was take, take, take and she would never forgive me. She's right. Just last night, Chester bailed me out of a situation. Afterwards, we got into a heated argument, mostly about me being a hot head."

"You're a hot head?"

"Sometimes I can be. I told him I was a grown ass man and asked him when he was going to stop treating me like his little brother. You know what he said?"

"What?"

"The day I die."

Paul paused to take another sip of his drink. "Victoria was right. Chester always tried to protect me from anyone that even looked like they were going to hurt me and today, he took a bullet for me and now dammit, he's gone!" This time, neither Paul nor Janice could hold back the tears.

By instinct, Janice reached over and hugged Paul. He hugged her back and held her tightly while he cried. They held each other for 10 minutes.

Paul was the first to pull away. He wiped his eyes and said, "Wow, I can't believe I did that. I don't even know you, but I feel like I've known you all of my life."

Janice too wiped her eyes. "It's okay. I feel the same way. Earlier, when I saw you in front of the hotel, I felt your pain across the parking lot."

"Can you feel me now? I feel like the entire world is on my shoulders."

"Well, maybe I'll loan you one of mine to help you carry it. I'll have to charge you a fee though—a vodka and cranberry juice."

Paul smiled and reached into his pocket. He gave Janice two of his business cards. "You have a good heart. I'd like to get to know you better."

"I'd like that."

Janice took one of Paul's cards and wrote her phone number on the back of it and gave it to him.

Paul took one last gulp of his drink. "When I came back here, I had every intention on drinking my $8,000 worth of liquor I paid for and just pass out. I'm glad you were here Janice. You're easy to talk to. Thank you for loaning me your ear and your shoulder tonight."

"You're very welcome Mr. Davis. I better get going."

Paul looked at his watch, "I can't believe we've been sitting here talking for three hours."

"I guess time flies when you're having vodka and cranberry juice."

"Let me walk you to your car."

When they got to Janice's truck, Paul offered Janice a mint.

Janice smiled and wondered if Paul thought he was going to get a kiss.

"No, thank you. It was very nice meeting you Paul. Take care of yourself and go home to your family. I'm sure they're all worried about you. I will keep you and your family in my prayers."

The entire time Janice was talking, she wanted to throw Paul down on her hood, but she already made one mistake tonight. Instead, she kissed him on his cheek, got in her truck and drove home.

When Janice pulled into her driveway, the clock on her dash flashed 4:05. She wondered how she even made it home.

Janice laid her head against her headrest and smiled. She could see Paul's face as clearly as she could see her hands on her steering wheel. She saw the two fine lines etched in his forehead, his bushy eyebrows over top of his medium brown eyes and full eyelashes, and his neatly trimmed goatee with a speck of gray encasing his narrow lips. Janice concluded that she was thinking about Paul too intensely because she could actually smell him.

Janice sat up straight and sniffed. When she thought about the 10-minute hug they shared when both of them cried in each other's arms, she looked down and smelled her blouse.

Janice laid back on her headrest and stared at her front door. "Compared to what Paul shared with me tonight, my problems are nothing."

Janice couldn't put her finger on it, but it was something about Paul that touched her in a way that was different from any other man she knew. She looked at Paul's card. "I would love to talk to you again, but I have enough problems as it is. Too bad, if I only met someone like you a few years ago, I wouldn't be going through what I'm going through now."

Janice tore the card in half and placed it in the side pocket of her door. When she opened her front door, it was pitch black. "Damn, I can't see anything." She felt on the wall until she found the light switch and flicked on the lights.

Janice jumped. "Marvin, you scared me."

"Do you know what time it is?"

Janice dropped her purse and took off her shoes. Without answering, she walked to the refrigerator.

Marvin raised his voice, "I asked you a question. Do you know what time it is?"

Janice casually looked at the clock on the kitchen wall. "It's 4:23."

"Where have you been?"

"I was at Dee's house."

"At Dee's, huh?"

"That's what I said."

Marvin got his crutches and hobbled over in front of Janice. "Well, did Dee tell you to bring home some orange juice?"

Janice's eyes began to flutter. "Orange juice?"

"I didn't stutter."

When Janice walked past him, Marvin sniffed. "Nice cologne you're wearing."

"Good night Marvin." Janice picked up her purse and quickly went upstairs.

When she got to her bedroom, she closed her door and grabbed her phone. She listened to Marvin's message and then she listened to Dee's message telling her that Marvin called and to bring home orange juice. "I should have checked my messages before I got in the house. Oh well."

Janice washed her face and changed her clothes. As soon as she got into bed, her phone rang. She answered, "Hello."

"I hope I'm not disturbing you, but I just wanted to make sure you got home safely."

"Yes, thank you. That was very considerate of you. Are you okay?"

"Yes, thanks for asking. Good night Janice."

"Good night Paul."

Janice sat on the edge of her bed with a huge smile on her face. "Wow!" Within seconds, Janice's phone rang again. "I know damn well this man is not calling me again."

"Tell your boyfriend not to call you at this hour."

Janice hung up on Marvin.

He called right back.

Janice yelled, "Marvin, what is it?"

"Come downstairs. We need to talk."

"Marvin, it's four o'clock in the morning."

"I know. That's why we need to talk."

"Talk to your harem. I'm going to sleep."

Again, Janice hung up on Marvin.

28

Marvin

Marvin threw his phone down on the bed, snatched up his crutches, and hobbled to the staircase. He looked up the 13 stairs and tried to climb one and almost lost his balance. When he tried again, he lost his balance, tumbled to the floor and knocked over a plant, a vase, and their 8 ½ by 11-inch wedding picture.

Janice ran downstairs and asked, "Marvin, what happened?"

Marvin was on the floor with dirt on his head and their wedding picture on his chest. "Ah, you do still love me." Marvin laughed.

"You scared me half to death."

Janice turned around and was about to go back upstairs when Marvin said, "Janice, come back. I need your help."

"I should let you sleep there tonight."

Three times, Janice tried to help Marvin stand up, but his weight was too much for her.

"Janice, let me try something else." Marvin dragged himself back to the stairs and pulled up on the railing. "See, there's more than one way to skin a cat. Can you hand me my crutches please?"

Janice gave Marvin his crutches and turned around to leave.

"Janice, don't go. You're already down here—let's talk."

"I'm tired Marvin. Let's do this in the morning."

"It is morning miss stay out till four o'clock in the morning. I'm not asking you to talk, just listen."

Janice crossed her arms and followed Marvin into the guest room. Marvin got himself situated on the bed and Janice sat in the chair across the room with her arms still folded tightly in front of her. "I'm listening."

"Janice, the first time I laid eyes on you, I fell in love with you and I've been in love with you ever since. Even when we weren't together, not a day went by that I didn't think about you and looked forward until the day we would be together. When I saw you again at the fundraiser, I promised myself that this time, I wasn't going to let you get away."

Janice looked away, but said nothing.

"You have it all wrong about Linda and me. That day you saw me at Linda's house, I was only there because I was working."

"Working?"

"Yes, working. Linda was one of my high profile clients. You see, last year Linda received threats on her life and the firm hired me to be her bodyguard. Everyday, I . . ."

"Marvin, this is the same story you told me in the hospital. What about the other fiancée?"

Marvin had a puzzled look on his face. "There's no fiancée. Janice, I love you. When I was in the hospital, I just wanted to die thinking about how much I hurt you."

"Marvin, while I was in your hospital room, a woman called and told me you had your accident leaving her house. Who was she?"

"Janice, I'm a married man and I have no fiancée."

"What about Linda? Are you telling me you and Linda were never in a relationship?"

"Yes."

"You never lived with Linda?"

"She would have loved for me to, but no."

Janice took a deep breath. "The little boy is not your son?"

Marvin looked Janice right in the eye and said, "No, he's not my son. Linda probably doesn't even know who his father is."

Janice stood up.

Marvin quickly asked, "Where are you going?"

"I'll be right back." Janice ran upstairs. When she came back downstairs, she stood in front of Marvin. "I'm going to ask you one more time. Is that little boy your son?"

Marvin looked at Janice's hand and wondered what was in the envelope. "No, she tried to pin it on me, but no."

Janice threw the unopened envelope at Marvin and yelled, "You lie too damn much. I don't believe a word that comes out of your mouth. For someone to deny his own flesh and blood, that's low Marvin. That's all I have to say."

Marvin looked at MJ's birth certificate and read Linda's letter. His breathing became erratic and his nostrils flared. He threw the papers on the bed, got his crutches and stood directly in front of Janice. She backed away, but he grabbed her by the arm. "Are you going to believe me or some Ho trying to find a father for her baby? I told you I'm not that boy's father. Linda and I never had a relationship, but I see you went out tonight and found yourself somebody else. Coming in here smelling like a sweet ass man and a liquor store looking like you just ate the forbidden fruit. And you got the nerve to get all self righteous with me like your shit don't stink!"

Marvin yelled even louder. "Where were you Janice and what the hell have you been doing until four o'clock in the morning?"

Janice yanked her arm away. "What are you going to do Marvin, try to kill me too?"

Janice walked out of the room and ran upstairs.

Marvin's anger almost reached his boiling point. He picked up the phone and called Linda.

"Hello," Linda answered.

"What the hell is wrong with you?"

"Who is this?"

"You know who it is. Why did you send Janice this damn letter and birth certificate?"

"Marvin, do you know what time it is?"

"Yes, answer me bitch."

"Marvin, it's too damn early for this. Yeah, I sent it. You know everything is true. Instead of calling me names, you should get down on your one good knee and thank your lucky stars I didn't throw your lying, married ass underneath the jail. And, the next time you wanna call somebody a bitch, you better go find your wife, that is, if she's stupid enough to still be with your lying ass."

After Linda hung up on Marvin, he threw himself down on the bed. "To hell with these damn women. As soon as my leg gets better, I'm getting another car and I'm through with all women, at least those two anyway"

Minutes later, Marvin closed his eyes and contemplated what type of car he was going to get, who was going to get it for him and once he got it, where he was going.

29

Paul

After Paul made sure Janice arrived home safely, he turned off the main highway and drove up his curved driveway to his four-acre Annapolis waterfront estate. He parked his car in his four-car garage, walked through his lower level and took the elevator that led straight to his master bedroom. Everything was just as he left it two days ago. His bed was unmade with his gun case on his pillow and the broken glass from the mirror was still on the off white carpet. Paul wondered why no one cleaned his room. "Tomorrow, I'm firing everybody."

For a few minutes, Paul stood in the middle of his room and looked in the mirror. With one quick move, he snatched off his bloody shirt, bald it up and threw it in the trash can. Paul completely undressed and went into his spa like bathroom to take a long hot shower. As the water dripped down over his head, Paul saw images of when Chester leaped in front of him and both of them fell to the floor. He closed his eyes and saw another image of Chester's lifeless body lying in a pool of blood.

Paul wrapped his arms around his lean body and wished he could wash away the shame, blame and guilt that consumed him. Tears fell uncontrollably down his face and blended in with the hot water that cascaded from the multiple showerheads. With both of his hands, he hit the shower wall and cried out, "Man, I told you to stop treating me like your little brother. Why didn't you just let me be a man this one time and take the bullet that was meant for me? Dammit Chester. Why? It should have been me, not you. I'm sorry, I'm so sorry. This time, I messed up bad. Now Victoria is without a husband, my nieces are without a father and I'm without my big brother. What the hell am I going to do without you in my life? You were the only person that truly had my back. If I had listened to you years ago, maybe none of this would have happened. I promise you Chester, if it's the last thing I do, I'm going to make Popeye and Desiree pay. I'm going to make them pay dearly."

Paul stayed in the shower for another 20 minutes. He cried, cursed and tried to beat the black out of the black and white marble shower wall. Emotionally drained and physically exhausted, Paul turned off the shower, draped a towel around him and fell across his king-size bed. He reached behind him to get his phone that poked him in his back and noticed he had 10 new messages. He listened to the first message—*hey Little Brother, before I forget, this is just a reminder. Take your butt down to the bank first thing Monday morning before Desiree lands you in the poor house. Don't worry. You're doing the right thing. You deserve to be happy. One day, true happiness will find you when you least expect it. Once again, Big Brother got your back. Don't forget, first thing Monday morning. Love you man.*

"You must have left that message the morning of the wedding while I was still asleep at your house. Even from the grave, you got my back."

Tears swelled up in Paul's eyes. He played Chester's message three more times and then saved it. Hearing Chester's voice again was all the comforter Paul needed to cover him while he closed his eyes and his mind to the worst day of his life.

Five hours later, Paul awoke to a rapid knock on his door. "Who is it?"

"Paul, it's Sarah."

Paul looked at the clock. "Damn, it's 11 o'clock. It felt like I just went to sleep."

Drudgingly, Paul sat up on the side of the bed and looked out the wraparound windows at his tennis court. Realizing his towel fell off sometime during the early hours of the morning—he reached for his robe and said, "Come in."

"Good morning," Sarah said and sat down a tray with a glass of orange juice, a cup of coffee, three sausages, two eggs, two toasts, and hash browns.

"I'm not hungry."

"Paul, you need to eat. I heard about Chester. I'm so sorry. He was a good man. We will all miss him."

Paul nodded.

Sarah looked around the room and then looked back at Paul. "How are you feeling this morning?"

"I don't know Sarah. I just can't believe he's gone."

"As long as you have him in your heart, he'll never be gone." On her way out, Sarah eyed the broken glass in the corner. "If you need anything, just yell."

"Sarah, why didn't anyone clean my room?"

"Did you forget? You gave the entire staff the weekend off so we could attend Miss Cynthia's wedding."

Paul rubbed his head and said, "I guess I did. Were you at the wedding?

"Sarah walked over to the window and looked out at the pool. She hesitated before she said, "Yes, I was sitting near the band."

"Hmm. If I gave everyone the weekend off, what are you doing here?"

"I thought you might need a nourishing breakfast. Now eat up. You need your strength. I'll come back later to clean up that mess."

Paul smiled at his loyal employee. "Sarah, you know how to take care of me and you run my house just the way I like it. Thank you, but the other staff can take care of it tomorrow. If I gave you the day off, you better take it. I don't know when the next time I'll be so generous. Go home and spend time with your family."

"Are you sure you don't need me?"

"I'm sure. Go home. I'll see you tomorrow."

Sarah left the room.

Paul looked at the hefty breakfast she prepared for him, carried his tray into his sitting room and turned on *TBN*. "No sense wasting good food."

When he finished, he said, "I guess I was hungry after all," and picked up his business card next to his orange juice. He turned it over—*shoulder for rent, Janice 301-555-2525.*

Paul smiled and thought about how he cried on Janice's shoulder like a baby. "Mmm-hmm. She must have thought I was some kind a punk. Damn, I can't believe I did that. It must have been the vodka."

Paul thought about Janice's beautiful smile and her pretty eyes. "One day, true happiness will find you when you least expect it. Where have I heard that? There's something about Janice. She touched me in a way that's different than from any other woman. One day, I'll call her to thank her, but now is definitely not a good time."

Paul put the card down and reached for his phone. Again, he listened to Chester's message. "Love you too Big Brother. No time like the present."

After Paul finished his phone call, he picked up the card with Janice's number on the back. Once he figured out that it was Janice who said the same thing Chester said about true happiness finding him, he laughed.

Paul listened to the rest of his messages and frowned when he heard the last message from a restricted number—*sorry about your brother—it was an unfortunate accident.*

"Where have I heard that voice before?" Paul replayed the message three more times, but he still couldn't recognize the man's voice. He decided to save the message and listen to it again later.

Paul debated several times before he finally dialed Janice's number. Half way through the number, his phone beeped. Paul disconnected the call and answered his other line. "Hey Dante."

"Dad, I've been trying to reach you all night. I left you two messages. Where were you?"

"Out."

"Are you okay?"

"Yeah, is everybody all right?"

"They're all hanging in there. Aunt Victoria is at home now with Aunt Marie. I'm on my way to pick up Aunt Janice to take her over. Are you coming?"

"Yeah, I'll be there."

"Good. I'll see you when you get there."

30

Desiree

Desiree woke up fully recharged and ready to tackle the aftermath of yesterday's catastrophe. To get her morning started, all she needed was coffee, toast, lightly buttered, and a long, hot luxurious bubble bath.

Desiree called for room service and went into the bathroom to run her bath water. While she waited, Desiree thought she would glance over the divorce papers. With all of the excitement, she only got as far as "Petition for Divorce."

Desiree skimmed most of it and just as Brent said, Paul charged her with adultery. She then went to the financial section and read it out loud, "The house located at yeah, yeah and a cash settlement of $1.7 million will be awarded to Desiree Davis."

Desiree flung the papers across the room. Most of them landed on the bed. "$1.7 million with all the shit we have. He has really lost his damn mind. I can spend that much as soon as I leave this hotel. If I have to stay married to his ass another 17 years, he's definitely not going to get away with this. I have no plans to live beneath the poverty level of $1.7 million for the rest of my life."

Desiree was on her way to the bathroom to check on her bath when she heard a knock at the door. "That must be room service."

Desiree opened the door to a tray filled with fruit, croissants, sausages, eggs, toasts, coffee, and juice. Desiree looked at all of the food. "I didn't order this. You must have the wrong room."

"This is room 310," the room service attendant said.

"Yes, it is."

"Well, this is your order."

"Wait just a damn minute."

Desiree ran back to the bathroom to shut off the water. When she came back into the room, the attendant was gone.

"Good morning Diva Darling."

"What the hell are you doing here? I thought you said . . ."

Brent pulled Desiree to him. "I said I wasn't going to spend last night or any other night with you, but I never said anything about mornings or days."

Desiree pulled free of Brent's tight hold. "Did you order all of this damn food?"

"Yes, I thought you needed a little more nourishment than toast and coffee."

"I'm getting real tired of your games Brent."

"Who's playing games?"

"You are."

"Diva, I brought you this magnificent breakfast and this is the thanks I get."

Brent grabbed Desiree, kissed her fervently on the lips and slid her robe off her shoulders.

Desiree pushed him away. "I don't have time for this. Right now, I have more important things to do than this lovey-dovey stuff with the likes of you."

Brent threw his hands up in the air and sat down on the bed next to Desiree's divorce papers. "Like charming your way back to hubby dearest? With $1.7 million, you can get your hair done and nails did for a long time."

Desiree snatched her divorce papers away from Brent. "Give me that."

"What's that about, $100,000 per year of marriage? The house is probably worth another couple of million. Considering the circumstances, I'd say that's quite generous."

"Brent, if you don't shut up!"

"And, what are you going to do if I don't? Yesterday, I let you get away with your little Diva tantrum, but don't get cocky and think I'll let you get away with something like that again."

Desiree stood with her arms folded across her chest. Brent picked up a plate and stacked it with everything he saw on the tray. "Sit down Diva. Your food is getting cold. When are you leaving town?"

"Tomorrow, after I go to the bank."

"Before you go, don't forget to grease my palms." Brent smiled.

"Is that why you're here?"

"No, that's why I'll be here tomorrow."

"How long do you think I'm going to pay you to keep your mouth quiet about something that happened 20 years ago? Hell, right now, you can sing like a bird. I have nothing else to lose."

"Diva, if I did sing, you wouldn't even have the settlement of $1.7 million."

"Who is calling me this morning? "Hello."

"Mrs. Davis, this is the front desk. There seems to be a problem with the credit card you left with us last night. Do you have another form of payment?"

"What the hell do you mean? There's nothing wrong with my credit card." "Ma'am, we ran it through twice and both times, it was declined."

Desiree yelled into the phone, "Well, run it again!"

"Just a moment Ma'am."

Brent stared at Desiree as she waited for the desk clerk to return to the phone.

"I'm sorry, it was declined again. Do you have another form of payment?"

"Yes, of course I do." Desiree reached for her purse, took out a VISA card and read off the numbers.

"Just a moment Ma'am."

Again, Desiree waited for the desk clerk to return to the phone. She looked at Brent eating and pretending not to hear what was going on.

A few minutes later, the desk clerk returned to the phone. "I'm sorry Ma'am, this one is also declined."

"Run it again! There must be something wrong with your damn system. I have one more card." Desiree read off a Discover card number.

"Ma'am, I'm sorry this one is declined. Please come down to the front desk with another form of payment."

Desiree slammed down the phone. "This is ridiculous. I hate all these damn hotels."

Brent smiled as he stuffed his face with a sausage. Desiree looked at Brent and asked, "What are you smiling at?"

"I guess grieving affects people in different ways. I see hubby got smarter and didn't wait until Monday. Damn Diva, it looks like you're a day late and millions short."

Desiree looked in her wallet at her three $100 bills. "That son of a bitch. What am I going to do? I don't even have enough money to pay for this room. Brent . . ."

"Hey, don't Brent me. What did I tell you? I told you don't even look my way just because you're having a sudden cash flow problem. I'll have my food to go."

"Why don't you do that and get the hell out of here with your broke ass."

"Now, now, is that anyway to talk to your baby daddy? You wouldn't want me to pay a visit to *our* daughter and ask her to help dear old dad out, would you?"

"You stay away from her. Paul is her father."

"No, Paul thinks he is her father and Cynthia thinks he is her father, but you and I know the truth. What were you thinking letting a 20-year old get married? Hell, you could have given me all that money you spent on that damn wedding. That little runt she married is just gonna get her pregnant, leave her home and go out looking for some other poor victim."

"Oh, like you did?"

"Diva, you know I didn't leave you by choice—I left you by force. I can't say the same about you. While I was in jail, you divorced me and married hubby dearest, pretending to be one big ass happy family with my child. I should have put a bullet in him back then."

"Brent, what the hell did you expect? Did you think I would wait for you for 10 years? Please, I may have loved you, but I wasn't stupid."

"No, I'll give it to you, stupid you're not. Lucky for me, you lucked up and married ole boy and he made himself into a millionaire. Now, we're both lucky, but I guess luck does have a way of running out sooner or later."

Desiree walked across the room. I should have never told you Cynthia was yours."

"Oh, Diva, quit crying over spilled sperm. I would have figured it out. I'm not stupid either. Hell, she looks just like me. Even Chester saw that. At the rehearsal dinner, you should have seen the way he looked at me then he looked at Cynthia and back to me again. Afterwards, he wrote something down on a pad."

Desiree covered her mouth. "Do you think he knew?

"No, like I said, you wouldn't have gotten that settlement if Chester spilled the beans." Brent raised his eyebrows. "You don't have to worry about him now, do you?"

Desiree lowered her head. "Pretty soon I'm not going to have any money to pay you, then what?"

"Then, we will have to come up with another plan. Sometimes people are much more valuable dead than alive.

Brent stood up with a napkin full of food. "Isn't that right Diva? I'll see you tomorrow. Eat up."

Desiree rolled her eyes and under her breath said, "Maybe it's time you become more valuable."

As soon as Brent closed the door, Desiree called the front desk and pulled out another credit card she hid in the back of her wallet.

"This is Mrs. Davis in room 310. I forgot that the cards I gave you earlier were all expired. I must have an old purse. I have a card for you now."

Desiree read the number from the credit card to the young lady. After a couple of minutes, the young lady said, "This one is fine Mrs. Davis. Will there be anything else?"

"No." Desiree hung up the phone, put her credit card back into her wallet, and dialed Paul's number.

"Hello," Paul answered.

"You son of a bitch, what am I suppose to live on? Do you realize I'm in a hotel and can't pay my bill?"

"Who is this?"

"You know damn well who this is? I have no money."

"Sure you do. I offered you the house, that's worth over $2 million and a cash settlement of $1.7 million. I'd say that's plenty of money."

"That's nothing compared to what we have."

"Desiree, we don't have anything but bad blood between us and a beautiful daughter. Perhaps you should have saved some of that money you stole from me throughout the years."

"I . . . I ne . . . ver."

"Save it. Chester told me years ago. Look, as soon as you sign the papers, your cash flow problem will be solved."

"Paul Darling, you're grieving and right now, you're not making a lot of sense. I still love you and I know you still love me. I don't want a divorce. I messed up and I'm sorry. Before you do anything else rash, take some time and think about this. We can go to counseling. Do you really want to throw away 17 years?"

"I didn't throw away 17 years, you did."

"Paul, let's talk about this."

"Nope, I'm on my way to Chester's. Besides, it will be hard for us to try again with you behind bars alongside your Popeye looking cellmate."

"Oh, the hell with you too!"

31

Janice

"Are you still in bed?" Beatrice asked.

"Hey Ma, of course I'm not still in bed."

Janice told her mother a little white lie and glanced at her alarm clock on her night stand. Her mouth flew open when she saw it was 1:05.

"Janice, what are you doing today?"

"Nothing much, why do you ask?"

"I need to talk to you about your sister, Elaine."

"Is she all right?"

"I'm not sure. That's what I want to talk to you about."

"Okay, I'll be over in about an hour."

"Janice?"

"Yes Ma."

"If you're still in bed at one o'clock in the afternoon, last night, you and Marvin must have *really* tied one on."

Janice giggled. *If you only knew.* "Ma, I told you I wasn't in bed."

"I know you're not, I'm just kidding Janice. I'll see you when you get here."

Janice hung up the phone and laughed. Ma always says what she means and right after, says she's kidding. I know she wasn't kidding." Slowly, she dragged herself out of bed. Her head throbbed as she felt the effects of the five vodka and cranberry juices she had with Davey and Paul.

She went to the bathroom, took two Advil, laid back down on the bed and wished she could stay there all day.

Janice covered her head and tried to get fifteen more minutes of sleep when her phone rang. "Dammit! Hello."

"The house is on fire."

"Hello Davey."

"Janice, I've been thinking about all that smoke we made in the hotel room last night. It was just like old times."

"Is that right?" *We must have been in two different rooms.*

Davey cleared his throat. "The room is still available. Meet me there in 30 minutes."

"Davey, last night was something that just happened. I'm not trying to make it into a routine."

"Are you saying you didn't feel anything last night?"

"No, I'm saying I never intended for it to happen."

"Neither did I, but I would sure like to intend for it to happen today."

"Davey, I have to go. Bye."

As soon as Janice pulled the covers back over her head, her phone rang again. "Oh, Davey, give me a damn break."

When she looked at her caller ID, she hesitantly answered, "Hello."

"Hello Janice, this is Paul."

With a huge smile on her face, Janice quickly sat up in bed. "Hello Paul, how are you?"

"I've been better. How are you?"

"I've been better too. Last night, I think I tried to be a big girl and drank a little too much."

"You should have taken two aspirins before you went to sleep." Paul laughed.

"Now you tell me."

"Janice, I want to apologize for crying like a baby this morning and ruining your blouse."

"There's no need to apologize. You went through something terrible. I would have cried too."

"I believe you did. I would charge you for my shirt if it wasn't already ruined."

"Excuse me."

"I'm only teasing." Paul laughed.

"I just felt your pain, that's all and I guess I let a little bit of my own out as well."

"Janice, I'm glad you were comfortable enough with me to let it out. With me, it was so strange because I don't open up to people that soon, if I open up to them at all. I never expected to run into someone like you ever, let alone last night when my only mission was to drink and pass out.

For the last two days, I've walked around and felt like I was suffocating. When I saw your beautiful face across the bar and heard the words that came out of those pretty lips, it was like a breath of fresh air. Last night, you gave me oxygen."

Janice quietly said, "Wow!"

"Last night, I believe God brought us together and when I heard Chester's message this morning, I was sure of it."

"Did you just say you heard from Chester?"

"It was a voice mail message he left me before . . . you know. I wasn't going to call you, but after that, I just needed to hear your voice."

Again, Janice quietly said, "Wow!"

"Janice, I need to protect my heart, especially after what I went through with my wife, but I would love to see you again. Once things settle down, maybe one evening we could have dinner?"

Janice was stunned yet flattered by what Paul said. Without thinking, she heard herself say, "Yes, I would love to see you again. Are you going to spend time with your family today?"

"Yes, I'm on my way now."

"That's good, because you need to surround yourself with family and the people who love you."

"Okay Miss Janice, I'm not going to hold you up any longer. I'll call you later."

"Paul, take care of you. Okay?"

"I will."

Janice hung up the phone and felt as giddy as a 16-year old. She didn't know someone her age could still feel giddy. "Well, so much for not talking to him."

She forgot all about the throbbing in her head and jumped out of bed and walked to the window. "I see AJ got Marvin. That's perfect. Maybe the fresh air will do him some good."

Janice continued to look out the window. "In 24 hours, I became an adulterer, a woman who doesn't give a damn about her husband and a giddy 47-year old thinking about a future with a strange man she just met in a hotel after having sex with an old lover. Who am I?"

32

Paul

Paul thought back to his earlier phone call with Desiree. He was amused by her unconvincing let's stay together for the sake of love plea that quickly ended with a very strong to hell with you too. "I guess that means I wasn't the only one that ruffled her feathers today. Thank you Chester and I'm sorry I didn't listen to you a long time ago. I'm on my way to see your wife. Please help me to help her see how sorry I am."

The closer Paul got to Chester's house, the more he felt he was suffocating. Paul pulled up into the driveway and turned off his engine. He stared at the red front door and remembered the conversations he and Chester had when he was in jail and up until the time they fell to the floor.

Paul reached into his glove compartment and took out his new flask that was filled to the top with vodka. For 15 minutes, he just sat in the driveway, drank his vodka and tried hard to get up enough nerve to face Victoria and his nieces.

"Hey Dad, what are you doing sitting in the driveway?"

"Hey Dante, I just got here."

Paul's sister, Janice, stood beside Dante and eyed the flask in her little brother's hand. "Paul, are you okay? You didn't call me back last night. I got worried that something happened to you."

"I'm sorry Janice. When I got back home, it was too late to call."

"After you left the hospital, where did you go?" Janice asked.

Dante looked at his father. Paul looked straight ahead as if he was in a daze and said, "I just went out to have a few drinks and then I got some oxygen."

Both Janice and Dante looked at each other and simultaneously asked, "Oxygen?"

Paul smiled and thought about the other Janice. "I mean air. Let's go inside."

When they stepped inside, Victoria was in the family room on the phone. *This is not going to be easy.* Paul saw Victoria gave a half smile to everyone except to him. He looked around at some of Victoria's relatives, a man Paul didn't recognize, and Chester's 22-year old twin daughters, Katrina and Kristina. He thought Katrina looked more like Chester and Kristina looked more like Victoria. "How are you two holding up?"

"Hey Uncle Paul," Katrina said. For several minutes, she hugged her uncle tightly. Kristina waved and walked away.

Paul asked, "Is Kristina all right?"

"Oh, she's been taking it really hard. We all have."

Katrina guided Paul to the other side of the room. "Uncle Paul, what happened? Mama said it was your fault Daddy is dead."

Paul shook his head, looked down to the floor and said, "I'm sorry to say Katrina, it is. Desiree and her lover were at the wedding. He had a gun. Your dad thought he was going to shoot me. He jumped in front of me and saved my life." A tear fell down Paul's cheek.

Again, Katrina hugged her uncle. "It wasn't your fault Uncle Paul. I know Daddy loved you. He would have done the same for any of us."

Paul held on to Katrina a little longer. Finally, he released her, wiped his eyes and said, "You don't know how much you sound like your father. I'm so sorry."

"I know you are. Have they caught the man that shot Daddy?"

"No, not yet, but I'm going to make sure they do."

"Good."

Looking directly into Katrina's eyes, Paul said, "Katrina, if you, your sister or your mother ever need anything, you call me."

Katrina nodded and softly said, "Give Mama some time. She'll come around."

Paul smiled at his niece as she walked away in search of her sister. He then looked over at Victoria and saw that she was crying again. He thought it best to stay on the opposite side of the room given that his presence seemed to upset her even more.

Dante walked over and stood next to Paul. "Cynthia is coming back tonight. She's cutting her honeymoon short."

"That's too bad. Dante, after the funeral, I'm going away for a couple of weeks."

"Where are you going?"

"Man, are you trying to keep tabs on me or something. You keep asking me where I've been and where I'm going like I'm your son."

Dante smiled and said, "Seriously Dad, I'm just worried about you, that's all.

"Don't be Son. Eventually, I'll be okay. I'm not sure where I'm going. I can do some work while I'm away, but I will need for you to hold down the forte until I get back."

"I'm on it."

Janice walked over to Paul, put her arm in his and whispered into his ear, "Let's take a walk outside."

"All right."

Janice looked around before she said, "You know Paul, we don't have but a little bit of family and we have to stick together.

"I know."

"Victoria is hurting right now. She loved Chester with all of her heart and she is going to need all of us."

"I don't think she needs me."

"Paul, you're wrong. Believe it or not, you were the closest person to Chester other than Victoria and the girls. Sure, he loved his sisters, but because you were the youngest, he acted more like your father instead of your brother."

"Tell me about it."

"Victoria loves you just as Chester did. I know she blames you right now, but in time, she'll come around. You'll see. What are you going to do about Desiree'?"

"I'm divorcing her."

"Hallelujah!"

"Now how long have you felt this way?"

"The day you married her."

"Is that right?"

"Brother, if you're happy, I'm happy, but I haven't seen you happy in years. Take some time so your heart can heal and after that, go out there and find yourself that special someone that truly makes you happy. You deserve it."

Paul didn't comment, but smiled as he thought about the other Janice.

"Oh, before I forget, don't go hiding out by yourself either. You stay close."

Paul looked at his sister and wondered whether she was through telling him what to do. "Janice, I'm going out of town for a couple of weeks. I need some time alone to think about things."

"Where are you going?"

"I thought about going to South Carolina."

"Chester has a house in South Carolina. You should stay at the Paulster."

"The Paulster?"

"Yeah, that's what he called it."

"Why?"

"I don't know. Go there and maybe you can figure it out. I assume it had something to do with you. He really loved you. Why, I don't know."

Janice smiled and Paul covered his face. She hugged him. "I'm here for you. The entire family is here for you. Never forget that."

Paul nodded.

Janice looked at the other family members that entered the house. "Well, I guess I better get back inside. Are you coming Paul?"

"I'll be there in a moment."

Paul got into his car and went straight to his glove compartment for his flask. He saw Dante staring at him through the living room window.

Desiree got out of her Mustang and walked towards the driver's side of Paul's Bentley. She pointed to the flask in Paul's hand. "I see grieving hasn't changed you one bit."

"Desiree, what the hell are you doing here?"

"I've come to pay my respects."

"If you have any respect for anyone, you'll turn around and leave."

"Why, I'm still family. Did you think a piece of paper was going to stop me from coming to support you and the family?"

Paul laughed and got out of his car to face Desiree. "There's no audience out here, so you can stop performing. This is not the time. Go back to wherever you came from and leave my family alone."

"You don't own everything Paul. I'm going in to pay my respects."

Paul stood in front of Desiree and blocked her path. "You are not going to bother my family."

"I'll bother you and every member of your damn family until you give me what's rightfully mine."

Desiree took the divorce papers and hit Paul on the chest with them and held them there. "Until then, you and your family are still my family."

Paul snatched the papers away from Desiree. "You are one trifling bitch."

Dante ran out of the house. "Desiree, you need to leave."

Desiree continued her frenzy. All of a sudden, she stopped yelling and her eyes got as big as silver dollars.

Both Dante and Paul turned around to follow Desiree's gaze and was shocked to see a shotgun in Victoria's hand pointed directly at Desiree.

Victoria shouted, "Get your hands off of him before I put so many bullet holes in you that *all* of your lies won't be able to cover."

Desiree jerked her hands away from Paul. Victoria aimed the gun at Desiree and shouted, "Why are you here? Haven't you caused me and my family enough heartache?"

Desiree held her head in the air. "I'm here to pay you my respects."

"What do you know about respect? Chester told me all about you stealing, lying, cheating, and . . ." Victoria briefly looked at Paul and then back to Desiree. "You're an evil woman. You killed my Chester and now you're going to pay."

Paul walked towards Victoria and pleaded, "Don't do this. Please Victoria, give me the gun. She's not worth it. Think about Katrina and Kristina."

Everyone ran out the door into the front yard. Kristina and Katrina cried out to their mother, "Mama, please don't do this. Put down the gun. We can't lose you too."

Paul got directly in front of Victoria and placed his hand on the gun. "It's okay. Give me the gun Sis."

Slowly, Victoria released the gun. Her arms dropped to her side. Once Paul had the gun safely in his hand, Desiree ran to her car and sped away.

Victoria held her head down and shook it from side to side. Paul gave the gun to Dante, gathered Victoria tightly in his arms and told her, "It's going to be all right."

Victoria hysterically cried and violently shook in Paul's arms. After a few moments, she reached up and held on to him as if she was holding on for dear life. She whimpered, "I'm so sorry Paul, I'm so sorry."

33

Janice

"I look good, I feel good, and I smell like "Knowing," as in knowing I am a strong woman with a good heart that knows what she wants and looks damn good for her age. Janice Perry, that's who I am."

After her pep talk in the mirror, Janice brushed on her neutral color eye shadow and used jet black eyeliner to define her lower lashes. While she put on mascara, she said, "I made a huge mistake when I believed in Marvin, and last night, I don't know what the hell that was with Davey. That must have been one of my "MGBP" moments. Oh well, like Lainey always says, "This too shall pass.""

Janice applied Revlon Spicy Cinnamon Lipstick and smiled as she thought about something Paul said to her. "Yeah, I do have pretty lips."

In her four-inch ankle boots, Janice left her house with pep in her step and a new attitude. On the drive over to her mother's house, Janice wondered what was wrong with Lainey. She felt guilty because with everything that happened with Marvin, she never got the chance to go see her or even call to welcome her back home.

Janice dialed Lainey's number. "Hey Lainey, I hear we're almost neighbors."

"Well, it sure took you long enough."

"I know. I'm sorry. I had a lot going on, which is no excuse."

"That's okay. I knew you'd call one day."

"So, where is this house? I know I'm close."

"Yeah, you are. You just passed it."

Janice quickly put on brakes. "I just passed it. Ma said you lived 20 minutes away from me."

"I told Ma that I lived at 2016 Minay Street."

"I was on my way to Ma's house, but let me turn around." Janice laughed.

When Lainey saw Janice, she dropped her water hose on her Azaleas. Janice jumped out of her truck and ran over to hug Lainey. "That's so funny. If I wanted to, I could walk to your house. How are you?"

Laney smiled at her younger sister. "I'm hanging in there. Look at you Janice, wearing your hooker heels and smelling like Estée Lauder Knowing. I could smell it before you got out the truck. I know that fragrance anywhere. It's so good to see you Little Sis. Come on inside."

Janice noticed Lainey moved very slowly and she lost a lot of weight. Her face no longer had its glow and her hair had a lot more gray in it than Janice remembered. When they got inside, Lainey had boxes all over the place which Janice thought was strange since she'd been there for three weeks.

"Can I get you anything Janice?"

"Yeah, some sense."

Lainey turned around to look at Janice. "Some what?"

"Nothing, how do you like being home again?"

"It's not Florida, but it's good to be back."

Janice looked around the living room at the built-in book cases, the newly done wood floors and the unique chandelier that hung in the foyer.

"Lainey, this is nice. Are you going to give me a tour?"

"Okay."

Lainey took Janice from room to room in her three-level, white and brick colonial. To Janice, it felt like Lainey took five minutes for each step she took and had bouts of shortness of breath. "Are you all right Lainey?"

"I'm okay. I've just been a little tired lately. That's why all of these boxes are still lying around. Let's go back into the family room."

Lainey slowly walked in front of Janice and sat down on the sofa. Janice sat down on the chair opposite Lainey and waited for her to catch her breath. She could tell Lainey's health was bad, but didn't want to start off with 50 questions quite so early in their visit. *This is what Ma wanted to tell me.*

After Lainey caught her breath, she asked, "How are my nieces and nephew doing?"

"They're all fine and getting old. Oh, Jasmine is an interior designer now."

"I know, she says she's going to hook up your event hall whenever you get one. I need to get her to come over here and help me out."

"When did she tell you that?"

"Jasmine calls me from time to time and keeps me up-to-date on the goings-on in Maryland."

"Does she now?"

"Yeah, that Jasmine is something else."

"You got that right. You know, Natalie is still a gospel rapper."

"Yeah, how is she?"

"She and her new hubby, Brandon, are living in South Carolina with my two granddaughters. Reginald, Mr. Money Bags, has finally found the love of his life and for once, I really like her. I betcha he's going to propose to her by Christmas."

"You're hoping he proposes just so you can plan an overpriced wedding."

"Something like that."

"And, how is hubby?"

"Don't ask.

"Didn't I just go to your wedding?"

"Yeah, eight months ago. Do you have anything to drink Lainey?"

"I have some vodka and cranberry juice."

Janice laughed. "I had too many of those last night. Don't you have anything else?"

"I have water."

"I need something stronger than that."

"Our brother and his girlfriend stopped by yesterday and gave it to me for a housewarming gift. I told Chester to take it with him because I didn't drink anymore. Stop stalling Janice, what's going on with you and Marvin?"

Janice got up to pour herself a vodka and cranberry juice. "Everything is a mess. That's why I haven't called you until now. I'll give you the short version. About three weeks ago, I found out Marvin lied to me ever since we got back together. He has two fiancées, a four-year old son and lived with me and one fiancée at the same time."

"Get out of here Janice. Marvin was always lively with his curly head self."

"He ain't so lively no more. He was in a bad motorcycle accident coming from one of the fiancée's houses. Now that he's all broken up, nobody wants him. Last night, he had the nerve to come back home and expects me to take care of him."

"Oh, my God Janice. How is he?"

"What do you mean how is he? He's lucky I didn't kill him.

"Be nice Janice."

"His leg is badly broken and AJ says his kidneys are all messed up."

"I see why you haven't called me. How did you find out all of this stuff?"

Janice took a sip of her drink. "By innocently coming home early, following my instincts and following him."

"Look and you shall find, but did you find what you were looking for or did you find out the truth?" Lainey laughed.

"Lainey, you sound like Ma and a lawyer."

"I am my mother's daughter and I am a lawyer."

"I forgot. One of Marvin's fiancées was a non-talking hoochie lawyer, but from the looks of things, got boo koo money. He drove around in her Bentley and they lived in, I hate to say this, but a magnificent home on the other side of town."

"Damn! You found out all of this just by following him."

"It was some more stuff. I told you I was giving you the short version.

This time, I believe I did find out the truth. Apart of me always knew something was up, but I guess I wasn't ready to face it until now. It's so weird because I feel relieved. I finally know something concrete and I'm out of that limbo stage. At first, I was hurt, but now, the love I had for him is gone and the thought of taking care of his broken up ass really pisses me off."

Lainey looked concerned and asked, "What are you going to do?"

"Divorce him and move on."

"Janice, are you sure you want to do that?"

"Yes, and I'm sure I *don't* plan on taking care of him either."

"Okay Janice, but sometimes, the plan we have for ourselves is not the plan that God has for us."

"What do you mean? After what Marvin did to me, God plans for me to take care of him?"

"I'm just saying, things happen for a reason and we don't always know what the reason is. We just always know that He is never wrong."

Lainey looked at Janice pour another drink. "Slow down girl."

"Speaking of wrong, last night, I ran into Davey."

"Davey, talk about a blast from the past. At one time, you two were hot and heavy."

"Yeah, last night."

"Last night?"

"Lainey, I did something so stupid. We talked, had a few drinks and we had sex right at the hotel."

Lainey's mouth flew open. "Janice, no you didn't."

"Yes, I did. I had a MGBP moment.

"Mind gone, body present. Yeah, we've all been there one time or another." Lainey laughed.

Janice nodded. "I didn't feel a thing. I mean, he still knows how to work it, but I had no feelings for him whatsoever. Afterwards, I felt bad. Not because I cheated on Marvin, but because it felt like a confirmation to the end of Marvin and a beginning of going backwards with Davey. I be damned if I go down that road again. I couldn't wait until he left. I took a shower, got my clothes on and went downstairs to the bar where I met this man.

"Didn't you have a busy night? Don't tell me you had sex with him too."

"Lainey, are you trying to call me a Ho on the sly?"

"No, just making sure my little sister hasn't lost all of her morals."

"I wanted to throw him on the hood of my truck, but I didn't."

Lainey shook her head at her sister.

Janice took another sip of her drink. "It's weird, because I could feel him even before I met him and when I did, it felt like I knew him all of my life. We talked for three hours about everything. Earlier that day, his wife's lover killed his brother at his daughter's wedding.

"Damn, poor guy."

"We exchanged numbers and he called to make sure I got home safely and he called again today. I tell you Lainey, it was just something about this guy and meeting him when I did."

"Ah Janice, that man was just out looking for a band-aid for his wounds and so were you. You just made him feel good and he made you feel good."

"Ouch!"

"I'm sorry Janice. What can you possibly know about a man you just met? Hell, you can live with someone all of your life and still don't know them."

"I'm telling you Lainey, it's something about this guy."

"It's something about all guys. Janice, you're a sucker for a hard luck story and you believe everything these damn men tell you."

"No, I don't."

"Yes, you do."

"I just give people a clean slate until something happens that brings up my antenna."

"Janice, you knew Marvin was a dog ten years ago."

"I thought he changed."

"Once a dog, always a dog. Stop believing in that love of my life, love at first sight, love never fails bullshit. It may look like it in the beginning, but that kind of love only exists in books and in movies."

Janice stared at Lainey and thought how bitter Lainey was about men.

"Damn Lainey. Tommy sure did a job on you."

Lainey looked at Janice and took a deep breath. "Yeah, he really did. I'm sorry Janice. I'm sure this dream man is everything you say he is. I just want you to guard your heart a little better and not put it out there for someone who isn't worthy of having it."

"Ah, my big sis loves me."

"Janice, you can be so silly at times. Just remember what I said. I thought Tommy was the love of my life. He was sweet, funny and everything to me. That man could do no wrong and no one could tell me he could do any wrong. I married him right out of high school, moved out of town away from my family and had his son. After a year, he beat me for breakfast, lunch and dinner.

"Oh, Lainey."

"If I put on something, it was either too short or too tight. One day, I wore shorts when I took out the trash and he accused me of enticing the trash man and beat me for it. From that day on, before I could leave the house, he had to inspect me. He didn't want me to wear makeup, nothing too low cut and nothing too short and none of his male friends were ever allowed to visit. One night, we were at a party with some friends, just having fun. He talked to women and men and I talked to women and men. Everybody knew one another. Talking about I embarrassed him in front of everybody. He actually pulled the hair right out of my scalp when he dragged me out of that party."

Janice put her hand over her face and asked, "Lainey, why didn't you tell me or tell somebody?"

"Janice, you were young and I couldn't tell Ma. At the time, I was in stupid love. I blamed it on myself and I told myself I wasn't good enough. After he became a lawyer, I studied to become a lawyer too so I could show him I was as smart as he was. I thought he would see that I was good enough—it didn't matter, he still beat me."

"Lainey, why did you stay?"

"He convinced me no one else wanted me."

"Are you kidding me? You're pretty and smart with a heart of gold. "Why would you think that of yourself?"

Lainey just shrugged her shoulders. Janice was hot as she thought about all of the pain her sister went through at the hands of her ex-brother-in-law.

"Tommy was a straight up A-hole that wanted to control you. It was easier for him to control you than it was to control his own crazy ass. He couldn't love you because he didn't even love himself. Where was Travis when all of this was going on?"

"He was there. When Travis turned fourteen, he started taking up for me. On one particular night, Tommy hit me and Travis came out of his room with his baseball bat and knocked him up side the head. Tommy fell to the floor. From that point on, he never laid his hands on me again. I believe that was the night Travis lost respect for me, because after that, he didn't listen to a thing I said. Tommy replaced the beatings with another woman, two children and making money. Travis was out running with the wrong crowd and I started putting all of my energy into helping other women, like myself, by making the men pay by hitting them where it hurts, in their pockets. I made a boatload of money doing it too."

"Lainey, you stayed with this man for thirty something years. Somewhere in that time, I grew up. Why didn't you tell me then?"

"I guess I didn't want you to lose respect for me too."

"I wouldn't have. I would have helped you, brought you home and paid somebody to beat Tommy's ass."

Lainey smiled. "You had your own life and I handled it the best I could."

"I can't believe you went through all of that for thirty years. You are one strong woman. Some people might say a woman who stays in that situation is weak, but regardless of why a woman stays, to endure that much pain for years, day in and day out, you have got to be a strong woman. I know I couldn't have done it. What made you leave now?"

"I was too weak to stay. When Travis moved out, I knew it was time for me to go."

"How is Travis?"

Lainey slowly walked to the refrigerator, took out a bottle of water and walked back to the sofa. "The last time I saw him, he was fine. You know, he became a chef. He's pretty good at it too. He said he would never become a lawyer because he'd heard enough arguing growing up to last him a lifetime. Travis said he opted to become a chef so he could put good food in people's mouths so they wouldn't be able to argue."

"That's smart. Where is he now?"

"He's in Delaware with some girl."

"Delaware is only an hour or so away."

"I know, that's one of the reasons I decided to move back home."

"I'm glad you're here Lainey, but tell me the real reason you came back. I can tell something is wrong. Let me help you now."

Lainey slowly walked to the closet and pulled out an oxygen tank. Janice's eyes got wide and moist.

Lainey dragged the tank to the sofa. "Janice, promise me you won't tell anyone, not Ma and especially not Travis."

"All right."

34

Marvin

AJ put on his seat belt and asked, "Okay Marvin, where to?"

"Anywhere, I just had to get the hell out of that house."

"Is anything wrong?"

"Everything is wrong. Janice came home at four o'clock this morning and told me she was with Dee. I called Dee last night—she hadn't even seen her."

AJ laughed. Where do you think she was all night?"

"I think she was with some damn man. Instead of us talking about this thing, she went out and made matters worst by sleeping with some loser. Then, that damn Linda sent her a copy of MJ's birth certificate and wrote a letter telling Janice all kinds of lies."

"No she didn't."

"Yeah, I called her up on it too."

"Let me get this straight. For the last year, you have been living with both of these women and you never told either one?"

Marvin was silent.

"You never told Janice you had a son?"

"Yeah, I told her. AJ, I can't be sitting in that house day in and day out with Janice. I need some wheels."

"Marvin, what do you need a car for? You can't drive."

"Once this cast comes off, I will and I can't wait. The first thing I'm gonna do is drive til the sun goes down and comes back up again. Hey AJ, make this right."

"Where are we going?"

"I want to see my son."

"Do you think that's a good idea?"

"I'm not going in. I just wanna see him. He should be in the front yard riding his bike about now. You can park across the street."

"If you say so."

AJ parked on the opposite side of Westbrook Lane and faced Linda's house. Just as Marvin said, MJ was outside riding his bike. Marvin looked at little MJ ride up and down the sidewalk padded from head to knee. "That little boy means everything to me. I'm not gonna let Linda get a way with keeping him from me."

"What are you going to do?"

"I don't know. Right now, I can't do anything but what I'm doing now—sit in a car with you and look at him."

AJ and Marvin watched Linda strut down the sidewalk in a very short red skirt and a multi-color halter top. Marvin shook his head. "Look at her. She got all that money and still buys clothes with less than a half a yard of material. MJ has no idea what kind of mother he got. Lord help him if he has to grow up only under her influences. He's gonna need a man in his life to show him how to be a man."

AJ pointed to the black convertible Corvette that pulled in front of Linda's house. "From the looks of things, he will."

Linda jumped in, kissed the driver and the two quickly drove off. Marvin said, "Aint that a bitch."

"It looks like all of your women have moved on." AJ laughed.

"I know damn well she didn't leave that boy home by himself."

"Marvin, you know MJ is not home alone."

"AJ, pull up closer to the house."

Marvin slowly got out of the car. As soon as MJ saw Marvin, he threw his bike down and yelled, "Daddy." MJ ran to Marvin and held on to his cast. MJ's nanny ran after him and yelled for him to come back.

Marvin put his hand up in a stop position. "He's okay."

With her arms folded across her chest, the nanny stood in the doorway and watched Marvin and MJ.

Marvin rubbed MJ's curly head. "Hey MJ, how's my boy?"

"I'm good Daddy."

"I see you have been riding your bike."

"Yep and I fell down too."

"You did?"

MJ pointed to his leg. "See, Mommy put a band-aid on it."

Marvin looked at MJ's leg. "You be all right."

"Are you gonna take me for a ride Daddy?"

"Not today son. Daddy can't drive with his leg all messed up, but I'll be back to see you soon." Marvin hugged MJ. "Go back to Nana."

The nanny picked up MJ and slammed the door behind them. Marvin hobbled back to the car and rubbed his forehead.

AJ asked, "Are you okay Marvin?"

"Yeah, go up the street and hang a right."

"Now, where are we going?"

"I'm going to check on my motorcycle."

"Why, it's not like you can ride it."

"Just make this right and another once you get to the top of the hill."

AJ did as he was told. When he stopped in front of the house, Marvin said, "It's just a friend of mind. I'll be right back."

Before Marvin got to the door, Karen opened it and stood in the huge doorway with a long, black silk robe. "What can I do for you Mr. Married Man?"

"Where's my motorcycle?"

"Why, it's not like you can ride it."

"Where is it Karen?"

"It's out back."

Karen followed Marvin to the backyard. Once outside, Marvin just stood there and examined what was left of his motorcycle. Karen hugged Marvin from behind and locked her arms around his waist. "You could have died on that thing. When I saw you lying in the street, I almost died."

Marvin unlocked Karen's arms from around his waist and turned around to look at her. "Yet, in two weeks, you didn't come to the hospital not once to see if I was dead or alive."

"I spoke to Mrs. Perry, your *wife* and she didn't say you were dead."

Marvin turned back around, looked at his motorcycle. *This is all Janice's fault.* "Karen, what are you talking about?"

"Marvin, do you think I'm stupid? I know you're married."

Marvin looked at Karen. "Did you and I get married while I was unconscious, because as far as I know, I'm a single man with a fiancée that left me high and dry in the hospital for two damn weeks?"

"I called the hospital and this woman answered and told me she was Mrs. Perry."

"And, you believed her?"

"Yes, I did."

"I don't know who answered the phone. I was knocked out for damn near the whole two weeks I was there. You should have come to the hospital instead of believing some strange woman on the phone."

Marvin put one of his hands over his mouth and started to laugh.

"What's so funny?" Karen asked.

"You are. I can't believe this. Now I know what happened. There was another man in the room named Carl Kerry. You were probably talking to his wife. Every time I woke up, that woman gave that man the blues. She yelled about some woman called her and said she was his fiancée. One time, security had to come in there and put her out for carrying on so bad. Sweetheart, was that you?"

For several minutes, Karen was quiet. "Does it hurt bad?"

"Yeah, right now it's killing me, but I had to see you and find out why you didn't come to visit me?"

"Marvin, I'm so sorry. When I heard that woman say, she was your wife, I . . ."

"Karen, you should have been there by my side. We can't get married if you're gonna believe any and everything somebody says about me."

Karen briefly looked away and turned back to look at Marvin. "Who's taking care of you?"

"Well, we both know it's not you. I've been taking care of my damn self. Why?"

"Stay here with me. I'll take care of you."

"No thank you. I need a woman that's gonna have my back, not bail on me soon as some other woman lies and says she's my wife or has my baby."

"Your baby?"

Marvin kissed Karen on her neck and whispered in her ear, "I'm mad at you. Sweetheart, you have to trust me. Do you trust me?"

Marvin took a few steps backward so he could see Karen's facial expression, but Karen looked to the side.

"Oh, so now you don't trust me. Hell, I'm not the one that left her fiancée high and dry."

"Marvin, this relationship is just . . . I don't know. There are other things too. That's why we haven't gotten married yet."

"Karen, how can I marry you and I'm all broken up? I don't have a car, a motorcycle and I can't work like this. Hell, I might even lose my job, my leg and my house. I don't know what I'm gonna do. Karen, I don't wanna lose you, but I love you too much to drag you in my mess."

Karen placed her arms around Marvin's neck. She kissed him on his cheek and on his forehead. "Baby, is that all you're worried about? I have plenty of money and plenty of cars. You want a car, just pick one. Which one do you want, the Vet, the 745 or the Escalade? I only drive them every now and then. Jackson takes me almost everywhere I go. I thought you were worried about something."

On the inside, Marvin smiled, but on the outside, he tried to maintain his distressed look. "How would I look taking one of your cars?"

"It would look like you would be driving, instead of walking."

"I can't drive anything right now until my leg heals."

"Like I said, come here so I can take care of you."

"I don't know about that Karen. You really hurt me leaving me alone in the hospital like that. I need some time to think about this. AJ is waiting for me. I got to go."

Again, Karen hugged Marvin. "Do you need anything else?"

"I'm just a little short on cash right now. While I was in the hospital, they stole my wallet with my money in it. Can you loan me $100."

"No problem."

Karen walked into the house and came back with a crisp $100 bill. Marvin stuck it in his pocket. He kissed Karen and said, "Thank you sweetheart. Everything is gonna be okay. I just need you to believe in me. I'll call you tomorrow."

Marvin hobbled back out to the car and got in. Karen stood in doorway and waved goodbye.

AJ looked at Marvin. "Who's that?"

"Just drive man."

"I guess all that stuff Janice said was true."

"What stuff?"

"You know the two fiancées."

"Man, I told you, she's a friend that's holding my motorcycle for me and is going to loan me one of her cars. Satisfied?"

"Marvin, you're gonna keep messing around til one of those women break your other leg."

"AJ, you let me worry about that. Stop at that liquor store. I want a Heineken for the game."

"Marvin, you know you're not supposed to be drinking with that medication?"

"I know you're getting on my nerves asking me a million questions like Janice and sounding like mother hen. AJ, just stop at the damn liquor store so I can get some beer."

Reluctantly, AJ pulled up to the drive-thru window. Marvin ordered 12 Heinekens and a fifth of Hennessey and handed AJ a $100 bill. "Here, get yourself something so you can loosen up."

AJ dropped the bag on Marvin's lap and gave him all of his change. Marvin saw AJ's disapproving smirk on his face and asked, "Is there a problem?"

"Nope."

AJ drove Marvin home in silence. He pulled into the driveway and left the engine running. He took Marvin's bag into the house and came right back out. "I see you later."

"AJ, don't you wanna watch the game with me?"

"No, I've seen enough games for one day."

"That's cool. I have a doctor's appointment on Tuesday at ten o'clock. Can you take me?"

AJ said, "Yeah," and backed out of the driveway.

Marvin hobbled into the house and went into the family room. With his beer at his feet and the remote in his hand, Marvin sat down in front of the TV and looked at his watch. "I wonder what she'll smell like tonight when she drags her all of a sudden, I'm single butt in here."

35

Desiree

As she sped through the subdivision, Desiree's hands and legs shook like a leaf on a tree in a hurricane. All she could see was the shotgun pointed in her face. "Victoria has really lost it. If Paul hadn't grabbed that gun, I think she would have actually shot me. That whole damn family is crazy."

Desiree ran through a red light and almost hit a man that tried to cross the street. She heard him yell, "It's a red light lady." Desiree continued to drive 40 miles over the 35-mile per hour speed limit until she slammed on brakes at the next stop light. With her fingers tightly gripped around the steering wheel, she lowered her head and cried out, "What have I done, what have I done?"

The light changed and a woman behind Desiree honked the horn for her to move. Desiree wiped her eyes and gave the woman a flip of the hand before she drove through the light. "I have to get out of town tonight. I need some time to clear my head."

Desiree turned the wheel in the direction of her estate. "Paul will be at Victoria's for a while. I'll pack a few things and be on my way."

Not wanting to be seen by Sarah, Desiree went in through the lower level, took the elevator straight to the master bedroom and closed the door. She ran into her closet, took out two Louis Vuitton monogram luggage and threw them on the bed. She made three trips into her closet and brought out two armfuls of her high-end label clothes, some unmentionables, a bottle of Dolce Garbana, a 22-carat gold leaf necklace, a pair of 18-carat gold diamond drop earrings, and an 18-carat yellow gold bracelet. "What else do I need?"

Desiree saw her easel floor mirror broken into tiny pieces. "He broke my damn mirror. I had that mirror for 30 years. Oh, he's going to pay for that. I think that's worth about $20,000."

Desiree opened the safe Paul hid in the wall behind his dresser. She reached in and took a stack of bills totaling $50,000. "I better not." She put back $30,000, threw $20,000 in her bag and closed the safe. "A few pairs of shoes and that will do it."

Desiree ran back in her closet and threw three pairs of shoes into her bag. One red sandal fell on the floor. Desiree bent down and saw Paul's gun case. She picked it up and laid it on the bed. "Please tell me he doesn't have it with him."

Desiree slowly opened the case. Just in case you get anymore ideas to point a gun at my head, I'll take this."

Desiree gently placed the gun in between her clothes and zipped up the bag. "Now, I'm done."

She picked up her luggage and took one more look around the room. "I'll be back. Mama just needs a mini vacation."

Desiree stopped when she saw the doorknob turn. In anticipation of another confrontation with Paul, she briefly closed her eyes. The door opened and Sarah stepped in. Desiree rolled her eyes. "Oh, it's just you. Sarah, what are you doing creeping around here? Make some damn noise. You nearly scared me to death."

Sarah looked at Desiree with her arms folded in front of her chest. "I find that hard to believe."

"What the hell does that suppose to mean?"

"It means I don't see you as the kind of woman that scares easily."

"Oh, get out of my way. I have to go."

Sarah blocked Desiree's exit. "I saw you."

"You saw me do what?"

"I overheard what you said at the wedding and I saw you guide that man's hand to shoot Chester."

Desiree dropped one of her luggage. "You don't know what you're talking about old woman and you better not go around telling lies about me either or I . . ."

"Or you'll what, do the same thing you did to Chester?"

"Get out of my way."

Desiree nearly knocked Sarah down when she ran out the door. As soon as she got to her car, she opened her trunk and threw in one bag. She bent down to pick up her second bag and froze when she felt a hand on her shoulder.

"Diva, don't tell me you were going to leave without saying goodbye?"

Desiree let out a huge sigh and threw her bag into the trunk. "Brent, have you lost your ever lasting mind coming here? Do you want to get us both killed?"

"Oh, calm down. Hubby is still over his brother's house. I had a feeling that you would be running scared after your sister-in-law almost blew you away and I was right."

"Have you been spying on me?"

"Let's just say, I've been keeping an eye on my investment."

Desiree nervously looked to her left and then to her right for any signs of Paul. "I was going to call you as soon as I left here."

"Diva, Diva, hubby might believe your little weak ass lies, but I know you all too well. You booked a flight to Jamaica, which leaves in two hours." Brent flashed the ticket Desiree had in her glove compartment.

"So, you rushed over here, packed some of your high-end garments, threw some unmentionables, jewelry, and a few pairs of shoes in a suitcase. Oh, and let's not forget the money you stole from hubby's safe. How much Diva? About $50,000 or did you get scared and put back half."

"Brent, I mean it, get the hell out of here. I'll meet you back at the hotel."

"You already checked out of the hotel, remember? Let's just say our goodbyes now. Hand it over Diva."

"I don't have any cash."

Brent grabbed Desiree by the arm and yelled, "I'm tired of playing games," and pushed Desiree aside. He leaned into the trunk and tore open one of her bags. He half closed it and opened the other. Brent saw the gun and picked it up.

Desiree screamed. With Paul's gun firmly in Brent's right hand, he unwillingly turned around to the sight of what looked like one hundred police officers on foot with their guns pointed directly at him and Desiree.

"Officer, he tried to kidnap me."

Brent looked at Desiree, shook his head and put his hands behind his back.

While the police handcuffed her and Brent, Desiree looked up and saw Sarah in the window smile at her.

"I'm going to get you old woman. You just wait!"

36

Paul

Katrina and Kristina cried, screamed and anxiously tried to get as close to their mother as they possibly could. Paul let go of Victoria and guided her to the open arms of her loving daughters. Both girls held on tight to their mother and all three continued to cry in a huddle. When Katrina looked up, Paul beckoned her to take Victoria and her sister into the house. After witnessing Victoria's breakdown, most of the other family members wiped their eyes and followed them into the house.

Janice walked over to Paul. "I tell you one thing, as soon as you get that woman out of your life, the better off we'll all be."

"Sis, not now."

"Yes, now. For years, everybody has been stepping on eggshells and holding their tongue where Desiree is concerned. We've tolerated her only because we love you. That woman is treacherous and no good for you. She's a habitual liar, a cheater and a thief. She has even tried to turn your own son against you, and now, she's killed Chester."

"Janice, Desiree is many things, but she's not a killer."

"How do you know? You didn't even know she was stealing from you until Chester told you. When did you find out she was cheating?"

"A few days ago."

"See, that's my point. That hasn't been the first time. You are so engrossed in work that you don't see anything until it's totally out of control."

Paul was tired of hearing Janice's obvious disapproval of his marriage. He wondered how she knew so much about what Desiree did. "Janice, I've been married to the woman for 17 years. I don't need you or anyone else to tell me how my wife is?"

"Well, somebody needs to tell you. Chester told me what your wife was doing."

"How did Chester know what Desiree was doing?"

"Chester kept a close eye on her, because he knew you didn't. He hired a private investigator."

"Why would Chester hire a private investigator for my wife?"

"To protect you, because you spent so much time working out of town. Years ago, he had your books audited and found out she embezzled money from your company."

"I know, Chester told me Desiree dipped into the travel account. I knew Desiree had expensive taste and loved to shop. It was a few thousand dollars, big deal."

"Ha! Is that what Chester told you?"

"No, I just assumed it was that. Besides, Chester told me he took care of it."

"At the time, that's what he thought. Haven't you noticed how Chester and Desiree never got along?"

"No."

"From that point on, Chester kept an even closer eye on the books, but it wasn't until a month ago when he discovered your wife, with the expensive taste and the heavy shopping habit, set up several dummy companies. Chester told me that over the last 10 years, she embezzled $2.3 million."

Paul's eyes flew open. "I don't believe it. How is it that you know this and Chester never told me?"

"He only found out a week ago. He confronted Desiree, but I convinced him to hold off on telling you until after the wedding."

Paul was so hot that sweat rolled down his forehead like running water in a faucet. "Janice, I don't want to hear anymore."

"Chester and Desiree were always getting into it. After he confronted her, she threatened that if he told you, she would make sure he never audited another book again."

"No, you've got this all wrong."

Janice put her hand on Paul's shoulder. "There's more."

Paul's phone rang. He put his hand up and answered, "Hello."

"This is Detective Lee Towson. Is this Paul Davis?"

"Yes, it is."

"Sir, we received a call that the woman and man who shot your brother were spotted coming from your house. I'm here now."

"Woman?"

"Yes, we believe they tried to burglarize the place."

"I'll be right there Detective."

"Janice, I have to go."

"What's going on?" Janice asked.

"Dante, move your car."

"What's wrong?"

"Someone just broke into my house."

"I'm going with you."

"Come on, you drive."

Before Paul got into Dante's Escalade, he went to his car and grabbed his flask. Dante looked at his father throw the flask to his head.

Paul yelled, "Don't look at me—drive!"

37

Janice

"Janice, I have a very bad heart," Lainey said.

"How long have you known?"

"It's been almost a year. I worked so hard to keep my practice going and one day, I just collapsed. They rushed me to the hospital and that's when I found out."

"Did Tommy know?"

"No and neither did Travis. After I got the practice from the divorce settlement, it got to be too much for me, so I sold it back to Tommy for double. Now, I don't have to work another day in my life."

Janice smiled. "Good for you Lainey, but what do the doctors say?"

"To keep doing what I'm doing. Keep taking all my medication—keep my appointments, and that kind of stuff."

Janice felt Lainey wasn't telling her everything, but decided to let it go for the moment. She reached out her hand and touched Lainey on the arm. "Let me tell Travis. If he knew, he would be with you."

"No! I don't want him to come out of pity and don't you tell him either. Promise me Janice."

Reluctantly, Janice said, "I promise. You know, I'll be dropping by quite a bit, so just in case you don't feel like getting up every time to answer the door, maybe you should give me a key."

Lainey stood up and slowly walked to the table and handed Janice a spare key. Janice expected Lainey to protest, but she didn't which confirmed her suspicions that Lainey was not being totally honest about her illness.

Janice twirled the key in her hand and silently prayed she never had to use it. "Lainey, I know we haven't always been close, but I'm here for you now. You don't have to do this alone. I love you and if you ever need anything, you call me day or night. Like Ma said, I'm only 20 minutes away."

Both Janice and Lainey laughed at their mother's good-natured mistaken directions. Not wanting to leave, Janice stood up and put her arms tightly around Lainey. "I better go."

"I love you too Janice, but don't forget, tell no one."

"I won't. Bye Lainey."

Janice pulled out of the driveway and wondered whether she would be able to keep Lainey's secret from her mother. She could definitely tell Lainey was a lot sicker than she let on. When Janice thought about the years of abuse Lainey went through with Tommy and now, she was dealing with possibly a life threatening illness, her eyes watered. Janice shivered at the thought of losing her only sister. Even though they were states apart, she always knew they were only a phone call and a flight away from each other.

The closer Janice got to her mother's house, the harder it was for Janice to hold back the tears. "I got to get myself together before I see Ma."

Janice thought about calling Paul. Just hearing his voice brought a smile to her face and right now, she desperately needed a reason to smile. "With everything that's going on with him, maybe he could use a pick me up as well."

She wiped her eyes and dialed Paul's number, but it went straight to his voicemail. Janice decided to leave him a message. "Hey Paul, this is Janice. I was thinking about you and thought I would send a little sunshine your way to hopefully brighten your day. Be good to yourself."

Janice hung up the phone and lit a cigarette. By the time she pulled up in front of her mother's all brick ranch style home, she felt calmer and confident that she could keep Lainey's secret.

When Janice saw her brother's brand new black 745 BMW parked in her mother's driveway, she said, "Perfect." Chester kept things lively and talked a lot, usually about everything and nothing, but today, Janice welcomed it. She put out her cigarette and checked herself in the mirror.

Chester cheerfully answered the door, "Hey Janice, what's shaken?"

"My hair." Janice shook her hair from side to side to show Chester her new highlights.

"Ah, you're just trying to cover up the gray."

"Whatever Chester. Where's Ma?"

"She's in the kitchen."

Janice said, a loud "Hey Ma."

Beatrice yelled from the kitchen, "Hi Janice."

Chester stood in the doorway and admired his very expensive new toy. "Hey Sis, did you check out my new ride?"

"Yeah, you can't help but to notice it. It takes up the entire driveway. When are you going to let me borrow it?"

"You can't even see over the steering wheel and no booster seats are allowed in my car for at least another 10 years."

"Oh, you got jokes."

Beatrice came from the kitchen, smiled at her daughter and said, "It's about time you got over here. What took you so long?"

"I stopped at Lainey's house. Ma, I thought you said Lainey lived 20 minutes away."

"That's what she told me."

"No, she said she lives at 2016 Minay. It's only five minutes away from me." Janice laughed.

Chester let out a hearty laugh. "I know. I was over there last night. Lainey looks real bad. She walked slow and could hardly catch her breath."

Janice cleared her throat and hoped Chester got the message. She glanced at her mother and saw the worried look on her face.

"Janice, is Lainey sick?" Beatrice asked.

"She's just coming down with something."

Chester looked at Janice and frowned. "Coming down with what? Whatever it is, it looks like it already came down. The girl looks bad."

"Chester, don't you have to pick up your girlfriend or something?"

"Not for 30 minutes Miss Timekeeper. What's your problem? Did curly head step on your toes in your hooker boots?"

Beatrice raised her voice. "You two stop that foolishness and tell me what's wrong with Lainey."

"Ma, nothing is wrong."

Janice tried to give her little brother the eye without her mother seeing her. "What did you want to talk to me about Ma?"

"I was just going to talk to you about throwing Lainey a welcome home party. Whenever I call her, she seems so depressed. Maybe this will cheer her up."

"Oh, that's nice. It would do her good to see family and old friends."

Beatrice nodded. "Did Lainey tell you what's going on with her?"

"Just that she has been tired lately and she misses Travis and Florida. We mostly caught up."

Beatrice folded her arms and looked into Janice's eyes. "I'm your mother and I can tell when I'm being lied to."

"Ma, I'm not lying."

Chester looked up in the ceiling.

Janice felt uncomfortable lying to her mother and decided to take the focus away from Lainey's illness. "Ma, did you know Tommy and Lainey had problems?"

"Not really."

"He did some terrible things to her."

"Like what?"

"He beat her for years."

Beatrice put her hand over her mouth and shook her head. "No, I didn't know."

Chester stood up. "Lainey should have told me. I would have taken care of Tommy for her. I never did like him. He was too damn quiet. You have to watch out for those quiet ones."

"I guess it's no need for anyone to watch out for you, huh Chester?"

"Whatever Janice. How is your curly head husband?"

"Not so good. He was in a motorcycle accident a couple of weeks ago."

"Serves him right," Chester mumbled.

Beatrice looked at Chester and then at Janice. "Is Marvin all right?"

Ma, he just has a broken leg and some bumps and bruises."

"You should be home taking care of your husband."

"I will Ma."

Chester frowned at Janice before he asked, "Did Marvin total his bike?"

"Yes."

"So, I guess he'll be driving the Bentley from now on?"

"Ah . . . we don't have a Bentley."

"That's right. Lainey is the one that has a Bentley, a black one right? They're nice. I thought about getting a glacier white one myself, but I changed my mind."

Janice turned around to look at her brother. She knew he was hinting around at something.

Chester stood up and kissed his mother on the cheek. "Well ladies, I have to go."

Janice jumped up. "Chester, I'll walk you out."

"Come on then, time's a wasting."

As soon as Janice got Chester out the door, she tapped him on the arm. "Do you have something you want to tell me?"

"Nope."

"What was all that talk about Bentleys?"

"Janice, you can lie to Ma all you want. I know Marvin has been driving around town in a glacier white Bentley and I know Lainey is sicker than what you say."

"Lainey didn't want me to tell Ma and how do you know about Marvin?"

"Girl, it's a small world. That same building your husband claims he works in is the same building I work in. He comes there almost every other day. Plus, my office window looks out into the alley—you'd be surprised at what goes on in that alley."

"Chester, Marvin does works there. I met him there for lunch."

"That man don't work there, at least the kind of work where you get paid. Marvin goes there to see some young lawyer that has those nasty looking hook fingernails and always wears her skirt so short that you can see *all* the land. Linda Franklin, that's her name."

"It is a small world. Why didn't you tell me?"

"Because you already knew."

"You didn't know that."

"Well, I don't see you all broken up about the news. When I mentioned Bentley, I could tell by the look in your eyes that you already knew."

Janice smiled at how observant her little brother had become. Chester opened his car door. "Janice, I just try to stay out of grown folks business. I don't know what you see in that curly head con anyway. He lies too damn much for me. You need to kick him to the curb and get you a good man or at least one that has his own Bentley. Well Sis, can't keep the ladies waiting. Let me know if you ever want me to put a foot up his . . ."

Chester kicked at the air. "Don't let these size tens fool ya."

"See you later playa playa." Janice laughed.

Chester leaned out of his window and said, "Bye Sis. Remember what I said."

When Janice went back into the house, her mother was on the phone.

"Get well soon," Beatrice said.

She must be talking to Lainey. As soon as Beatrice hung up, Janice asked, "How's Lainey?"

"That wasn't Lainey. That was Marvin."

"Marvin? What did he want?"

"He told me my daughter came in at four o'clock this morning. What did he say? Smelling like a liquor store and a sweet man. He also said since his accident, you've been leaving him home alone, not taking care of him and acting like you don't want to be married anymore. He sounded pretty upset."

Janice was angry that Marvin involved her mother in their problems. She walked to the window and said, "I can't believe he called you."

"Is it true? Are you stepping out on Marvin?"

"Ma, no."

"Janice, you just got married. Marriage is work, hard work and never let anybody tell you any different. You're going to have your ups and downs, but when you bring that third party in—it only brings hurt for everyone."

Janice wanted to tell her mother the truth about Marvin, but decided that was another secret she was going to keep. "I hear you Ma. Well, I guess I better go home and take care of my husband."

Janice kissed her mother on the cheek.

Beatrice kissed her back and said, "I love you."

"I love you too Ma."

38

Paul

Paul and Dante arrived just moments after the police cruisers left with Desiree in one car and Brent in the other. Several officers checked the sides and the back of the house and three officers searched the black Mustang that was parked in the driveway.

Paul and Dante immediately got out of the car. A tall man dressed in a black suit with a short haircut extended his hand to Paul and asked, "Are you Mr. Davis?"

"Yes, I am."

"I spoke to you on the phone, I'm Detective Towson. Both the man and woman are now in custody. When we got here, they were already outside and the man had this gun in his hand."

"That's my gun."

"We'll have to keep it for now."

"What did the man look like?"

"He was bald, about six-feet tall, around 240 pounds, and very muscular."

Under his breath, Paul said, "Popeye."

"Mr. Davis, we believe they were already in your house. You may want to search for missing items. Afterwards, we need you to come down to the Annapolis Police Station to see if you can pick them out in a live lineup. We're off of Taylor Street. Once you get there, ask for me."

"I'll be there."

Paul and Dante ran through the house and checked every level to make sure nothing was missing. They started on the main floor and looked to the left to the living room and to the right in the formal dining room. They went through the large kitchen to the family room, the library and the guestroom. Everything seemed untouched. They ran up the dramatic staircase and looked in the den, the exercise room, four of the bedrooms, the mini office, and the other family room.

Paul stopped at his master bedroom door. "Dante, go to the first level and check the theatre room, the rec room, and around the bar area. I'll meet you outside."

Paul saw that Sarah cleaned his room anyway and nothing there seemed to be out of place. He stood in the middle of the room and looked at a picture on the wall. "I better check my safe." Right away, he noticed stacks of money had been moved around. "That thieving bitch. I know it was her. If anybody else was going to rob me, they would have taken it all, not just $20,000."

Paul looked in Desiree's closet. "Good, she took some of her clothes. That will make the load lighter when she gets the rest of her damn things out of here. I should leave her ass right in jail for stealing from me and bringing that damn Popeye in my house."

Paul slammed the closet door. "This time, she's gone too damn far, too damn far!"

By the time Paul and Dante met outside, Detective Towson and the other officers were gone, but the Mustang was still parked in the driveway. Paul opened the door, reached into the glove compartment and looked for the owner's identity. "Desiree, what did you do with my damn money?"

He opened the trunk and looked through Desiree's luggage. Hidden between her blouses was a stack of bills. "I'll take this. Dante I'll be right back."

Paul ran into his house and cursed all the way to his bedroom.

"You can go anywhere you want to, but I'll be damned if you'll go with any more of my money."

Paul put the $20,000 back into his safe. "Tomorrow, I'm moving this damn money and changing all of the locks and security code."

On his way out, Paul ran into Sarah. "Oh, you're still here."

"Did they catch them?" Sarah asked.

"Yeah, so it was you that called the police?"

"Yes, I saw her when I went to clean your room."

"Did Desiree bring that man into my house?"

"No, inside, Desiree was alone. After she left, I looked out the window and saw the two of them arguing. I recognized him from the wedding and that's when I called the police. I tried to call you, but you didn't answer."

"Good job Sarah, but why did you tell the police Desiree was involved in Chester's shooting?"

"When I was at the wedding, I overheard that man ask Desiree was she ready to become a widow? She said that wasn't part of the plan. When you walked towards them and Chester tried to catch up with you, I saw her guide that man's hand with the gun and pointed it right at Chester. Then, the gun went off and that's when I saw you and Chester fall to the floor."

Desiree isn't a killer. Paul just stared into space.

Sarah lightly touched him on his shoulder. "Are you all right?"

"I told you to take the day off. When I tell you to do something, I expect you to do it. You better leave now."

"Yes sir." Sarah hung her head down and as instructed, left the house.

As soon as Paul got into Dante's truck, he said, "That damn Sarah called the police and told them Desiree was involved in Chester's shooting."

"Dad, do you think Desiree had anything to do with it?"

"Son, like I told your aunt, Desiree is many things, but she's no killer. She is undoubtedly a thief and according to Janice, a damn good one. Do you know in 10 years, that damn woman stole over $2 million from me?"

Dante sprayed Paul with his water. "Sorry Dad, $2 million, that's impossible. Chester always kept a close eye on the books."

Paul pulled out his flask, took another drink and put up his hand. "Janice just told me Chester did an audit last week and found several dummy companies Desiree set up years ago."

"Damn! That's a lot of money. I know that's your wife, but do you think Desiree shot Chester so he wouldn't tell you?"

"Now, here you go. Desiree is no killer and I don't want to hear another word about it."

Dante turned on Taylor Street and pulled into the Annapolis Police Station. As soon as they walked in, Detective Towson escorted them back to a room with a two way mirror. "Mr. Davis, you can see them, but they can't see you. The person who shot your brother may or may not be present in this lineup. The perpetrator may not appear exactly like they looked on the day of the incident."

Moments later, five men walked across the platform, stopped and looked straight ahead. Brent was number two.

"Mr. Davis, just take your time," Detective Towson said.

Paul took no time and pointed out Brent as the man that shot Chester. "That's him."

"Mr. Davis, are you sure that's the perpetrator?"

"Yes, I'm positive."

Detective Towson alerted the officer to secure number two and instructed the other men to leave. Shortly thereafter, Desiree and four women walked across the platform. Desiree was number three. Paul looked at Dante and turned back to look at Desiree. Dante did all he could not to laugh at the unsightly mess of his stepmother. Desiree's hair was sticking up in different places, her makeup was smeared, her jewelry was gone and her arms flapped up and down. Although no one could hear her, Paul and Dante knew she was yelling. Detective Towson pushed the button and instructed, "Number three, settle down in there."

As Paul stared at his wife of 17 years, the only things he could see were Desiree in the arms of his brother's killer and her stealing millions of dollars from him. The thought of Desiree having something to do with shooting Chester was more than he could handle.

Detective Towson pointed to all five women and asked, "Mr. Davis, do you recognize seeing any of these women the night of your brother's shooting?" Paul didn't answer.

"Take your time."

For five minutes, Paul stared at Desiree and read her lips as she said every curse word in the book. Finally, he said, "No, number three is my wife. Let her go."

With a surprised look on Detective Towson's face, he quickly looked at Paul. He then looked at Dante, who had a mischievous smile on his face, and looked back to Paul. Detective Towson tried to conceal his own amusement, but let out a chuckle and said "Very well sir."

By the time Paul and Dante got to the front of the police station, Desiree was released and ran towards them. "Paul, thank God you're here. They handcuffed me and finger printed me. They locked me up like I was a common criminal."

Two officers were in the corner and started to laugh. Desiree yelled, "I'll have your heads for this! Paul, this is a huge mistake. You know I would never do anything to hurt your brother. I loved Chester."

With sheer contempt in his eyes, Paul looked at Desiree and asked, "How is it possible that every time I see you, you sink even lower than the time before?"

Desiree grabbed Paul by his arm. "Please, you've got to believe me."

Paul looked down at Desiree's hand on his arm. "Get your hands off me."

Desiree slowly removed her hands. Without saying another word, Paul walked out of the station.

"Son, take me back to my car."

"Okay Dad. Are you all right?"

"Yeah, I will be."

The entire drive back to his Aunt Victoria's, Dante played his father's favorite music, Oldie but Goodies. When he pulled into the driveway, Paul got out and said, "Thanks Son."

For a few minutes, Dante sat in the driveway and watched his Dad as he walked up the sidewalk towards Katrina. Paul sensed Dante was still there and waved goodbye. Dante backed out of the driveway and drove off.

"Hey Katrina, how is your mother?"

"She's sleeping now. Kristina is looking at TV."

Paul took both of Katrina's hands in his and said, "They caught the man that shot your father."

"Thank God."

Through tears of joy, Katrina smiled and gave her uncle a big hug. "I'll tell Mama when she wakes up."

"Tell your mother and sister that I'll be back tomorrow. You try to get some sleep tonight."

"I'll try. Good night Uncle Paul."

"Good night Katrina."

39

Janice

As soon as Janice walked through her front door, she was ready to give Marvin a piece of her mind. She dropped her purse in the foyer and headed straight for the guest room. "Marvin, I can't believe you called my mother."

When Janice didn't see Marvin in the guest room, she searched the half bath and the mini office. "Marvin, where are you?"

Marvin didn't answer. Janice let out a deep breath. She walked towards the kitchen and looked in the direction of the family room where she found Marvin passed out on the sectional sofa. "Look at all this beer and liquor. He knows he's not supposed to be drinking alcohol while he's taking all that medication."

Janice stood in the middle of the floor and looked down at Marvin. "I don't know what's worst, not having a home to go to or having a home that you don't want to go to." *My home used to be my sanctuary.*

Janice grabbed her purse and out the door she went. For an hour, she drove down Interstate 495, listened to Jazz and mostly thought about Lainey. As hard as it was for Janice to hear about her sister's abuse and illness, she was glad Lainey finally told her. With Lainey just down the street, Janice can frequently stop by and make sure she's all right.

Again, Janice ended up at the Gaylord. As soon as she parked her truck, her phone rang. She answered, "Hello."

"Thanks for sending sunshine my way. You don't know how much I needed it today."

Janice smiled as she heard Paul's voice on the other end of the phone. She would have much rather heard from him earlier when her mood was a little better, but she tried to sound as upbeat as she could.

"You're having a bad day, huh?" Janice asked.

"Let's just say I feel like I've been to hell and back."

"I'm sorry to hear that. Is there anything I can do?"

"Just hearing your voice is plenty."

"Glad to be of service."

"Janice, is something wrong?"

"Why do you ask?"

"You seem a little down, in spite you trying to sound upbeat."

"Very observant Mr. Davis. I'm fine. Today, I just received some bad news about my sister."

"Do you want to talk about it?"

"No, but thanks."

"Janice, I have my own stuff going on, and I could very well just accept your no, but I don't like to hear you down. Despite all my troubles, I haven't been able to stop thinking about you. I remember how your words rescued me. I may not be as good as you, but I'll do my best. Let me share with you some of my sunshine that earlier, a very pretty lady sent to me."

Janice was quiet and felt that peacefulness she desperately needed. To her surprise, she started telling Paul about Lainey. "Today, my sister told me she's very ill. She made me promise not to tell my mother or her son."

"That must be hard on her as well as you."

"I asked her for a key, just in case . . . She gave it to me without any protest. That was so unlike her. I know she's not telling me everything about her illness. I don't know if I can handle losing my only sister. Paul, I'm really worried."

"Janice, where are you?"

"I went for a drive to think. When things get a little heavy, driving seems to calm and relax me."

"I do the same thing."

"Right now, I'm standing across the street from the Gaylord."

"What are you doing there?"

"I don't know exactly. Like I said, I was driving and the highway led me here. Why do you ask?"

"Because I see you."

When Janice saw Paul park his Bentley next to her truck, she hung up her phone and walked over to him. "Wow! I can't believe you're here."

Both she and Paul smiled from ear to ear and hugged each other tightly. Paul pulled slightly away from Janice and looked into her eyes. "I'm here. I'm here for you."

As unplanned as the drive was to the Gaylord, so was their first kiss. Paul kissed Janice passionately and Janice felt peace, love and happiness, along with a burning desire to throw him across the hood of his car. Paul let go of Janice, but continued to look into her eyes. He smiled and said, "You really do have pretty eyes."

"Thank you."

"Well, Miss Janice, since we're here, let's have that dinner."

"Okay."

Paul held out his hand for Janice. They both walked hand in hand into McCormick and Schmick's.

Two hours went by with Janice and Paul talking, laughing, drinking, and eating scallops, shrimp, and crab cakes, which turned out to be both of their favorites.

Paul leaned back in his seat. "Can I get you anything else Pretty Lady?"

"No, I'm stuffed. Thank you."

Paul kissed Janice on her neck. "I'm so glad I ran into you."

"Me too."

"I feel sorry for your ex-husband. He must be crazy to let you go. If you were my wife, I'd never let you go."

A deep voice said, "But, she's not your wife—she's mine."

Both Janice and Paul looked up to Marvin dressed in all black standing in front of their table trying to balance himself on his crutches.

Janice's eyes got huge. "Marvin, what are you doing here?"

Marvin looked at Paul and then at Janice. "I should ask you the same, but I can see what you're doing here. I guess this is your sweet smelling man you were out with until four o'clock in the morning."

"Janice, is your ex-husband giving you problems?"

"Is that what my little sweetheart told you? Janice, I'm sorry I let the cat out of the bag, but it sounds like you haven't been totally honest about your marital status to your sweet smelling man here." Marvin laughed and turned towards Paul. "We are very much married. We still live together in the same house and like a good little wifey, she's been taking care of me in *sickness and in health*. I guess she just needed a little break and decided to get out and find a new toy to play with for a while. Sweetheart, I'm sorry

I've been such a burden. See you when you get home." Marvin reached down and took a shrimp off of Janice's plate and hobbled towards the door.

Paul finished his drink in one gulp and threw a $100 bill on the table. Janice touched his arm. "Paul, I can explain."

"No need to explain. I'm not your husband—he is."

Paul pointed to Marvin still making his way out the door. "Look, I just got rid of one lying ass, cheating woman. I definitely don't need another. Playtime is over Janice. Go home. Take care of your husband."

Janice sat at the table alone and felt like Marvin stuck a knife in her back while Paul stuck a knife in her heart.

40

Desiree

On her way to the bathroom, Desiree thought she was sure she could get one of the officers to take her home. She looked in the mirror. "Ewe, don't I look crazy? No one would even look at me like this, let alone want to take me anywhere."

Desiree emptied the contents of her purse onto the counter and transformed herself back into Diva style. Again, she looked in the mirror. "That's more like it."

When Desiree left the bathroom, she saw the officers take Brent down the long narrow hallway. She tried to go around the corner before he saw her, but was unsuccessful.

Brent lunged forward and yelled, "Diva, get me out of here! If I go down, you go down!" The officers yanked Brent back and continued to escort him to a cell.

In pure Diva form, Desiree walked up to the three officers who previously laughed at her. "Would one of you fine gentlemen be so kind as to take a lady in distress to her car?"

A handsome six-foot, 170-pound picture perfect Officer Goode was the first to speak up. "I'm just getting off my shift. I'll be happy to take you to your car."

"I'll be waiting."

Just give me a couple of minutes," Officer Goode said.

Detective Towson walked up to Desiree and chuckled. "Mrs. Davis, I see you clean up real well."

Desiree turned up her nose.

"You have a good day. I have a feeling we'll be seeing each other again very soon."

Under her breath, Desiree said, "I wouldn't count on it. By this time tomorrow, I'll be in sunny Jamaica Mun."

As promised, Officer Goode returned to give Desiree a ride to her car. "Thank you so much officer."

Officer Goode took his business card from his pocket and rubbed it on Desiree's wrist before he laid it on her lap. "If you ever need anything, please don't hesitate to call and I do mean anything."

Desiree took the card, gave Officer Goode a wicked smile and got out of the Stinger Yellow Dodge Challenger. Not taking any more chances on Paul catching her with yet another man in front of their house, she jumped into the Mustang and quickly drove down the curvy driveway.

Desiree looked in her rear view mirror. "What a day. One minute I have a gun pointed at me and the next I'm being hauled off to jail. I'm not spending another day in this hell hole. I can't believe Brent showed up at my house. He can't be that damn stupid. It really serves him right. Hell, I'm going to Jamaica. What can he do, he's in jail. I'll deal with him when I get back and I'll also deal with that damn nosey ass Sarah for calling the police on me. That's okay Sarah. The day I come back home is the day I'll toss you right out on your nosey old ass.'"

In route to the Ronald Reagan National Airport, Desiree took Highway 395. She pulled onto the parking lot in front of the Avis Rent-A-Car and said, "Jamaica, here I come." Before she turned in her rental car, she opened her trunk and looked in her luggage for her $20,000. "Security will stop me with all this money."

Desiree didn't see the money and kept pulling out her belongings until all her clothes were on the floor of the trunk. "Dammit! Either the police took it or Paul took it."

Desiree put everything back into her two bags and stood in the parking lot while she debated her next move. She took her luggage out of the trunk and turned in her keys. "I guess this trip is on me. That's the first time this ever happened and will definitely be the last time I spend my own money."

Desiree walked into the airport and looked around to see where she needed to exchange her ticket. She got no more than 20 feet inside the airport before she heard Cynthia yell, "Mother."

Desiree briefly shut her eyes. *Oh no.* "Cynthia Darling, fancy meeting you here." Desiree hugged Cynthia. "Hello Brian."

"Hello Mrs. Davis."

"Cynthia, how was your honeymoon?"

Cynthia put her arm into Brian's arm. "It wasn't as long as we wanted it to be, but it was still nice. When we heard about Uncle Chester, we decided to cut it short. Mother, where are you going?"

"I'm going to Jamaica."

"Why Jamaica?"

"Why does anyone go to Jamaica—to have a wonderful time of course?"

"I mean with Uncle Chester and all, why would you pick now to go on a vacation? Daddy must be really torn up behind all of this. He and Chester were really close."

"That's right darling, they were. You should go to him now. I have to go. Bye."

Desiree grabbed her luggage and scurried down the hall in search of the Air Jamaica desk.

41

Marvin

Marvin got into the car with AJ and laughed so hard he could barely speak. AJ took one look at Marvin and he too began to laugh. "Marvin, what happened in there?"

"Boy, you should have seen Janice's face when I stood in front of her and Sweet Daddy."

"Is that why you wanted to come out here, to catch Janice with a man?"

Marvin tried to catch his breath. Yeah and I planned it just right. She didn't know what hit her in there. Damn I'm good. Something told me she was gonna meet her man again today and I was determined to catch her in the act. That's why I asked you to come back. Earlier, I called her mother and told her I was so upset and hurt because Janice stayed out until four o'clock in the morning and some more stuff. I knew Beatrice would tell her and I knew Janice would be hot enough to come home to confront me. That's why I told you to park around the corner. Like clockwork, my little sweetheart came home to tear me a new ass-hole. You were out back on the phone when she came in. I pretended to be passed out on the couch. Just as I thought, she left right back out and went to meet him. When I walked up to that table, you'd think she'd seen a ghost."

AJ shook his head. "What did you do?"

"Oh, I was cool. I didn't act like a jealous husband or anything. Ole boy didn't know Janice was still married. So I just told him the truth."

"Then what happened?"

Marvin pointed to Paul as he walked down the street. "You see him leaving. That ought to tell you what happened."

"Where's Janice?"

"She's still in the restaurant. Let's get out of here before she sees me."

"Too late, here she comes now," AJ said.

Janice jumped in her truck and pulled off. When she spotted AJ and Marvin behind her, she sped up. Marvin laughed. "Oh sweetheart, don't be mad. How do you think I felt when you showed up at my mansion and blew my whole world into pieces? Now, maybe you'll stay off my case."

"Two wrongs don't make a right. In your case, 10 wrongs don't make a right."

Marvin gave AJ a look that told him he didn't appreciate or agree with his comment. "Boy, you're too soft. You got to show these women who's the man. A woman can wear pants all she wants, but it will never make her a man. A man can have five women and he's a playa. If a woman has five men, she's a Ho."

Again, AJ shook his head at Marvin.

"Hey, I didn't make the rules. I'm just trying to keep my sweetheart a good girl."

"Doesn't it bother you that she was with another man?"

"Not really, she doesn't care about him. I know she was just trying to get back at me."

"You know your woman."

"Yes, I do. I know all my women."

Janice pulled in the driveway, jumped out her truck and went into the house. Marvin laughed. With AJ's help, he got out of the car. "Thanks man. I'm gonna show my wife how hurt I am and ask her how she could cheat on her loving husband. I'm sure we'll be talking about it all damn night."

"See ya Marvin."

"See ya tomorrow AJ."

Marvin hobbled in the door. Janice was in the kitchen. "Hey sweetheart, don't tell me you're mad at me because you got busted. I'm the one that should be mad. I just found out my wife is cheating on me."

Janice looked at Marvin and said nothing. She grabbed a bottle of wine out of the refrigerator, her wine glass from the rack and walked right past him up the stairs to her room and slammed the door.

Marvin yelled up the stairs, "You better be glad I can't get up those stairs!"

He opened up the refrigerator and took out a beer. "Damn, she didn't say nothing. That's a first. In a week, she'll forget all about ole boy and things will be back to normal. I can't have both of us cheating. What kind of marriage is that?"

42

Paul

Paul was baffled by the rapid intensity of his feelings for Janice. He was angry at her for lying to him, but he was furious with himself for feeling the way he did, disappointed and surprisingly hurt. "Women, all of them are just sneaky and conniving. Can't trust none of them. From now on, they can go find another sucker, because I'm safeguarding my heart and my damn money."

Paul sat in his driveway and put in his Oldie but Goodies CD. He threw his flask up to his head and drank the rest of his vodka. "I see the Mustang is gone. Good, two cheaters bit the dust."

Paul walked up the six stairs to the side entrance of his home. He stood in the middle of the huge living room and looked around at all of his expensive furnishings, pictures, and vases Desiree bought over the years. For the first time, he realized he had more valuable things in his life than valuable people.

All of a sudden, Paul felt the emptiness in his house and in his heart. Other than his family, he really didn't have anyone he could say was truly valuable to him. He longed to have that one person in his life that he could tell his most intimate feelings to and not have to worry about being judged or taken advantage of. The only person Paul ever felt totally comfortable sharing his feelings with was Chester and now he was gone.

Paul silently counted each of the 24 steps he took to his bedroom. He threw his jacket on the bed and headed to the mini bar. Paul poured himself a hefty drink and turned on his calming music, instrumental Jazz. He then took off his clothes and sat in the chaise lounge chair next to his bed. With drink in hand, Paul laid his head back on the chair and closed his eyes. He tried to let the music soothe his soul, but thoughts of his entire day ran through his mind. He thought about when Victoria pulled a gun out on Desiree, when Janice told him Desiree stole millions

166

from him, when he identified Brent in a lineup, when he saw Desiree in a lineup, and ran into Janice and her husband.

Paul shook his head and looked at Desiree's picture. "How can I make millions of dollars and be so stupid when it comes to women? In the many years I've lived with Desiree, I would have never guessed she would have turned out to be the kind of woman she is today."

Paul took another drink. "I don't actually know Janice, but from the moment I met her, I felt there was something special about her. I could definitely tell she was sweet, kind and had a good heart, but I never thought she was as much of a liar and cheater as Desiree."

Paul sat up straight and looked out the windows at the lights that shined over his four acres. He thought about the look on Janice's face after Marvin left and wondered why she looked like someone betrayed her instead of the other way around.

"I guess it's time for another drink. Paul kicked off his shoes and walked to the mini bar. He thought about the unplanned kiss he and Janice shared and how he felt like a giddy teenager. Paul smiled. "I didn't know older people could still get giddy, but that's the way I feel whenever I talk to that damn woman. I've never felt this way with Desiree, not even in the beginning of our relationship."

He wanted to believe that Janice was just like Desiree and kick them both to the curb, but something deep inside him wouldn't let him. As much as Paul didn't want to admit it, Janice was already in his heart. He took a huge gulp and held his glass high in the air. "She's married to a broken up pretty boy. No thank you, I'll leave that one alone."

Paul's phone rang. He saw that it was Janice and let it go to his voicemail. A few seconds later, Paul's message light lit up and he listened to her message—"Paul, I don't blame you for not wanting to talk to me. I just wanted to say I'm sorry for not being totally honest about my marriage. My life is so complicated right now. Maybe one day, I'll get to explain it to you, but for now, I guess it's best this way. Be good to yourself. Again, I'm really sorry."

Paul listened to the message again and put the phone back down. He closed his eyes and said, "Not as sorry as I am Janice." Again, Paul's phone rang. He quickly picked it up and answered, "Hello."

"Hi Daddy, I'm back."

"Oh, hey Baby Girl."

"Oh hey, what kind of greeting is that?"

"I'm sorry. I thought you were someone else."

"Who, a woman?"

"No, why would you say that?"

"No reason, I'm sorry to hear about Uncle Chester. Are you okay?"

"Thanks Baby Girl. I'm hanging in there. Where are you?"

"Brian and I are still at the airport. We just ran into Mother. She's on her way to Jamaica."

Under his breath, Paul said, "She ought to go somewhere."

"What did you say Daddy?"

"I said it must have been some airfare. You know last minute and all."

"Daddy, do you want us to come over?"

"No, you two go on home. How was the honeymoon?"

"Short, but we enjoyed ourselves."

"That's good. How's Brian?"

"He's fine."

"That's good."

"Daddy, are you sure you don't want us to come over?"

"Yeah, I'm sure. I'm just going to turn in early."

"Okay Daddy, I'll see you tomorrow."

"Bye Baby Girl."

As much as Paul loved his daughter, the only thing he wanted to do was listen to his music and drink until he passed out.

43

Janice

The next morning Janice decided not to go to work. She knew she didn't want to stay all day in the house with Marvin, but wasn't quite sure what she wanted to do. Janice made her way into the shower. As the warm water hit her body, she came up with a plan to call Jasmine and surprise Lainey with putting her house in order.

Janice got out of the shower, dried herself off, and called her daughter. "Hey Jasmine."

"Hey Mommy. What's up?"

"You are."

"Huh?"

"How would you like a job?"

"What kind of job?"

"A few weeks ago, your Aunt Lainey moved up the street from me and needs help with her place. Do you think you can come over today?"

"I knew she was talking about it, but I didn't know she was here already. Yeah, what time?"

"Today, at around noon. I'll even feed you."

"Sounds good Mommy. I'll pick you up in my new ride."

"Bye sweetie."

Janice ran downstairs to start her morning coffee. Her back was turned, but she could hear Marvin's squeaky crutches, which told her he was near. Out the corner of her eye, she saw him sit down at the kitchen table.

"Good morning sweetheart," Marvin said.

"Good morning."

"Janice, are we going to talk about this?"

Janice ignored Marvin and continued to make her coffee.

Marvin banged on the table. "Dammit Janice, I'm talking to you!"

"It's too early for this. What do you want to talk about?"

"I've been up half the night thinking about you and Sweet Daddy. I feel betrayed and I don't like it one bit. You hurt me Janice."

Several minutes went by and neither Janice nor Marvin said a word. Marvin looked at Janice and asked, "What do you think?"

"I think I have to go to work."

"How long have you been seeing Sweet Daddy?"

"Who?"

"Who hell—the damn man you were with yesterday."

"I'm not seeing him. I met him a few days ago. Over dinner, we talked about an event he wants to book."

"When did you become a liar?"

"I'm not lying, that's your specialty."

"I saw you big as day on the parking lot kissing him. What was he booking, your lips?"

Janice turned around to get her coffee. *Damn, he saw that.* Janice turned to face Marvin. "I don't know why you're interrogating me and you're the one that has a harem out there. I didn't ask you to come back here. I left your ass in the hospital and I never came back. That should have told you something."

"I told you there was nothing going on between Linda and me."

"Marvin, I know what you told me, but I don't believe you. For years, I tried to believe in you. All you do is lie. Did you honestly think I believed all of your lies or did you think you had me where you wanted me? Just because I don't call you up on everything you do, don't think I don't see what's going on. I'm not stupid. I've just learned to pick and choose my battles. It's less frustrating and less exhausting that way."

Marvin was quiet. Janice shook her head. "Marvin, you're like a serial cheater and your victims are always women with money. Tell me something. I don't have that kind of money. Why did you marry me?"

"Because I love you dammit! What in the hell is it gonna take for you to believe me? I told you nothing is going on with Linda and me. I don't have a son, and I definitely don't have a fiancée."

"Will you please stop insulting my intelligence? You're lying. This time, I know you're lying and nothing you say will convince me otherwise. I can't trust you. I want "Wows," not "Woes," and for years, woes are pretty much what you've given me. This is not what I want."

Marvin stood up. "What the hell do you want Janice?"

"I want you out of here!"

"Why, so you can cuddle up to Sweet Daddy?"

"No, I don't give a damn about him or you. I'm not happy and I know now I shouldn't have married you. If there are problems before you get married, the same problems are there after you get married."

Marvin threw the chair across the kitchen. "Oh, you shouldn't have married me, huh?" Is that what you said?"

Janice backed off.

Marvin nodded. "You're right Janice. You shouldn't have married me and I should have married Linda or even Karen. Hell, both of them have the money I need and both of them are just waiting for me to put a ring on that finger. If you hadn't been so damn nosey driving by my house to stir up shit, I could have been in my mansion with my son and driving my Bentley."

Tears of fury streamed down Janice's face. She looked Marvin right in the eye and in a slow but steady voice said, "I want you out of here today."

"Okay, if that's what you want. Just give me 30 days to find another place to live. Until then, I'll stay out of your way."

Janice didn't respond and continued up the stairs. She sat her coffee cup down on her dresser, went into her closet, and pulled out a jogging suit. When she bent down to get her sneakers, her phone rang. Janice looked down at her caller ID and saw that it was Davey. "I really shouldn't answer this. Hello Davey."

"Hello yourself. I was beginning to think you were screening your calls."

"I've just had a lot going on. How are you?"

"I'm fine now. I was calling to tell you the house was on fire. Is there any chance you could come and put it out?"

"Nope."

"Hey, you can't blame a brother for trying."

"I guess not."

"Hey Janice, are we still friends?"

"Yeah, we're still friends."

"All right then, I'll be calling to check on my friend real soon."

"Bye Davey."

When Janice hung up the phone, she noticed her message light was on. She smiled when she saw it was from Paul. "He and Davey must have called at the same time."

Janice listened to Paul's message—"Hey Pretty Lady, I got your message. I think I would like to hear that explanation. I am at my office. The address is on my card. You can reach me here until three o'clock.

"Wow! He's actually going to give me a chance to explain. That's what I'm talking about. I'll call him back after I leave Lainey's house."

When she heard Jasmine's Honda Civic outside, she quickly put on her jogging suit and sneakers. Jasmine yelled from downstairs, "Hi Mommy."

"Come on up. I'm almost ready."

"Where's the food?"

"I didn't say I would cook anything. I said I would feed you."

"Oh, I didn't eat anything and I'm starving."

Janice laughed at her high spirited and spoiled rotten daughter. "Jasmine, before we leave, I have to tell you something."

"What Mommy?"

"Lainey is very ill, but you can't tell anyone."

"What's wrong with her?"

"She has a bad heart."

"Will she be okay?"

Janice looked away for a moment and said, "I hope so. Anyway, that's why I wanted to do this for her. Right now, she has boxes everywhere."

"Mommy, does she have any furniture?"

"She has the basic stuff—a sofa, bed, table, and chairs. Jasmine, I see that sparkle in your eye, the one you get when you're about to spend someone else's money."

"That means she'll need some more furniture." Jasmine giggled.

"You're the interior designer and knowing you, I'm sure you'll incorporate new furniture into your design, but keep in mind that I'm paying for this."

"Okay Mommy."

Janice and Jasmine pulled into Lainey's driveway. Jasmine looked at her mother and said, "Mommy, Aunt Lainey practically lives next door to you. We could have walked."

"Yeah, I know. Isn't it great?"

Janice jumped out of the car and rang the doorbell. A few minutes went by and there was no answer. Janice rang the doorbell a second time and again, there was no answer. Janice took a deep breath and reached into her purse for the extra key Lainey gave her.

"Mommy, did she know we were coming?"

"No, it's a surprise."

When Lainey didn't answer the door on the third ring, Janice was about to put her key in the lock and Lainey opened the door. Janice let out a sigh of relief. "Hey Lainey, we're here to surprise you."

Lainey smiled. Janice thought Lainey looked much better than she did the last time she was there.

"Surprise," Jasmine yelled.

"Yes, this is a surprise. Come on in."

"Hi Aunt Lainey," Jasmine said as she hugged her aunt.

"Jasmine, look at you. You're all grown up."

"Are you ready for me to do my magic?"

"Your magic." Lainey laughed.

"We've come to give your home a makeover," Janice said.

"Help yourself. I was getting tired of looking at all these boxes."

Jasmine went through the house with her pen and pad while Janice and Lainey sat at the kitchen table.

"Lainey, how are you feeling today?"

"I'm feeling good today. I appreciate you two helping me out. I didn't know when I was going to get all of this stuff done."

"Jasmine and I will have your house looking like a picture in no time. You just sit there and relax."

Janice got up and unpacked some of Lainey's boxes.

Lainey had a mischievous smile on her face and asked, "So Janice, what have you been up to? I talked to Ma and she says your hubby gave her a call."

Janice stopped unpacking and looked at her sister. "Ma and her loose lips telling all my business."

"Well, spill it."

"Lainey, it's been crazy. Yesterday, I went for a drive and ended up back at the Gaylord. Paul, remember the guy I told you about?"

"Yeah, your *Wow Man*."

"I just got out of my truck and he called me. We talked and the next thing I see is him pulling up right next to me. It wasn't planned or anything. We hugged each other and kissed. It was my first time kissing him and my entire body tingled. Since we were close to McCormick and Schmick's, we went in and had dinner. We were there for two hours having a great time. When dinner was over, he said if I was his wife, he would never let me go."

"What did you say?"

"I didn't say anything, but Marvin said, "But she's not your wife—she's mine.""

"Janice, you got busted." Lainey laughed.

"I could have strangled Marvin for telling Paul we were living together and I was taking care of him like a good little wife."

Lainey looked puzzled. "Well, you are."

Janice looked away and put Lainey's dishes into the cupboard. For several minutes, she said nothing.

"Janice, you didn't tell your Wow Man you were married?"

"I did and I didn't. I told him no, in my heart, I'm not married."

"My goodness, haven't we become the little liar and cheater these days."

"That's exactly what Paul said. He told me he just got rid of one lying cheating woman and he didn't want another."

"You can't blame the guy for that."

"I did leave him a message and apologized for not being totally honest."

"What a tangle web we weave."

"I know. This morning, Marvin and I had a huge argument and I told him to get out."

"I hope it wasn't because you're thinking about playing house with your Wow Man."

"No, but Marvin and I were arguing about Paul when he finally admitted to his harem. He had the nerve to tell me if it wasn't for me snooping around, he would still be in his mansion with his son and driving his Bentley. That's when I told him to get out."

Lainey's eyes widened. "Ouch. That's a confession all right. Is he going to leave?"

"He asked me to give him 30 days to look for something."

"That is the law. What about this other guy?"

"He did call me this morning. He said he wanted to hear my explanation."

"Janice, are you sure it is over between you and Marvin?"

"Yeah, I'm sure. I can't trust him. I've tried and he let me down more times than I can count. Marvin loves money more than me. I shouldn't have married him in the first place."

Lainey looked at her little sister and said, "I'm concerned about your life changing events. Janice, I know your heart is doing flip flops for this other guy, but I hope your decisions were not based on him."

"No, it wasn't. When I left Marvin in the hospital, I knew it was over. It had nothing to do with Paul."

Lainey smiled. "Good, just checking. Take it slow with this one."

"Yes, Big Sis."

Jasmine came out of the room with her pad full of notes and sketches. While Lainey and Jasmine talked, Janice slipped outside to return Paul's call.

When Janice stepped back inside, she instantly noticed the gigantic smile on her daughter's face. Jasmine showed Janice the check Lainey wrote. Janice's mouth flew open. "Lainey, I was going to do this for you, not that lavishly though."

"Janice, didn't I tell you I don't have to work another day in my life? Besides, Jasmine can put this down on her resume. I'm her first real client."

"Thanks Aunt Lainey. Come on Mommy, I have to go shopping."

Janice hugged Lainey. "I guess she's ready. All of the boxes are emptied so I'll take these out front on my way out. Lainey, do you need anything?"

"No, I'm fine. A friend of mine is bringing me lunch."

"Oh, anyone I know?"

"I doubt it."

"Okay, I'll call you tomorrow."

Janice put on her seatbelt and looked at Jasmine. "I can't believe she wrote you a check for $25,000. Lainey is loaded."

44

Paul

Paul was in his office bright and early taking care of as much business as he could before Chester's funeral and his two-week sabbatical. As he did every Monday at 11 o'clock, Paul grabbed his files and went next door to Chester's office to go over important business and talk.

Paul sat in Chester's chair, looked around his office and noticed how their styles were very different. Chester liked the traditional oak and mostly used his desk as a filing cabinet. "Man, he got papers all over his desk, but he could always find whatever I needed whenever I needed it."

Paul put both of his hands over his face and wondered how he was going to function without Chester. He was more than Paul's big brother—he was his father, his best friend and his lawyer. Paul had so many questions that only Chester could answer. He missed his brother terribly. He missed their talks and he missed hearing Chester's voice.

Paul uncovered his face and smiled when he remembered he saved a message from Chester. He was about to listen to it when Vivian came in. "Mr. Davis."

"Yes, what is it?"

"There's a lady on the phone by the name of Janice Perry. I tried to take a message, but she said she was returning your call."

"Put her through right now."

"Mr. Davis, for future reference, what company is she with?"

"She's with the Pretty Lips Foundation." Paul smiled.

Vivian hesitated before she said, "I'll send her right through."

When Vivian walked back to her desk, under his breath, Paul said, "Thank you Vivian with your nosey self."

Paul was about to see why Vivian took so long to put through Janice's call when Chester's phone rang. "Hello Pretty Lady. I'm sorry for the wait."

"Hey Paul, that's okay, I know you're a busy man. I'm so glad you called."

"I hope I can say the same after I hear your explanation."

"I felt terrible about what happened yesterday. I was up half the night thinking about it."

"So was I. That's why I decided to call you this morning and hear you out."

"Thank you. I have some errands to run right now. Can I meet you somewhere later?"

"Today, I don't have much time, because I'm wrapping up a few things before I head out of town."

"Oh, when are you leaving?"

"Tomorrow, right after the funeral."

"How are you holding up?"

"It's a bit rough, but I'm hanging in there. Hearing your voice helps."

"Paul, we can talk about this later."

"No, I still want to hear your explanation. I'm leaving here at three o'clock and I have to meet my family at four o'clock. Can you meet me in the parking lot at my office?"

"That's a strange place, why the parking lot?

"I think that's a pretty safe place. I wouldn't want your husband to hit me with one of his crutches."

Janice was quiet. In a low voice she said, "Okay, I'll see you at three o'clock in the parking lot. Bye Paul."

Paul hung up the phone and smiled. "I see she didn't like my last comment." He picked up the picture of him and Chester on the desk. "Well Chester, at three o'clock, I'll hear what the lady has to say."

Paul grabbed his files, closed the door and poked his head into Dante's office. "Hey Son, when you get a minute, come over to my office."

Paul's office was in between Dante and Chester's office. He liked having both of them close to him.

In less than five minutes, Dante was at his father's door. "Hey Dad."

"Dante, close the door. Here are the files I need you to take care of while I'm gone. My phone will be on, so you can reach me at anytime. I'll check my emails, but I will only respond to the ones marked urgent. I've asked Vivian to call everyone and tell them I had a family emergency and for the next two weeks, you'll be handling things in my absence."

"Okay, but who do I contact for our legal issues?"

"For right now, we're going to use one of Chester's partners at his firm, but if anyone in here asks, just tell them to give all legal issues to you."

"I can't believe Uncle Chester worked for you and still kept his practice. Where did he find the time?"

"He always had time for me."

"Dad, are you going to be okay?"

"Yeah Son. Another thing, be careful of what you say and give to Vivian. She's my executive assistant and is good at what she does, but she's nosey as hell and very close to Desiree. During the next two weeks, I want you to work more closely with my admin, Kim.

Dante had a big smile on his face. "No problem, I'll work with Kim. Did Cynthia call you?"

"Yeah, she called last night. She told me she was back and she saw her mother at the airport on her way to Jamaica."

"Seeing Mommy dearest in a lineup with her hair all over her head, I guess after yesterday, she decided to fly the coop for real." Dante laughed.

Paul looked at his son and let out a deep breath.

"Oh, Cynthia said to tell you she's coming to see you today."

"Did she say what time? I'm leaving at three o'clock and then I'm going to see Victoria."

"No, she just said this afternoon."

Paul leaned back in his chair. "So Son, are you ready to be the head man in charge?"

"I got it Dad. Don't worry about a thing. What I need help with, I'll call you."

"I guess you're all set. On your way out, send in Vivian."

Vivian walked in with her pad and sat down in the chair in front of Paul's desk. "Yes Mr. Davis."

"Vivian, can you please get me a turkey sandwich?" Paul handed Vivian a $20 bill. "I would go myself, but I'm trying to wrap up some things before I leave. Also, please hold all of my calls, except for Ms. Perry. We have some unfinished business."

Vivian grunted as she took the $20 bill and left Paul's office. In 15 minutes flat, Vivian was back in Paul's office and handed him his lunch. "Mr. Davis, here is your sandwich. This envelope just came for you. It's marked confidential."

Paul took the envelope from Vivian's hands. "Thank you." Vivian didn't move. She watched Paul open the envelope.

"Are you going out of the country?" Vivian asked.

"No."

"Yeah, the beach is nice this time of the year."

"Yes, it is. Vivian, thank you. Please close the door behind you."

Paul watched Vivian walk to the door. She grabbed the doorknob, looked at a piece of paper and shoved it back into her pocket.

Paul looked at his airline ticket to South Carolina. "Finally, now I can finish this contract so I can get out of here on time."

For the rest of the day, Paul made calls and packed up files to take with him. He looked at the clock and saw that it was 2:55 in the afternoon. "I guess Baby Girl changed her mind."

Paul picked up his box of files and locked his office. "Vivian, for the next two weeks, Dante's your man."

"You just take it easy. I'll make sure everything here continues to run smoothly."

"I appreciate that."

"Mr. Davis, you didn't say where you'd be staying."

"No, I guess I didn't."

Kim tried not to laugh at Vivian's obvious attempt to be nosey. Paul winked his eye at Kim. "While I'm gone, Dante is going to need your help."

Kim said, "Yes, Mr. Davis."

"Vivian, only call me if it's an emergency."

"Yes sir. Oh, here are your messages."

"Give them to Dante."

"This one is from Cynthia."

Without looking at the message, Paul put it in his pocket. "Ladies, I will see you in two weeks."

Paul took the elevator down to the lobby. He walked out to the parking lot and Janice was standing outside her truck dressed in a beige jogging suit and white sneakers.

Paul thought without her heels, Janice was really short, but just right for him. "Fancy meeting you here Ms. Perry."

"Well, Mr. Davis, I couldn't very well ignore a summons to a parking lot."

Paul smiled and put his box of files into his trunk. "Please join me in my satellite office."

He opened the door and Janice got into the passenger side. She watched as Paul took off his Brooks Brother jacket and flung it in his back seat. Paul sat behind the wheel, loosened his tie and rolled up his sleeves on his crisp white shirt.

"Mr. Davis, I'm sorry I'm not appropriately dressed for this oral examination, but I was doing chores for my sister."

Paul smiled and looked at Janice's sneakers. "Yeah, you look like you're ready to run away."

Janice wiggled her foot. "Usually, I do run away, but lately I find myself wanting to run to you."

"That's a good thing, isn't it?"

"I hope so."

While Paul waited for Janice to speak, he fumbled through his CDs.

"Marvin is moving out. About a month ago, I found out he has a four-year old son and two fiancées."

Paul raised his eyebrows, but kept quiet and let Janice continue her explanation.

"The whole time we've been married, he's been living with me and one of the fiancées.

"Busy guy."

"He was in a motorcycle accident the same night I found out about him having a son with one fiancée and when I went to the hospital, I found out about the other fiancée. After that, I was through. I left him in the hospital and never went back. For two weeks, I didn't hear from him and then he showed up expecting me to take care of him."

Paul stared at Janice and thought her story sounded too crazy for her to make up. She doesn't look like she's lying. He didn't feel she's lying, but then again, he didn't catch it when she lied to him the first time."

"When I told you no, I wasn't married, I didn't really lie to you. When I left that hospital, in my heart, I wasn't married."

"Janice, how long have you been married?"

"Eight months, but we've been together off and on for over 10 years."

"Eight months. People go through things, especially their first year of marriage. This is something that just happened. Are you sure about all of this? Sometimes things aren't what they seem to be."

"Oh, I'm positive."

Paul turned his body around to look Janice directly in her eyes. "I just need to know, is there any chance for reconciliation?"

Without hesitation, Janice said, "No, he's moving out within the next 30 days."

For a few moments, Paul was silent. He took Janice's hand in his and said, "I know I'm taking a chance on you, but if I'm going to take a chance on someone, I rather it be you. This may sound crazy, but I fell in love with you the moment I saw you."

"It was on the Gaylord parking lot for me."

"I'll be gone for the next two weeks. I'm going to South Carolina to visit one of my brother's houses he named after me. I don't know why he did that, but I'm going to find out."

"I can tell Chester really loved you by what you've said about him. Once you see it, you'll know exactly why he named it after you."

Paul kissed Janice's hand. "I'm really dreading this funeral tomorrow."

"I can only imagine what you're going through. I know I get upset just thinking about losing Lainey."

"How is your sister?"

"She looked a lot better today."

"I'll keep her in my prayers."

"You remembered my sister. Thank you."

"Well, Pretty Lady, I have to meet my family."

"I guess that means I'm dismissed."

"For now."

"Take care of yourself and if you ever need to talk, call me."

"Thank you, that's sweet of you."

Paul leaned over and kissed Janice passionately. "I miss you already. I'll call you."

Paul got out of his car and went around and opened Janice's door. She put one hand on Paul's face and kissed him softly on the lips. "Be good to yourself."

"You do the same Pretty Lady."

Paul pulled out of the parking. He looked in his rear view mirror for Janice, but she was still in her parking spot. "Why is she still there? Paul slowed up but a SUV honked its horn for him to move. "I'll call her later."

45

Desiree

Cynthia yelled into the phone, "Mother, you were right. Daddy is having an affair. I'm on the company parking lot and I just saw them in the car, wrapped all up in each other's arms kissing like 16-year olds. I walked right in front of her truck and stared her down."

Desiree was quiet. When she told Cynthia the story about Paul cheating, she never considered he was actually seeing anyone. She always thought he worked too much to cheat and when he wasn't working, he was either drunk or sleep.

"Cynthia, what did she look like?"

"She looks like she could be Daddy's age or a little younger. She had brown shoulder length hair with highlights, looked short, nice looking."

Desiree grunted.

"Mother, I can't believe Daddy is having an affair."

Desiree's mind drifted as she thought about the strange woman who now had Paul's attention and who could be a potential threat to her getting back her millions.

"Mother, are you there?"

"Yes darling, neither can I. I have to go, but keep me posted."

"I will. Bye."

Desiree hung up the phone and paced back and forth. "How in the hell did I miss that? The nerve of him cheating on me. Then again, this could be good for me. I just have to figure it all out."

An unavailable number popped across Desiree's phone. "I know that's nobody but Brent. He's been calling all day. I'm not paying his damn bail. $250,000, I don't think so. Try again in 20 years loser."

Desiree's message light was on. She listened to Brent's message—"Diva, I know what you're doing. It would definitely be in your best interest to talk to me. If not, I'll have no choice but to ask our daughter to bail out her old man. A little birdie told me she got back in town last night. I will let her rest for now, but Diva, if you don't answer my next call, I'll drop two bombs tomorrow, one to her and the other to that drunken hubby of yours. I'll call you back in two hours."

Desiree screamed. I came to Jamaica to get away from my problems. Okay, his bail is $250,000. 10% of that is $25,000. Damn, at this rate, I'll be broke before I get back home."

Desiree turned on her computer and searched for a bails bondsman that was near the police station. She called them and made arrangements to wire Brent's bail. As the person who put up bail, Desiree used the name, Shelly Baker. The bondsman assured her that once they received the money, Brent would be out in a few hours.

"That's one down," Desiree said as she dialed Paul's office.

"Davis Graphics," Vivian answered.

"Vivian Darling, how are you?"

"Hello Desiree, you just missed Paul."

"Actually, I called to speak to you."

"Oh, what can I do for you?"

"Lately, has there been any strange women coming around the office or calling Paul?"

"Desiree, women call here for him all the time."

"Vivian, you know what I mean. Women who aren't calling for business."

"Why do you ask? Is everything all right between you two?"

Desiree hesitated before she said, "I don't know if Paul has told you, but currently, we're separated."

"I'm very sorry to hear that Desiree."

"I think he's having an affair."

"Well, today, a woman named Janice something called. The way he was acting, it seemed personal."

"Vivian, the next time she calls, get me more information."

"Okay, I'm on it."

"Did Paul say where he was going?"

"He wouldn't tell me."

"As long as it's not Jamaica, I don't care. Vivian Darling, you've been very helpful. We'll have to do lunch some time."

"Sounds good."

Desiree hung up the phone and thought about the new woman in Paul's life. "Nice looking, huh? That chair is nice looking."

Desiree looked in the mirror at her curves. "I bet she doesn't beat my time. Oh well, I can't do anything about that until Vivian finds out more information. For the moment, that's number two off my list. One more to go and I can get back to enjoying the rest of my vacation."

While Desiree waited for Brent to call back, she sat outside her four-bedroom villa in her lounge chair near the 40x20 aqua-glass tiled pool and watched the spectacular views of the Caribbean Sea. "Until I sign the papers, this villa is *mine*. As a matter of fact, I want to keep this one. I'll end up selling the estate anyway. Giving me a measly $1.7 million with all the stuff we have. Please, my Mama didn't raise no damn fool."

One of the staff came out by the pool and asked, "Mrs. Davis, what would you like for dinner?"

"Let me ask my guest what he would like. Officer Goode, what would you like for dinner?"

"Anything is fine with me."

Desiree smiled at Officer Goode and said, "Just surprise us."

"Yes Ma'am."

Desiree sat down on Officer Goode's lap. "I'm glad you decided to join me even if it's only for a couple of days."

"Now, how could I say no to a beautiful woman like you?"

"You can't. Tell me, how long have you been a police officer?"

"10 years."

"So, I take it you know your stuff."

"I'd like to think so."

"How about the pay?" Desiree asked.

"What about it?"

"Have you ever thought about making more money?"

"Who hasn't?"

Desiree thought Officer Goode could be very beneficial to her in making sure Brent took the rap alone for Chester's death. "I have a proposition for you."

With Desiree in his arms, Officer Goode stood up and walked her to the edge of the pool. Desiree laughed and held on tight. When her phone rang, she knew it was Brent calling her back. "I have to answer it."

"Just let it ring."

"No, put me down. I really have to answer it!"

Officer Goode turned around and quickly put Desiree down and walked away.

Desiree ran into the villa and answered Brent's call. She yelled into the phone, "Hello!"

"Diva Darling, don't tell me I interrupted something."

Desiree was silent.

"I'm glad you saw fit to answer my call. It's a damn shame how you just left me high and dry. I won't forget that."

"Brent, I didn't leave you high and dry. You should be getting out in the next couple of hours."

"Oh, really?"

"Yes, really. Now get the hell off my back."

"Just because you're in Jamaica, don't think you can talk to me any kind of way."

"How did you know I was in Jamaica?"

"Diva, Diva, I always had my eye on you, that's nothing new. The only thing new is that now you know. Since I'm getting out of here, I guess tomorrow your world won't come crashing down after all. Do you need any company in Jamaica?"

"You, hell no. Brent, I've bailed you out. Now consider your palms greased."

Desiree hung up on Brent and walked back out to the pool. Desiree danced her way towards Officer Goode. Where were we?"

Again, Officer Goode picked up Desiree and held her in his arms. "I believe I was holding you in my arms and getting ready to . . ."

Officer Goode threw Desiree into the pool. Desiree screamed, "What the hell is wrong with you? Have you gone crazy?"

Officer Goode smiled and looked at Desiree curse and splash water all over him. "That's for being so damn rude. You have no idea how to accept good treatment from a man."

Desiree climbed out of the pool, stood in front of him and wiped the water out of her eyes. "Why don't you teach me?"

For the third time, Officer Goode picked up Desiree, walked her over to the lounge chair, and gently placed her down. He went over to the bar, brought back two drinks, handed her one, and sat down beside her in the other lounge chair.

Desiree looked at Officer Goode. "What is your first name?"

"Officer, isn't that what you've been calling me?"

Desiree smiled and sipped her drink.

"Roberto, my name is Roberto Goode. Now, sit back, relax and take in this breathtaking view."

Desiree looked at Roberto. "Oh, I am, indeed I am."

46

Paul

"Janice, are you all right back there?"

"Yeah, a woman walked out in front of my truck and just stood there staring at me. It was the weirdest thing."

"Maybe I'm not the only one that can't keep their eyes off of you." Paul laughed.

"I don't know. She looked at me like I owed her money or something."

"Janice, I have another call. I'll call you later."

"Paul Davis."

"Detective Towson here."

"Yes Detective."

"I thought you should know an hour ago, Brent Foster made bail."

Paul let out a huge disappointing sigh and a very loud "Damn! Do you know who posted his bail?"

"Yes, a Shelly Baker."

"What do we do next?"

"We don't do anything. I'll be gathering evidence for the trial."

Paul was quiet. He wanted to tell Detective Towson that he could find all the evidence he wanted because when he found Brent, there won't be a need for a trial."

"Mr. Davis, let us handle it."

"I'll do my best."

"I'm warning you Davis. If you take matters into your own hands, you'll be sharing a cell with Brent Foster."

"I'll let the police handle it."

"Good, before I go, tell me what kind of relationship did your wife have with Mr. Foster?"

"He was screwing her."

"I think I have all that I need right now. Mr. Davis, I'll be in touch."

Knowing Brent was now free to wreak more havoc on anyone he came in contact with, Paul was livid. He weaved in and out of traffic. "Shelly Baker my ass. Desiree, so help me, if I find out you bailed out that murderer with my damn money. I'll . . ." Paul banged on the steering wheel.

When he got to the edge of Victoria's driveway, he looked at the house and wondered how he was going to tell Victoria, Katrina and Kristina they released the man that shot Chester.

Paul could see most of his family members had already arrived. Before he faced them, especially Victoria, he knew he needed more time to calm down. Paul turned his steering wheel and drove past the driveway. He drove another 20 minutes and turned on Route 714. "Hmm, the Colossal Lounge, never heard of it, but it'll do."

Paul pulled into the parking lot and parked his car on the opposite side of a glacier white Bentley identical to his. "Someone has good taste."

Paul went in, took a seat at the far end of the bar and ordered a vodka and cranberry juice. He looked around the dim lit Jazz and old R&B lounge and thought the place had a nice vibe to it. "This is just what I needed."

Paul drank his vodka and cranberry juice and thought about what was immediately ahead of him, telling Victoria Brent made bail, the funeral and life without Chester. It seemed like the more he thought about things, the faster his drink disappeared. Paul ordered another vodka and cranberry juice. As he waited on the bartender, he kept hearing an annoying sound. He looked across the bar and saw a man with curly hair on crutches hobble over to a booth. A few minutes later, a young woman in a very short skirt slid into the same booth.

The bartender handed Paul his drink. Paul sipped his vodka and watched the pair in the booth. To Paul, the two appeared to be arguing about something. For a moment, the curly head man looked in Paul's direction and turned back around to the young woman that pointed her long nails in his face. Paul shook his head in disbelief and under his breath, said, "That's Janice's pretty boy husband."

Paul slightly turned his body to the left so Marvin wouldn't be able to see him, but he could still watch them. After about 30 minutes, Paul saw the woman get up and slide in beside Marvin. They kissed and fondled each other as if they forgot where they were. Paul rubbed his forehead, took a big gulp of his vodka and tried to refrain from getting up and punching the lights out of Marvin. He got angrier by the moment and realized how much Marvin had obviously hurt his precious Janice.

Several minutes later, Paul saw the woman leave. Marvin got up and hobbled across the floor. When Marvin got almost to the door, Paul discreetly put out his foot. Marvin lost his balance, crutches went one way and Marvin fell on his face. Paul gulped the rest of his drink down and laughed to himself when he heard the oohs and ahs from the few people that rushed over to pick Marvin up off the floor. Paul paid his bill and left.

Immediately, Paul called Janice.

"Hey Pretty Lady."

"Hey you. Are you okay?"

"I'm better now. I just wanted to hear your voice again and tell you, I gotcha."

"You got me, got me?"

"I gotcha."

"Paul, I gotcha too."

Unknown to Janice, her words confirmed Paul's feeling of satisfaction about defending her honor. "That's what I needed to hear Pretty Lady. I'll call you later."

Paul hung up the phone and felt satisfied, calm and ready to meet with his family.

Again, Paul pulled up to the edge of Victoria's driveway. This time, he went past the driveway because there was nowhere to park.

As soon as Paul stepped inside, he saw Victoria crying. As many times as he's seen her cry in the last few days, it still tore him apart. Everyone else stood around eating and talking. Paul saw Cynthia across the room. She waved and quickly turned her head. Paul waved back and thought that was strange considering earlier, she wanted to see him and didn't show."

When he saw Dante walk towards him, he smiled.

"Hey Dad."

"Hey Dante, what's up with your sister?"

"I don't know. She's been acting strange ever since she got here."

"You don't think she and Brian are fighting already?"

"No, at least they haven't been since I've been here."

Paul walked over to Cynthia. "What kind of greeting is that for your old man?"

"Hey Daddy."

Cynthia gave Paul a very weak hug.

"Now that you're married, all the loving is for your husband, huh? That's all I get?"

"Seems to me you've already had enough hugs and kisses today." Cynthia walked away.

"What the hell is that supposed to mean?"

Paul walked across the room and started a conversation with some of his other family members. From time to time, he saw Cynthia stare at him. He wasn't sure, but he could have sworn she rolled her eyes at him too. Under his breath, Paul said, "What in the world is wrong with her?"

"Hey Janice."

"Hey Little Brother. You know we never finished our conversation."

Paul hugged his sister and said, "Not today Janice, please."

Janice folded her arms across her chest. "Victoria told me you decided to go to the Paulster."

"Yeah, I wanted to see what all the fuss was about."

"Yeah, you do that." Janice handed Paul an envelope with the key and address to the Paulster and walked away.

"Now, she has an attitude with me."

When Paul saw Victoria walk towards him, he regrouped. "Hello Victoria."

"Oh, Paul, Katrina told me they caught the man that killed my poor Chester."

Paul didn't have the heart to tell Victoria that Brent already made bail and was no longer behind bars. He just hugged her and looked over her head at Cynthia.

After a few seconds, Victoria let go of Paul, "When you come back from visiting the Paulster, stop by and see me, okay?"

"I will. Victoria, how are you doing?"

"I'm good one moment and bad the rest of the time. It hurts so much. Sometimes, I want to stay in bed and not get up at all."

"I know what you mean, but with the grace of God, we will both get through this."

Victoria looked like she was about to cry again. "Will I Paul? Will I ever stop feeling the pain that I feel right now?"

Paul looked at Victoria and wondered the same for himself. "Probably not. I think with time, we just learn how to cope better and as a result, the sharpness of the pain gets duller and eventually, we find a way to move on."

Victoria smiled and squeezed Paul's hand. Another family member came over to Victoria and Paul excused himself and walked over to Cynthia. "Baby Girl, is there a reason you've been rolling your eyes at me?"

Cynthia ignored her father.

"Baby Girl, I asked you a question."

"Yes, I do have a problem Daddy. I have a problem with you cheating on Mother and throwing her out of her home just to be with some whore!"

Paul looked surprised and so did the rest of the family. Everyone stopped what they were doing and all eyes were now on Cynthia and Paul. He took Cynthia by the arm and pulled her out the door. Cynthia jerked her arm away from him.

Once outside, Paul asked, "What are you talking about?"

"How could you Daddy?"

"How could I what?"

"How could you cheat on Mother and throw her out of her home?"

"I've never cheated on your mother."

"You're lying. Today, I saw you kissing that whore in your office parking lot."

"You were there? I didn't see you."

"I saw you very clearly and I told Mother too. She shouldn't have to be in the dark why you threw her out."

"Your mother knows why I threw her out."

Paul briefly closed his eyes. He was beginning to lose his patience with Cynthia. "Baby Girl, I wish you hadn't done that."

"So, it's true, you are having an affair with that whore?"

"Stop saying that and she's not a whore. You really don't understand what's going on."

"I understand all right. You're a liar and a cheater. Poor Mother is crying her eyes out in Jamaica."

Paul laughed. "The only time your mother cries her eyes out is when she's putting on a performance for someone or her money well is about to dry up."

"Daddy, how could you do this? I always looked up to you, but now all I see is a lying, cheating man who I'm embarrassed to say is my father."

"Look girl, there are a lot of things you don't know."

"Tell me then."

"No, this is not the time."

Cynthia yelled even louder than before. "This is exactly the time. I'm not going to let you hurt Mother anymore!"

Family members were still coming in and some were leaving. As they walked by, Paul could tell they stretched their necks and tried to hear what was being said between him and Cynthia. "Baby Girl, I'm asking you not to do this here. Don't do this now."

Cynthia went on and on about her mother and what Paul's affair was doing to Desiree. Paul couldn't take it anymore. He threw his arms up in the air and yelled, "Cynthia, grow the hell up! Your mother doesn't give a damn about anybody but herself."

Tears streamed down Cynthia's face. "You're wrong Daddy. You're the one that doesn't give a damn."

Paul looked at Cynthia with sadness and disappointment in his eyes. "If you feel that way, get the hell out of my face and go be with your saint of a mother."

Cynthia burst into tears. Paul walked away. Brian came out the door. "Please take her home.

"All right Mr. Davis."

"Hey Brian, you can call me Paul."

"Okay Mr., I mean Paul."

Paul went back into the house. As usual, Dante was close by. "Dad, are you okay?"

"You know if I had a dollar every time you've said that in the last few days, I'd have enough for my flight."

Paul hugged Dante. "Thanks for being so concerned Son, but right now, I'm concerned about your sister. Look after her while I'm gone. Her mother has been feeding her a bunch of bullshit."

"Dad, to tell you the truth, I don't know what's going on."

"Take a walk with me."

Paul and Dante walked outside to the far corner of the yard. "This is between you and me."

"Okay."

Paul thought the only person he ever confided in was Chester. This was the first time he wanted to confide in his son about his personal life. "I found out your stepmother was having an affair with the man who shot Chester."

Dante's eyes got big, but he said nothing.

"The night before Cynthia's wedding, I caught them together. As a result, I spent a few hours in jail. Your Uncle Chester bailed me out. At the wedding, we, I mean, I served Desiree divorce papers. Janice seems to think Desiree had something to do with Chester's shooting because he found out she embezzled money through several dummy companies. Desiree must have told Cynthia I was the one having an affair and that I kicked her out to be with another woman. Now Cynthia is all upset thinking I have wronged her crazy ass mother. I can't tell her what's really going on."

"You're having an affair?"

"Here you go. No, I met this woman the night Chester was killed and we've been talking ever since. She's wonderful, but I've only seen her twice. Cynthia came by the office today and saw us kissing in my car."

"Kissing in your car, go Dad." Dante smiled.

"Son, this is serious."

"Okay, seriously Dad, I can believe Desiree had something to do with Uncle Chester's death and all of it. I've never put anything past her."

"You and everyone else in this family. It seems like I'm the only one that didn't pick up on anything until it was too late. I've had a rough day. I was going to spend the night, but I think I'll go home and come back in the morning. Let's go back inside."

When Paul and Dante went back inside, Janice announced to the family that tomorrow morning at ten o'clock, she wanted everyone to meet back there to load up in the family cars. Paul said, "That's my cue to leave." He kissed and hugged everyone and said his goodbyes. One of his family members gave him his card for a business he just started. Paul put the card in his pocket and felt a slip of paper. He reached in and saw Cynthia's message—will be by to see you at 2:45. "I wished I looked at this message when Vivian gave it me. Cynthia was the woman Janice said stared her down. Damn."

Paul drove home in silence. "This time tomorrow, the funeral will be over and I will be miles away at the Paulster. I'm glad I'm already packed because as soon as I get home, I'm going to take a shower and go straight to bed."

It seemed as if Paul had just fallen asleep when it was time for him to get up again. He showered, dressed, grabbed his luggage and headed back to Victoria's house. Everyone was dressed in black with their hearts full of despair and waited for the family cars to arrive. To Paul's surprise, neither Victoria nor the girls were crying. Victoria was looking out the window while the twins were looking into space.

The family cars arrived and Janice called everyone to load up. The 20-minute ride to the Baptist Church seemed like it took forever. For the entire ride, the car was silent except for the gospel music that played on the radio. Every so often, Paul looked over to Victoria. When the car turned on Brightseat Road, all you could see were people and cars everywhere. It looked like rush hour traffic.

When they got inside, a church that held 1,500 people no longer had any seats available—only standing room. Paul felt a sense of pride when he saw how many people loved and respected his brother. He was thankful that the viewing and the funeral was on the same day. He couldn't bear to watch his brother lay in a casket for two straight days. Before the two-hour service was over, they announced for people to take their last viewing of Chester. Victoria went up and kissed her husband one last time on his cheek before they closed the casket. Paul thought she would break down, but she didn't. He did notice that she had this far away look in her eyes as if she wasn't even there. Katrina and Kristina cried and other family members hugged them and tried to comfort them as best they could.

Chester had been in the military and was given a 21-gun salute at the cemetery. After the soldiers rolled up the flag, they said a few words and handed it to Victoria. She took it, said thank you and held it close to her heart. When the Pastor gave the Benediction, all Paul could think about was getting a stiff drink and getting as far away as possible. He was glad that the funeral finally came to an end.

When they all got back to Victoria's house, Paul reached into his pocket, pulled out his flask and took two huge gulps of vodka. Cynthia walked past her father and did not speak. He couldn't and didn't want to deal with her, so he too said nothing.

Janice walked over to Paul and took away his flask. "Drinking won't bring him back. I'm worried about you. I'll tell the family goodbye for you. Go to the Paulster now. You'll see Chester there."

Paul nodded and beckoned his driver. He hugged his sister, got into the limo and headed to the Ronald Reagan National Airport for his four o'clock flight to South Carolina.

47

Janice

For two straight weeks, Janice practically worked around the clock to keep up with her increased workload and the demands of taking care of her chronically ill sister. Everyday during work and everyday after work, Janice ran Lainey's errands, drove her to her many doctor's appointments, cooked her meals, made sure she had everything she needed, and went back to work. Janice was exhausted and badly in need of a break.

She looked at her calendar and sighed. Just to rejuvenate, Janice tried to pinpoint a time when she could take a couple of days off. "It's been three weeks since I last spoke to Paul. Why hasn't he called me? He should be back by now."

Janice dialed Paul's number, but her call went straight to his voicemail. At the last minute, she decided to leave a message—"Hey Paul, I haven't gone anywhere. I'm still here. If you want to talk, I'm just a phone call away. Hope you've been good to yourself. Take care."

Slightly disappointed that Paul didn't answer, Janice hung up the phone. On one hand, she missed talking to him, but on the other hand, she was thankful for the silence between them. Janice had so many of her own issues to deal with that she didn't have anymore energy left to give to anyone, including Paul.

The connection Janice and Paul shared was the one part of her life that she loved to think about. She wanted to keep it that way for as long as she could.

When Janice got back from her two-hour long management meeting, she was drained. She listened to her messages and perked right up when she heard Paul's message.—"Hey Pretty Lady, I got your message. I apologize for not calling, but these last few weeks have been a little rough for me. I'm still in South Carolina. I stayed longer than I originally planned. I'll be back tomorrow and would really love to see you. I've missed talking to you. While I've been gone, I hope you've been good to yourself. Hope to see you tomorrow."

Janice listened to Paul's message twice. She thought about how much she wanted to see him, but with everything going on in her life, it wouldn't be fair to drag him into her mess. She didn't want to let him go, but felt it was the right thing to do. Janice decided that tomorrow, she would tell him just that.

Janice's phone rang. She answered, "Hey stranger, where you been hiding?"

"I should be asking you that. The last time I saw you, you ran out my house like the police was after you. I thought maybe you plucked off Marvin and you were on the run," Dee said.

"I see you didn't try to find me."

"Oh, I knew you were all right. I talked to Chester. I figured you would call me sooner or later."

"What are you doing in about an hour?"

"Nothing, why?"

"Let's go out for a drink."

"Okay, at the usual place?"

"Yeah."

One hour later, Janice and Dee met up at the Radisson Hotel off of Basil Court. Janice arrived first and saved Dee a seat on the left side of the bar, next to the wall, under the 40-inch TV. A few minutes later, Dee arrived. "Hey Girl, what's been going on?"

"Everything and nothing."

"Hello ladies, what can I get for you?" The bartender asked.

Dee ordered a Chardonnay.

"Vodka and cranberry juice," Janice said.

"Aren't we drinking heavy these days?"

"I've got a lot on my mind."

"Tell Dr. Dee what ails ya."

"Where do I start? A month ago, Lainey moved back home."

"How is she?"

"She's very ill. I've been taking care of her."

"What's wrong with her?"

"She has a bad heart."

"Oh, no."

"Dee, I just have this bad feeling that Lainey isn't being totally honest with me."

"Why do you say that?"

"Because, she's getting weaker and weaker. She doesn't want me to tell anybody about her illness and she doesn't want anybody to stay with her either. I've been running back and forth, taking her to her doctor appointments and making sure she has everything she needs."

"Janice, I hope you're wrong about her. Tell me something good. Have you kicked out curly head yet?"

"No, he's still there. He spends most of his time in bed. We rarely talk to each other."

"Hmm, sounds like guilt is eating him up."

"I don't know Dee. He seems worst now than when he came from the hospital."

"Why didn't one of his fiancées take him in?"

"Since he was all broken up, I guess nobody wanted him. I didn't want him either, but he was really ill and AJ said no one else would take him in. AJ agreed to take care of him and that's why he's there."

"That's messed up.

"Who you telling.

Janice asked the bartender for another vodka and cranberry juice. Dee looked at her friend and took a sip of her wine that was still half full.

"Did I tell you Marvin finally confessed to everything?"

"You mean to tell me curly head actually admitted to something."

"Believe me. I was shocked too. I told him to get out."

"It's about time. What did he say?"

"He agreed to leave. He told me to just give him 30 days, which is one week from today."

"Good."

"It would be, but the way he looks, I doubt if he'll be able to move out next week."

"After what he did, I'd kick his ass out anyway."

"I know you would."

"Janice, you're going to blow my buzz before I even get one. This time, tell me something *good*."

"Well, I did meet this guy."

"Excuse me Mrs. Perry."

"I met him at the Gaylord, right after I had sex with Davey."

Dee coughed several times. Janice laughed at her friend and patted her on the back twice.

Dee cleared her throat. "Back up. Did you say you had sex with Davey?"

"It was a MGBP moment. Something stupid that just happened."

"Now tell me, was Davey good? Dee smiled.

"Yes and no. I didn't feel anything for him, but he's still good in that department."

"Mrs. Perry had sex with a man other than her husband. Way to go."

"I'm not proud of it, but it happened."

"Okay, tell me about this guy you met after your one night stand with Davey."

Janice blushed and sipped her drink. "His name is Paul. He's my gift from God. I can't explain it. On the first night I saw him, I felt something really powerful between us. We've been talking on the phone and I've seen him twice. We had dinner and somehow, Marvin followed me and showed up at the restaurant."

"Wait a minute. Janice, you mean to tell me you got busted on your first time out cheating. I can tell you don't know what you're doing."

"Whatever Dee."

"What did ass-hole do?"

"He told Paul we were still married and I was taking care of him like a good little wife should. When we got back home, you know he tried to put everything on me."

"I'm not surprised. Are you and your guy still talking?"

"Somewhat, he's away right now. His brother died and he's taking it pretty badly. He'll be back tomorrow, but as much as I like him and as much as I want to see him, it just isn't right. Technically, I'm still married and I have so much going on that it wouldn't be fair to drag him in my mess."

"Girl, please. You have to be a mighty poor rat to have one hole."

Janice looked puzzled. "What does that mean?"

"It means you should always have a spare man like you have a spare tire. So, if that man is your gift as you say, I wouldn't let him go."

"I don't need a spare man. Marvin is on his way out. I don't want to let Paul go, but it's not right."

"Janice is he married?"

"He's in the process of getting a divorce."

"Hell, technically, you're both married. Go on and see the damn man. Have some fun. Lord knows your no good husband has had fun enough for the both of you."

Janice sipped her drink and thought about what Dee said. She didn't think it made any sense that just because she and Paul were both married, that made it okay to see each other.

"Dee, the fact that we're both married makes it wrong. I understand what you're saying, but I don't want to hurt him and I've been doing a lot of wrong things lately."

"Girl, he's a man. He'll get over it. If I were you, I'd kick Marvin's ass out and see your gift of a man and call it a day."

After Janice left Dee, she was torn between whether she should continue to see Paul or tell him it was over before it began. She thought about the many issues they both had to deal with and in such a short period of time, how much joy he's brought into her life. "I'll sleep on it and decide tomorrow."

Janice pulled into her driveway. Right away, she saw something on her front step. She jumped out of her truck, dropped her purse and fell to her knees. Marvin was stretched out on the sidewalk unconscious. Janice yelled, "Marvin, Marvin," but he never moved. A neighbor rushed over to see if he could help.

Janice called 911.

48

Paul

The moment Paul laid eyes on the Paulster, he felt Chester's presence all around him. The longer he stayed, the stronger he became. Before he knew it, two weeks passed by and he was still there.

The Paulster was nothing like Chester's four-bedroom colonial he shared with his wife and twin daughters. The Paulster was double the size and was fully staffed with two housekeepers, a chauffer, and a chef.

Paul sat on the third floor deck, looked out into the blue ocean and talked to Chester, something he did everyday that he was there. "Big Brother, it's time for me to go. I don't want to leave, but I have so much unfinished business back home. For one, I have to make sure I put Desiree and Popeye behind bars."

Paul lowered his head. "I miss you man. You never cease to amaze me. Now, I know why you named this place after me. It looks like an island version of my house, only it feels like home—a feeling my house hasn't had in years. I promise you, I'll be back. I look at your beautiful family, your law practice, your homes, this place and all of your other accomplishments you made. I see how successful you were in every area of your life. I envy that. I have a successful business, money, great kids and a great home. Beyond that, I don't know, but I'm going to work on that. I love you man. I was always proud of you. I just hope one day, you'll be proud of me too."

In his white shorts, green tee shirt and bare feet, Paul took the stairs down to the backyard. He walked a hundred feet until he was along side the edge of the water. He relished the sand between his toes and the warm breeze against his bald head. Paul felt totally relaxed and wanted to feel that peacefulness all of the time, but with all of the stressors waiting for him back home, he seriously doubted it. "I should stay another week, but I've imposed on Dante long enough."

As soon as Paul reached for his phone, it rang. He answered, "Miss me already?"

"Hey Dad, are you ready to come back?"

"Son, it's been very relaxing down here. Nothing but peace and quiet. You should see the ocean, it's beautiful. I've gotten so much work done. I almost hate to leave."

"You are coming back, right?"

"Yeah, Son, my flight leaves tomorrow at two o'clock."

"You scared me. I'm happy you entrusted me and all, but I'm *sure* looking forward to you coming back and running things again."

Paul laughed. "I appreciate all of your hard work. I've heard nothing but great things about you from our clients. I'm proud of you Son."

"Thanks Dad."

"How has your sister been doing?"

"I talked to her a couple of times. She's still mad as hell with you though."

"Is she now?

"You didn't tell her anything, did you?"

"No, I just told her there were two sides to a story and she shouldn't listen to everything her mother says about you."

Paul smiled. He thought that was good advice Dante gave to his sister. "Sounds like something I would say. How did that go over?"

"Not so good. She told me to get the hell out of her house."

"That's the "me" in her. I'll talk to Cynthia when I get back. The way I feel right now, I can tackle just about anything. I'll see you tomorrow."

"Okay Dad."

Paul looked up at the sunset and thought about how Janice made him feel at a time when he was at his lowest. "Chester, before I left, Janice and I had a very strong connection. I would love to bring her to the Paulster to live and forget all about the outside world, but right now, the timing is bad. Her husband doesn't deserve her. I know I haven't known her for long, but I know she's a good person. She just married the wrong man like I married the wrong woman. I know she's the one and if you were here, I know you would agree."

Paul followed the sound of Gospel music to a white one-story building that played a few hundred feet away. He heard a young man sing Deitrick Haddon's "Well Done." When Paul got closer, he saw a young woman on stage that for some reason looked very familiar to him. He listened to the rest of the song and sang, "Just wanna make it to heaven." *I know Chester is in heaven.*

When the song ended, Paul clapped his hands and looked around at 60 or so people that sat at small square tables on the huge patio. Although the children played in it, Paul liked the large fountain in the middle of the patio. He smiled at the rectangular table that was filled with all types of fruits, cakes and cookies. People brought him cake, cookies and refreshments. *They sure are friendly.*

Paul accepted a plate of fruit and walked closer to the stage. An older woman said, "I love this place. We're so sorry to hear about your brother. We all loved him."

"Thank you," Paul said.

A man said, "I'd like to reserve next month for my daughter's graduation party. Please tell me it's available."

"I don't know."

Under his breath, Paul said, "How would I know? That's strange. Maybe I look like the owner." Paul walked around the building and looked up at the sign that read, "Paulster II." Tears swelled up in his eyes. He opened the double doors and walked in. "It's an event hall."

Paul looked around the huge ballroom at the beautiful hardwood floors, wrap around windows and several chandeliers that hung from the ceilings. A mini stage was at the far-end and out of each window, a breathtaking view of the ocean. A huge picture of Paul and Chester hung on the wall in the hallway. Around the corner were two small offices and two bathrooms.

Paul sat down in the office chair and let out a deep breath. He picked up the schedule book and saw the calendar was pretty much booked for this month, next month and the month after that. "I guess I'll tell the guy it's booked." Paul thought about whether Victoria knew half the stuff Chester owned. He made a mental note to help her sort through all of Chester's businesses and figure out who was going to run his law practice and Paulster II.

On his way out, Paul saw the same man and told him the place was booked. He walked back to the Paulster and sat back down on the deck. Again, he looked out at the ocean. "Janice, that's who that woman on stage reminded me of. She could be her daughter. I can't wait to see Janice tomorrow. I wished Cynthia hadn't told Desiree about her. Knowing Desiree, she'll drag Janice into our divorce. "Damn, I have to end it. I care too much for Janice to ever hurt her or place her in a position where she might get hurt. As much as I don't want to let her go, right now, not seeing her is the only way I can protect her. When all of this mess is straightened out, maybe we can find our way back to each other again. Tomorrow, when I see Janice, I'll tell her I just want to be friends. I guess I better go back in and pack."

It was Paul's last night at the Paulster. As he walked through the elegant living room, the chef's kitchen, and the formal dining room, he wondered how his life would be once he got back home. Without the tranquility the Paulster brought him, would he be able to deal with all of his issues? Paul shook his head and went in Chester's office. It was so different than the office at his company. The office was decorated in dark woods and everything was neat as a pin. Papers on his desk were neatly stacked in piles. Paul sat down behind the desk and smiled as he looked around. It almost looked like his office at Davis Graphics, only it was larger. On Chester's desk, there were pictures of Victoria, his girls, and his sisters, Janice and Marie. Paul saw another picture of him and Chester together. He picked it up and held it tightly in his arms. Tears began to stream violently down Paul's face. After the funeral, It was the first time he actually cried.

Paul held on to the picture and felt something on the back. He turned it over and it was a key with two initials and a number, PD1. Paul took off the key and looked around the room. He saw two file cabinets, but the key didn't fit in either cabinet. He walked around the office and stuck the key into places he thought the key would fit, but nothing opened. He went back to Chester's chair and sat down. Paul thought long and hard. He tried to figure out what the key opened. He thought about his own office. "I have a safe in my wall behind the file cabinet."

Paul went to the file cabinet and moved it an inch from the wall. Behind it was a silver plate with a keyhole. Paul put the key in and it opened. He moved the file cabinet away from the wall so he could look all the way inside. There was one long, slim box. Paul took it out.

He sat back down at the desk and looked inside the box. There were several papers and sealed envelopes. The papers were ten contracts with names of companies that Paul didn't recognize that were dated as far back as 1992. There was another set of the same contracts but were dated more recently. "These must be the dummy companies Desiree created."

He looked inside an 8 ½ x 11 sealed envelope. There were several pictures, including one of Desiree when she was pregnant and standing in front of a correctional institution. There was a second picture of Desiree standing in front of a correctional institution with Cynthia when she was just a baby. A third picture with Desiree and Cynthia when she was about four at the same correctional institution. "Why would Desiree take my child to a correctional institution?"

There was a fourth picture of a man that looked familiar to Paul and a fifth picture of Desiree with the same man hugging Cynthia. Paul finally recognized the man in the picture. "They're all pictures of Popeye with hair and before he got bulk."

Paul dropped the pictures. "This can't be true. Chester, this is all wrong." Paul got up and left the office.

Several minutes later he went back and pulled out another envelope with recent pictures of Desiree with Brent coming out of different hotels.

Paul's name was on the third sealed enveloped.

"*Hey Little Brother,*

> *If you're reading this letter, I must have kicked the bucket. Just the way it should be, the older brother going first. I wanted to make sure you knew everything that I knew. I know all of this must be a shock to you. I'm very sorry that I can't be there with you to help you through it all, but I'm going to do my best. Regarding the contracts, I've known for quite a while that your wife embezzled large funds from Davis Graphics through 10 dummy companies going as far back as 10 years. I just had to make sure I could prove everything. Along with them, are account numbers of where the monies were deposited. Brace yourself Little Brother. It was a grand total of $2.9 million. Don't worry. For the last few years, Desiree hasn't received any money from these companies. I'm sure that's why she hated my guts.*
>
> *I know you've seen the pictures. Ever since the day I met her, I've had my suspicions. You see, I always knew one day, you would be very successful and Desiree seemed more interested in money than anything or anyone. Throughout the years, I hired a private investigator to follow her. I wanted to protect you.*

Little Brother, what I am about to say will hit you like a ton of bricks. Promise me you won't do anything stupid that will land you in jail. Remember, I'm not there to get you out. Desiree was married to Brent Foster before she married you. Around the time you two met, Brent was serving a 10-year sentence for armed robbery. About six months after she moved in with you, Desiree divorced Brent.

I wish there was an easy way to say this, but I don't believe Cynthia was a premature baby. I also believe there is a possibility that Cynthia is not your biological daughter. I believe her father is Brent Foster. This, I cannot prove. I just have my suspicions. I know hearing this hurts and I wish I was there to comfort you, but I thought you should know. You have always been the only father Cynthia knows. She loves you and always will love you.

Several years ago, I confronted Desiree about this and she told me to mind my own damn business or I would be sorry. I also confronted her about the dummy companies. She threatened that if I tell you, it would be from my grave. I guess she was right.

I love you Little Brother and I have always been very proud of you. You have a good heart, a little selfish at times, but other than that, I know you're a good man. I know you've seen the Paulster. Looks just like you, huh? See, you're not the only one that likes the lap of luxury from time to time. Take good care of it and yourself. Stop that drinking. Find yourself someone who truly loves you. You deserve it.

Now you know what I knew. I trust you will do with it what you feel is best. I know you're hurting right now, but just know that as long as you keep me in your heart, I will always be with you.

Love Forever,
Big Brother Hubbard Chester"

49

Janice

Janice could hear the sirens blaring from the ambulance that raced down her street. Three of the four paramedics rushed over and immediately attended to Marvin while one paramedic asked Janice several questions.

"Ma'am, are you his wife?" The paramedic asked.

"Yes, I am."

"How long has he been unconscious?"

"I don't know. I just got home."

"Is he on any medications?"

"Yes."

"What are they?"

"I don't know."

Out the corner of her eye, Janice saw the paramedic shake his head and frown. With a slight attitude, the paramedic asked, "What happened to his leg?"

"He was in a motorcycle accident a couple of months ago."

"Ma'am, we need to move him into the house."

Janice opened the door and the paramedics followed her inside. They placed Marvin on the sofa in the family room and inserted an IV drip into Marvin's arm. Slowly, Marvin came to.

Loudly, the paramedic asked, "Sir, can you hear me?"

Marvin tried to get up, but the paramedic told him to stay down.

"Do you know what happened?" The paramedic asked.

"Mmm Hmm."

"Do you know how long you were out?"

"Mmm Hmm."

"Sir, when was the last time you ate?"

Marvin looked dazed and finally said, "Two days ago."

Janice, along with the paramedics looked surprised. "Two days ago." Janice thought the paramedic looked at her as if she was the worst wife in the world.

"Ma'am, you mean to tell me you haven't fed your husband knowing he can't get it for himself."

"Someone else was taking care of him."

"It is the wife's job to take care of her husband, in *sickness and in health*. Do you remember that?"

"Sir, is my husband going to be all right?"

"He should see a doctor, but right now, he needs a good meal and not a sandwich."

Janice turned her head away from the judgmental paramedic. One of the other paramedics with better bedside manners came over to Janice. "We just gave your husband some fluids to stabilize him, but he does need to eat something right away."

The paramedic left Janice and went over to Marvin. "Sir, do you want to go to the hospital?"

Marvin said "No, I'll be all right."

"Okay, sign this paper and we'll be on our way."

"Ma'am, he should be fine once he gets some food into his stomach, but if he loses consciousness again, call us back."

Janice let out the paramedics and slammed the door behind them. "Marvin, why haven't you been eating?"

Marvin didn't answer.

"Where the hell is AJ?"

"I haven't seen AJ in three weeks."

"Three weeks! Why?"

"I don't know."

"Well, when was the last time you went to the doctors?"

Marvin put his hand over his face. "About a month ago."

"This doesn't make any sense. I can't do this."

"Janice, no one asked you to take care of me. I can take care of my damn self."

Marvin started to get up, but fell back down. Janice went into the kitchen and looked for something she could quickly prepare for Marvin. In 30 minutes, Janice handed Marvin a plateful of spaghetti, salad and corn. Marvin sat up, took the plate, and didn't wait for it to cool before he began eating.

Janice went back into the kitchen and brought Marvin a glass of orange juice. She sat down in the chair and watched in amazement as he devoured the plate of food in 10 minutes flat.

"Can I get you anything else?"

"No, this is fine."

"Marvin, you need to go to the doctor."

"No, I don't. I'm fine."

"No, you're not."

"Janice, drop it, I said I'm fine."

"How can you say that and you were passed out on the front lawn?"

"I'm not going to tell you again, I'm fine." Why don't you get the hell out of my face and go back to your Sweet Daddy!

"Damn, you're ungrateful. Maybe I should have left you where I found you."

Janice grabbed her purse and cursed all the way upstairs. As soon as she reached her bedroom, she pulled out her phone and searched for AJ's number.

Janice was fired up and ready to give AJ a piece of her mind. "I can't believe his number is disconnected." She was in the middle of redialing his number when she heard a loud noise that came from downstairs.

"Marvin, what was that?"

He didn't answer.

"Marvin!"

Janice ran downstairs. For the second time, Marvin passed out. He was on the kitchen floor unconscious. Janice dialed 911. In minutes, the same paramedics came back to the house and this time, they rushed Marvin to the hospital.

Slowly, Janice followed behind the ambulance. When she got to Southern Maryland Hospital, she parked her truck, but kept the engine running. For several minutes, she sat in her truck and gazed out of her window. She tried to will herself the courage to walk across the parking lot into the emergency room doors. Apart of her was genuinely concerned about Marvin's health while the other part of her was annoyed for being back at the place she hated the most.

Janice thought about how lately, nothing happened the way she planned and tonight was no different. She had a strange feeling that once she went inside the hospital that her life was going to change drastically and not for the better.

She turned off her engine and at a snail's pace, crossed the parking lot into the emergency room doors. She looked around the semi-filled waiting room at the 20 or so irritated people that occupied themselves by looking at the TV that hung in the ceiling. Janice wasn't eager to hear about Marvin's condition. She sat down to prepare herself for whatever the doctors told her.

In less than an hour, a doctor asked, "Is there anyone here for Marvin Perry?"

"I am," Janice said.

"Are you his wife?"

"Yes, how is he?"

"Well, right now, he's stabilized, but we're going to admit him. His kidneys are the real problem. We're going to run several more test before we put him on dialysis."

Janice's eyes got big. "May I see him?"

"We'll be moving him to a room in a moment, but yes, you can see him."

Janice followed the doctor to a curtain where Marvin laid helplessly on the bed with wires attached to his chest, monitors beeping and an IV drip. She touched him on his arm. "Is there anything that you need?"

Marvin didn't look at Janice. "Nope."

"Would you like me to call your sister?"

"Did I ask you to call my sister?"

"No, but . . ."

"Janice, just go. I don't need you here."

"Fine, I'm gone."

"Good," Marvin said as he closed his eyes and turned his head to the other side.

Janice gladly and regrettably left the hospital. She drove home as fast as her truck would take her. Along the way, she couldn't help but to think about Marvin and the seriousness of his condition. She also thought about him not moving out as originally planned.

Janice opened her front door and immediately went to the kitchen to pour a huge glass of wine. She sat down on the sofa and took two big gulps and then refilled her glass. Janice wished she was the kind of person that didn't have a conscious so she could just throw Marvin out and be done with it like Dee said. She didn't want to feel anything for Marvin, but the truth was, she was very concerned and still cared about what happened to him. Janice hated the position she was in and was mad at Marvin for putting her in it. Just the thought of staying married to Marvin and the likelihood of being forced to take care of him was more than Janice could bear. She didn't want to do either, but things in Janice's life were changing rapidly for the worst and she didn't know what, if anything, she could do about it.

Janice poured herself another glass of wine, and another, and another until she was numb from all of the pain she was feeling.

The next morning, Janice woke up on the sofa with the same problems accompanied by a gigantic headache. She was in no shape to go to work, but made an honest attempt to try, which only lasted about five minutes. Janice laid back down on the sofa and tried to get one more hour of sleep when the phone rang.

"Hello," Janice answered, but the phone continued to ring. Slowly, she got up from the sofa and found Marvin's phone on the kitchen floor not far from where he passed out. She looked at the caller ID. When she saw the initials L.F., Janice answered, "What do you want Linda?"

For several seconds, the person on the other end of the line didn't say anything. Janice pushed the end button, turned off Marvin's phone and threw it on his bed.

Once upstairs, Janice's sleepiness was replaced with anger. "I knew he was still talking to that damn Linda. She should be the one taking care of him, not me. This entire situation is just crazy."

Janice took a shower, put on her clothes and went to work. She hoped her day would go by quick and leave her no room to think about her problems.

Janice got exactly what she hoped for, a day filled with little time to do nothing but work. Her day zoomed by with meeting after meeting, call after call and one crisis after another. By the time she got a chance to sit at her desk, it was already three o'clock. Janice was thankful she made up her mind to go to work after all. She checked her phone and saw several calls from the hospital. *Something bad happened.*

Janice immediately called the hospital.

"Hello Marvin, what's wrong?"

"Nothing, I just need you to bring me some clothes and my phone."

"You called me five times for that. I thought something was wrong."

Marvin rattled off a few items he wanted Janice to bring him. Janice pretended to write them down. "Okay, I'll see you later."

Janice hung up the phone. "I think not. Let Linda bring you your clothes and your phone."

With her mind less on work and more on her problems, Janice tried to come up with a way to get Marvin out of the house and find someone else to take care of him. She called Gloria, Marvin's older sister by about 15 years.

"Hello Gloria, this is Janice, Marvin's wife. How are you?"

"Oh, I'm hanging in there."

"Gloria, Marvin is in the hospital."

"Oh no, what's wrong with him?"

"Well, he was in a motorcycle accident a couple of months ago and now the doctors think his kidneys are damaged."

"Ah, I hadn't heard."

"He's not able to take care of himself and needs someone to be with him during the day and since I work, I can't be there."

Gloria was silent.

"I was hoping when he gets out that he could stay with you?"

Gloria cleared her throat. "Janice, I'm an old woman and I can barely take care of myself. I can't do it."

"I understand Gloria, but Marvin just needs someone to be in the house with him."

Again, Gloria was silent.

"Please, I just need some help, that's all."

"No, I'm sorry. Like I said before, I can't do it. You're his wife Janice. You are just going to have to find a way to take care of your own husband. I have to go. Bye."

"So much for sisterly love."

Still nowhere near a solution to her problem, Janice packed up her desk and left her office. On her drive home, she thought about going to the hospital again and quickly decided against it. She had to check in on Lainey and check in on her mother.

Janice's phone rang. "Please let it be something that brings a smile to my face."

"Hello Pretty Lady."

Janice smiled. "Hey Paul, how are you?"

"I've been better. How are you?"

"I'm good."

"You don't sound good."

"I've seen better days. When did you get in?"

"I got in about an hour ago. I was on my way to my office and wondered if I could persuade you into having a drink with me?"

She thought this was as good a time as any to tell Paul she won't be seeing him again. "Okay, but first, I have to make a few stops."

"That's cool. Can you meet me at my office and we can go from there? Shall we say 6:30?"

"That's fine. I'll see you then."

Janice hung up the phone and felt both happy and sad. She was happy that she was going to see Paul again and sad that it would most likely be her last time. Janice thought about a hundred reasons to keep seeing him, but none of them seemed fair to Paul.

Janice called her mother. "Hello Ma."

"Hi Janice."

"Do you need anything?"

"If you don't mind, I just need you to pick up my medicine."

"No, I don't mind. After I leave Lainey's house, I'll drop it by. Have you talked to her today?"

"Yes, I did. She didn't sound so good. Let me know how she's doing."

"Okay Ma. I'll see you in a little bit."

That's the last thing Janice wanted to hear. She hoped she could skip Lainey and just check on her by phone.

Janice pulled into Lainey's driveway and rang the doorbell. Lainey slowly answered the door. "Hey Janice."

"Hey Lainey, how are you today?"

"I've been better."

"A lot of that is going around. Can I get you anything?"

"No, I'm fine."

Janice thought Lainey didn't look fine. She looked like she hadn't showered and was in bed all day.

"Did you eat anything today?"

"I had a little something," Lainey said.

Janice opened the refrigerator. "I'll fix you dinner."

"Janice, you don't have to do that."

Janice looked at Lainey and said a firm, "Yes, I do." *I don't want you passing out like Marvin.*

Janice prepared a salad, baked fish and potatoes.

"Thank you. Are you going to have any?"

"No, I am supposed to meet Paul in an hour."

Lainey looked confused, "Oh, your Wow Man."

Janice gave Lainey a half-hearted smile. "Yeah, but I'm going to tell him I can't see him anymore."

"Why?"

"Marvin is in the hospital and at the moment, things are just so complicated. Lainey, I'm really going to miss him."

"Well Janice, if it's meant to be, you telling him you can't see him now will only be temporary."

"How long is temporary?"

"Less than permanent,"

"Thanks for your wisdom Big Sis. Are you sure you're all right?"

"Yeah, I'm fine. Go meet your Wow Man. By the way, how is Marvin?"

"Not good. The doctors said it's his kidneys. He may have to go on dialysis."

"Hmm, I hope he doesn't have to. I hear that's rough,"

"I just don't know how I'm going to take care of him and . . ."

"Take care of me too?"

Janice held her head down. "I'm sorry Lainey, it's not a problem. It's just hard."

"Janice, I do appreciate what you're doing for me, but you don't have to come here everyday."

"I better go. I'll call you later."

"Bye Janice."

Janice left Lainey's house, dropped off Beatrice's medicine and headed out to meet Paul. Since it started to rain, Janice thought she should cancel her date with Paul, but realized she was just making excuses not to do what needed to be done. When she arrived at Paul's office, he wasn't at his car. She was five minutes early and looked in her mirror to give herself a look over before he came out. As she closed her mirror, she saw Paul dressed in jeans and a white shirt and carried two pieces of luggage. For some reason, Janice loved to see a man in a white shirt.

"Hello Mr. Davis."

"Right on time."

Paul put his luggage down and hugged Janice. She almost melted in his arms and thought about what she'd rather do with him than what she was about to do.

Paul held her close and whispered into her ear, "I've missed you." Janice said nothing and let go of him. Paul put his luggage in his trunk and opened the door for Janice. When he got in, Janice nervously took his hand and rubbed it. Paul looked at Janice, picked up her hand and gently kissed it.

When he reached to start his engine, Janice said, "Paul, wait a minute. I'm really going to miss you."

"Are you going somewhere?"

"I'm sorry, but I think it's best that we don't see each other."

Paul didn't say a word, but his eyes said it all. They were full of sadness and disappointment. Janice looked at Paul as he stared straight ahead. She wanted to take it all back. Until she got up enough nerve to continue, she focused on the spots the raindrops on the windshield made on his face.

"Paul, Marvin isn't moving out."

"So, you're getting back together with your husband?"

"No."

Paul continued to look straight ahead. "You said your marriage was over. Were you lying then or are you lying now?"

"It's not like that. We will be in separate rooms. Things are just so complicated."

"I knew I was taking a chance with you. If you're going back to your husband, that is, if you ever left him to begin with, I wish you well. As long as you're under the same roof with him, I wouldn't have continued seeing you anyway. Have a good life Mrs. Perry."

Paul's words cut Janice deeply. "Paul, it's not what you think. I just don't want to drag you in my mess. Please don't give up on me. This is hard for me and so unfair to you. If the situation was different, believe me, I would never let you go."

"Janice, he doesn't deserve you. He's only going to make you miserable and continue to cheat on you, but if this is what you feel you need to do, I understand."

Janice reached over and hugged Paul tightly. He held on to her and kissed her long and hard before he let her go.

Paul walked around and opened Janice's door. "Take care of yourself Pretty Lady."

One tear slid down Janice's cheek as she watched Paul get into his car and drive away.

50

Desiree

For the last three months, Desiree kept a low profile and hid out in her Jamaica, Florida, and New York properties, all of which, Paul neglected to put in her divorce settlement. Desiree was tired of running and tired of playing with her boy toy, Officer Goode. She decided it was time she went back home to find out what's been going on in her absence.

"Cynthia Darling, how are you?"

"Hi Mother, I'm fine."

"How is your father? Is he still seeing Ms. Nice Looking?"

"I don't know. I haven't spoken to him in a couple of months. The last time I saw him was when he came back from South Carolina. He kept staring at me and hugging me tight and saying stuff like you will always be my baby girl. It was weird. I've tried calling him, but he's always gone somewhere and he hasn't been returning my calls."

"That is weird. I'll have to check that out."

"Mother, I almost forgot. This man called looking for you."

"What man?"

"I think his name was Brent Forrester. He said you ordered a designer dress and he was trying to deliver it."

"Cynthia, did he leave a number?"

"No, he said you already had the number."

"Thank you darling. We'll have lunch tomorrow. Bye."

Desiree screamed, "I can't believe that damn Brent. I told him to stay the hell away from Cynthia." She quickly dialed Brent's number.

"Hello," Brent answered.

"Brent, I've warned you to stay away from Cynthia."

"Diva Darling, I thought that would get your attention. Where in the hell have you been?"

"Away, and none of your damn business."

"Now, that's where you're wrong. Everything you do is my business. If I hadn't heard from you today, I was going to New York to drag you back."

How does he always know where I am?

"Like I told you Diva, I've always had my eye on you. I'm glad you're back though. My trial comes up next month and this lawyer is costing me a pretty penny."

"And, the reason you're telling me this?"

"Look, if it wasn't for you, I wouldn't even be in this mess or have you forgotten since you've been away jet setting to all of your ex-husband's properties?"

"He is *still* my husband."

"Whatever Diva. I didn't call you to talk about your marital status or your drunken ex-hubby. I need cash and your testimony."

"My testimony?"

"Yeah, your testimony. I need you to testify that your hubby threatened me and that's why I had a gun. I also need you to say your hubby was drunk and he accidentally shot his own brother when he tried to shoot me."

"Who is going to believe that?"

"The jury will if you back me up and plant my gun in your hubby's office."

Desiree shook her head from side to side. "Brent, I can't do that and I won't do that to Cynthia's father."

"Dammit Diva. I'm Cynthia's father and don't you ever forget it! That's one thing neither you nor your drunken hubby will ever be able to change. Don't play with me Diva or I'll get on that stand and tell the world whose Cynthia's father really is and who really killed Chester. You know what, forget the gun. I'll just get on the stand and tell the truth."

Desiree took the phone from her ear when Brent hung up on her. She dialed him right back. Before she could say anything, Brent said, "Diva, I thought you would see it my way."

"You win Brent. Where is the gun?"

"Meet me at my office in 30 minutes. Do you know where it is?"

"What do you think?"

This time, Desiree hung up on Brent. "Damn, I wish I had stayed gone." Desiree paced up and down her Sheraton Hotel suite. She had 29 minutes to decide between Paul and Brent, who would be the lesser evil and how much she was willing to give up. Desiree didn't want to lose Cynthia and she definitely didn't want to lose her millions. One thing was for sure, Desiree had no plans to go back to jail today, tomorrow or ever.

Desiree dialed Paul's office.

"Davis Graphics," Vivian answered.

"Vivian Darling, how are you?"

"Hello Desiree. It's been a while."

"I know. I'm just getting back in town. I have been on a very long much-needed vacation."

"Sounds good, what can I do for you?"

"Is Paul around?"

"No, he's out of town, but he's due back sometime today."

"I need to leave him some papers. I'll drop by and we can do lunch."

"Okay, I'll see you when you get here."

Desiree headed out the door to meet Brent and literally ran right into Officer Goode. "Roberto, what are you doing here?"

"We are supposed to have lunch. Did you forget?"

"Actually, I did, but I'm glad you're here. Maybe you can help me with a little problem I have."

Roberto pulled Desiree close to him and whispered, "I'm here to serve."

"Not that kind of problem dear, but maybe later. "Actually, this is a police matter."

"Lay it on me sweetie."

A light bulb went off in Desiree's head and she began to smile mischievously. "Second thought, let me lay something else on you first."

Desiree called Brent to let him know she was on her way.

"Diva, where the hell are you? You should have been here 15 minutes ago."

"Calm down, I'm here."

Brent heard a knock on the door. "It's about damn time you got here." He opened the door to Officer Goode and three other police officers standing in his doorway.

"Are you Brent Foster?" Officer Goode asked.

Brent said, "No," and tried to close the door.

Roberto forced it back open. "Foster, you're under arrest."

"For what?"

"Assault with a deadly weapon and attempted murder."

While the officers placed Brent in handcuffs, he squirmed and pleaded, "You have the wrong person. I didn't assault nobody. Whoever said it is lying. Who did I allegedly assault?"

"Mrs. Desiree Davis."

"I'll kill her!"

"See, that's exactly why you're being arrested."

"No, I didn't mean it like that. You're making a huge mistake."

"What have we here? Look guys, it's a gift for Mrs. Davis, a .357 Magnum wrapped up all pretty in a shiny red gift bag. I'll take this.

"That bitch set me up!"

"Take him to the Upper Marlboro jail. I'll be there shortly. Desiree, did you get all that?" In his ear piece, Roberto asked.

"Loud and clear my darling hunk of an officer man. You did a fabulous job."

Desiree was parked on the BB&T parking lot and could see right through Brent's Melwood office. When Roberto walked past her car, he lifted up the gift bag and winked. She blew him a kiss and drove off doing the happy dance in her seat. "That will teach Brent's ass to stop trying to bleed me dry. I have no use for him anymore. I have invested too much time ensuring my lifestyle and I'll be damned if I'm going to give it all up for my mistake of a baby daddy. Besides, Roberto is looking mighty good to me these days. I'm getting hungry. Paul's office is about 15 minutes away. I guess I'll have lunch with old Vivian after all. I need to catch up on what's been going on with Paul and my companies. Now that Chester is gone, maybe I can start getting the money to flow again."

Feeling extraordinarily powerful from her victory with Brent, Desiree walked into Paul's office like she owned the place. Dante was right on her heels and asked, "Desiree, what are you doing in here?"

"Dante darling, how are you?"

"I'm fine. I asked you what you're doing in here."

"I have to speak to your father."

"He isn't here."

"Darling, I can see that. When will he be back?"

"Sometime tonight."

Desiree picked up a contract off of Paul's desk. Dante snatched it out of her hands. "Give your father a message for me. Tell him I will sign the divorce papers over drinks tonight. He can reach me at the Sheraton Hotel."

"Yeah, I'll give him the message."

"Thank you darling. You're looking more and more like your father everyday."

"Bye Desiree."

Desiree walked out of Paul's office and stood in front of Vivian's desk. "Vivian, are you ready to go?"

"I'm ready."

"Well, come on then. I don't have all day."

51

Paul

Kim and Dante looked at each other and laughed. "Those two sure make a dangerous pair," Dante said.

Kim smiled at Dante. "Are you going to give your Dad the message?"

"Give me what message?" Paul asked.

"Hey Dad. Welcome back."

"Hey Son. Hey Kim. What message?"

Both Kim and Dante smiled at Paul. "Dad, your wife was just here on her broom snooping in your office."

Paul frowned.

"Don't worry. I went in right behind her. She wanted me to tell you that she will sign the divorce papers over drinks tonight at the Sheraton."

"I'm not falling for that one."

"Oh yeah, she and Vivian went to lunch together."

"I don't know what it is, but Vivian follows Desiree around like she has a pork chop in her pocket. Those two are a dangerous combination."

Again, Kim and Dante looked at each other and laughed. Paul looked through all of his messages. "Kim, did I get any other messages?"

"No sir."

Paul went into his office and Dante was right on his heels.

"Who are you looking for a message from? Dante asked.

"None of your business."

"It wouldn't be that woman Cynthia saw you kissing, would it?"

"Hell no. I haven't talked to her in three months. I'm just looking for a message from someone I met when I was in Atlanta."

"Hmm, aren't you the ladies man these days?"

"Dante, don't you have some work to do?"

"Yes, but right now, I'm on my way to lunch. As a matter of fact, I think I will take Kim out to lunch since she's been working so hard lately."

"Is that right? Who is going to answer the phone while she's gone?"

"Well, I was thinking we would transfer them to the receptionist."

Knowing what Dante was up to, Paul smiled. "Go ahead, but don't make this a habit. I need her focused on her work, not you."

"That will probably be hard to do, if you know what I mean."

"Get out of here. I'm timing you."

Paul put his head back on his chair and looked out the window into the parking lot. The truth was everyday, he hoped Janice would call. There wasn't a day that went by that he didn't think of her, but he refused to call her. He did decide that if she should call him that he would definitely talk to her. Paul sighed and thought about Brent's trial coming up next month and how Desiree was still fighting the divorce every step of the way. How happy he would be if things were different in his life and Janice's life.

Paul rubbed his head and tried to warn off an impending headache.

"I have something for that darling," Desiree said.

"I bet you do. What do you want Desiree?"

"I came to say hello. Did Dante give you my message?"

"What message?"

"That I'm ready to sign the divorce papers."

"No, I guess he forgot. Where are they?"

"Not so fast. I thought we could have a drink and toast to the demise of our long and happy marriage."

"At least you got one part right. I don't have time. Just give them to me now."

Desiree retouched her lipstick. "If you want the papers, you will meet me at the Sheraton. You know the one, Jennifer Road. Tonight at seven o'clock sharp. Be there or stay married."

Desiree turned around and walked out of Paul's office and left a scent of her cologne behind.

Paul shook his head and checked out Desiree's rear-end as she walked away. "It's been too long, much too long. Down boy. That's nothing but trouble with a capital T."

Paul's phone rang. "Yes Kim."

"Mr. Davis, you have a call from a Detective Towson."

"Put him through please. Detective Towson, it's been a while."

"Yes, it has. I wanted to let you know Brent Foster is back in jail. I just got word that they picked him up today for assault and attempted murder on your wife."

"My wife? Hmm, I wonder what she's up to now."

"I don't know, but the gun they found in Foster's office matched the gun that killed your brother."

Paul jumped to his feet. "That means he'll be in jail for a long time."

"I can't promise you anything, but it's looking good."

"Thanks Detective."

Paul hung up the phone and smiled. "Maybe, I'll have that drink with Desiree after all."

52

Janice

"Hey stranger."

"Hey Dee, what's been going on?" Janice asked.

"I just got back from Miami and thought I'd check on the inmate."

"Ha, ha, very funny. Miami, that sounds so nice. I am beginning to feel like I'm under house arrest."

"Well then, let me take you out to dinner for good behavior and you can tell me all about it."

"I do need to get out of this house and Marvin is asleep right now. Okay, I'll meet you in an hour."

Janice took a quick shower, threw on a pair of jeans, a black knit top and stepped into her four-inch heels. She peeked in on Marvin and he was sound asleep. She wrote him a note and left out the door happy to be going somewhere that didn't involve illness.

As soon as Janice pulled into Olde Towne Inn's parking lot, Beatrice called. "Hey Ma."

"Janice, have you talked to Lainey today?"

Janice thought she had, but she was so busy taking care of Marvin that she forgot to call Lainey. "No, not yet, but I talked to her last night. Why do you ask?"

"Since this morning, I've been calling and calling. She doesn't answer."

Janice could hear the concern in her mother's voice. "Maybe she's just sleeping. I'll try calling and if she doesn't answer, I'll swing by after I leave the restaurant. Right now, I'm having dinner with Dee."

"Okay, let me know what's going on."

"I will and Ma, don't worry."

As soon as Janice hung up from Beatrice, she called Lainey. Just as her mother said, there was no answer. *I'll try her later.*

Janice saw Dee approaching her. "Hey Dee."

"Hey Janice, what's with the long face?"

"Oh, I just got a call from Ma telling me Lainey hasn't been picking up her phone today."

"Do you want to leave?"

For a second, Janice thought she should leave. "No, I'm sure Lainey is okay. She's probably sleeping. Ma just got all worked up over nothing. I'll go by after I leave here."

"Okay, let's go eat."

With mixed emotions, Janice followed Dee inside the restaurant. She wanted to get together with Dee for a catch-up, but ever since her mother called, all Janice could think about was Lainey.

"All right Janice, what's been going on with you?"

"Oh, I've been running back and forth to Lainey's house helping her out and taking her to the doctors. Then, I go back home, take care of Marvin and take him to the doctors, and so on and so on. I'm worn out. Because I couldn't take care of both of them and still work, I had to take Family Medical Leave."

"Janice, not that I care, but how is that curly head husband of yours doing?"

Janice knew Dee really didn't care how Marvin was doing, but appreciated her asking. "I know you don't, but he's on dialysis three times a week now. Most of the time he's weak as a kitten and the little bit of strength he does get back, he uses it to get on my last nerve. I don't know how much more I can take of this. His leg is taking longer to heal and he's still on crutches. Sometimes, when he comes past me hopping on those damn things, I think about sticking out my foot and clipping him. I imagine him with mash potatoes all over his face, crutches hitting him in the head, and him falling on his ass."

"Now that's funny."

"Dee, I know I'm wrong, but damn he gets on my nerve. Lately, I've been so afraid to leave the house because when I walk back in the door, I don't know what I'll find. It just looks like he's giving up on getting well."

Dee looked around at the booth next to them. "I need a drink and so do you."

"Oh, please, I've been drinking like a fish and smoking like a chimney. These days, alcohol and cigarettes have become my two best friends.

"I don't know how you do it or why you do it. I told you a long time ago to kick Marvin's ass out."

"I know and I have. One week before the 30 days was up—he was rushed to the hospital. Now, because he's on dialysis, he can't be left alone and no one else will take care of him. I didn't plan any of this. I may not love him anymore or want to be married to him, but I still care what happens to him. I couldn't just throw him out in the streets like that."

"I could. He better be glad he wasn't married to me. I'd be in jail right now."

Janice smiled at Dee knowing she meant every word. "It's hard Dee. Most of the time, I can't stand to look at him. One time, he passed out and for a moment, I thought about not calling 911."

"Damn girl, I didn't realize things were that bad."

"Unfortunately, they are. I just pray for strength and hope God will guide me in the right direction."

"Hang in there Janice. God will bless you for it. I'll be right back. When the server comes, order me a White Russian."

"I'll try Lainey again." Janice dialed Lainey's number and under her breath said, "Please pick up." After six rings, there was still no answer. As soon as she hung up, her phone rang. *That's Lainey.*

"Hello."

"Janice, I don't feel good."

"What's wrong Marvin?"

"I don't know. Just come home."

"Marvin, I'm having dinner."

"With Sweet Daddy?"

"Marvin, I'll be there shortly."

"Janice, I really don't feel good. Please come home."

"I said I will be there shortly. Bye."

Both irritated and concerned, Janice hung up the phone.

"Is everything all right?" Dee asked.

"I guess so. That was Marvin telling me he wasn't feeling well."

"Do you have to leave?"

"No, he thinks I'm out with a man."

"Hell, I'm no man, but that's not a bad idea. So, when was the last time you spoke to your Wow Man?"

"I haven't spoken to Paul in three months."

"Three months, why?"

"Well, with everything that's going on, I told him I couldn't see him anymore."

"Janice that was a dumb move."

"Dee, things are just so complicated. I told you I didn't want to drag him in my mess, but I do miss him. There is not a day that goes by that I don't think about that man."

"Then, call him."

"I want to, but I don't know what to say."

"Tell him that you're horny and because you two didn't get the chance to do the wild thing that he owes you one for the road."

Janice laughed and almost spit out her drink.

"Girl, you better call that man and relieve some of that stress before you burst."

"There are other ways to relieve stress."

"Yeah, I know, but wine and cigarettes can't do what a man can do for ya."

Dee and Janice ate their cat fish nuggets, talked about everything and laughed about everything. For the next two hours, Janice was full of joy and felt like her old self again.

Out of nowhere, Janice got a bad feeling in the pit of her stomach that told her something just wasn't right. Janice hugged Dee and said, "Thanks for dinner and drinks. That's exactly what I needed."

"You're welcome and don't forget to call that man and go do the wild thing. You'll thank me later."

"Bye Dee."

When Janice got in her truck, she still felt like something just wasn't right. She pushed the redial button and again, Lainey didn't answer. Janice was scared, but she shook it off and told herself that everything was fine. The 15-minute drive to her house felt more like an hour. Janice pulled into the driveway. She slowly got out of her truck and looked around as if someone was following her. She took a deep breath and walked towards the door. Janice's keys were in her hand, but banged on the door and yelled, "It's Janice, open up." No one came to the door.

Janice searched for her key and again, banged on the door. Still, no one answered. When she finally realized her keys were already in her hand, she nervously put the key in the door.

Slowly, Janice turned the key and pushed open the door, but a chain across the door prevented it from opening all the way. Janice peeked in, but couldn't see anyone. She cried hysterically. "Hold on, I'm coming!" The more Janice pushed the door, the more upset she got. She pushed again, but the door wouldn't budge. Not knowing what to do, she called her brother. When Chester answered his phone, Janice cried out, "Chester, I can't get the door open. The chain is on the door. Something is terribly wrong."

"Janice, I'll be right there. I'm 10 minutes away."

Janice couldn't wait for Chester. She had to get into the house now. With tears streaming down her face and strength that could only come from above, she stepped back a few feet from the door, took her shoulder and pushed the door open.

Janice knocked off the chain that previously held it closed. She ran in under the fragments of wood dangling from the sides of the door and stopped dead in her tracks.

53

Desiree

"Paul Darling, I knew you'd show."

"I'm only here for the papers."

"That's what you say now."

Paul was about to respond to Desiree when the bartender asked, "What can I get you sir?"

"A vodka and cranberry juice," and Desiree, that is what I will say later too. I heard your friend was arrested for attempted murder on your life."

"Something like that." Desiree laughed.

"Desiree, what's the deal with you two?"

"What do you mean?"

"You know what the hell I mean."

"He was just someone I met years ago. You were working so much and one night, I went out and one thing led to another."

Paul looked at Desiree, briefly turned his head to the other side and looked back at her. "How many years ago did you meet him?"

"Oh, about five years ago. I'm sorry Paul. He means nothing to me. You were the one that I loved. I mean, you are the only one that I love."

Paul laughed and took a sip of his vodka. "Yeah, I can tell how much you love me by the amount of money you stole from me."

"Darling that was just pocket change for my expensive shopping habit."

"Pocket change, huh? Is that what they're calling $2 million these days?"

Desiree coughed and said, "$2 million, that's absurd! At the most, it was only a few thousand dollars."

"Cut the crap. I have proof that you created 10 dummy companies and over the years, you've stolen $2.9 million from me. I should throw your ass in jail right along with Popeye."

"Darling, you don't want to do that. Perhaps we can work out something. How would you explain it to Cynthia? Do you think she will forgive you for throwing her mother in jail? You know how she acted when she found out you cheated on me."

"You know damn well I've never cheated on you."

"Then who was the bitch you kissed in the parking lot?"

"Olive Oyl."

"With the long hours, the so-called overnight trips and your Largo condo, I knew you were having an affair long before this. What's the slut's name?"

Paul didn't answer.

For several seconds, Desiree watched Paul look in a daze. "Don't tell me you're thinking about that slut."

"Drop it Desiree. You have some damn nerve. Remember, I caught you and Popeye in a hotel room or have you forgotten?"

Desiree rolled her eyes and was about to say something else, but thought she better stop before Paul throw her in jail.

"Paul Darling, that's water under the bridge. Why don't you forgive me so we can go home and make mad passionate love like we used to before you started your company?"

"That will never happen."

"Oh darling, never say never."

Paul ordered another drink. Desiree watched Paul's eyes roam around the luxurious hotel restaurant and lounge area. "Are you expecting someone?"

"No, why do you ask?"

"Because you keep looking around at everything else instead of what's right in front of you."

"Desiree, where are the damn papers?"

"They're in my hotel room."

"Why did you leave them there when you knew I was meeting you at the bar?"

"I simply forgot. When we finish our drinks, you can walk me to my room and I'll get them for you."

"Desiree, you need to stop playing games. I'll be right back."

While Paul stepped outside the hotel, Desiree made a phone call. When she saw Paul returning to the bar, she immediately hung up.

"No need to hang up on my account," Paul said.

"I didn't." Desiree smiled at Paul take a big gulp of his vodka.

"Desiree, go get the papers."

"Oh calm down. I'll get them. First, let me finish my drink."

Desiree looked at Paul sway back and forth on the bar stool and rub his head. "Desiree, my head is spinning. I need to leave."

"I have just what you need in my room."

"What?" Paul slowly asked.

Desiree put her arms around Paul's shoulder. "Come darling. Let me get you something for that head of yours."

Desiree told the bartender to put the drinks on her tab and beckoned to Vivian to come over and help her with Paul.

"What wrong with Mr. Davis?"

"Nothing. While he was outside, I just slipped him a little something that will ensure his cooperativeness. In a couple of hours, he'll be fine. Just help me get him to the room."

By the time they got Paul to Desiree's suite, he was totally out. Desiree and Vivian threw him down on the king-size bed.

"Desiree, are you sure he's not going to wake up?"

"Vivian, doesn't he look like he's out? Did you bring the camera?"

"Yeah."

"How about the papers? Did you bring them?"

"They're right here."

"Good. You know his signature better than I do. Sign them and I'll sign after you."

Desiree created five more dummy companies and contracts for each one.

"Now with that nosey ass Chester gone, I can get the money train started again. Five more dummy companies and contracts for each one of them."

Desiree looked at the new divorce papers her lawyer created that included all the properties she visited and a settlement of $5 million instead of the $1.7 million Paul previously proposed.

Vivian's hands shook as she signed Paul's name to the contracts. Desiree also signed the contracts and gave them back to Vivian. "Now make sure I get a copy and input them into the system tomorrow."

"Okay."

Desiree signed her version of the divorce papers and laid them on the side table. She and Vivian took off Paul's clothes and positioned his head on the pillow.

"Vivian, take off your clothes and lay beside him."

"Desiree, this is too much. I'm going to lose my job. Do I have to?"

"Stop your whining and just do it."

Desiree took several compromising pictures of Vivian and Paul. When Desiree was done, Vivian quickly dressed. "Now tell me again, why are you doing this?"

"Just for insurance darling. You never know when I'll have to use these."

"Desiree, I'm going to lose my job for sure."

"Oh Vivian, will you stop the damn whining? You'll always have a job with me. After I'm done, I'll be able to pay you double what Paul is giving you. Get his phone. I want to call your number so it looked like he called you."

Desiree was about to dial Vivian's number when Paul's phone rang. The caller ID said Pretty Lady. Desiree switched it to go directly to his voicemail. "I'll deal with that later. Vivian, get out of here. I'll call you tomorrow."

After Desiree dialed Vivian's number, she saw Paul begin to twist and turn. Desiree quickly took off all of her clothes and slid in bed next to Paul. He moaned, "Janice, what's wrong?"

Desiree said, "Janice" and smacked Paul across his jaw. "I got your Janice all right."

Paul moaned something incomprehensible and threw his arm across Desiree's waist. She threw his arm off, picked up her phone, and called Dante.

"Dante Darling, this is your stepmother. I hate to bother you, but your father had too much to drink and has passed out in my hotel room. Do you think you can come and get him?"

"I'll be right there," Dante said.

"Good. Bye darling."

Desiree hung up the phone and smiled. "I feel like $5 million."

Paul groggily asked, "What happened?"

"Darling, I'm hurt that you don't remember. We just made mad passionate love just like we use to do when we first got married."

Paul sat up on the edge of the bed and held his head. "You have got to be kidding."

"Do I look like I'm kidding?"

Paul turned around and looked at Desiree's naked body in bed next to him. Desiree got on her knees and hugged Paul from behind. "Darling, you really don't remember? We were downstairs at the bar talking, laughing, drinking, and having a wonderful time. You came with me to my room to get the divorce papers. We sealed the deal with one last hurrah of great lovemaking."

Desiree handed Paul her version of the divorce papers. "See, signed, sealed, and now delivered."

Paul grabbed the envelope. "I got to get out of here." When he heard a knock on the door, he said, "Don't answer it."

Desiree got out of bed and put on her robe. "That must be room service." She opened up the door and Dante stood in the doorway. Paul looked at Dante and closed his eyes. "Son, what are you doing here?"

"Desiree called me."

"Yes, I did. I couldn't let you drive home drunk. What kind of wife would I be?"

"No kind. Son, I'll be right out."

Dante left the room and stood out in the hallway. Paul quickly put on his clothes. He looked at Desiree smiling at him like a kid who just stole candy from the candy jar. "This will never happen again."

"Never say never," Desiree sang.

Paul grabbed his phone and slammed the door behind him.

54

Janice

Janice screamed to the top of her lungs. "Lainey, oh God, no! What did you do, what did you do?"

Lainey was in her family room, stiff as a board, seated on her sofa in a pink bathrobe that slid off her shoulders and exposed her naked body. In her left hand, she held an empty pill bottle. On the coffee table in front of her was a half cup of water.

Although Janice had never seen a dead body up close and personal before, she knew without even touching her sister that she was dead. Janice ran from room to room and cried hysterically as she looked to see if anyone else was there. She went back to the family room and put her hand on Lainey's forehead. Lainey's head was as cold as a block of ice. Again, Janice screamed, "Lainey, oh God, please no.

She ran to the kitchen for Lainey's phone, but it wasn't on the charger. Janice fumbled through her purse until she found her cell phone and dialed 911.

When the emergency dispatcher answered, Janice screamed, "I'm at my sister's house and she's dead. Lainey is dead!"

"Ma'am, please calm down. Now tell me what your emergency is."

"My sister is dead! Please, will someone please help me? Please help me."

The dispatcher didn't respond.

"Did you hear me?"

Janice's phone lost its reception. She ran into Lainey's bedroom and picked up her phone off the bed. Again, Janice dialed 911, but that phone didn't have a dial tone. The 911 operator called Janice back on her cell phone.

"Did someone just call 911?" The emergency dispatcher asked.

"Yes."

Janice stopped crying long enough to talk to the dispatcher. "I walked in and found my sister dead."

"Ma'am, is anyone else in the house?"

"No."

"What is the address?"

"2610 Minay Street."

Janice sobbed on the phone. "Is someone coming? Please send someone."

"Ma'am, stay on the line. I'm sending help now."

"Okay."

Janice stayed on the phone. While she walked from room to room, she cried and screamed. Each time she passed Lainey's body, she cried louder and each time, the dispatcher said, "Someone should be there any minute Ma'am."

A tall man dressed in a black suit with a pad in his hand walked in Lainey's front door. Janice looked at the man and told the emergency dispatcher, "Someone is here now."

"Okay Ma'am."

The man looked at Lainey's dead body on the sofa and then turned his attention to Janice. "Ma'am, my name is Detective Towson. Are you the one that called 911?"

"Yes."

"Can you tell me what happened?"

"I was at the restaurant and my mother called to ask if I'd spoken to Lainey because she couldn't reach her all day. I came over to check on her and I found her like this."

"Was she ill?"

"Yes, she had a heart problem."

"Do you know the name of her doctor?"

Numerous times, Janice took Lainey to her doctor appointments, but at that particular moment, she could not remember the doctor's name.

Detective Towson walked over and picked up the pill bottle. "Do you know if this bottle was full?"

Janice covered her face with her hands. For a split second, she wondered if her sister committed suicide because her illness got to be too much for her to handle. Janice removed her hands from her face. "I don't know."

"I'll call her doctor," Detective Towson said.

The doctor verified that Lainey had an enlarged heart and other health issues unknown to Janice. He also explained that even if Lainey took the entire bottle of 20 pills, that alone would not have killed her and what happened to Lainey was typical of her illness.

Tears violently fell down Janice's cheek as she thought about Lainey not telling her the entire truth about her condition. Regardless of how much Lainey protested, if Janice had known the truth, she wouldn't have left Lainey alone so often.

Chester ran in. He threw both of his hands in the air and yelled, "No, oh no!" He looked at one of his sisters dead on the sofa and his other sister looking like a zombie. He ran over to Janice and hugged her tightly. "How did you get in?"

"I broke down the door."

Chester shook his head, hugged her even tighter and looked over her head at Lainey's naked dead body. He looked at Detective Towson and said, "Cover her up please." Detective Towson got a white sheet and covered Lainey's naked body.

Within minutes, the entire house was filled with police officers going from room to room making sure there was no fowl play involved. Chester was on his phone and Janice sat at the kitchen table in a daze. In an effort to keep Janice calm in between making his phone calls, Detective Towson sat across from Janice and made small talk.

"Ma'am," Detective Towson said.

"You can call me Janice."

"Okay, Janice. I've called the coroner and he should be here any minute. Have you contacted your family?"

"No.

"Go make your call Janice. I'll be here for a while."

"Okay, I'll be right back."

Janice felt light-headed. She knew her mother was going to take Lainey's death very hard. She wanted to ask Detective Towson to break the news to her mother, but after thinking about it, she knew it would be best if it came from her.

Before Janice dialed her mother's number, she smoked a cigarette and braced herself.

"Hello," Beatrice answered.

Janice took a deep breath. "Ma, Lainey is gone."

Beatrice screamed, "Oh my God, no!" Although Beatrice dropped the phone, Janice could still hear her mother scream and cry out, "Oh my God, no, not Lainey!" Janice stayed on the phone until her mother picked it up again.

"My Lainey is gone."

"I know Ma."

"Is Marvin with you?"

Janice totally forgot about Marvin until her mother mentioned him. "No, I was on my way home, but first, I needed to check on Lainey. Chester is here with me. Ma, are you going to be all right?"

Beatrice didn't answer. Again, Janice heard the phone drop to the floor. She stayed on the line and listened to her mother in the background cry and yell, "My baby is gone. My baby is gone."

As she felt her mother's pain through the phone, tears streamed down Janice's cheeks. She knew how she felt losing her sister, but could only imagine how her mother felt losing her first born child.

Janice hung up the phone and called Marvin.

"Janice, where are you?"

"Marvin, Lainey is gone. I found her in her family room dead."

"Oh, sweetheart, I'm so sorry. I wish I could come to you. Are you okay?"

"I'll be all right."

"Listen, I'm fine. I was just feeling sorry for myself earlier. You stay there as long as you need to. I'm here for you."

"Thanks Marvin."

Janice's phone beeped. "I have to go. Hello."

"Janice, are you all right?"

"Paul?"

"Yes, it's me. Are you all right? You sound upset."

"No, I'm not. I, I . . ."

"Baby, what is it?"

"I just found Lainey dead."

"Ah, Man, I'm so sorry. I know I haven't talked to you in a while, but I had a strong feeling that you were in some kind of trouble. That's why I called you earlier. Is there anything I can do?"

"No."

"Okay . . . okay. Day or night, call me if you need anything."

"I will."

Janice hung up from Paul and dialed Lainey's son.

"Travis, this is your Aunt Janice."

"Hey Aunt Janice."

"I need you to come over to your mother's right away."

"I'm on my way now. I was going to surprise her by bringing over her grandson."

Again, tears began to swell in Janice's eyes. "She would have liked that "Travis, just get over here as fast as you can."

"Aunt Janice, what's wrong?"

"Travis, come now."

Not wanting to tell Travis over the phone that his mother just died, Janice hung up the phone and went back inside. A few moments later, Beatrice walked in. She looked at Lainey, sat down beside her, put her hand on hers and again, cried. Detective Towson gave Beatrice a tissue and said, "I'm sorry for your loss Ma'am."

"Thank you."

Detective Towson looked at Janice and also gave her a tissue. "You will need to call a funeral home to remove the body. Do you know one?"

"No."

"I have a number to one if you would like it."

"Yes, I would really appreciate it. Thank you for being so kind to me and my family."

"I'll be here for as long as you need me to be."

"Thank you."

When Travis and his son walked in, Janice was on the phone with the funeral home. Travis' eyes instantly went to the sofa where the white sheet covered his mother's body. For several minutes, he stared at the body and then looked at Janice. She nodded her head and confirmed that it was his mother.

With his son in his arms, Travis turned around and bolted out the door. Chester followed him. About 15 minutes later, Chester and Travis walked back in. Travis went over to the sofa and removed the sheet from Lainey's head. For what seemed like an entire hour to Janice, Travis just stared at his mother. Little Travis started to cry. Travis placed the sheet back over Lainey's head and looked around the room. Janice went up to Travis and put her arms around him and his son.

Travis cried. "I didn't even know Ma was ill."

"I know. She made me promise that I wouldn't tell you."

"Aunt Janice, if I had known, I would have been there for her."

"She knew that, but she didn't want to be a burden to you or anyone for that matter. Lainey loved you so much. Never forget that. Whatever happened between you two, she forgave you. I hope you have forgiven her too."

"I did Aunt Janice. I did. That's why I'm here now to finally let her see Little Travis for the first time, but now she'll never see him and he will never know his grandmother."

Janice held her nephews in her arms and vowed that she would look after Lainey's family for her.

Finally, the funeral director arrived. "Would you all please go to another room while we place the body on the stretcher?"

Beatrice, Chester, Travis and Janice all went into one of the bedrooms. As soon as it was done, the funeral director yelled, "Everyone can come out now."

Seeing Lainey in a bag on a stretcher was too much for the family, especially Beatrice. When they rolled Lainey's body out the door, she cried and cried. Chester hugged his mother and tried to comfort her as best he could. Travis hugged his son tightly in his arms. Janice stood beside Detective Towson and watched her family in so much pain. Although she could crawl into a corner somewhere and never come out, at that moment, she realized she had to be strong for her family.

Detective Towson turned to Janice and gave her his card. "I'm really sorry for your loss. If you ever need anything Janice, please don't hesitate to call."

"Thank you. I really appreciate you staying with me so long."

"You take care. Goodnight everyone and again, I'm sorry for your loss."

Janice let out Detective Towson. Everyone else followed. Janice locked Lainey's door behind them and looked at her mother cry. Janice hugged Beatrice and placed her in the car with her friend who was nice enough to bring her there and nice enough to take her back home.

Janice knew she had to be strong, but seeing her mother continuously cry broke her down bit by bit. "Are you going to be all right Ma?"

"No."

"I'll be over later."

"Okay."

Janice looked over at Travis. "Where are you staying?"

"He's staying with me," Chester said.

Travis looked at Chester and agreed. Chester looked at Janice and asked, "Where are you going?"

"Chester, I need a strong drink."

"I know what you mean."

Chester hugged Janice tightly. "Are you sure you're okay?"

"Yes, I just need to be alone right now."

"I understand Sis. You be careful and call me later."

Janice drove to the nearest liquor store and bought a pint-size bottle of vodka, a 16 ounce bottle of cranberry juice and three plastic cups. Before she pulled out of the parking lot, she poured herself a generous "on-the-go cocktail." Janice threw the cup up to her head, drank it down in one big gulp and frowned when the alcohol burned her throat. She picked up the phone and called Dee.

"Hello," Dee answered.

"Dee, Lainey is gone."

"Janice, I'm so sorry. What happened?"

"After I left the restaurant, I stopped by and found her . . ."

"Oh, my God. How's your mother?"

"Not so good. She's home now."

"Where are you?"

"I'm at the liquor store."

"Janice, I'll come and get you."

"No, I'll be fine. I needed a drink and time lone. I just called to let you know."

"Are you sure you don't want me to come and get you?"

"Yeah, I'm sure."

"Okay, you get off of that lot and don't be driving around drinking."

"I won't."

"Janice, call me anytime."

"I will. Bye Dee."

Janice knew she couldn't stay on the liquor store lot and drink, but she wasn't ready to go home either. Janice poured herself another generous cup of vodka and cranberry juice and pulled off of the lot.

Against Dee's good advice, for hours, Janice drank her vodka and cranberry juice and drove around town. Her final destination was Mercantile Drive, Davis and Graphics' well lit parking lot.

Janice sat on the empty parking lot, listened to Jazz, and drank her vodka and cranberry juice. She thought about Lainey and wondered if she would ever be able to get the image of Lainey's dead body out of her mind. The more she thought about it, the more she cried in between lifting the cup to her mouth. Janice drank half the bottle and began to feel its effect.

A car pulled up and shined bright lights into her eyes. Janice put her head down on her steering wheel. "After everything that happened tonight, all I need is to be arrested for drunk sitting." The car pulled up beside Janice's truck and stopped. Janice kept her head down. Moments later, she heard someone tap on her window and call out her name, "Janice, Janice." She looked up and it was Paul. Immediately, she burst into tears.

"Baby, what are you doing here? Open the door."

Janice opened the door and practically fell into Paul's arms. He caught her just before she hit the ground. "Ah Baby, I'm taking you with me."

Paul grabbed Janice's keys out of the ignition, her purse off of the front seat, and locked her door. He then guided Janice's wobbly body into the passenger side of his car. Janice put her head back on the headrest, cried and looked out the window. "Baby, I gotcha. Everything is going to be all right."

On his way to his condo, Paul shook his head. "If I hadn't pulled up when I did, I don't know what would have happened to you. Here we are Janice."

Paul walked around his Bentley and opened the passenger's door. Janice looked at the strange three-story brick building. "Where are we?"

Paul said, "Home."

He picked up Janice and carried her up two flights of stairs. When they got inside, he gently placed her down on his brown micro-suede sofa. Janice rubbed her temples. Paul took off her shoes and smiled. "I would offer you a drink, but I can tell you had enough."

Paul went into the kitchen and returned with two cups of steaming hot coffee. "Here, drink this."

With one eye shut and one eye opened, Janice took the cup. "Thank you."

"You're welcome," Paul said and again, smiled at Janice. "Now, what were you doing on my parking lot? Were you by any chance looking for me?"

Janice took one sip of her coffee and then stared into her cup. "No, I wasn't looking for you. I was . . . I don't know what I was doing."

"It's okay if you were."

With her eyes filled with tears again, Janice looked up at Paul. "I went to the parking lot to feel you."

Paul put his cup on the table and sat down beside Janice. "Feel me now." He put her coffee cup down and held her in his arms. "Janice, I'm so sorry about your sister. I wish you didn't have to go through this. Believe me—I know how hard it is to see someone you love die right in front of you."

Janice nodded and remembered Paul too had just been through the death of his brother. "I was at dinner with Dee. By the time I got to Lainey's house, it was too late. I had the key, but there was some kind of chain on the door. I broke down the door and I found her dead."

Again, Janice cried. "Maybe if I hadn't gone to dinner first, I could have saved her. I wasn't there for her when she needed me. Paul, she died alone. No one should die alone, especially when you have so many people that love you."

Paul's eyes began to water. He kissed Janice on the top of her head and held on to her tightly. "Janice, you can't blame yourself. There was no way you could have saved her. If it was, you would have. It was God's plan. You did your part. God knew you would find her and He knew you could handle it. That's why you were given the key."

Paul, I'm trying to handle it, but it's hard."

"Janice, everything is going to be all right."

Paul moved over and guided Janice to lay her head on his lap. For two hours, he gently rubbed her head while she silently cried and drifted in and out of sleep.

Paul was beginning to fall asleep too. "Janice, would you like to really lie down?"

Janice sat up. "Yes."

Paul led the way into his bedroom. He turned on the fireplace and then pushed in a CD and played soft Jazz. Janice stood in the middle of the floor and looked at the king-size bed. Janice wasn't ready to have sex with Paul, but she did want to stretch out all the way.

Paul removed his shoes, but kept on his clothes. He laid down on top of the beige comforter and reached his arm out to Janice. "Come on. Let's get some sleep."

Janice climbed into bed and nestled into Paul's arms. In a soft voice, she said, "Being in your arms feels like home."

"That's because it is."

Janice and Paul laid in each other's arms fully dressed and listened to the Jazz music that softly played. Paul looked at Janice's tear-stained face through the dim light from the CD player and fireplace. He took his finger and lifted Janice's chin up and kissed her lightly on the lips. "I've missed you."

Janice's eyes slowly opened. As he climbed on top of her, she gazed into Paul's eyes. With his hands in hers, he took both of her arms and gently placed them over her head and intensely kissed her on her lips, on her neck, and back to her lips again.

For a few minutes, he stared at Janice and stopped. He lowered his head, shook it from side to side, rolled off of Janice, and laid back down beside her.

Janice was taken aback by Paul's sudden change of plans. Apart of her felt like she was in a world where just the two of them existed while the other part of her was numb and felt nothing but heartache and pain.

Janice laid beside Paul, looked up at the ceiling, and tried to resist the urge to tear off Paul's clothes.

This time, Janice was the one to climb on top of Paul. Staring into each other's eyes, Paul grabbed Janice from behind and held her close to him until her back arched. Janice felt Paul rise beneath her through the thick fabric of his jeans. The two kissed, fondled each other's bodies, and moved to the music as if they were actually making love.

Janice stopped and said, "I'm sorry Paul," and laid back down in his arms. Both breathed heavily. Paul kissed Janice on her forehead. "You look so good in my bed, just like you belong here. Sleep Pretty Lady. I gotcha."

Within minutes, Janice felt the effects from the vodka and fell fast asleep in Paul's arms.

55

Marvin

As if someone just let jack out of a box, Marvin sat straight up in bed and shouted, "Finally, I thought this day would never get here. Today is the day I get this damn cast off and I can drive."

Marvin pulled back the ivory drapes to let the sunshine in and take a look at the street that he would soon drive down. He noticed Janice's truck was not in the driveway. "She must have stayed over Beatrice's last night. Let me call my sweetheart. She must be a wreck. Plus, I need to remind her that I have a doctor's appointment at 10 o'clock."

"Hello," Beatrice answered.

"Miss Beatrice, this is Marvin. I'm really sorry to hear about Lainey."

"Thank you Marvin. It was a shock to us all. How are you?"

"I'm doing good."

"Glad to hear it. How is Janice doing this morning?"

"Uh, she's as well as could be expected. She's sleeping right now."

"Tell her to call me when she wakes up."

"I will. You take care Miss Beatrice."

"You do the same Marvin."

Marvin hung up the phone and wondered where Janice could be. He dialed Janice's cell phone, but it went straight to her voicemail. He redialed the number and again, it went to her voicemail. "Damn, I don't wanna call Big Mouth."

He hobbled out to the kitchen and contemplated whether or not he should call Dee. "If she's not over Dee's house, she must be with that damn Sweet Daddy. Forget it. Since she's grieving, I'll let her have this one. I have a great day planned and nothing is gonna spoil it. I'll deal with her later. Right now, I need some wheels. Time to call my second sweetheart."

"Karen Sweetheart."

"Hey sweetie, what are you doing up so early?"

"Today is the day."

"For what?"

"My cast finally comes off."

"That's great. I'm happy for you Marvin."

"Hey, does that offer still stand to loan your future husband some wheels?"

"Future husband? What a joke. What's in it for me?"

"Knowing that you're helping me to get back on my feet should be plenty."

"Yeah, yeah, which one do you want?"

"The 745 will be fine."

"When are you coming to pick it up? I have to go out of town today."

"First, I have to go see the doctor and after I'm done, I'll need a ride from there . . ."

Karen was quiet.

Marvin was on the other end of the line and tried to figure out how to get to Karen's house from the doctor's office.

Finally, Karen spoke. "I'll just give the keys to Jackson."

"Now, you know Chunky Monkey don't like me."

"That's because you keep calling him names. I told you to stop. He's sensitive and if you want the car, promise me you'll be nice to him."

"Yes Miss Karen, I'll play nice with Jackson."

"Good, I'll tell him to pick you up around noon."

"Perfect sweetheart. Have I told you lately how much I love you?"

"Marvin, I already said you can use the car."

"No, I'm not saying it because you're loaning me a car, I'm saying it because I mean it."

"I love you just the way you love me Marvin. I have to go. Have a great day and I mean what I say. Be nice to Jackson and I will check on you later."

"Thanks sweetheart."

Marvin hung up the phone and smiled from ear to ear. "To hell with Janice. I don't need her. I'll just take a cab to the doctor's office."

Marvin hobbled back to his room and almost fell. "I have got to get my strength back. All I need to do is get behind the wheel again and everything will be fine."

Marvin sat down at the kitchen table and thought about his doctor's warning that if he didn't take better care of himself that his kidneys and other organs would soon fail. "Lainey and me are the same age." Marvin held his head in his hand and cried. Lainey's death hit him harder than he thought it would, mostly because it reminded him of his own mortality.

He shook his head at some of the bad decisions he made in his life that led him up to this point. "I don't have the energy to fight for you anymore Janice." Marvin knew it was over between them, but he hated the thought of her being with someone else. He had so many regrets and not enough time to even begin to make them all right.

Marvin wiped his eyes and made up his mind that whatever time he did have left, he was going to spend it doing exactly what he wanted to do and if someone got hurt in the process—so be it. The first thing on his agenda was getting his cast removed. After that, he was going to see MJ and drive, drive, and drive.

With a new found strength and a new perspective on life, Marvin got up again and stayed up. He made his way into the bathroom and back into the kitchen where he cooked two scrambled eggs, four strips of bacon, and two slices of toast. As he sat at the table and ate his breakfast, his mind switched back to Janice's whereabouts.

Marvin picked up his phone and dialed Dee.

"What Marvin?"

"Dee, is my wife there?"

"Good morning Marvin."

"Oh, good morning. Is my wife there?"

"Yes, but she's asleep. She had a rough night and I'm not going to wake her up. You know what she's been through."

"Yeah, for once you're right. Just tell her I'm taking a cab to my doctor's appointment this morning."

"Anything else Marvin?"

"Just tell her I'll call her later."

"Yeah, you do that."

Marvin hung up on Dee and went back to finish his breakfast. After his soul cleansing and hearing from Dee that Janice was with her and not some place where she shouldn't be—he felt better. Marvin had a big day planned. He no longer wanted to waste time thinking about his regrets. He promised himself that from now on, he was only going to focus on what was happening at the present time, and presently, he needed to get dressed, call a cab, get his cast removed, and get behind the wheel of a 745 BMW.

Three hours later, Marvin was dressed in a crisp white shirt, jeans and stood in two snakeskin cowboy boots. He walked with a limp, but was glad he no longer had to sport the metal crutches. His curly hair was slicked back and he felt like a new man. He couldn't wait to get behind the wheel again. In some strange way, driving gave him strength and the freedom from whatever and whomever he wanted to get away from.

At 11:55, Jackson pulled up in front of the hospital and Marvin jumped in the backseat of the Lincoln Town Car. The entire drive to Karen's house, neither Jackson nor Marvin said a word to each other. Marvin didn't care. He just wanted to get to the car and drive.

Jackson pulled into Karen's driveway. "We're here."

"Man, do you have a problem?"

Jackson turned his huge frame around in his seat. "Yeah, I do have a problem. I have a problem with guys like you that give guys like me a bad wrap."

"Man, you don't know me."

"I know you. I know you use women like Miss Karen and that's why when a good man comes across her path, she doesn't trust him because she thinks they always want her for what she has and not for who she is."

"Just give me the damn keys."

Jackson threw the keys in the backseat. Marvin caught the keys and laughed. "Don't hate me because I got something you wish you could get. She don't want you anyway. Karen likes her men slim and debonair like me. Lose about 200 pounds and maybe then, you'll have a shot at riding Miss Karen instead of driving Miss Karen."

Jackson didn't respond. Marvin touched Jackson's shoulder. "Hey, I'm just giving you a tip. Thanks for the ride Chunky Monkey."

Marvin got out of the car, laughed and limped all the way to the 745 BMW that was waiting for him in the garage. As soon as Marvin slid behind the wheel, he instantly felt the power he missed the last several months he was immobile. Nothing was on his mind but to put his foot on the pedal and drive until he can't drive anymore. Marvin popped in a "Dance Party" CD and turned it up to its highest volume. He adjusted the mirror and slowly pulled up beside Jackson. Marvin smiled and danced in his seat, slapped the steering wheel, and made horse sounds to Jackson.

"Ride her. Don't drive her." Marvin laughed and squealed tires out of the driveway.

The first thing he saw when he sped down Linda's street was MJ happily riding his bike in the front yard. Marvin stopped the car and jumped out. Fearing he would cause MJ to fall if he called out his name, Marvin silently stood at the end of the driveway. He smiled and looked at MJ attempt to do a wheelie.

After a few moments, MJ looked up and yelled, "Daddy!" He threw his bike down and ran into Marvin's anxious arms. "Did you come to take me with you Daddy?"

"No Son, Daddy just came to visit. I see you're doing wheelies now."

"Yeah, do you want to see?"

"I just saw you. Have you been a good boy?"

"Mmm Hmm. I miss you Daddy."

"I missed you too."

Linda stood in the doorway and watched Marvin and MJ.

"Well, well, I see you sporting a new set of wheels. Did wifey give you a present for getting off the crutches?"

Marvin didn't answer.

Linda rolled her eyes at Marvin and told MJ it was time to come inside. With MJ in his arms, Marvin walked closer to Linda. "I haven't seen him in a long time. You can't keep him from me."

"I can and I will, but since you look good today, maybe I'll make an exception. You can come in."

"I can't stay today. I just needed to see him. Can I come back on Thursday?"

"Yeah."

Marvin kissed MJ and handed him to Linda. He looked at Linda and kissed her on the cheek. "Thank you."

"You're welcome." Linda smiled.

Marvin rubbed MJ's head. "I'll see you later MJ."

"Okay Daddy. I love you."

"I love you too."

Now that Marvin had seen MJ, he was ready to hit the highway. He was tired, but wanted to go for the long drive that for months, he dreamed about. He drove two hours, non-stop to Delaware. Once he got there, he was pleased that he still had it and patted himself on the back. After the long drive, Marvin was worn out, but refused to give in to his fatigue. "I need something to eat before I take that long drive back home."

While he waited on his food, Marvin called Janice.

"Hello," Janice answered.

"Hey sweetheart, how are you?"

"I'm okay."

"Where are you?"

"I'm at the funeral home with everyone. Can I call you back?"

Disappointedly, Marvin said, "Yeah" and hung up the phone. He wanted to share his good news about his cast removal and his drive to Delaware. Then again, he thought he should leave out the part about whose car he drove. He knew Janice would have a fit. Sick or not, that would surely land him on the other side of the door. Marvin knew he had to keep it to himself and park the car down the street and around the corner.

The four-hour drive almost wiped out Marvin's energy level. He was so tired that he could barely walk the block to his house. When he opened the door, he could feel the sweat on his forehead and felt his heart beat faster and faster. Marvin leaned up against the door and tried to muster up enough strength to walk the few steps to his bedroom when he saw Janice coming down the stairs. Not wanting her to see how drained he was, Marvin put on a big smile. "Hey."

"Hey yourself. Where have you been?"

"Getting off my cast and hanging out." Marvin stuck out his leg.

"Congratulations. How did you get there?"

"AJ took me."

"AJ is back in town?"

"Yeah, he came back yesterday."

"Oh, that's nice."

Marvin noticed how despondent Janice seemed. "Come here Janice." Reluctantly, she walked towards him. Marvin held her securely in his arms. He hadn't touched her in awhile and was thankful she at least allowed him the chance to console her. Marvin thought about how they used to make love and how she used to light up whenever she saw him. He kissed her on the top of her head and said, "I'm so sorry about Lainey."

Marvin missed being close to Janice and lingered a little longer than she would have preferred because she pulled away.

"Thank you. Why are you sweating?"

Disappointed that she pulled away, Marvin hung his head down. "I just overdid it today, that's all: I'm going to bed."

Janice smiled at Marvin as he limped to his room. She yelled, "I'm happy to see your cast was removed and you look like your old self again."

Marvin yelled back, "I'm glad to be my old self again."

56

Paul

"Talk about cruel and unusual punishment. What the hell are you doing here Drunk Davis?" Brent asked.

"Brent, this isn't a social call. I've come for answers and unfortunately, you're the only one that can give them to me."

Brent leaned towards the glass with a gleam in his eye. "What's in it for me?"

"Well, if you tell me the truth, I'll make it worth your while."

"Okay, I'll play along. What do you want to know?"

"When did you first meet Desiree?"

"Uh, Diva and I go way back." Brent laughed.

"How far back?"

"Over 20 years."

"Were you two ever married?"

"Davis, are you having second thoughts about divorcing your wife and my lover?"

Paul balled up his fist in his lap and clinched his jaw shut. Brent sat back in his seat and laughed. "I can save you both time and money. Our Diva is not wife material and never has been. She's the kind of woman that will eat you up, spit you out and screw you all in the same breath."

"You still didn't answer my question."

Brent turned his head and said nothing. For a few moments, Paul stared at Brent through the glass before he yelled, "Brent, answer the damn question!"

"All right, all right, yes, we were married. While I was in prison, she divorced me and married you. Does that sound accurate?"

"When did you go to prison?"

"Davis, cut through the chase. You know when I went into prison. Ask me what you really want to know."

Paul hesitated. He wanted to know the truth yet he feared the next words that would come out of Brent's mouth. Slowly, Paul asked, "Are you Cynthia's biological father?"

Brent didn't answer Paul right away. He licked his lips and smiled. "Oh yeah, Cynthia, a beautiful girl. She reminds me of the daughter I never had. A little young to be married, but seems to be quite happy in her make-believe world. It would be a shame if her fairytale life came crashing down when she least expects it."

Paul stood up and banged on the glass between them. The correctional officer turned around and walked towards Paul. Brent put up his hand and the officer stopped, but kept his eye on them. In a lower voice, Paul said, "Brent, if you ever do anything to hurt Cynthia, I'll . . ."

"You'll what Davis? Pull a gun on me and get beat down or get somebody else killed because you're too drunk and stupid to see what's really going on. Sit your ass down and listen to me."

Reluctantly, Paul sat back down. The veins in his head protruded as if they were about to burst. Brent smiled at Paul. "Davis, you already know the answer. I don't know why you came down here huffing and puffing ready to blow the jail down. Consider yourself lucky that for the last 20 years, you had the pleasure of raising my baby girl. My only regret is that she never knew the truth, but as they say, better late than never. What do you think Davis?"

"Brent, you're playing with fire. Cynthia will always be my baby girl!"

"Davis, she was *never* your baby girl! She is my daughter!"

The officer inched closer to Brent and he lowered his voice.

"You and Desiree stole her from me and pretended to be one big damn happy family. For years, ya lied to that girl, but now it's time."

"What the hell are you talking about Brent? I just found out a couple of weeks ago."

"My daughter deserves to finally know the truth."

"What truth, that her sperm donor is a con artist and a murderer. You don't give a damn about anybody but yourself. You've killed my brother and now you want to destroy my daughter."

"Davis, I didn't kill your brother."

"As far as I'm concerned, you can take Desiree and stick her up your ass, but Cynthia is off limits. So if you have any plans in that twisted mind of yours to tell her anything, I'll make sure you never see the light of day."

Brent didn't even blink at Paul's threat. "I tell you what Davis. Perhaps you and I can come to some kind of agreement that will make us all happy."

Paul knew he was going to regret selling his soul to the devil, but he had to protect his daughter. He left the jail feeling as if a Mack Truck just ran over him.

Paul jumped into his car and sped out of the parking lot and never saw Desiree run into the jail.

57

Desiree

"Brent, you son of a bitch."

"Today must be my lucky day. Diva Darling, I was wondering when you were coming to see me since it's your fault I'm here."

"I got your damn messages. How dare you threaten me and my family like that?"

"How dare I? You have some damn nerve. You set me up and you think I'm going to lie down and play dead. You must have forgotten who you're dealing with."

"Look Brent, the trial begins in two days."

"I know this."

"I need you to promise me that you won't mention anything about you being Cynthia's father."

"What's in it for me?" Brent leaned back in his chair.

Desiree rubbed her forehead. Her only worry was how she was going to protect Cynthia from finding out the ugly truth that Brent is her father and not Paul. She hoped that somewhere deep inside, Brent had enough compassion for their daughter to spare her from the heartache and pain, but his last threat made it clear he was sparing no one.

"What else, money."

"How much money Diva?"

"$50,000."

"Not enough. Since I've been locked up, my businesses have suffered. It will take more than pocket change to keep my mouth shut."

"$100,000."

Brent took his hand and gestured for Desiree to go higher.

Desiree let out a deep breath and said, "Okay, $250,000."

"Higher Diva."

"Look Brent, I don't have anymore damn money."

"Diva, stop lying. People who lie about not having money eventually end up not having any. One day, you'll remember I told you so."

Desiree rolled her eyes. "How much do you want Brent?"

"You can roll your eyes until they're stuck in that crazy head of yours, but if you want me to keep my mouth shut for life, it should be enough money to cover the rest of my life, wouldn't you say?"

Brent smiled at Desiree before he told her $1 million.

"Are you out of your damn mind? Where am I going to get that kind of money?"

"Not my problem Diva. Take down this number. *Before* the trial starts, wire the money into my account. If the money isn't there when I call tomorrow, I'll tell my lovely daughter where she got her perfect genes from."

Desiree took down the number and slammed down the phone. She watched Brent lean back in his chair and laughed uncontrollably.

She knew once she set up Brent that she stepped into merciless territory. At the time, she thought she had the perfect plan that would rid Brent of his power over her and bring her closer to the perfect life—one without him in it and lots of money.

Desiree left the jail and cursed all the way out the door. "There's no way I'm going to let that son of a bitch destroy my Cynthia. One way or the other, I'm going to find a way to bury the truth once and for all."

58

Janice

Janice woke up and already dreaded the day ahead. It was the day she would bury her only sister and Beatrice would bury her first-born daughter. Janice didn't know how she was going to get through the day because she was having a hard enough time just trying to put one foot on the floor. The more she thought about the funeral, the longer she stayed in bed.

Another forty-five minutes went by and Janice was still in bed. She slowly turned her head to look out the window. The sky was bright and perfectly blue without a cloud in sight, but all she could see was gloominess and the horrendous night she found Lainey. A few tears streamed down Janice's cheek. She didn't want to see her sister lying in a casket, but knew she didn't have much of a choice.

Janice forced herself to get out of bed. She went into the bathroom to wash her face, but just stood there, stared in the mirror and yet again, wondered would she ever get the image of finding Lainey out of her mind?

Again, a few tears streamed down Janice's cheek. She washed her face and walked downstairs.

Marvin sat at the kitchen table and eyed Janice as she slowly sat down. "Good morning sweetheart. How are you this morning?"

"I'm fine. What's all of this?"

Marvin cooked Janice three strips of bacon, hash browns, toast and one scrambled egg.

"It's breakfast for you sweetheart."

"Thank you."

Janice moved the food around on her plate, but she didn't put any of it into her mouth.

Marvin touched Janice's shoulder. "Sweetheart, I know you're hurting. I just wanted to do something to comfort you."

For several moments, Janice just looked at Marvin and said nothing. Finally, she said, "Last night, I couldn't sleep. I came downstairs and it was dark so I lit a candle. I sat down at this table and started talking to Lainey about the night I found her. I told her how sorry I was that . . ."

Marvin touched her hand but said nothing.

"For a few minutes, the candle flickered and then it stopped. All of a sudden, the entire room brightened as if someone turned on the lights. I looked around to see if it was you, but it wasn't."

"No, it wasn't me," Marvin said.

"Lainey was here. Last night, I went out to dinner with Dee. By the time I got to her, she was already dead. I should have been there for her. I could have saved her. Lainey, I'm so sorry."

Marvin got up and hugged Janice. "Sweetheart, it wasn't your fault. You can't blame yourself. There was no way you could have known Lainey was going to die."

"Marvin, I felt something was wrong and I stayed at the restaurant anyway. I shouldn't have gone and now Lainey is dead."

Janice didn't shed one tear. Marvin frowned and continued to hold her tightly in his arms for as long as she would allow.

"I don't know if I can do this today."

Marvin slightly pushed Janice away from him so he could look in her eyes. "You can get through this Janice. I will be right by your side. Besides, your mother needs you. I know you have lost your sister, but Miss Beatrice has lost her daughter. I can only imagine what she's going through."

Janice put her hand over her mouth. "Oh, my God Marvin, you're right. Ma does need me."

Janice ran upstairs. When she got half way up the stairs, she turned around. "Thank you."

Four hours later, Janice and her family arrived at Jenkins Funeral Home. There were so many cars that it took the driver 15 minutes just to get from the parking lot to the front entrance. When she saw the many people that obviously loved Lainey and came out to pay their last respects, Janice smiled and felt a warm feeling inside.

Chester took his heart-broken mother by the arm and walked her into the funeral home with Travis and little Travis behind them. Janice walked in with Marvin and dreaded every step of the way. She looked straight ahead and never paid any attention to the many eyes that were on them. Janice fought the onset of a panic attack until she stood directly in front of the white casket and saw how beautiful Lainey looked dressed in the burgundy chiffon dress she and Beatrice picked out for her. There was one spray of flowers on top of the casket, 19 baskets of different bouquets of flowers, and three wreaths that were positioned all around the casket.

Janice felt calm as she smiled down on her sister. She couldn't get over how peaceful Lainey looked. "She looks just like she's sleeping."

The service lasted for two hours and surprisingly, Janice did not shed one tear. Beatrice took it pretty badly and so did Travis. When Janice walked behind the casket, she spotted Paul standing in the back next to Lainey's ex-husband. Their eyes met and Paul winked at her. Janice felt Marvin's arm tighten around her shoulder. She smiled back at Paul. *How sweet of him to come.*

On the way to the cemetery, everyone was quiet. The only sounds in the family car were the gospel music coming from the radio. Janice stared out the window and wondered whether Lainey was now happy. While the sun continued to shine brightly, without warning, sheets of rain fell from the perfectly blue sky.

Janice smiled and looked at her mother. "See Ma, Lainey is happy."

"Yes, she is."

59

Paul

Given that Brent's trial for the murder of Paul's brother was scheduled to begin in just a few hours, Paul had little hope that the day ahead would be nothing like his last two days. From making a deal with one devil to protect his daughter to witnessing another devil wrap his arm around the woman he was in love with, Paul was not looking forward to what havoc the day would bring. For a brief moment, he wondered if his life will ever calm down and get to a place where he is truly happy. Not seeing it happen anytime soon, Paul slowly got out of bed.

Seconds after his feet hit the floor, Paul's phone rang.

"Now what? Hello."

"Hey Dad."

"Hey Son, what's going on?"

"I'm coming with you to court this morning and Cynthia wants to come too."

"No! I mean, you two don't need to come."

"I want to come and so does Cynthia. We both loved Uncle Chester and we want to be there to see the man who killed him go to jail for the rest of his life."

"Dante, listen to me. Keep Cynthia away from the courthouse. I don't care if you have to lock her in the closet, just keep her away."

"I don't understand."

"Son, I know you don't. Please trust me on this. Will you do this for your 'dear ole dad'?"

Dante was silent.

Not liking the silence, Paul yelled, "Dante, I don't have time for this. Just do what I ask!"

"All right!" You know how Cynthia can be when she has her mind set on something."

"I know and that's why I'm counting on you to do this for me. I'll talk to you later."

As Dante dialed Cynthia's number, he vented out loud. "None of this makes any damn sense. Now I'm my sister's keeper. 'Dear ole Dad' needs to get a dog if he wants somebody to jump when he says jump and roll over when he says roll over. I'm a grown ass man."

"Son, is there a problem?"

Dante dropped the phone when he heard his father's voice on the other end. "Dad, I didn't mean . . ."

Paul laughed. "Oh, you meant it. "From the heart, the mouth speaks." That's why I listen more than I speak. I'm just sorry I've been so preoccupied that I haven't listened to you."

"Dad, I am sorry."

"No, I'm sorry I've made you feel that way, but the next time you want to talk behind my back, make sure you hang up the damn phone first."

Dante laughed.

"Son, I realize I've asked a lot of you, especially in the last few months. If I haven't said so, I appreciate everything you do and believe me I do know you are a 'grown ass man.' I don't expect you to jump and roll over for me. If you don't want to do something, just say so. Not just at Davis Graphics, you're very valuable to me period. I love you, I respect you and I trust you. That's why I come to only you with my sensitive matters. Are we okay Son?"

"Yeah Dad, we're okay."

"Are you sure?" Paul jokingly asked.

"I'm sure."

"Good, because if I hear you talking about me like that again, I may have to show you how fast a grown ass man can hit the ground.

Dante chuckled and said, "I'll find Cynthia."

"All right. I need to get dressed and you . . . you know."

"Yes Dad, I know. Don't worry. I'll take care of it."

"I know you will."

An hour later, Paul's phone rang.

"Yeah Dante."

"Dad, I can't find Cynthia."

"What do you mean you can't find Cynthia?"

"I just left her house and she's not there. Brian doesn't know either and she's not answering her phone."

"Keep trying her. She has got to be around here somewhere."

"Okay Dad."

Paul worried about what would happen if Dante was unable to keep Cynthia away from the courthouse. He thought about the outrageous deal he made with Brent and the false testimony he was about to give. Helping his brother's murderer go free made Paul literally sick, but he told himself that was the only way to protect his daughter. Paul still wasn't convinced that the man who was capable of doing just about anything wrong would keep his end of the agreement. He prayed that just in case Brent reneged on his word, Dante would find Cynthia and keep her away.

Five minutes before the trial started, Paul's driver let him out in front of the courthouse steps. After he was cleared through the metal detector, he ran to the information desk and asked for directions to the courtroom. As he opened the huge wooden doors, Paul took a deep breath.

He looked to the right and saw Brent was already there dressed in a black suit and sitting next to his lawyer. Desiree was also there. She sat next to a man with a folder in his hand. Paul thought Desiree got a lawyer just in case the finger of guilt pointed in her direction.

He continued to look around and was surprised to see that Victoria and the twins were not there. Paul was about to sit down right behind Brent when Dante rushed in. Briefly, Paul closed his eyes and cursed under his breath.

"Dante, what are you doing here? Where is Cynthia?"

"Dad, I promise you, I looked all over town for her. I can't find her. I must have left her a dozen messages. She's not answering her phone."

Before Paul could say another word, the bailiff loudly announced, "All rise, court is now in session. The Honorable Judge Traylor is now presiding."

Paul patted Dante on his shoulder. The prosecutor and Brent's lawyer delivered their opening statements—each was very compelling. The prosecutor called several hotel employees who testified they saw Brent on the day of the shooting and once shots were fired, they saw him run out of the hotel.

Officer Goode took the stand and testified that he arrested Brent for attempted murder and the same gun was used in Chester's shooting.

Paul took the stand. As agreed, he testified that he didn't actually see the gun in Brent's hand. When asked, why did he and his brother fall to the floor? Paul lied and said he heard someone yell, "He has a gun," but it was not Brent.

During his testimony, he saw Desiree fold her arms across her chest, roll her eyes at him, and shake her head from side to side. When he finished his testimony, Paul saw Brent smile and lick his lips.

As Paul stepped down from the witness stand, he saw Cynthia, Victoria, Kristina, and Katrina enter the courtroom. Cynthia waved at Paul and sat down in the back row next to Victoria.

Paul rubbed his bald head and quickly walked back to his seat. He whispered into Dante's ear, "Your sister just walked in."

Dante looked over his shoulder at Cynthia and then back to his Dad.

The prosecutor called Desiree to the stand. In true Diva fashion, Desiree switched her way to the witness stand.

"Do you promise to tell the truth, the whole truth and nothing but the truth so help you God?" The Prosecutor asked.

Under his breath, Paul said, "Not in this lifetime."

"I do," Desiree said.

"Please state your name."

"Desiree Davis."

"What was your relationship to the defendant?"

"At one point, we were married. Brent never got over me divorcing him and marrying the love of my life, Paul."

"What do you mean Mrs. Davis?"

"Well, once he found out we were rich, for years, he harassed, threatened, and blackmailed me. It was unbearable."

Paul looked at Brent's reaction to what Desiree said. He heard Brent say, "Tread lightly Diva."

"On several occasions, he even raped me. He said if I told anyone or went to the police that he would kill my husband, so I kept quiet."

Paul saw Brent lean over to his lawyer and overheard him say, "She's lying."

The prosecutor looked at Brent and wrote something down on his pad.

"Mrs. Davis, what happened the night of the shooting?"

"Well, it was also the night of my daughter's beautiful wedding. Everything was going splendid until Brent came uninvited. I begged him to leave, but he wouldn't. He marched right on stage as if he owned the damn place and started singing. When he finally got off the stage, he pulled on my arm and threatened me. He said if I didn't leave with him that he would kill my husband. When he saw Paul walk towards us, he took out his gun and shot my brother-in-law who I dearly loved. I was devastated. Before he ran out, he told me that was a warning and if I didn't comply with his demands that next time, it would be Paul."

"What were his demands?"

"For me to steal millions of dollars from my loving husband and to be with him. I couldn't let that happen. I just couldn't." Desiree wiped her tears away.

"No further questions," the Prosecutor said.

Paul looked at Dante and shook his head. *Know goodness well, she wasn't crying."*

Dante cleared his throat. Paul looked back at Victoria on the back row and saw she was crying. Cynthia had a frown on her face.

Again, Paul saw Brent lean over to his lawyer and this time, he overheard him say, "I'm not going back to jail for no one. Bury the bitch and I mean hold nothing back."

Brent, we had a deal. Paul tried to get Brent's attention, but Brent ignored him. Paul looked back at Cynthia who still had a frown on her face.

Brent's lawyer stood in front of Desiree

"Mrs. Davis, are you able to continue?"

"Yes." Desiree dabbed the corner of her eye.

"Isn't it true that you were still in love with Mr. Foster and you were the one that wouldn't let go?" Brent's attorney asked.

"No, I love my husband. It was him that wouldn't let go."

"Mrs. Davis, you were never raped. Isn't it true that for years, you and Mr. Foster were having an affair?"

"No, no, he raped me."

"We have several witnesses that will testify on several different occasions, they saw you with Mr. Foster. In fact, isn't it true that your own husband caught you in a hotel room with him the night of your daughter's wedding?"

"That's not true. I was only there to pay Mr. Foster the money he forced me to steal."

"Mrs. Davis, how did you go about stealing money from your husband's company?"

Desiree squirmed in her seat. She briefly looked at Paul and dropped her head. "I invented dummy companies."

"I'm sorry Mrs. Davis. I didn't hear you."

"I invented dummy companies!"

"How much money would you say these dummy companies made?"

"Not much, just a few thousand. Most of it went to him." Desiree pointed her finger at Brent. Brent's lawyer gave Desiree a sheet of paper. "Where did the other $2,000,000 go?"

Ahs and oohs came from the courtroom. Desiree's eyes got huge. "That's ridiculous."

"Not according to Mr. Chester Davis. He found out you stole from your husband and he confronted you about it. Isn't that right Mrs. Davis?"

"No!"

"Your brother-in-law told you he was going to tell your husband and on the night of the wedding, it was you who shot Chester Davis."

"No, no, it was Brent, not me. He shot Chester and threatened to kill Paul. I tell you he was blackmailing me."

"Mrs. Davis, it's time to tell the truth. Mr. Foster never raped you, he never threatened you, and he never blackmailed you. Under your own volition, you stole that money from your husband's company to pay Mr. Foster not to tell your husband and your daughter that Brent Foster is in fact your daughter's biological father!"

"Objection!" the Prosecutor shouted.

Desiree cried and looked out into the courtroom at Cynthia then at Paul.

"Answer the question Mrs. Davis. Brent Foster is your daughter's biological father, you stole money from your husband, and you killed Chester Davis!"

"Objection!"

"No!" Desiree yelled.

Brent's lawyer went over to the table and brought back a piece of paper and handed it to Desiree. "This is a DNA test taken 15 years ago. Would you please tell the court what it says? Remember, you're under oath."

Desiree took the paper.

"Read it out loud Mrs. Davis."

Desiree silently read the paper.

"I believe it says Brent Foster is 99% the father of your daughter, Cynthia Davis." Brent's lawyer said.

Paul looked back at Cynthia crying and then looked at Desiree throw the paper at Brent's lawyer and jump off of the witness stand. Desiree ran over to Brent and yelled, "You son of a bitch, I paid you to keep your damn mouth shut. How could you? We had a deal."

The bailiffs grabbed Desiree. Brent straightened up his jacket and laughed in Desiree's face. "You didn't hear me say a word."

Desiree tried to get away from the bailiffs. "Let me go. If it's the last thing I do, I'll get you for this Brent."

Loudly, the judge demanded, "Order in the court, order in the court! We will take a 20-minute recess. Mrs. Davis, you're in contempt. Bailiff, take her out of here now."

Desiree kicked and screamed all the way out the courtroom, "Cynthia, Cynthia, come back. I'm so sorry."

Dante looked over at his father cover his face with his hand. "Dad, I'm sorry I couldn't keep Cynthia away."

Paul uncovered his face. He too had tears in his eyes. "I know Son. Look after Victoria and make sure she's all right. I have to find Cynthia."

"Okay Dad."

Before Paul left the courtroom, he walked up to Brent. "Why? Why did you have to do that?"

"The Diva made me do it."

Paul thought, he offered Brent a million dollars to not reveal that he was Cynthia biological father and he still couldn't keep his mouth shut. Paul wanted to hit Brent and wipe that smirk off of his face, but saw Victoria approaching him. He walked away and immediately hugged Victoria. "How are you holding up?"

"By the grace of God, I'm still standing. I should be asking you the same. That Desiree. If I had a gun, I'd shoot her right off that stand."

Paul chuckled at his sister-in-law as he remembered not so long ago—she did have a shotgun aimed at Desiree. "Get in line."

"Paul, I know what you've heard must be a shock. I'm so sorry. Are you okay?"

"I will be. I've had a few weeks to digest it."

"Who told you?"

"Chester."

"Chester, how can that be?"

"He told me in a letter that he left for me at the Paulster."

"Even from his grave, Chester is still looking after his little brother. Chester and I spent many nights talking about whether to tell you or when we should tell you."

"We? Victoria, you knew?"

"Yes, for quite some time now. You will always be Cynthia's father. That won't ever change."

Paul nodded.

"You go now and find your daughter. Oh, I almost forgot. Here's her phone. She stopped by the house last night and left it behind."

Paul took Cynthia's phone, kissed Victoria on the cheek and left the courtroom in search of his baby girl.

60

Janice

At eight o'clock in the morning, Janice braced herself for yet another day of family members and friends stopping by to give their condolences and unsolicited advice. As she pulled herself up in bed, she remembered Lainey's funeral was yesterday and she had no place she needed to be. Janice was relieved that she was alone and free to be whatever way she wanted to be without anyone passing judgment. She knew her family meant well, but she was fed up with them telling her what a traumatic experience it was to find Lainey's body. Repeatedly, Beatrice, Chester and even Marvin told Janice to let it out and when she didn't, they soon became disappointed and just walked away. That irritated Janice. She wanted to let it out every time she thought about Lainey, which was pretty much every minute of the day, but she couldn't, at least not the way her family wanted her to. Deep down, Janice was afraid that once she started to cry, she wouldn't be able to stop. Finding Lainey's body and blaming herself for not being there to save her was just too much for Janice's mind to deal with. Unknowingly, she pushed it aside to be dealt with when she was strong enough to face it. Meanwhile, she handled it the best way she could, only allowing a few tears to flow at a time.

At noon, Janice got out of bed and skimmed through some of Lainey's personal papers. She couldn't believe Lainey was gone, but whenever she closed her eyes, she was constantly reminded. Again, Janice wondered if she would ever get that image out of her head. She knew she had to do something to take her mind off of Lainey or it would drive her crazy. Janice wanted to talk to someone other than her family whose only objective lately was for her to cry buckets of tears.

She thought about how Paul always made her feel better and feeling better was exactly what she wanted. Janice smiled as she thought about him showing up at the funeral to support her. She missed him and desperately needed to hear his voice. Earlier, she left him a message and thanked him for coming to the funeral. She also called again this morning, but he never returned her calls.

Janice put down the papers and walked over to the window and looked out into the empty street. She thought about the night she laid in Paul's arms after their trial lovemaking. She wanted to look into his beautiful eyes and feel his strong arms wrapped around her while hearing him say, "I gotcha." She needed him, all of him. At that moment, Janice decided she was ready for the real thing. She was ready to give herself to Paul.

She ran over to her purse and searched for her phone. She dialed Paul's number and prayed that he would answer.

"Paul Davis."

"Hey Paul."

Janice heard Paul let out a deep breath before he said "Hello baby, I was just about to call you."

Janice too let out a deep breath. "Do you want me to hang up so you can call me?"

"No, now that I have you, I'm not letting you go."

Janice smiled as Paul already made her feel better. "Well Mr. Davis, how are you?"

"I've seen better days. Baby, I'm sorry I didn't return your calls and I wasn't there for you. I think about you all of the time."

"You do?"

"I do. You wouldn't believe the mess I've been dealing with."

"Things have just been so crazy for me over the last couple of days and today was no exception."

"Yeah, I know what you mean."

"I'm sorry Janice. I didn't ask how you're doing."

"Like you, I've seen better days."

"Well, it sounds like we both need to do something about seeing better days."

Janice thought that was her cue to set her plan into motion. "How about seeing a better night? Will you meet me at the Radisson's bar at seven o'clock?"

"I miss you too and I'll see you at seven o'clock."

Janice was pleased that Paul accepted her invitation. She walked back over to the window. "Paul, you don't know how much I need you right now."

After Janice reserved a hotel room at the Radisson, she flipped through the clothes in her closet and searched for the perfect "give me all of you attire." She pulled out a short, silk, soft peach colored gown with spaghetti straps and a criss-cross back. She went over to the mirror and placed it in front of her and looked from side to side. To see the full effect, Janice changed into it. She put on her four-inch strapless bone colored heels and stood in front of the mirror. Liking what she saw, Janice danced one of her sexy moves and sang to one of Smokey Robinson's songs. When she turned around, Marvin stood in the doorway.

"Marvin, what are you doing up here?"

"Don't you look like a sexy kitten that just swallowed the canary? Planning me an evening of love, sex, and lies?"

"No, I was just cleaning out my closet and tried to decide what I needed to throw away."

"I guess it's just an evening of lies. Carry on."

Marvin turned around and went back downstairs.

"Dammit, I forgot he can come upstairs now. I need to remember to close the door." Janice closed her door, took off the gown, put it back into her closet. "I guess that answered my question. I don't want to wear something I already wore for Marvin. Time for a shopping trip."

For the rest of the day, Janice shopped and prepared for her big night with Paul. At two o'clock, she decided to end her shopping spree, go home, take a nap, and leave back out around 5:30. That would give her plenty of time to check in and get the room ready for a night they would never forget.

61

Paul

Paul waited on the courthouse steps for his driver to pick him up. He was pleasantly surprised that Janice missed him as much as he missed her. He looked in the sky and underneath his breath said, "Janice, you don't know how much I need you right now."

Paul got into the limo and told his driver to take him directly to Cynthia's house. On his way there, he called Brian.

"Hello," Brian answered.

"Brian, this is Mr. Davis. Have you heard from Cynthia?"

"Hey Mr. Davis, didn't you see her in court this morning?"

"Yes, but . . ."

"Sir, what's going on? This morning Dante called looking for her and now you call."

"Cynthia was in court this morning. She heard some things that I know hurt her badly."

"What things? Where is she?"

"I don't know. I was hoping she contacted you."

"Mr. Davis, what happened?"

Not sure how to explain the situation to Brian, Paul took a deep breath. "At the trial, Cynthia found out that I'm not her biological father." That was the first time Paul said it out loud. The words almost stuck in his throat.

"What do you mean you're not her father? Cynthia must be devastated. Mr. Davis, we got to find her."

"I know Brian. No one can reach her, because I have her phone. If she contacts you, call me right away."

"I will sir."

Paul reached down in the compartment next to him and took a big gulp of vodka. When he looked up, the first thing he saw was Desiree crazily running towards the limo.

Paul quickly got out and stood directly in front of her.

"Paul, have you found my baby?"

"No, I haven't found her. Why do you think I'm here? This is all your damn fault. Telling one callous and spiteful lie after another and messing with that damn no good Popeye. Look at all of the lives you destroyed. Mine, Chester, Victoria and now Cynthia. If something happens to her, you have only yourself to blame."

"Paul, I know, I know. I'm sorry. I just want to find my baby." Desiree cried and flung herself into Paul's arms.

Paul stood there with his arms by his side. A small part of him felt sorry for Desiree. Slowly, he put his arms around her shoulders and said, "We'll find her."

When his phone rang, he quickly let go of Desiree.

"Paul Davis."

"Dad, have you found Cynthia?"

"No Dante. I'm at her house now, but she's not here. Call all of her friends. I have her phone and that's why you couldn't reach her earlier."

"Dad, how did you get her phone?"

"Victoria gave it to me. Cynthia left it over her house yesterday. Son, please find her, please."

"I'll find her Dad."

Paul looked at Desiree yell to the sky and scream, "My baby, my poor baby."

He shook his head at Desiree before he said, "Dante is going to call all her friends. He and Brian are out looking for her now. We'll find her."

Paul walked back to his car and Desiree ran after him. "Paul, what do you want me to do?"

With eyes no longer of pity, but full of anger, Paul looked at Desiree and said, "Go to hell."

Paul got in the limo and instructed his driver to pull off. As each hour passed with Cynthia still nowhere to be found, Paul's hopes of finding her himself dwindled. He was tired, hungry, and tipsy from drinking vodka on an empty stomach. "Bernard, drive me home please."

"Yes Mr. Davis."

Paul decided that for now, he would go home, eat, take a nap, and leave the search to Dante and Brian. On his way home, he closed his eyes and allowed his mind to focus on something pleasant. He thought about the night Janice laid in his arms after their almost lovemaking and how much he needed and wanted all of her. A warm feeling came over Paul, a sense of peace and calmness.

Bernard pulled up in front of Paul's house. "Mr. Davis."

Paul didn't answer.

Bernard turned around in his seat. "Mr. Davis! We're here sir."

Paul quickly opened his eyes and looked around in a daze. "Thanks Bernard. I can get the door. Come back and pick me up at six o'clock."

"Yes sir. Mr. Davis?"

"Yeah."

"I'll continue to look for Cynthia."

"Thanks Bernard. You're a good friend."

Paul stumbled to his front door and went straight to his bedroom. He fell on his bed like a ton of bricks and within minutes, he was fast asleep.

By the time Paul woke up, it was already 5:30. "Damn, I didn't mean to sleep that long." Paul jumped to his feet and called Dante.

"Hey Dad."

"Dante, did you find her?"

"No, but we're still looking."

"Who is we?"

"Brian is with me now. We've called all of Cynthia's friends and no one has seen her."

"You mean to tell me she hasn't even called Brian?"

"Afraid not."

"Now, I'm really worried."

"Dad, do you think we should call the police?"

Paul thought about the message Desiree left him about Officer Goode helping, but wouldn't allow himself to hang any hope on anything Desiree said.

"Not yet. Besides, they won't do anything until she has been missing for 24 hours. Dante, I'll be leaving shortly, but call me the minute you hear anything."

"I will Dad."

Paul called downstairs for Sarah to bring him something light to eat. He removed his wrinkled clothes and stepped into the shower. When he came out of the bathroom, Sarah left a tray with soup, salad, and bread. Paul ate in between putting on his beige linen shirt, jeans, and cashmere brown cowboy boots. *Now, I feel better.*

Paul knew he was running late, but as always, wanted to look his best. For the last time, he stepped over to the mirror to check himself out. A huge smile stretched across his face as he struck a pose. "Not bad for an old man."

Paul was really looking forward to seeing Janice, so much so, he was actually giddy. Even though he was still worried about Cynthia, he just couldn't stop smiling.

Paul grabbed his wallet and headed downstairs. As promised, Bernard was outside waiting by the limo.

"Mr. Davis, you're sure in a good mood. Did you find Cynthia?"

"No, I still haven't heard from her."

Bernard closed the door behind Paul and then got into the driver's seat. "I drove around on the other side of town and I didn't see her either."

"Thanks for doing that Bernard."

"Where to Mr. Davis?"

"The Radisson."

"The one on Basil Court?"

"Yeah, that's the one."

Paul smiled and was unaware that he hummed Al Green's "Love and Happiness."

"It must be someone really special that has put that little boy smile on your face. Bernard chuckled.

"Am I that bad?"

"Yes sir."

"Bernard, this woman is beautiful inside and out. She's intelligent, funny, and sweet and she loves me. I can feel it in here." Paul pointed to his heart. "She makes me feel like I'm 16 years old again. The moment I saw her, I instantly fell in love. I can't believe it myself let alone say it out loud."

"If you don't mind me saying so sir, you sound like you're 16."

Paul shook his head and tried to get a grip on himself. "Bernard, I tell you, I think about this woman all the time and when we're together, I don't want to leave her. I miss her the minute after she's gone."

Bernard let out a slight grunt. "She sounds too good to be true. Mr. Davis, don't take this the wrong way, but you're a rich man. How do you know this woman isn't in it for your money?"

"Bernard, I'll admit the woman could probably sell ice to an Eskimo, but I ain't no Eskimo. Janice has a good heart. She's not like that."

Bernard nodded. "This Janice sounds like a keeper."

"I plan to once . . . well, it's a little complicated right now. With my divorce not finalized yet, I don't want to give that damn Desiree any ammunition to use against me. She's already got far too much of my money as it is. Bernard, let's just keep this conversation between us."

"I hear you sir."

Bernard slowed down to almost a crawl.

"What's going on up there?"

"Sir, it looks like a bad accident up ahead with lots of police, ambulances, and a couple of fire trucks blocking the roadway."

Paul rolled down his window and tried to see what was going on. "What the hell! Bernard, pull over."

Paul jumped out of the limo and walked over to a man that stood on the corner of Brightseat Road and held a bloody cloth up to his face. The man looked at Paul and asked, "You've come to finish the job?"

"Brent, when did you get out?"

"What, no hello, how the hell are you, nice seeing you again."

Paul was silent.

"Thanks to your accommodating testimony and Diva's calamity on the witness stand, it presented more than enough reasonable doubt. After you left, my lawyer motioned to have *all* my charges dropped. Lucky for me, the judge agreed. Once he said Mr. Foster, you're a free man—I didn't see any point wearing out my welcome."

Angry with himself for placing an ounce of trust in someone so untrustworthy, Paul quickly turned away. "Had I known you were going to double-cross me, I wouldn't have changed my testimony."

"Should of, could of, would of. Life's a gamble Davis. You should know that by now."

Paul wanted to knock that sheepish grin off of Brent's face, but knew Brent would have no problem calling one of the twenty police officers that were a few feet away to press charges against him.

"Brent, you are rotten to the core. Do you give a damn about anybody but yourself? My little girl is devastated. She's missing all because of your greed and pure evilness."

Brent's expression changed to one of seriousness and concern. "Cynthia is missing?"

"Yes, because of you, she's missing.

"Davis, listen. I didn't want to, but Desiree was up on that stand ready to nail my coffin shut. If I didn't want to spend the rest of my life in jail for a crime I didn't commit, I had to do something. Honestly, I didn't want to hurt my little girl. I figured she wouldn't care because to her, you will always be her father."

"Well, you figured wrong."

Brent looked down the street where the ambulances were. "I tried to tell crazy cakes that, but she tried to run me over anyway and now her crazy ass is wrapped around that pole over there. It serves her right."

Paul's mouth fell wide open. Like a bullet, he took off up the street towards the fire trucks, ambulances, and police cars.

The police shouted, "Sir, you can't go in there."

"My wife is in that car!"

"We're trying to get her out. Please stay back."

62

Janice

Smiling every mile she drove, Janice arrived at the Radisson at 6:20, which gave her plenty of time to prepare the room for her Wow Night with Paul. Once inside, Janice decorated the hotel suite. She placed one dozen of roses in a vase on the coffee table and strategically placed the other dozen throughout the entire suite. She carefully placed rose pedals on the king-size bed and put a bottle of Moscato in an ice chest on the table along side two of her finest crystal wine glasses.

For the special occasion, Janice also bought a red negligee and a pair of the perfect color red four-inch heels that would undoubtedly accentuate her ensemble. She then placed them in the closet and out of sight until she was ready for that part of the evening when she would put them on and dance to one of Paul's favorite songs.

Janice looked around the room at her handiwork and made sure she didn't miss anything. Pleased with her work, she closed the door and headed downstairs to the bar. "All right, it's seven o'clock and time to get this show on the road."

The moment Janice got off of the elevator, she expected to see Paul. Slightly disappointed that he hadn't arrived yet, Janice sat on the left side of the bar underneath the TV. While she waited, she ordered a glass of Chardonnay to calm her nerves.

Janice drank her wine and listened to R&B music. Each time a person walked in, she looked and hoped the next person would be Paul. Twenty minutes passed and still no Paul. Janice dialed his number, but it went straight to his voice mail. Not sure what to do next, she hung up without leaving a message. As each minute passed without hearing from Paul, Janice worried that something may have happened to him. She finished her glass of wine and ordered another.

At eight o'clock, Janice concluded that Paul was a no show. Again, she dialed his number. This time, it rang several times. Janice was about to hang up when she heard Paul answered, "Paul Davis."

"Paul, are you all right?"

"Yes Miss Perry."

"Are you on your way?"

"No, I'm afraid I won't be able to make our meeting. I will call you later to reschedule."

"No problem. I've already left the hotel. I just called to make sure you were okay."

For a couple of moments, there was dead silence on the line. While she waited for Paul to respond with some kind of explanation and an apology for standing her up, Janice looked at the bartender pour her third glass of wine.

In a hurried whisper, Paul said, "I'll call you later."

Without saying goodbye, Janice pushed her end button.

She sat at the bar disappointed, confused, and felt as if she was all dressed up with no place to go. As she put the wine glass to her lips, she muttered into it, "He stood me up. I can't believe this and to think I was ready to give all of me to him."

Janice took a generous sip of her wine and tried to make sense of what just happened. The more she thought about Paul standing her up, the more her previous concern for him shifted to anger. She would have never pegged him to be the kind of person that would be so cavalier as to not call if he couldn't make it or not apologize for keeping her waiting for an hour. Perhaps, she misjudged him and misread what was between them.

Janice finished her wine and headed up to the suite. She opened the door, stood in the middle of the floor and glanced at all of her decorations. She kicked off her shoes and slowly walked into the living room area and put in one of their favorite CDs, *When Time Flies* by Smokey Robinson. Janice bought one for Paul and one for herself. It became their favorite CD to listen to, especially when they were apart.

Janice lit two vanilla scented candles and a cigarette. She then opened the bottle of wine that was nicely chilled and filled up her crystal glass. With her wine glass in one hand, a cigarette in the other, she flopped down on the sofa and just stared at the blank TV screen. She didn't know whether to be mad at Paul or mad at herself for allowing her feelings to run so deep so fast for a man she hardly knew.

Before she knew it, she smoked half of a pack of cigarettes, drank the entire bottle of wine and danced to everything from Jazz, Reggae, and Tina Marie to Al Green and back to her favorite CD. It was midnight and she was both physically and emotionally tired.

Janice went around to each room, removed her decorations and cleaned up her mess. She went to the closet, took out her red negligee and heels and placed them in her bag. She looked around and thought that tonight was supposed to be their Wow Night, but instead, it was a night filled with disappointment, pain, uncertainty, old habits, and great music."

As she turned off the lights and closed the door behind her, she vowed to do what Lainey told her before she died, "Guard your heart a little better and not put it out there for someone who is not worthy of having it."

63

Paul

Paul stood behind the caution tape and watched the team of firefighters and police work to free Desiree from what was left of her rental car. Dante and Brian finally found Cynthia and rushed her to the accident. They all stood quietly beside Paul and looked at the firefighters as they carefully cut and pried away pieces of the Mustang.

After two hours, they finally freed Desiree from the car and placed her into the ambulance. Thankful that Desiree was still alive, Paul dropped his head and said, "Thank you." He looked at Cynthia staring at the cut up car and asked, "Cynthia, are you all right?"

"Yes, Paul."

Paul was shocked that Cynthia called him by his first name and not Daddy as she had done for the last 20 years.

"Baby Girl, I know you're upset, mad and more. In every way that counts, I'm still your father."

"If you say so Paul."

Paul was hurt by Cynthia's comment, but decided to ignore it.

"I'll see you at the hospital Baby Girl."

"I'm not going to the hospital. As far as I'm concerned, she's already dead."

"Cynthia! I know you don't mean that. Regardless of what Desiree did, she's still your mother—your only mother."

"Like you're my only father?"

"Come to my house and we'll talk about this."

"There is nothing for us to talk about Paul. You are not my father, my mother has lied to me and case closed."

Cynthia walked away and left Paul with his head hung down. He felt hurt, disappointed, and terribly betrayed.

"Mr. Davis, she'll come around."

"For her sake Brian, I hope she does. She's too young to keep hold of so much bitterness."

Paul looked at Dante. "Let's go to the hospital."

Dante didn't move.

"Are you coming?" Paul asked.

"Dad, I'm tired and I'm going home to a warm bed and hopefully to a warm body. Desiree is not my mother and case closed." Dante smiled.

"Now, here you go."

Both Dante and Paul laughed. Paul was grateful that he still had a solid relationship with his son. Dante gave his father a pat on the back. "Dad, everything is going to be all right. Call me later old man."

"I got your old man."

Paul walked back to the limo. "Bernard, drive me to Southern Maryland Hospital."

"Is Desiree going to be all right?"

"I don't know, but at least she's still alive."

"I see Miss Cynthia is okay."

"Yeah, she's okay, but she's mad as hell."

"She'll come around sir."

Paul poured himself a vodka and cranberry juice and drunk it in one big gulp. He poured another, let out a huge sigh and laid his head back on the black leather seat.

Bernard watched him through his rear view mirror.

"Rough day, huh?"

"Rough doesn't begin to describe it. I tell you Bernard, I was all ready for a lovely evening with Janice and now this. She called while I was standing out there. I didn't want to take the call in front of Cynthia so she could get all stirred up, but I wanted to somehow let Janice know that I wasn't going to make it. I didn't want her to think I stood her up."

"What did you do?"

"I talked to her like she was a client."

"Why didn't you just step away?"

"I don't know, but I know I hurt Janice because she hung up without saying goodbye."

"Why don't you just call her now and explain to her what happened?"

"No, what's done is done. The last thing I want to do is drag her in my mess. Before I hurt her anymore, I'll hurt myself. No, until I get a grip on things, the best thing I can do right now is to just stay away."

"Sir, if you don't mind me saying so, I think you're making a big mistake. If you feel the way you say, staying away from her and shutting her out will only make it worst not better."

"Bernard, she's not going to wait around until I get my life straight. It's just as well, she'll probably turn out and act just like Desiree, cheat, lie, and try to take me for everything I got."

Paul took another big gulp of vodka. Bernard shook his head at his employer. "Mr. Davis, all women aren't the same. It sounds to me like you're trying to protect yourself, not Miss Janice. Too bad, it sounds like you two were a match made in heaven."

Paul turned a deaf ear to Bernard and continued to drink his vodka. "Let me know when you get to the hospital Bernard."

"Yes, Mr. Davis."

Bernard turned on the Oldie but Goodies station and without another word, drove Paul to the hospital.

"Here we are sir."

"Thanks Bernard. I'm sure I'll be here half the night. I'll just take a cab home."

"Good night Mr. Davis."

Paul walked into the hospital emergency room. He thought about the last time he was at Southern Maryland Hospital, he waited for news about Chester. He knew they took Desiree directly into surgery, so he sat down in one of the waiting room chairs and prepared for a long night.

Hours went by and still no one came out to give him an update on Desiree's condition. Paul noticed a police officer sat in the next row that waited just as long as he waited. The officer looked familiar to Paul, but he couldn't place where he seen him before.

The officer walked over to Paul and extended his hand. "My name is Roberto Goode."

Paul shook Roberto's hand and asked, "Do I know you?"

"I know Desiree. We've been seeing each other and I'm in love with her."

"Is that right?" Paul chuckled. "Well, I guess once she is released, you'll be taking her home with you to care for her."

Roberto looked at Paul. He was about to answer him when the doctor came out. "Is anyone here for Desiree Davis?"

Simultaneously, Paul and Roberto answered, "Yes."

"I am her husband," Paul said.

The doctor directed his attention to Paul. "As you know, your wife was badly injured. She made it through surgery, but she's lucky to be alive. She suffered internal injuries, trauma to the head, a broken arm and leg. Now, we just wait. The next 24 hours are crucial."

"Is she conscious?" Roberto asked.

"No, she's in a coma," the doctor said.

Roberto dropped down in the chair, shook his head from side to and whimpered, "Oh no, oh no."

Paul frowned at the young tall officer. *He's about to cry like a baby.* Paul shook the doctor's hand. "Thank you Doctor." He then turned back to Roberto who had full blown tears in his eyes. "You really love her, don't you?"

Roberto never looked up. He just shook his head and said, "Yes, I do."

Paul put his hand on Roberto's shoulder. "I feel sorry for you young man. Take it from me, save your tears. She's not worth it."

Paul left Roberto to his mini meltdown and called a cab. When he arrived at his condo, it was two o'clock in the morning and all he wanted to do was go to bed and forget the day ever happened. Paul took off his clothes and fell into bed. He hoped sleep would come quick, fast and in a hurry, but instead, it came slow, full of visions about Janice and what she must be thinking.

After Paul tossed and turned for an hour, he finally gave up on sleep. He got out of bed and reached for his phone. Slowly, he dialed Janice's number. Before the number connected, Paul changed his mind and hung up the phone. "Nope, I'm not going to do it. From now on, I need to guard my heart a little better."

With that piece of self advice, Paul got back in bed, turned on his side and within minutes, fell asleep.

64

Janice

"Hello Auntie Janice."

"Hi Travis. How are you?"

"I'm hanging in there."

"How is little Travis?"

"He's fine. Auntie, they're going to read Ma's Will today."

"Today?" Janice jumped up.

"Yeah, didn't you get the notice?"

"Travis, I haven't read my mail in days."

"I was wondering if you wanted to go together."

"I'd loved to. What time is the reading?"

"It's at three o'clock."

"Oh, I thought you were about to say in 30 minutes. I'm glad you called me Travis."

"Jasmine is mentioned in the Will too."

"That's why she left me so many messages. We have been playing phone tag. I'll call Jasmine as soon as I hang up."

"Auntie, I'll pick you up at two o'clock."

"Okay Travis, I'll be ready."

Janice hung up from Travis and dialed Jasmine.

"Jasmine, this is your mother."

"I know who it is. What do you think Auntie Lainey left me?"

"Oh Jasmine, why didn't you tell me the reading of the Will is today?"

"Mommy, I thought you knew. I called you, but you've been busy, busy, busy."

"Travis wants us to go together. He'll be here at two o'clock. Come over and ride with us."

"Sounds like a plan, I'll be there."

"Okay sweetie."

"Looks like someone is going to be rolling in the dough," Marvin said.

"Why are you eavesdropping on my call?"

"I'm not eavesdropping. I just happened to walk by the moment you were talking. I call that listening with my ears. Isn't that what they're for?"

"Marvin, I don't feel like listening to your smart aleck remarks right now."

"Janice, you never feel like listening to anything I have to say. How long are we going to go on like this?"

Janice let out a huge sigh. "If I remember correctly, you were supposed to be gone by now and for the record, there is no we."

"I see you're still singing that same old tune. Are you still waiting around for Sweet Daddy to call? The man is married and back with his wife. You were just his little chick on the side to make him feel good while he went through a few trials and tribulations with the Mrs."

Janice just stared at Marvin. She hadn't heard from Paul since he stood her up.

"Face it Janice, the man is married and so are you. Sweetheart, if you come to your senses, we can make this work. Don't mess around and lose the best thing you ever had waiting on that rich bum. Besides, after the reading of the Will, we'll probably be rich too. Word on the street says your sister was worth *millions*."

Marvin laughed as he dodged the coffee cup Janice threw at him.

"Temper, temper, don't make me call your mother on you and tell her how you've committed adultery and attempted to inflict bodily harm on your loving husband."

"Marvin, get the hell out of my room. There is no damn we. You got that? Just get out and leave me alone!"

Janice slammed her bedroom door and almost crushed Marvin's foot. She reached for a cigarette and lit it. She didn't want to admit it, but what Marvin said made a lot of sense, given that she hadn't heard from Paul since he stood her up. Janice continued to puff on her cigarette and pace back and forth. "How could I have been so gullible and allowed myself to get so sucked in by Marvin and now Paul? What's wrong with me?"

Janice put out her cigarette and lit another. She tried to figure out who she was mad at the most, Marvin, Paul or herself. Janice's phone rang. She looked at her caller ID. To her surprise, it was Paul. She threw her phone on the bed and walked away. After Paul left a message, Janice picked up her phone and listened to his message.—"Hello Janice. I know I haven't called you in awhile and I'm sorry. Call me when you get a moment."

"After not hearing from you in two weeks, that's the best you can do. I don't think so."

Janice put out her cigarette and went downstairs to get another cup of coffee. She went into Marvin's room to tell him he had 30 days to get out, but he already left. "That's strange. I didn't hear AJ. I wonder who picked him up. Oh well, I'll just tell him later."

Janice got a fresh cup of coffee and headed back upstairs. For the next two hours, she went through her mail and wrote checks for her overdue bills. "There has got to be a better way."

Janice laid her head back on her brown leather chair and closed her eyes. She daydreamed about starting her own business, performing her customer service seminars and showcase her books—all best sellers in her event hall. At Paul's suggestion, Janice started her first romance novel. She hadn't made much progress, but once things settled down in her life, she planned to write more.

Janice opened her eyes, walked to the window and looked toward the sky. "Oh Lainey, I never expected you to leave me anything, but if you did, I promise you I will make you proud of me. When you look down from Heaven, you will be so pleased with what I've done. I miss you so much Lainey."

A tear slid down Janice's cheek. Time got away from Janice. She looked at the clock and it was already 12:30. Quickly, she jumped to her feet and hit the shower. When she came out of the bathroom, Jasmine was sprawled across her bed.

"Jasmine, you scared me."

"Hi Mommy."

Janice smiled at Jasmine and thought whenever she called her Mommy, she still sounded as if she was four years old. "Jasmine, get your shoes off my bed."

Jasmine gave her mother a sour look. "Mommy, aren't you excited? I'm going to get a brand new car this time and a house of my own. No more roommates for me."

"How do you know Lainey left you anything?"

"Oh, she did. My Auntie loved me."

Janice laughed at her high spirited daughter eating her out of house and home in just 15 minutes. While Jasmine text her multitude of friends, Janice dressed in a black pantsuit and silver blouse. After she approved herself in the mirror, Janice was ready to go downstairs. "Come on Jasmine. Travis should be here any minute."

Five minutes later, Travis rang the doorbell.

"Hey Auntie. Hey Jasmine. Look at you all grown up," Travis said.

"I know. You look good cousin."

"Thank you."

"Where is the little one?" Jasmine asked.

"He's with his mother right now. Are you all ready to go?"

"Ready as I'm going to get," Janice said.

As Janice, Jasmine and Travis pulled into the parking lot to the lawyer's office on 17th and K Streets, NW, Chester and Beatrice pulled up beside them.

"A family reunion," Jasmine yelled out from the back seat of the Toyota Camry.

Before Janice spoke to her mother and brother, she took a deep breath.

"Hi Ma. Hey Chester."

Beatrice gave Janice a disapproving look. "What's wrong with your phone Janice? I've been trying to get a hold of you for a week now."

"Ma, I called you, but you were out."

"I haven't been out all week."

"I miss you too Ma." Janice smiled.

"Hey Sis, you all right?

"I'm fine."

"What are you going to do with your million?"

"Chester, here you go spending money you don't have. You're just as bad as Jasmine."

A stocky, but very well dressed man came out into the waiting area to show everyone to a conference room. He wasted no time telling them Lainey's estate was worth over $5 million in money, stocks, bonds, cars and real estate.

Janice, Beatrice, Chester, Travis and Jasmine sat around the huge conference table and gave their undivided attention to the Executor as he read Lainey's Will.

"To my loving mother, I leave $1 million for you to live the rest of your life happy and free of worry.

To Chester, I leave my Bentley and $250,000. Little brother, you know what to do. Have fun and take care of my Bentley.

To Jasmine, I leave my red Mercedes Sports, my house that is fully paid for and thanks to you, now beautifully decorated and $100,000. Jasmine, make your new home your show place for your interior design business. I know one day, you will be a very successful interior designer.

To Janice, I leave you a vacant building, $500,000 and my silver on silver convertible BMW 128I. Don't let anyone or anything stand in your way of realizing your WOW dreams and I mean all of them.

To my heart, Travis, if I let you down as a mother, I am so sorry and I hope one day, you will forgive me. Always remember that I have always loved you and I always will. I leave to you the bulk of my estate totaling over $3.6 million. Continue to make people smile with your good food. Love my grandson for me. I'm just sorry I never got the chance to meet him. I know if we had more time, you would have brought him to me. I've also set up a trust fund for Little Travis so he will never have to worry about money.

I love you all. In time, I hope you all will stop grieving and enjoy the gifts I have given you. Always remember, family is everything. Take care of each other.

Love always,
Lainey"

When the Executor finished reading the Will, everyone cried bitter sweet tears knowing the only reason they had such good fortune was because Lainey was no longer with them. No one knew how much Lainey was worth and how much love she had for her family to leave such huge amounts of money. For 15 minutes, everyone just sat there in silence and looked from one to another.

Chester looked across the table at Janice and Beatrice. "Ma is a millionaire, Janice is a half a millionaire, I'm a quarter of a millionaire,

Jasmine is a hundred thousandnaire and my man Travis is a 30-year old multi-millionaire. Oh, and let us not forget who has the Bentley."

Janice smiled and shook her head at her car struck brother.

"Travis, are you okay?" Janice asked.

Travis cried and said, "I just wish I spent more time with my mother and taken Little Travis to see her sooner. I'm going to open up my own restaurant and name it after her."

Janice hugged her nephew. "I'm sure she would love that. Okay family, let's go."

Janice hugged her mother and got into the car with Jasmine and Travis.

"Wow, I can't believe this."

"I can Mommy. See, I told you Auntie Lainey loved me. I got just what I said, a house, a car and even money."

Janice stared out the window and felt both happy and sad. When Travis turned on North Berry Court, she thought she saw Marvin get into a black 745 BMW. Janice jerked around to make sure it was actually Marvin. "Travis, pass my house and go back to the corner please."

Travis shrugged his shoulders and did what his Auntie asked. By the time they got back to the corner, there were no cars in sight, but Janice made a mental note to check it out later.

Travis dropped off Janice and Jasmine in front of Janice's house. Again, Janice hugged Travis. "Don't be a stranger. Before you go back home, bring Little Travis by."

"I will. See ya cuz."

"Bye Travis," Jasmine said and jumped in her car and sped off.

Janice smiled and shook her head. "I know she's ready to tell everyone she's a rich woman with $100,000, a new house and a car. What a blessing."

As soon as Janice opened her front door, she saw Marvin standing in front of her with a big smile on his face.

"Well, don't keep me waiting. Are we rich?"

Janice looked at Marvin and walked past him into the kitchen. Marvin followed her.

"Well, tell me, are we rich?"

"Marvin, we are nothing and to answer your question, no. Lainey didn't leave me anything except a building."

"A building? What the hell are we going to do with a building, but sell it? Where is it? How much is it worth?"

"Marvin, don't be an A-hole all of your life.

Janice grabbed a bottle of water and slammed the door behind her. She got into her truck and headed towards the highway. Images of Lainey's dead body flashed across her mind. Again, tears began to swell in Janice's eyes. She shook her head and said, "At the same time, Lainey's death changed my life both in a good way and in a bad way. She left me a building and $500,000. Wow! Don't let anyone or anything stand in your way of realizing your WOW dreams and I mean all of them. I won't Lainey. I promise."

Janice decided that from this point on, whenever she thought about Lainey, she would only concentrate on the good and do exactly what Lainey told her. "It's time to celebrate. I'll give Dee a call and see if she wants to have a drink with me."

Before Janice could find her phone, it rang. She looked at her caller ID and it was Paul. Again, she decided to let it go to her voicemail.

Janice turned into the Radisson parking lot. She picked up her phone and listened to Paul's message—"Miss Perry, I called you earlier today and asked you to give me a call and still, I have not heard from you. I'm calling again to reach out to you. I know you're upset with me and have good reason not to speak to me, but I really wish you would. I have some things going on and am trying to handle them. Janice, you will always be a part of my heart. I do love you and it is not about just getting you in my bed although that would be nice too. Seriously, I would be lying if I said I didn't want to make love to you. I want your whole body, mind and soul. I want all of you. When you get some time, give me a call. Honey, I'm not trying to hurt you. The last thing I want to do is hurt you. If I never hear from you again, I want you to know you will always be a friend of mind because I will always be a friend of yours. I hope you're okay, take care."

Janice closed her eyes and said one word, "Wow!" It took her but a second to dial Paul's number.

"Davis Graphics," Vivian answered.

"Paul Davis, please."

"May I tell him whose calling?"

"Janice Perry."

"And what company are you calling from?"

"He's expecting my call."

After a few minutes, Vivian put through Janice's call.

"Janice, I'm so glad you called. How are you?"

"I'm good and you?"

"I'm better now. Janice, I've missed you and I'm sorry. Can we talk? Where are you now?"

"Actually, I'm not too far from your office. I'm at the Radisson having a bitter, sweet drink."

"Is everything okay?"

"Everything is wonderful."

"Janice, may I join you?"

"Sure."

65

Paul

Paul was so overjoyed at Janice's acceptance of his invitation to join her that for a brief moment, he totally forgot about his last two horrendous weeks. While he sang Smokey Robinson's "You're The One for Me," Paul shut down his computer and walked past Kim and Vivian. "Ladies, I'm leaving for the day."

Vivian ran after him and yelled, "Mr. Davis, Desiree wants you to bring her a pint of butter pecan ice cream."

Paul threw his hand up in the air and continued to walk to the elevator. The mentioning of Desiree's name quickly brought back the thoughts of his last two weeks. "Nope, tonight, I am going to put my problems aside and totally focus on just being with Janice."

When Paul got to the Radisson, he walked through the beautiful contemporary lobby and met Janice in the hallway that led to the octagon bar. With his head slightly cocked to one side, he smiled and took in Janice's beautiful face smiling back at him. Paul felt the powerful energy between them. He walked towards Janice and immediately hugged her, and almost lifted her up off her feet. They stood there in the hallway and held each other tightly oblivious to anyone else walking past them.

After a few moments, they both sat down at the high top table and neither said a word, but their smiles and eyes spoke volumes. In unison, they both said, "I've missed you."

Paul laughed and took Janice's hand across the table. "I'm so glad you agreed to see me. In the last two weeks, you have been weighing heavily on my mind. So tell me Pretty Lady, how have you been?"

"I've been wonderful."

Paul frowned. He didn't like the idea that Janice was wonderful while he was miserable without her.

"Well, not the whole time. Let's just say today I'm wonderful, because my sister gave me an extraordinary gift. She made the dream of owning my own business come true."

"Sweetheart, that's wonderful. I'll help you any and every way I can. I'll do your signs, logo, printing—you name it. I also have the perfect driver for you."

"Driver? Why would I need a driver?"

"Janice, we both know you get lost going around the corner. You'll need someone to drive you to all of your meetings, seminars, the airport, and to my office."

Janice laughed at Paul's enthusiasm about her future success. Paul nodded. "Yep, Jarrod will take good care of you."

"Who's Jarrod?"

"He's a good friend and my back up driver when Bernard isn't available. Janice, I know you will be successful. I'm so happy for you."

"I'm happy for me too, but it's bitter sweet."

Paul thought about Chester leaving him the Paulster. "Yeah, I know what you mean, but your sister obviously wanted you to have this opportunity. Accept it and make her proud."

Janice nodded. "Enough about me, how have you been?"

Paul hesitated and let out a sigh of relief when the server came over to ask for their order. He was thankful for the interruption because he needed more time to think about how he would answer Janice's question. While Janice gave their order to the server, Paul thought about helping to free the man responsible for killing his brother, Cynthia disowning him, Desiree's near death experience, waiting for her to come out of her coma, moving her back into their Annapolis home and finding out he is still very much married to her.

"Okay, now how have you been?"

Paul decided not to share the gory details of the past two weeks with Janice. Instead, he just said, "My last two weeks have been spent working and missing you."

The evening went by with Janice and Paul talking, laughing, eating, and just enjoying each other's company. Janice looked at her watch. "Paul, it's getting late, I better get going."

Reluctantly, Paul agreed and walked Janice outside to her truck. He took her in his arms and kissed her long and passionately. Janice was the first to break away. "Good night Paul."

As Janice turned around to get into her truck, Paul said, "Janice, come back to me. Stay with me tonight."

Janice stopped and turned back around. "I thought you'd never ask."

On a night when planning was out the window and fate stepped in, Janice and Paul's night was full of lovemaking that overflowed with the deepest passion that usually happens when two hearts are mutually filled with love. Janice and Paul finally had their Wow Night. It was more than she ever planned and more than both ever imagined.

66

Janice

Still feeling the effects of her Wow Night with Paul, Janice tiptoed into her house at seven o'clock in the morning. She peeped into Marvin's room and expected to see him asleep or waiting for her with some snide remark. To her surprise, Marvin was nowhere to be found and his bed hadn't been slept in. "I see I wasn't the only one that spent the night out."

Janice went to the kitchen and made herself a fresh pot of coffee. As she let the aroma fill her nostrils, she beamed with joy and thought about how much her life instantly changed for the better. In just 24 hours, Janice's finances drastically increased, her dream became a reality, and her relationship with Paul was stronger than ever.

Janice smiled and said, "With the exception of Marvin, life is finally good again and getting better by the moment. Now that Marvin's health has improved, it's time for him to keep his end of the agreement and get out."

Janice sat at the kitchen table and planned her day. The first item on her agenda was to see the extraordinary gift Lainey left her. Not wanting to be alone, she decided to ask Dee to join her. It was still early, but Janice knew Dee would be up. Just as she was about to call Dee, her phone rang.

"Good morning sunshine. Just making sure my baby got home safely and she's still thinking of me."

Janice smiled and listened to Paul's deep morning voice before she said, "Always."

"I'm going to hold you to that. What are your plans for the rest of the day?"

"I'm going to try and find the building Lainey left me and see what I need to do to turn it into my dream event hall."

"I could have Jarrod take you. That way, the two of you could get acquainted."

"No need, I can find it on my own."

Paul laughed. "Okay, have you thought of a name yet?"

"Yes, I'm calling it Ambiance, the place where the ambiance says Wow."

"I like that. Baby, after you're done, come to my office. I have a surprise for you."

"A surprise for me?"

"Yes, that's the least I could do for you since you kept me up all night. Now I have to drag into work, all tired with bags under my eyes and try to get through the day with you all on my mind."

Janice laughed. "I'll just have to make sure I keep you up all night again."

"You better. Okay Pretty Lady, I got to go to work. Don't forget. Make sure you stop by my office anytime after three o'clock."

"I'll see you then."

Janice smiled from ear to ear as she dialed Dee's number.

"Good morning Dee."

"Janice, what's so good about it?"

"Everything, life is wonderful."

"Oh, Janice, it is way too early for me to look into your rose colored glasses. Where have you been anyway and why haven't you returned my calls?"

"I'm calling you now. Listen, today at 11 o'clock, I need you to go somewhere with me. Can you make it?"

"That depends on two things. One, where we're going? Two, are you going to feed me?"

"Well, one, it's a surprise and two, yes."

"I'll go. Lucky for you, I'm hungry and I don't have any appointments until three o'clock.

"I'll pick you up at 10:30, so be ready."

"Yes Miss Janice."

Again, Janice's phone rang.

"Don't I have a hotline this morning?"

"Good morning," Janice answered.

"Hey Sis."

"Chester, is everything all right?

"Yeah."

"Oh, you scared me. I don't usually get calls from you this early."

"Girl, calm your nerves. So, how are things?"

Janice frowned and slowly said, "Things are good. Today, I'm going to see the building Lainey left me."

"That's good. Let me know how that goes. Hey, how is Marvin?"

"Chester, why are you acting so strange? Marvin is fine, but he's not here right now. AJ probably took him to the doctors."

Chester was silent.

"Chester, are you still on the phone?

"Girl, stop yelling in my ear. Hey Janice, does AJ have a 745 BMW?"

"No, not that I know of. Why?"

"Nothing, I just asked."

"Come on Chester. I know you didn't call me early in the morning to chit chat. What is it that you don't want me to know?"

"All right, I'm standing in my office window and it looks like Marvin in a 745 BMW, but I can't be sure. I do know the woman, that attorney that wears the short skirts. Linda something."

"Did you say a 745?"

"Yeah."

"Is it black?"

"Yeah."

"I thought I saw him driving one the other day, but like you, I wasn't sure."

Chester took Janice off of speaker. "What's with you two anyway?"

"Marvin and I are through, but he's dragging his feet on moving out, especially now since he thinks Lainey has left me a boatload of money. If I find out he's still up to his old tricks that will help me get him out of here sooner rather than later."

"Handle your business Sis."

"Thanks Chester."

"For what?"

"For having my back."

"Anytime Sis, anytime."

Janice poured herself a cup of coffee and went upstairs to her mini office. She decided that now was as good a time as any to quit her job. She sat down at her desk and came up with one idea after another for her consulting business in extraordinary customer service and her event hall, Ambiance.

Pleased with her wave of creative juices, Janice finished her coffee and jumped into the shower. When she came out, she heard the downstairs door close. Just in case Marvin made his way back upstairs again, Janice quickly locked her bedroom door. After she put on her makeup and curled her hair, she put on her black and gray pin-striped pants suit and white blouse. She was ready to do business today and wanted to look the part.

Janice opened her bedroom door and almost ran smack into Marvin. Just as she thought, he was on his way to her bedroom.

"Going somewhere Mrs. Perry?"

"Yes, if you must know, I have some business to tend to. Why are you up here?

"My clothes are still in the closet or did you take them all with you to wherever you spent the night?"

"Look at the pot calling the kettle black. You have some damn nerve."

"Now what do you think I did? Unlike you, I was here all last night. Can you say the same? Where were you last night Janice?"

"Where were you this morning Marvin?"

"I just came from taking a walk around the block."

Janice laughed. "Sure you were Marvin."

"Janice, if you have something to say, just say it."

"Marvin, I have plenty to say, but right now, I don't have time."

Janice ran past Marvin and out the door. On her drive over to pick up Dee, Janice had nothing on her mind but her new life ahead—one that didn't include Marvin. As soon as she pulled up, Dee stood in front of her building.

"Aren't you the punctual one?" Janice asked.

"You told me to be ready. So, where are we going?"

"It's a surprise. Here is the address of the building."

"I know where this is. It's off of 100 west, before you get to Baltimore. It should take us about 30 minutes to get there."

"See, I knew there was a reason I asked you to join me."

"Yeah, because you would have gotten lost."

"Why does everyone say that?"

"Because you get lost going around the corner. You need to start paying attention just in case you have to make a speedy get away one day."

"Whatever."

"What's been going on?"

"Everything and nothing."

"By the look of that big smile on your face, it must be everything."

"Nothing really. I'm just enjoying life."

"I know you're lying Janice. I'll get it out of you at lunch. Hey, get ready to make a left and whatever it is should be right there."

As soon as Janice saw the building, she yelled, "Oh my God, Lainey!" Tears began to swell up in Janice's eyes.

"What Janice?"

"Dee, I can't believe it."

Immediately, Janice parked the truck, jumped out and stared in amazement at her new building. Dee too jumped out and again asked, "What?"

"Oh, Dee, this is a dream come true."

"If you say so? Is that Jasmine's car?"

Janice momentarily took her eyes off her building to look at the car Dee pointed to. "Yeah, it looks like it. What would she be doing here?"

Janice nervously and excitedly put her key in the door. When she walked inside, again, she couldn't believe her eyes. More tears of joy flowed down Janice's cheek. It wasn't just a building—it was her hall that was all decorated and ready for business. On the outside of the building, the name "Ambiance" was displayed in huge letters for everyone to see as they drove by.

As Jasmine took in her mother's shocked, but happy reaction, she too had tears in her eyes and a big smile on her face.

"Mommy, how do you like it?"

"Jasmine, I love it, but you knew about this?"

"Yes, I've been working on it for the last six months. Lainey was going to give it to you for your birthday."

While Janice was in awe of her hall, she still loved the fact that Ambiance was finally a reality.

With her hands on her hip, Dee looked from Jasmine then to Janice. "Is anyone going to tell me what the hell is going on?"

Jasmine laughed. "Hey Dee, welcome to Mommy's Ambiance."

Dee's eyes got huge. "You mean this is Janice's hall? Are you kidding me?"

"Nope, it's Mommy's."

"Jasmine, you did all of this?"

"Yes Ma'am."

"You're good girl. I need to get you over to my place."

Jasmine handed Dee one of her cards.

"Well, all right. Janice, this is wonderful."

"Mommy, let me give you the grand tour."

As Janice went through her hall, she looked at the lobby that was decorated with light and dark mahogany wood floors with a big cursive A in a circle as soon as you walked in. There were two glass showcases on each side of the walls for Janice to display her books. Chandeliers hung from the ceilings and sconces that looked like miniature chandeliers hung on the sides of the walls. Two winding staircases joined together at the middle to form one wide staircase. A huge ballroom that would hold up to 350 people was upstairs. There was a huge balcony fully furnished with lawn furniture that looked out onto a patio with a fountain. There were two bathrooms upstairs and a bedroom suite down the hall. Downstairs, there was another ballroom that would hold up to 200 people, one big office in between two smaller offices. Each was furnished in dark mahogany furniture. There was a kitchen and two more bathrooms were down the hall.

At the same time, Janice smiled and cried. "This is so beautiful Jasmine. You incorporated everything I wanted."

"You really like it Mommy?

"I love it."

"I remembered everything you told me Mommy. When it came to the office area, Lainey gave me a few suggestions. She said you would probably hire an assistant and one other person."

"Wow! The only things left to get are tables and chairs."

"That's already done. Follow me please."

Jasmine led her mother to a storage closet filled with round and rectangular tables and hundreds of chairs with gold colored cushions."

"Jasmine, you've thought of everything."

Janice walked over and looked at the A in the floor. She closed her eyes and under her breath said, "Oh, Lainey, I promise I'll make you proud of me."

When Janice opened her eyes, she saw Dee crying. "This is beautiful. I'm so happy for you Janice. Whenever I find a man, we're going to get married right here."

"I'll give you a discount."

"Discount nothing. I better get it for free."

"If the woman who has a commitment phobia that disguises it by finding everything in the world wrong with a man says she's getting married here for free, I guess I have no option but to say no charge."

"That's more like it, but I don't have a commitment phobia. When I find the right person, I'll marry him. I want to do this thing one time and one time only."

"That's really the way it should be. You know Dee, for so many years, I was wrong when I thought about marriage. With the kid's dad, I was young so I thought if it didn't work out, there was always divorce. With Marvin, I thought we loved each other on and off for so many years, that we should get married. Again, I thought if it didn't work out, there was always divorce. Until recently, I never looked at marriage as spending the rest of my life with someone."

"What changed?"

"Paul."

"The Wow Man you met three months ago?"

"Yes, I really believe he's my gift from God and with him, I can see myself spending the rest of my life with just him."

Dee rolled her eyes. "That's nice Janice."

"Mommy, when will you open?"

"Very soon. Jasmine, I'm so proud of you. You have become just what Lainey said you would, one hell of an interior designer. I love you sweetie."

"I love you too Mommy. I'm going to throw a party here next week."

"Now, here you go."

Dee's stomach growled. She laughed. "Let's go eat."

"Do you want to join us Jasmine? Janice asked.

"No thank you."

"I can't believe you're turning down a free meal."

"Mommy, I'm tired. When Chester told me you were coming this morning, I rushed over here so I could surprise you. I'm going back home to get my beauty sleep."

"Chester knew about this too?"

"Yeah, I told him."

Janice didn't think the day could get any better. She was now on cloud nine hundred and ninety-nine. She and Dee pulled into Ten Buck Two, a seafood restaurant 10 minutes away from Ambiance.

Once inside, Dee and Janice were immediately taken to their tables. Both ordered Chardonnay and looked around the rustic restaurant.

"I've never been here before," Janice said.

"Me either, but we're going to toast to Ambiance. That Jasmine of yours is going places."

"Yes, she is."

Dee turned her head to look around the restaurant. "Hey, is that Davey over there and who is that gorgeous piece of chocolate with him?"

Janice followed Dee's eyes in the direction of Davey and a bald head muscular man.

"Dee, I don't want Davey to know I'm here."

"Sorry Janice, you have your Wow Man. I'm trying to book your hall. I think I've just found my husband."

"Dee, don't go over there."

Dee hurried over to the table where Davey and the unknown man sat. Janice could see Davey smiling. She smiled back at him and waved. A few minutes later, Dee came back to their table.

"They want us to join them."

"Why did you do that?"

"Come on Janice. Make Davey's day."

"Very funny."

Janice and Dee walked over to Davey's table.

"There's my girl," Davey said. He hugged Janice and pulled out a chair for her.

Dee didn't wait for anyone to pull out her chair—she just sat down really close to Davey's friend.

"Janice, I want you to meet an old friend of mine, Brent Foster. He's the guy I went to the wedding with the night we ran into each other. Brent, this is Janice Scott."

"Excuse me Davey. "It's Perry."

"That's right, she married some bum."

Janice ignored Davey's comment. "Nice to meet you Brent."

"I like how you handled Davey. Nice to meet you Janice Perry. Dee tells me you two are here to celebrate your new business."

"Yes, I have a consulting business that specializes in delivering extraordinary customer service and I also have an event hall. The name of it is Ambiance."

Davey looked surprised, but said nothing.

"Sounds intriguing." I have a few businesses and a lot of business contacts that could definitely use some customer service overhauling. Do you have a business card?" Brent asked.

"Not yet."

Brent smiled as he placed his business card in the palm of Janice's hand and rested his hand over hers. "Feel free to use it anytime."

Janice blushed. "Thank you."

Both Dee and Davey frowned and curiously eyed Janice and Brent.

For the next two hours, Janice, Dee, Davey, and Brent ate, laughed and talked about almost everything. Janice looked at her watch and saw that it was 2:15. "I hate to break up this party, but I have an appointment at three o'clock."

"So do I," Dee said.

Brent looked at Janice. "It was very nice meeting you Janice and very nice meeting you Dee. I hope we have a chance to get together again real soon."

Dee handed Brent her business card. "I have my card. Feel free to use it anytime Brent."

Brent took Dee's card and smiled. Davey stood up and hugged Janice. While his arm was still around her, he whispered into her ear, "I'm still waiting for you to put out that fire."

"Goodbye Davey."

When Janice and Dee got to the car, Dee just stared at Janice.

"What's wrong with you?"

"Brent was hitting on you."

"No, he wasn't."

"Janice, you had to be blind not to pick up on that. Poor Davey. I thought he was going to faint when Brent put his hand over yours. Davey still has it bad for you. Poor guy. Are you going to call Brent?"

"Sure, for business."

"Well, you call him for business and I'll call him for pleasure."

Janice laughed at Dee as she kept going on about how good she and Brent will look together when they get married in her hall.

Janice dropped off Dee and headed over to Paul's office. She took a few minutes to give herself a once over before she went upstairs to his office. As soon as Vivian saw Janice, she stood up. "Hello, may I help you?"

"I'm here to see Paul Davis. My name is Janice Perry."

Vivian's eyes got huge and looked Janice up and down.

Kim shook her head at Vivian and looked at Janice. "Hi, my name is Kim. I'll get Mr. Davis for you."

"I am his executive assistant. I'll get him," Vivian said.

"Stop acting so crazy and go get him then."

As she witnessed a mini cat fight between the two ladies, Janice smiled at Paul standing in his doorway.

"No one needs to get me, because I'm right here."

Paul smiled at Janice and Janice smiled back. Both Kim and Vivian looked at each other as Paul reached out for Janice's hand. "Hello Janice, come right in."

Paul closed his door and immediately took Janice into his arms. "I've been waiting to do this all day."

"Is that right?" Janice chuckled.

"Yes, that's right. How was your day so far?"

"It was so great that I can't even put it into words."

Paul kissed Janice again and said, "Good."

"I'll just have to show you."

"First, let me show you what I've been working on all day."

Paul took Janice by the hand and guided her to his small conference room. "Feast your eyes on Ambiance, the place that says Wow!"

"Wow!"

Inside, there were signs, logos, business cards, letterhead, envelopes, and everything else Paul could think of that would be essential to Janice's business.

"All we need is an address, a phone number and your okay. Sweetheart, what do you think?"

"Oh, Paul, this is wonderful." Again, tears began to swell in Janice's eyes. "You did all of this today?"

"Yes, as soon as I got here this morning, I started working on everything and I just finished 15 minutes ago. I do have some bad news for you. I did some research and found out there's another hall by the name of Ambiance off of 100 west. I'm sorry, you have to change the name, or maybe you can just change the spelling."

Janice laughed at Paul's puzzled look. She handed him her phone with a picture of Ambiance.

"Is it this one?"

"Hey, that sign looks like some of my work."

"This is your sign?"

Paul studied the photo a little longer and smiled. "Yeah, it's mine."

"Wow! Oh Paul today has been a dream that I hope I never wake up from. Lainey has done everything. All I have to do is open up shop."

"That is a dream comes true. I'd love to see it."

"What are you doing now?"

"Going to see Ambiance. That way, I can get the address."

"Janice, before we leave, there is someone I want you to meet."

Paul dialed Dante's number. "Can you step into my office now?"

Moments later, a much younger version of Paul with hair appeared in the doorway.

"Janice, this is my son and right hand, Dante Davis. Dante, this is my Janice."

Dante smiled and extended his right hand. "I finally get to meet Miss Janice Perry. It's very nice to meet you."

Dante looked from Paul to Janice and smiled. "Don't you two look like a pair of bookends?"

Paul and Janice looked at each other and saw they both wore black and gray pin-striped suits. Paul hugged Janice and both laughed.

Dante walked over to the table. "So, this is what you've been working on all day with your door closed."

"What do you think?"

"Not bad old man. I see you still got it."

Janice smiled at Dante as he joked with his Dad and noticed their close relationship.

"Dante, did we do this sign?" Paul asked.

Janice showed Dante the picture on her phone. Dante smiled. "Yeah, I did this one myself. I remember it because I liked the name and the funny young lady that had a lot of energy. What was her name? Jasmine Scott, that's it."

"That's my baby girl," Janice said.

"Small world," Dante said."

Paul shook his head. "First, our paths crossed personally and now in business. I guess I'm a part of your dream too."

"I guess you are." Janice said.

Dante cleared his throat. "I hate to interrupt your undercover flirting Dad. Miss Perry, do you have a marketing person?"

"You can call me Janice and no, not yet."

"Well, if you need any help, just give me a call. Here's my card."

"Thank you Dante."

Paul smiled at Janice and Dante as they exchanged marketing ideas.

"It was very nice meeting you Janice."

"Son, I'll walk you out. Janice, I'll be right back. Do you want anything to drink?"

"Water please."

"I'll tell Vivian to bring you in a bottle."

Janice went back to Paul's office. When Vivian walked in with her water, Janice was looking at a picture of Paul, Dante and two women she didn't know. Vivian stood behind Janice and had no problem filling her in.

"That's Paul's wife and his daughter. Nice looking family, wouldn't you say?"

"Yes, a very nice picture. Thank you for the water."

Janice thought Paul's wife looked like an older version of Linda, only heavier with a short spike hair cut. Under her breath, Janice said, "That could be Linda's mother."

Janice looked at Vivian and wondered why she was still standing there.

"Miss Perry, may I get you anything else?" Vivian asked.

"No, I'm fine."

"Glad she's gone. Wife, huh? I'll make a mental note to ask him about his divorce."

Paul walked back over to his office. "Hey Pretty Lady, did you miss me?"

"Always."

Paul packed up some of his proofs. "I'll take some of these with me in case you inspire me along the way. Shall we go to your dream?"

"I'm already there." Janice smiled

67

Desiree

"Desiree, they're walking out right now."

"Vivian, speak up, I can't hear you. Who is walking out?"

"Your husband and that Janice Perry woman. You should have seen them smiling up in each other's faces like a Cheshire Cat. I tell you one thing, she's not a business associate and you better do something about it fast or you can kiss your fortune goodbye."

"It looks that serious?"

"Yes, it's that serious."

"What else do you know about her?"

"Well, I'm in his conference room and you wouldn't believe all of the stuff he has for her business. He did everything from signs, letterhead, business cards, and some more stuff."

"What's the name of her business?"

Vivian looked at one of the signs. "It looks like an event hall. Oh, here it is. The name of it is Ambiance, over on 100 west. Desiree, what are you going to do about it?"

"I don't know yet. I need to think."

"You better not take too long. I didn't do all of those things just so I end up with nothing to show for it."

"Vivian Darling, I told you I will take care of you. Let me worry about it and you just continue to keep your eyes and ears open.

"Desiree, I have to go, bye."

Desiree looked at the phone and rolled her eyes. "Janice Perry. I need to find away to get rid of her."

Desiree's phone rang again.

"Desiree, I'm sorry about that. Kim came in and I had to get rid of her. She is so nosey and stuck up Dante's butt and always in my business. Dante doesn't want her."

"Vivian, I don't have time for your rambling. Is there anything else?"

"Oh, yeah, they're on their way to her hall."

Desiree started moaning, groaning, grunting and making all kinds of weird sounds. "Vivian, I have to go think."

Desiree hung up on Vivian. She threw her head back on her pillow and tried hard to devise a plan that would ruin Paul and Janice's relationship, but the pain medication interfered with her concentration. Desiree's eyes were just about to close when her phone rang again.

"Hello," Desiree slowly said.

"Diva is alive!"

Desiree sat straight up in her bed. "Yes, I am alive and to hell with you Brent. I'm not finished with you yet. You destroyed me!"

"Ah Diva, you destroyed your own crazy ass. You're lucky I didn't file attempted murder charges on you."

Desiree offered an insincere "Thank you."

"So, how are you Diva?"

"As if you care."

"I called you, didn't I?"

"I'm coming along. I'll be better once I get this damn cast off."

"I hear you're back in the mansion. To tell you the truth, I didn't think you could pull it off. I guess Drunk Davis decided to stop the divorce and take you back."

"Well, you were wrong. Paul and I are tight as thieves. So, if you still have any inkling about us getting back together again, you can forget it."

"Diva, I told you once and I'll tell you again, you think too damn highly of yourself. Nobody wants your broken up ass. I saw this beautiful sweetie today. She has her own business, she's sweet, and nothing like you. So Diva Devil, you don't have to worry, I won't be knocking down your door. Oh, I forgot, you don't have a door. I won't be knocking down Davis' door anytime soon." Brent laughed.

"Good for you Brent. If you don't mind, I was busy."

"No problem, I was just about to call my potential sweetie, Janice Perry."

Desiree coughed uncontrollably.

"Diva, are you all right over there?"

"Yes, did you say Janice Perry?"

"Yeah, do you know her?"

Desiree's head became clearer as she thought of the perfect plan to tear Janice and Paul apart. "Yes, I know her through a friend of mine. Actually, I just got off of the phone with my friend. She told me Janice just opened Ambiance. That's her hall over there off of 100 west. My friend is on her way to her open house. It's at six o'clock. If you hurry, you might be able to make it."

"Diva, it was nice talking to you, but I have to talk to some important people. Take care of yourself and the next time you want to try and run over somebody, especially me, don't. As far as not being finished with me yet, you're right."

Desiree laughed when Brent hung up on her. "I never thought I would be thanking my lucky stars for Brent Foster to be back in my life again. About now, he should be making his way over to the Open House for Ambiance and breaking up that little rendezvous between Paul and that husband steeling Perry woman. Once Paul sees Brent, whatever they planned today will be out the window. When Paul gets home, I'll casually drop the names of Brent and Janice."

As she became more and more convinced that her plan to sabotage Paul and Janice's relationship will actually work, Desiree fell back on her pillow and laughed so hard that she had tears in her eyes. "I'll take a nap. When I wake up, "Brent should be calling me to tell me the good news."

Two hours later, Desiree's phone rang.

"Hello Darling."

"It's going to cost you Diva."

Desiree silently laughed. "Brent Darling, what on earth are you talking about?"

"You know damn well what I'm talking about. Again, you set me up. Had me walk in there and Drunk Davis getting his freak on with my sweetie."

"Freak on?" What were they doing?"

"What did I just say? You knew there was no open house. You sent me there because you knew Janice and Drunk Davis would be there."

"So if I did. I know how you get when you see something or someone you want. I know you're not afraid of a little competition. I was just helping you out."

"As always Diva, you were helping out yourself. What's your plan? Just to see your drunken hubby drink himself into oblivion and lose some of his millions, I might even do this one for you for a discount."

"Brent, I'll get back to you very soon." Desiree smiled.

"Yeah, you do that Diva."

Desiree hung up the phone, laid back on her pillow and gloated over her latest scheme. "I told you Janice Perry, you'll be sorry you ever laid eyes on my husband. Paul Davis will always be my husband."

68

Marvin

Marvin stood in what used to be his bedroom and looked from one side to the other. "If Janice thinks she's going to spend all of that money without me, she has another damn thing coming. There has got to be something in here that will tell me how much Lainey left us."

Marvin picked up the stack of papers Janice left on the night table and flipped through the pages. He opened up the drawer and saw an envelope. Marvin carefully opened the envelope and saw the words $500,000 and a building on a document. "Yes! I knew Lainey was loaded. Janice can have the building but half of that money is mine. Now, I can give Karen back her car and get me another Bentley. I'll even have enough left over to get me some more suits, cowboy boots, another watch, rings . . . Damn, I almost forgot. I need to get a condo on the other side of town. This time when she says, get out, I'll have some place to go."

Marvin sat on the bed and further thought about his wish list. He shook his head and smiled. "$250,000 doesn't go far. I'll take $400,000. Janice will be all right with $100,000. She can sell the building and then we'll be even. Now, let's see where she put our money."

Marvin continued to look through papers until he came across two deposit slips. One slip for $400,000 was deposited in their old business account he and Janice started years ago and the other slip was for $100,000 in a personal account with Janice's name only. "Hot damn, she even agrees with me on the split. I knew marrying Janice would pay off one day."

Marvin carefully placed Janice's papers back into the envelope and in the drawer. He was about to call Karen when the doorbell rang. Marvin looked out of the bedroom window. "What the hell does he want?"

Marvin closed the bedroom door and casually went to answer the front door.

"Brother-in-law, Janice isn't here."

"I didn't come to see Janice. I came to see you," Chester said.

"Okay, come on in. What can I do you out of?"

"For starters, you can tell me what you were doing dropping Linda off this morning in a 745 BMW that I know does not belong to you."

Marvin looked at Chester and didn't say a word. He rubbed his curly head from front to back and walked over to the refrigerator. "Do you want a beer?"

"No, I want you to answer my damn question."

"Well, I'll have one."

Marvin took a sip of his beer and turned around to look at Chester. "First of all, I don't know where you get off coming into my house accusing me of doing something I didn't do. I'm married to your sister, remember? Besides, I was here all night and here this morning, except for when I took my morning run. You know, trying to get my leg back to where it used to be."

Chester put his balled up fist into his pockets and turned his head to look out the window. "Marvin, you might be able to lie to Janice, but you can't lie to me. I saw you this morning. I've seen you plenty of mornings, days and evenings. I work in the same building Slick Rick."

Marvin's eyebrows went up as he took a long sip of his beer. "You don't say. I guess I'm busted then. What do you want Chester?"

"I want you to stop hurting my sister. If you want to be with Linda, just move out."

"It's not that simple young blood."

"The hell it is. Janice would never do to you what you're doing to her. My sister is a good woman and if you ask me, she's too damn good for you."

"No one asked you."

"Look Marvin, I'm not going to continue to watch while you run around with your Hoes and drive their cars pretending you are Big Daddy Curl while Janice takes care of you."

"What are you going to do little man, run and tell your sister her husband is cheating on her? She's not going to believe you. Janice knows I love her and I am 100% faithful. She won't leave me."

Marvin knew every word he just said was a lie, but Chester didn't need to know what's really going on between him and Janice.

"Marvin, don't underestimate Janice. Just because she hasn't said anything to you, don't think she doesn't know what you're up to. You'll look up one day and without notice, she'll be gone."

"You know your sister so well."

"Yes, I do. I don't want to tell her, but if I have to, I will. Look Marvin, Janice doesn't deserve what you're doing to her. Before things get any worst, just leave."

"Man, please! You don't half know. Your sister's shit stinks just like the rest of us and at this very moment, your so-called sanctimonious sister is out there screwing another man."

Chester's eyes and mouth flew wide open. Marvin put his hand up to his ear. "What, what was that? I don't hear you saying anything Chester. So, don't come at me about hurting your sister. Your sister deserves every damn thing she gets. She's as much as a Ho than any of the Hoes I've ever dealt with."

Before Marvin realized it, Chester punched him across his jaw and he sailed across the kitchen into the family room. Marvin half sat up near the sofa table and the lamp dangled above his head. Chester walked over to Marvin and rubbed his fist. "Let that be your thirty day notice Mr. Drive Every Woman Car. And, by the way, my sister is nobody's cheap Ho!" Chester slammed the door behind him.

"You're right—she's a $500,000 Ho!" Marvin laughed and dragged himself up off of the floor.

Marvin rubbed his jaw and felt the swelling. "Ouch. Little Man got a powerful punch. That's okay. I'll leave. Thirty days is plenty enough time to make my withdrawals. By the time Janice notices anything, I'll be long gone. For the next few weeks, I'll be the model husband. I'll agree to anything and everything for the sole purpose of my wife's happiness even if it means letting her go. Hell, I'll even start right now."

Marvin dialed Janice's number, but the call went straight to her voicemail. "Why am I not surprised? Janice, this is Marvin. I've been thinking about you sweetheart. I'm sorry I've caused you so much pain. I love you and all I care about is your happiness. As much as I don't want to let you go, I know I have to. If you still want a divorce, you got it. Within the next three weeks, I promise I will be out of your hair. I just want you to be happy. That's all I care about. Can you please come home so we can talk about this? I'll see you soon."

Marvin hung up the phone and smiled. "As soon as by baby gets that message, she'll be home within the hour."

69

Janice

The next three weeks Janice educated herself on how to run Ambiance. She contacted old business associates and prepared for her open house that was just two weeks away. Janice had tunnel vision and was totally focused on making Ambiance a success. Within the three-week period, she only saw Paul once and although Marvin was still at the house, she barely saw him either.

Janice offered the Assistant position to Antoine, a 23-year old who previously worked with Janice on a temporary basis at her old job. Antoine typed letters, made phone calls, gave private tours of the hall, scheduled Janice's appointments, ran her errands, picked up her lunch, told her jokes, and guarded her from unwanted visitors.

"Hey Miss Perry. Everything is all set for the open house. I just got off the phone with Elaine's and the food is confirmed."

"How is my nephew?"

"He's fine. He said to tell you Hi."

Janice smiled as she thought about Travis doing just what he promised he would do—opened up his own restaurant and named it after his mother, Elaine.

"I know Lainey is as proud of him as I am."

"Miss Perry, I also confirmed the drinks and the entertainment. That's everything."

"Are you sure Antoine?"

"Yep, that's everything."

"How about the guest list? No sense having all of that if no one is coming."

"Ah, Miss Perry, that's done too."

"How many people are we expecting?"

Antoine flipped through his notes. "The count is 248, give or take a few."

"With that many people in and out, we will need some type of security. Call some of the police stations and discreetly see if any of the guys would be interested in moonlighting for the night. We will probably need about three."

"Okay Miss Perry. Here are the invoices. All they need is your Janice Hancock."

"Thank you Antoine." Janice smiled.

"Miss Perry, I'm going to get something to eat. Would you like me to bring you back something?"

Janice looked at her watch. "It's three o'clock. We've been working hard for the last three weeks. When you get your lunch, keep going and I think I'll do the same."

Antoine jumped for joy. "You're right Miss Perry. The last time I worked this hard is when I tried to . . ."

"Okay Antoine. I'll see you tomorrow."

"Thank you Miss Perry."

Janice gathered up her papers and held her head in her hands. She was tired and very hungry. She signed the invoices Antoine gave her that totaled $23,245.68. "Damn, I forgot my business checks."

She placed the invoices in her briefcase. "I'll write the checks out tonight and have Antoine mail them in the morning." Janice grabbed her purse, turned off the lights and locked the door. When she got outside, she looked in the sky and took a deep breath. It had been weeks since she left when it was still daylight.

Janice drove home and thought about how good her life was again. She was living her dream, both personally and professionally. Her relationship with Paul was still strong and both of their divorces seem imminent.

Janice turned the corner and almost passed Jasmine's house. She hadn't been there since the night she found Lainey's body. It was hard for her to drive past it let alone go inside it. To Janice, it will always be Lainey's house. Ever since Jasmine moved in, Janice made excuses to her why she couldn't come to visit.

Janice saw Jasmine's car in the driveway and decided she would muster up the strength and go in. As she pulled into the driveway, Janice saw Marvin driving down the street in a black 745 BMW. "I know that's him. Marvin, I see you're still up to your old tricks."

Janice rang the doorbell, but Jasmine didn't answer. "I finally get up enough nerve to visit and she won't even answer the door."

Janice dialed Jasmine's number.

"Hi Mommy."

"Hi Sweetie. Let me in. I'm at your front door."

Jasmine laughed. "I would, but I'm not home."

"Your car is in the driveway."

"Mommy, you forget, I have another car, a red Mercedes."

Janice laughed. "That's right. I forgot you're a multi-car owner. Well, you just missed a visit from your mother."

"Sorry, next time, call first."

"Excuse me."

"I mean, I don't want you to waste your time."

"It's okay. I was on my way home anyway."

"Stop by tomorrow Mommy."

"All right sweetie. I'll talk to you later."

Deep down, Janice was glad Jasmine wasn't home, but was proud of herself for finally making an attempt to overcome her anxiety about going back to Lainey's house.

Janice was on her way home to finally relax for the day. She was about to pull into her driveway and came to a screeching halt when she saw the black 745 BMW in her driveway. Janice just stared at the car. "Damn, either he's gotten bold or just thought I wouldn't be home until late."

Moments later, Marvin backed out of the driveway and headed down the street opposite Janice. "Where are you going Marvin?" Janice debated whether to follow Marvin or go home, as originally planned, but curiosity got the better of her. She followed Marvin down Route 214. She had a strong sense of Déja vu when she followed him months ago into the same subdivision.

Marvin drove past Linda's house, made two more rights, drove up a hill and stopped in front of another multi-million dollar home. Janice parked at the corner. When Marvin got out of the car, a middle-aged woman dressed in a long, silver silk robe stood in the doorway behind the glass storm door. "Here we go again. At least I don't see any signs of anymore children. I wonder how long he's been seeing this woman. Okay Marvin, if you're well enough to be up to your old tricks again, its time for you to go."

Janice drove to the nearest Lowe's and picked up two sets of locks for her doors. On the Lowe's parking lot, she called Chester.

"Hey Sis."

"Hey Chester."

"What's wrong?"

"Nothing, but I need you to do me a favor."

"What kind of favor?"

"I need you to come over and change the locks on my doors."

"What's wrong?"

"I just saw Marvin driving the 745 and I followed him to yet another female's house. Chester, I'm tired of his shit. He has to go."

"About time Sis. I'll be right there."

When Janice pulled into her driveway, Chester was already there. "Damn girl, can't you drive that thing any faster than that. I've been here waiting for half an hour."

"Chester, I just got off the phone with you. How fast were you driving?"

"As soon as you said you're putting out that no good curly head fool, I broke all of the speed limits getting here. See, I even brought my own tools."

Janice laughed at her very eager brother, handed him the locks and went inside. Twenty minutes later, Chester replaced both locks and was handing Janice her new keys.

"Thank you Chester."

"Anytime Sis. Are you okay?"

"Yeah, I'm fine. I think I'm going to stay at a hotel tonight. I don't want to be here when Marvin returns."

"I'll stay here with you. I would love to see his slick face when he puts his key in that door and it doesn't work."

"I'm sure you would, but I just want him gone with the least amount of drama."

"Have it your way Sis, but can I sit outside in the bushes?"

"Go home Chester."

"I'm not going home, but I will leave yours."

Janice hugged Chester. "Thanks again."

"You're welcome. Do you want me to wait while you pack a bag?"

"No, I'll be okay."

"All right Sis, call me later. I'll keep a key just in case I have to come back here and put a foot up curly head again."

"What do you mean again?"

"Nothing, see you later."

Janice went upstairs to pack a bag. She was on her way out the door when she remembered to get her business checks. "I almost forgot. Tonight, I will write my first of many business checks."

Janice put the checks in her black overnight bag and walked downstairs. She looked around the kitchen and family room, closed the front door and locked it with her new set of keys.

As Janice drove to the Radisson, her stomach growled. "I really need to eat something. Since I skipped lunch, I'll go straight to dinner after I check in."

Janice opened the door to her hotel room and threw her suitcase on the bed. She grabbed her phone and dialed Paul's number, but her call went straight to his voice mail. Janice left a message—"Hey Paul, I was hoping you could have dinner with me tonight. I'm at the Radisson. Give me a call." Janice knew she had been really busy, but lately, she noticed whenever she called Paul in the evenings and nights, he wasn't answering his phone. Most of the time, it would take him an hour or more to call back and sometimes, he didn't return her call until the next day.

Janice went downstairs to the hotel restaurant.

"How many will be dining with you this evening?" The server asked.

"It's just me."

"Follow me please."

Janice sat down at the square table alone and looked around the hotel restaurant. Under her breath, she said, "I'm a big girl and I'm hungry. I can eat by myself if I want to."

A server walked up to Janice's table and asked, "Can I get you anything to drink Ma'am?"

"Yes, I'll have a Chardonnay please. On second thought, make that a vodka and cranberry juice. I need something strong tonight."

"Yes, Ma'am."

Janice looked down at her phone and thought about who else she could ask to join her for dinner. When the server brought back her vodka and cranberry juice, she saw Brent at the bar waving at her. She waved back. Slowly, Brent made his way over to her table.

"Brent, what are you doing here?"

"I got to feed these muscles sometimes."

Janice smiled as she looked at Brent's muscles bulging beneath his white cotton shirt. "Yes you do. How have you been?"

"I've been great. How about yourself?"

"I'm good."

"Janice, are you dining a lone this evening?"

"It appears that way."

"May I join you?"

Janice hesitated before she said, "Why not, sure."

"Are you sure? I wouldn't want to impose."

"No imposition."

"All right, I think I will join you."

For the next two hours, Janice and Brent sat in the hotel restaurant and ate, talked, and laughed. Janice laughed so hard and had such a good time that she forgot about Paul not returning her call. She truly enjoyed Brent's company and liked the way he periodically touched the small of her back when he talked. Janice also liked all of the undivided attention Brent gave her which was something in the last few weeks Paul did on an inconsistent basis.

"Dessert?" Brent asked.

"No, I'm fine."

"Check please."

Janice picked up the check and Brent took it out of her hand. "This one is on me. I hope we can do this again sometimes."

"Maybe we will." Janice smiled.

"Let me walk you out to your car."

Janice didn't want Brent to know she was staying at the hotel so she walked outside with him.

Brent stood there and smiled at Janice as he waited for her to lead the way to her car.

"Oh, I forgot something. You go ahead," Janice said.

Without warning, Brent pulled Janice close to him and kissed her on the lips. Janice was startled, but let Brent kiss her. Brent was the first to pull away. "Thanks for allowing me to crash your party. Drive home safely."

Brent walked across the parking lot. Janice just stood in the circle and stared at Brent until he was out of her sight. Janice's phone vibrated and she looked down at her caller ID. "Now he calls." Janice let Paul's call go to her voice mail. "Hmm, he didn't leave a message."

Positive that Brent was long gone, Janice turned around, went back into the hotel and up to her room. She thought about Brent's kiss and shook her head. "Wow, this night sure turned out to be different. Brent is no Paul, but on the surface, he's damn close."

Again, Janice's phone vibrated.

"Hello," Janice answered.

"I had a nice time tonight Janice. I almost followed you home to make sure you got there safely, but didn't want you to think I was stalking you or anything. I hope calling you doesn't display any stalker tendencies."

"No, calling was definitely the wiser choice. I had a nice time too Brent and yes, I am home. Thank you."

"We need to do this again."

"Brent, I don't know about that. I'm married."

"Oh, yeah, Davey said you married some bum."

Janice wrinkled up her nose.

"Well, if you ever just want a dinner partner, give me a call."

"Okay, I'll remember that. Oh, Brent, I'm having an open house in two weeks at my event hall. It would be nice if you could come."

Brent chuckled. "I would love to, but I will be out of town."

"Too bad. Good night Brent."

"Good night Janice."

As soon as Janice hung up the phone, for the third time, it vibrated. "I know Brent isn't calling back. No, it's probably Paul." Janice looked at her caller ID and it was Marvin. She waited for him to leave a message, but like Paul, he too didn't leave a message. A few minutes later, Marvin called again and again, but still didn't leave a message. "I guess Marvin knows the locks are changed. Oh well, I'm sure he has some place to lay his head."

Janice removed her clothes, took a quick shower and wrote out her first business checks. She tried to concentrate, but her mind drifted back to Brent's unexpected kiss.

70

Desiree

"Desiree, what the hell are you doing in my bedroom?"

Desiree laid across Paul's bed dressed in a long, deep purple gown with a split up to her hip that exposed her entire right leg.

"Our bedroom darling and I'm waiting for you. I was hoping we could celebrate. See, I finally got that dreadful cast off of my pretty leg. It's smaller, but none the less, still pretty."

"Good, now use it and get out of my bedroom. Better yet, get out of my house."

"*Our* house darling. Paul, have a drink with me."

Desiree got up and poured one drink for her and one for Paul. "How was your day darling?"

"Desiree, I don't have time to play games with you. What do you want?"

"I want you to have a drink with me. Here."

Desiree shoved the glass into Paul's free hand. Paul looked at his phone and let out a deep breath. "Dammit!"

"Hmm, sounds like someone stepped on your corns."

"I don't have corns, but I do seem to have a pain in my ass right now."

Desiree rolled her eyes at Paul, but decided not to comment. She could see the conversation wasn't getting her anywhere and decided to shift gears.

"Darling, you seem stressed. Why don't I give you a massage like old times?"

"Desiree, before I let you touch me again, I would have to be broke, stupid and on crack. Why don't you go find your boy toy? Better yet, go find your baby daddy."

"Brent, please, I'm through with him."

Paul laughed. "Oh, you'll be with your baby daddy again. You two are like crabs in a barrel. You won't stop until the other is down in the barrel. In your case, you two won't stop until you're both six feet under."

Desiree turned her head. A wicked smiled formed on her lips as she thought about the perfect reply to Paul's statement. "This time darling, you're wrong. I've decided to cut my losses. I'm no longer interested in getting back at Brent or getting with Brent. Besides, Cousin Jacqueline told me he has a new love interest that has his nose wide open. Some pretty, short woman that owns an event hall over on 100 west."

Desiree looked at Paul's eyes widened as big as the hoop earrings in her ears. When Paul took a huge gulp of his drink, she smiled. "What was her name? "Jean, Joann . . . no, Janice, Janice Perry, that's it. So you see Paul, I'm through with him and he's definitely through with me."

Paul gulped down the rest of his drink. *I got him now.* Desiree choked back a giggle. "Paul Darling, can I get you another drink?"

Paul jetted out the room. Desiree flung herself back onto the bed and laughed her head off. "I better call Brent."

While Desiree was on the phone, Paul stormed back into his bedroom and poured himself another drink.

Desiree hung up on Brent. "Is everything okay darling? You bolted out of here like the house was on fire."

After Paul took a huge gulp of his vodka, he turned around to look at Desiree. "Are you still here? Yes, everything is fine."

Desiree knew she succeeded in making Paul doubt Janice. "As I was saying, before you left so abruptly, Brent has found a new love interest. That was Jacqueline on the phone. She just told me she saw them at dinner tonight over at the Radisson. Good riddance. Now, he can stay the hell out of our lives."

Desiree eyed Paul for his reaction. Paul clinched his jaw and took another huge gulp. Desiree fought back the laughter that was building up inside.

"Desiree, what makes you think I give a damn about Brent's love life or yours for that matter?"

Desiree walked over to Paul and caressed his back. Paul didn't notice that Desiree practically chewed the buttons off his shirt. When he realized what she was doing, he grabbed both of her arms and stared into her eyes. In one quick movement, Paul threw Desiree on the bed, pulled his pants down to his knees and began to release all of his frustrations. When he was done, he stood up, buttoned up his pants and walked out of the room.

Desiree jumped up in bed and yelled after Paul. "Darling, where are you going?"

Paul didn't answer.

Desiree laid back on the bed and smiled. "Well, it wasn't what I hoped for, but it was a start. You'll be mine again Paul, you'll see."

71

Paul

Paul was on his way to the Radisson to see for himself if Janice and Brent were together. As he recklessly drove to the hotel, he wondered how long Janice has known Brent. Were she and Desiree cut from the same mold? Paul envisioned Brent making love to Janice and again, rage surged through his veins. He dodged in and out of traffic as the visions of Janice and Brent together became more and more vivid. When he stopped at a red light, he violently hit the steering wheel. Paul was hurt and confused, but mostly disappointed in himself for having sex with Desiree and falling in love with yet another woman that has betrayed him with his brother's murderer.

As Paul pulled up to the hotel, he looked around the parking lot to see if Janice's truck was there. When he saw the black BMW truck, his heart skipped a beat. He stopped the Bentley, looked down in his lap and shook his head. When he looked at the hotel, he had a strong sense of Déja vu only this time, he didn't have Chester to call.

Paul sat in his Bentley, poured himself a drink of straight vodka and looked at Janice's truck. He tried to fight the deep rage within and an overwhelming desire to get rid of Brent, but they were too powerful. Paul turned off his ignition, got out of his car and walked across the parking lot.

Paul's phone rang. He looked at his caller ID. "It's Janice."

"Yeah," Paul answered.

"Paul, this is Janice. Is everything okay?"

Paul was silent.

"You called me four times and left me a very stern message. Surely, now that you have me on the phone, you have something to say."

Paul didn't want Janice to hear the desk clerk, so he put his hand over the receiver and walked back out to his car.

"Okay, why did you leave me that message?"

Paul still didn't answer until he was situated behind his wheel.

"Hello Pretty Lady."

"Do you have a problem with me?"

Paul wanted to know for sure whether she was out with Brent and whether he could trust Janice.

"Are you out?"

"Yes, I am."

Before he asked his next question, Paul took a deep breath. "Where are you?"

"I'm on the other side of town working."

"Did you eat yet?"

"Actually, I just had dinner with a potential client."

Paul cringed as he heard Janice refer to Brent as a client.

"A client, huh?"

"Not yet, but I'm working on it. Why are you giving me the third degree?"

"Janice, I know it's late, but I can't stop thinking about you. I need to see you. Can you meet me?"

"Paul, I do miss you and any other time, I would love to see you, but I have to get this work done. I'll stop by your office tomorrow at four o'clock. Is that okay?"

Paul took a sip of his vodka and thought about Janice not inviting him up to her room and not telling him her whereabouts. Paul concluded she must still be with Brent.

"Yeah, that's fine. I'll see you tomorrow Janice. Bye."

For a few minutes, Paul just sat in the parking lot and drank his vodka. "How could this shit be happening to me again?"

Paul looked at the people as they entered the hotel and then looked around the parking lot. "I'll be a . . ." Paul saw Brent get out of a silver Mercedes-Benz CLK500 with his phone up to his ear walking towards the hotel. Paul dropped his drink, jumped out of his car and yelled, "Brent!"

Brent turned around. "Well, if it isn't Drunk Davis. Fancy meeting you here. What can I do you out of tonight?"

"Brent, I don't know what you're up to, but stay the hell away from Janice!"

"Who?"

"You know damn well who I'm talking about."

Brent laughed. "Don't get it twisted Davis. You're married to Desiree, not Janice. I saw you kissing up on Janice and throwing her on the bed. You should be ashamed of yourself. That's no way for a married man to act. Go home to your wife and I will see who I damned well please."

"Brent, I'm warning you."

"Davis, we've been down this road before. Carry your drunk ass home before I give you a repeat performance."

"Not this time."

"Before Brent could blink an eye, Paul knocked him to the ground. He continued to hit Brent over and over again. Paul was in a rage and couldn't stop himself. Blood gushed from Brent's nose and his mouth. He was about to hit Brent one last time when someone caught him by the arm.

Paul turned around to see who held his arm. Brent staggered to his feet and wiped the blood from his nose and mouth onto his shirt.

"Officer, I want this man arrested. Hold up, I know you. You're that bastard that helped Desiree frame me." Brent swung at Roberto, but missed when Roberto blocked his punch and hit him across his jaw. Brent landed right back on the ground, only this time, he didn't get up.

Roberto turned to look at Paul. "Like you told me, she's not worth it."

"It wasn't about Desiree," Paul said.

Roberto looked down at Brent. "He's not worth it. Go home Paul. I'll take care of this."

Paul shook Roberto's hand. "Thank you. You're a good man."

Paul decided to take Roberto's advice and go home. As he got into his car, his phone rang. When he saw that it was Janice, he cursed under his breath and let the call go to his voicemail.

72

Marvin

Marvin wasn't the least bit angry that Janice changed the locks. On the contrary, he was relieved. Whether Janice wanted him there or not, Marvin knew he would have hung around forever. This way, he had no other choice but to stay away. Marvin's conscience began to get the better of him. He knew some of the things he did in the past badly hurt Janice. He also knew the things he did within the last two days will also hurt Janice. Marvin just hoped that one day she will find it in her heart to forgive him for all of the wrong things he's done.

Marvin went back to Karen's house. He was thankful that he had the place to himself. "Thank goodness Karen is out of town for a couple of days because I definitely don't want to hear her mouth about how tired she is of me coming in and out of her life with no promise of a future. Hell, I'm tired myself. I just need some peace and quiet and a bed for my aching body."

As Marvin laid his head on the soft pillow, thoughts of his past wrongs rushed through his mind like a roller coaster that switched from Janice to Linda to Karen to MJ to AJ and others that he told lies to and scammed.

Marvin picked up his phone to call Janice. Marvin knew it was the end of the road for him and Janice. "The only thing left to do is go back, get my clothes and be done with it. I know she's not going to pick up, so I'll just leave her a message—"Janice, this is Marvin. I understand. In a couple of days, that's Thursday, I'll send AJ to pick up my clothes. I'll get everything and you'll be rid of me forever. Janice, I'm really sorry about everything. I will always love you and hope one day you will forgive me. Bye."

Next, Marvin dialed Linda.

"Speak to me," Linda answered."

"Hey, this is Marvin."

"Well, well, what can I do for you Mr. Marvin?"

"Linda, I just want to say I'm sorry for everything I've done to you."

"What? I can barely hear you."

"I said I'm sorry for everything I've done to you. I know I haven't always been the best person I could be and I have stolen from you and not treated you the way I should have. I'm sorry. You're a good mother. Take care of MJ and tell him I love him and Linda, I love you too."

"You sound strange. You going somewhere?"

"Not right now. I just had you and MJ on my mind and wanted to tell you that. How is he?"

"He's fine."

"Good, make sure he stays that way. I have something for him. I'll have AJ bring it by in a couple of days."

"Okay Marvin."

"Linda, you take care of yourself. I'm sorry. I'll talk to you later. Bye"

Marvin had one more phone call to make.

"Hello," AJ answered.

"Hey AJ."

"Hey Marvin, what's happening?"

"AJ, there's something I need you to do for me."

"Marvin, you sound strange. Are you all right?"

"Yeah, I'm just tired. Janice changed the locks on the door. In a couple of days, I need you to go over there and pick up my clothes."

"Where are you now?"

"Right now, I am over Karen's, but I'll be leaving here soon."

"Where are you going?"

"Some place far away from all of this craziness. I need you to go to the bank for me too. Take down these numbers."

Marvin gave AJ two bank account numbers. "I want you to get a certified check for $200,000 and give it to Linda for MJ."

"Did you rob a bank or something?"

"No, just some back money I had coming to me. There should be $150,000 left. The rest, I want you to put in another certified check and bring it to me."

"Marvin, the bank won't let me take out that kind of money."

"Yes, they will. When I opened up the account, I put your name on it too just in case . . ."

"I don't like the sound of this Marvin. Just in case what?"

"Just in case I wasn't feeling well and needed you to get it for me."

AJ let out a huge sigh and said, "Oh."

"AJ, I love you. You're always here for me."

"Marvin, now you're scaring me. What's going on?"

"Nothing, just promise me you will do what I ask."

"I promise."

"Good. I'll talk to you later AJ."

"Bye Marvin."

Marvin put down his phone and closed his eyes. He felt a little draft so he pulled the covers over top of his head. Instantly, he fell into a deep sleep.

73

Paul

Paul knew if it wasn't for Roberto, he would be in jail instead of in his plush executive office. He tried to concentrate, but thoughts of him and Desiree having sex and Janice and Brent having sex monopolized his mind. Paul shoved his chair back and walked over to Dante's office.

"Hey Dante."

"Hey Dad, what's up?"

Paul was silent and walked over to Dante's window. Dante looked up at his father and noticed the bandage on his hand.

"Dad, are you okay?"

"No Son, I'm not."

Dante leaned back against his chair and waited for his father to continue.

"I've messed up really bad. Last night, I went to the hotel and beat the hell out of Brent. I kept hitting him and hitting him and I couldn't stop. I wanted to kill him. If it wasn't for Officer Goode, I'd be in jail right now. I can't believe I fell for that woman's lies. I keep doing the same damn thing."

"Dad, I told you step mommy dearest is nothing but trouble."

Paul turned around to look at Dante. "I'm not talking about Desiree—I'm talking about Janice."

"Janice, the woman I met the other day?"

"Yeah."

"Wait Dad, I'm confused. Brent is the man Desiree was married to and Cynthia's father, right?"

"I'm Cynthia's father."

"Sorry, I mean sperm donor. What does Janice have to do with you beating up Brent?"

"Janice has been seeing Brent behind my back. I went to the hotel last night to see for myself. I saw Brent walking to the hotel and I lost it."

Paul walked over and sat down in the navy blue leather chair in front of Dante's desk.

Dante frowned. "I can't believe this."

"I can't believe it either. I talked to her last night. She didn't want to see me and she wouldn't tell me she was at the hotel. Then, I see Brent on his way up to her room."

"Tell me something Dad. If Janice didn't tell you she was staying at the hotel, how did you know?"

"Desiree told me."

"Desiree? Now, I'm totally confused. She knows Janice too?"

"No, Desiree told me Brent had a new love interest named Janice Perry and they were at the Radisson. That's how I knew. When I got there, I saw Janice's truck parked outside and Brent was walking up to the hotel."

Dante sat up straight and looked his father in the eye. "You didn't see Janice and Brent together, did you?"

Paul hesitated before he said, "No, but she was there and I know he was there."

"Think about it Dad. Think about who told you about Janice and Brent and where Janice would be and where Brent would be. It's just too perfect. I've only met Janice once and she doesn't seem like she would do that to you. On the other hand, I've known step mommy dearest for years and I don't put anything past her."

"Desiree doesn't know about Janice and me."

"Are you sure about that? Vivian tells Desiree *everything* Dad."

Paul got up out of his chair and paced back and forth. "Hmm, Desiree will do anything to stay in the house."

"I bet you, she planned the whole thing."

"This all makes sense. Desiree was feeding me the whole time. She knew how I would react. After I left last night, she must have called Brent. What a fool I was, but I'm still not sorry for beating the hell out of Brent. He deserved it. Janice must have thought I was crazy last night. I left a message and I told her, rather sternly, that I wanted to know what she was doing at that very moment and she needed to call me right now."

"Did she call you?"

"Hell no. She's supposed to swing by here today at four o'clock. I'll try to explain in a way that won't incriminate myself too badly." Paul laughed.

"If you don't mind me saying so, I know Desiree has hurt you, but try not to make Janice pay for her mistakes. Believe me. They are two entirely different women. She's nothing like Desiree. Janice seems like she's good people, and if you'll let her, she can be good for you."

"You're very wise in your young old age. I'll remember that."

"Dad, I wasn't going to tell you this today, but I guess this is as good of a time as any."

"What?"

"It's about your divorce. It was my fault your divorce papers weren't filed when you thought they were and it's my fault you're still married."

Paul looked puzzled. Dante pulled out the original set of divorce papers and the set of divorce papers Paul gave him the night he picked him up from Desiree's hotel room.

"Remember the night I found you at the hotel with Desiree?"

"Don't remind me."

Dante pointed to the latest set of divorce papers. "You gave me these. Look at them both. They're different."

Paul read through both sets of papers. He banged on the desk. "That bitch! Call Mr. Anderson. I want the original papers drawn up again and served today! Have someone go over to my house and pack up Desiree's things. By the time I get home, I want her gone."

"I'm on it."

"Dante let me know as soon as it's done."

"I will."

Paul walked over to Kim's desk. "At four o'clock, I'm expecting Janice. I don't care where I am, find me and don't let Vivian anywhere near her."

"Yes, Mr. Davis," Kim said as she smiled at Vivian walking towards them with a frown on her face.

Paul went in his office and closed the door. He didn't want anything or anyone to interfere with their visit. Even though Janice didn't have a clue what went on last night, Paul felt he had so much to make up for.

Dante knocked on his father's door. "Dad, they're ready for us."

"I'll be right there."

For the next few hours, Paul and Dante were in a board meeting. Paul's body was there, but his mind was on Janice. He looked at his watch.

It was 3:55 and the board meeting was still going on. Paul thought Janice should be there by now.

Five minutes later, Kim stepped in and gave Paul a note that read, *"Miss Perry is here."*

Paul wrote on the note, *"Show her to my office."*

Kim left the conference room and took Janice to Paul's office. Janice walked over to the wall of pictures and looked at the one with Desiree in it.

"Hey Pretty Lady, I hope I didn't keep you waiting long."

"No, I just got here."

Paul went over to Janice and hugged her tightly. "I've missed you terribly. I wanted to see you so bad last night. Don't ever forget how much I love you. Promise me."

"Why did you leave me that message last night?"

Paul hugged Janice even tighter. "I'm sorry about that. I had a rough night and I guess I took it out on you. It won't happen again."

"You damn right it won't happen again!"

Both Paul and Janice looked at the door that swung open with Desiree in the doorway. Janice tried to pull away from Paul, but he wouldn't let her go.

"Listen, you gold digging little tramp. Get your damn arms from around my husband!"

"Desiree, what the hell are you doing here?"

"I was at home waiting for you like a good little wife should. I decided to surprise you and finish our lovemaking from last night."

Janice pulled free from Paul's arms. "I have to go."

"That's right bitch, you better go!"

Paul glanced over at Janice looking as if she was about to jump out of his window. "Janice, you stay."

Paul grabbed Desiree by the arm and took her out of his office.

"Desiree, get the hell out of here. Didn't you get the real divorce papers today?"

"Yes and I'm not going to sign them."

"I don't give a damn whether you sign them or not. When we go to court, I'm going to tell them all about your dirty dealings, lying, the millions you stole from me and how you conspired to kill my brother. There's not a judge in the world that will make me stay married to your ass. Just make sure by the time I get home, you're gone."

Paul saw Kim looking at him and Desiree. "Kim, you can go home."

"Yes sir," Kim said.

Dante looked out of his office. "Dad, is everything all right?"

"Yeah son."

Paul rushed back in his office and locked the door behind him.

Janice looked out the window. Paul put his hand on Janice's shoulder. "Baby, I'm so sorry about that."

Janice turned around. Paul expected to see tears in Janice's eyes but instead, her eyes were dry and cold as ice. "What are you sorry about Paul? Are you sorry for lying to me for months or are you sorry I found out what a lying, cheating bastard you are?"

"Janice, it's not what you think."

"You have no idea what I'm thinking. Tell me Paul, when will your divorce be final or have you even filed for one?"

Paul lowered his head. In a very low voice, he said, "No, it's not final. I just filed it today."

"I can't believe this. You've been lying to me all of this time. You're still living under the same roof with your wife, seeing me on the side and telling me how much you love me."

"Janice, it's not like that."

"She does live with you right or did she just happen to come over last night to make love to you?"

"Yes, no."

"Which is it Paul?"

Paul let out a deep breath. "After her accident, Desiree moved back in and now she's moving out again. It's complicated."

"You've lied to me from the beginning and you're still lying."

"Honey, I'm not lying to you now. I mean."

"Are you still married to the woman who just left here?"

"Yes, but . . ."

"That's all I need to know." Janice walked towards the door.

Paul grabbed her arm. "Janice, I'm sorry if I hurt you."

"I'm sorry too Paul. If your divorce ever becomes final, give me a call."

Paul threw up his hands. "If that's what you want Janice."

"Yes, that's what I want. I just got rid of one lying ass, cheating man. I definitely don't need another. Playtime is over Paul. Go home to your wife.

Paul briefly closed his eyes as he remembered he told Janice those same words when Marvin showed up at McCormick and Schmick's. Paul let out a deep sigh and looked Janice in the eye. "You're beautiful."

"Thank you."

"Honey, you will always have a special place in my heart."

Paul hugged Janice and kissed her on the top of her head. He could feel Janice's body stiffen in his arms.

"Janice, are you okay?"

"I will be."

"Please don't give up on me. Things will work out. You'll see."

"Take care Paul."

Janice pulled away from Paul. Without another word, she opened the door, walked past Dante, and walked down the hall to the elevator.

Dante walked into Paul's office. "Are you okay Dad?"

"Son, what do you think?"

Paul reached into his drawer, pulled out his vodka and poured himself a huge glassful.

"Do you want to talk about it?"

"No."

"You know where I am if you need me."

"Close the door behind you."

74

Marvin

"I see Marvin is here," Karen said.

"Yeah, your boy toy came here Monday night and hasn't moved since," Jackson said.

"It's Thursday. That's strange for Marvin."

"He must be tired of driving your car all around town day and night."

"I take it you don't like Marvin very much."

Jackson turned around in his seat. "Karen, you can do a lot better than that con artist. He's just using you. You need a real man who will love you for the beautiful woman that you are. Karen, I love you. I always have."

Karen's eyes widened. "How long have you felt this way?"

"For a long time now."

"Jackson, I'm not stupid. I know Marvin is a player, but deep down he's a good man."

Jackson coughed.

"I know there's not a future with Marvin. I just keep him around because he's familiar and I know what he's about, but I'm tired of it. I need something more. For your information, I've already decided that I was going to end it with him. Now that he's here, I guess it is no better time than the present."

Jackson opened the door for Karen. She looked at him and kissed him on the jaw. "Jackson, you're sweet. I just never looked at you in that way, but maybe I should start."

Karen went into her house and yelled, "Marvin, we need to talk. Where are you?" Karen went from room to room until she saw a lump in her bed.

"Marvin, what are you doing sleeping this time of the day?"

She pulled back the covers. "Marvin what's wrong with you?"

Marvin slowly opened his eyes. He could barely talk, but he slowly said, "Karen, I'm sorry. You can have your car back," and closed his eyes.

Karen shook Marvin, but he didn't answer her nor did he open up his eyes. "Marvin, Marvin!" Again, Marvin did not answer.

Karen picked up the phone and dialed 911. As she talked to the emergency dispatcher, she walked out into the long hallway. Karen heard a banging sound coming from her bedroom. She hung up the phone and ran back into her bedroom. Again, she shook Marvin, but he didn't move. "Marvin, Marvin!"

She ran downstairs to get Jackson. "Jackson, come quick. I think something is wrong with Marvin."

Jackson walked into the house and up the stairs.

"Where is he?"

"He's in there."

Karen pointed to her bedroom. Jackson went over to Marvin and looked at him. He felt for a pulse, but there wasn't any. Jackson looked at Karen and casually said, "He's dead."

"What?"

"He's dead."

"Jackson, he can't be dead. I was just talking to him. Do something. Do CPR."

The sirens blared outside. Jackson put his hand on Karen's shoulder. "The paramedics are here now. I'll show them upstairs."

In less than five minutes, the paramedics rushed upstairs and immediately started CPR on Marvin. Kim cried uncontrollably and yelled, "What's wrong with him. He can't be dead."

"Ma'am, please go downstairs while we work on your husband," one of the paramedics said.

Reluctantly, Karen went downstairs. With tears streaming down her cheeks, Karen looked at Jackson. "Oh no, what do I tell his wife?"

"His *wife*, you mean to tell me that scum was married too?"

Jackson shook his head and reached for Karen's hand.

Twenty minutes later, the paramedics hurried downstairs with Marvin strapped down on a stretcher with an oxygen mask on.

Karen jumped up. "Will he be okay?"

On their way out, one of the paramedics said, "We're taking him to Southern Maryland Hospital Ma'am. You can come there."

Again, Karen looked at Jackson. "What am I going to do? I can't call his wife. I have to tell someone in his family. I can't believe Marvin died in my bed. He was probably here all alone for three days and no one to help him."

Karen put her hands over her face and cried out, "This is all my fault."

Jackson put his arms around Karen. "You had no way of knowing he was ill, did you?"

"No, I knew he wasn't himself, but I didn't know he was ill. He didn't stay here that often. I didn't know he was here until we pulled up."

"Well then, you can't blame yourself. You can't help what you don't know."

"I have to call someone. I know he has a younger brother. I think his name is AJ. Marvin told me if I couldn't reach him on his phone that I could always call him."

Karen searched through her phone directory. "Here it is."

"Hello," AJ answered.

"AJ, this is Karen. I'm a friend of Marvin's."

"Karen, Marvin isn't here."

"No AJ, I'm not calling Marvin. Actually, he was just here."

"AJ . . ."

Jackson motioned her to continue.

"AJ, I don't know how to tell you this, but I think Marvin is dead."

"What is this, some kind of joke? I just spoke to him last night."

"I was out of town. I just got back and I found Marvin in my bed, practically unconscious. Right before he closed his eyes, he managed to mumble something. He wouldn't wake up again and that's when I called 911. While I was on the phone, I heard him bang on the wall, but when I went back in, he didn't move or respond to me. The paramedics took him over to Southern Maryland Hospital. I'm sorry AJ."

AJ hung up the phone and rushed over to the hospital. "I have to call Janice, but what am I going to say, Marvin's girlfriend called me and told me she thinks he's dead? No, I need to wait and find out what's really going on."

AJ sat in the emergency room and waited for word on his brother.

75

Janice

With her nose to the grindstone, Janice was at Ambiance getting ready for her open house. Working was the only thing that kept her mind off of Paul being still very much married.

"Miss Perry, we have a problem."

"What is it Antoine?"

"You know I love you, right?"

Janice smiled and said, "Yes."

"I would work for you for free, but I got bills. My paycheck bounced."

"Antoine, I don't have time for your jokes this morning. The open house is right around the corner."

"Miss Perry, I'm not joking."

Antoine handed Janice the check with "NSF" stamped on it.

"That's impossible." *I have $75,000 in it.* "Don't worry Antoine. It must be a mistake. I'll take care of it right now."

Antoine walked back to his office. Janice called her bank.

"This is Ms. Jacobs, how may I help you?"

"Yes, this is Janice Perry. Yesterday, one of my employees brought over his paycheck and it was stamped NSF. I know I have the money to cover it. Can you please check my accounts? I have one business and one personal account. I will give you the personal account number first."

"Mrs. Perry, your balance is negative $2,483."

"That's impossible."

"I see there were five checks totaling $23,245.68."

"Yes, that's right," Janice said as she eagerly waited for more information.

"I also see on the 8th and the 9th, you made two sizeable withdrawals—one for $200,000 and another for $170,000."

"I didn't make any withdrawals!"

"Ma'am, please calm down. I'm sorry Mrs. Perry. It was your business partner, Marvin Perry who made those withdrawals."

Janice's heart raced and she could hardly catch her breath. "Check my business account."

"Ma'am that was your business account."

Janice wrinkled up her nose. "No, I only deposited $100,000 into my business account and $400,000 into my personal account that only has my name on it. Please check my personal account."

"Ma'am, in that account, your balance is $100,103."

Janice was almost in tears. In a shaky voice, she said, "Please transfer $50,000 into the business account and please take Marvin Perry's name off of it right now."

"Yes Ma'am. Is there anything else I can help you with today?"

"No thank you."

Janice hung up the phone and tried to hold back her tears. She walked into Antoine's office and gave him his check back.

Janice forced a smile. "Antoine, everything is fine now. Just what I thought, a mix up. Now go to the bank, cash this check and pay those bills."

"Thank you Miss Perry."

"I have to run out for a moment. Hold down the forte."

Janice ran to her truck and let out a scream. Tears swelled up in her eyes. "I'm going to kill you Marvin!"

She picked up her phone and dialed Marvin's number, but the call went straight to his voicemail. She redialed the number and again, the call went to his voicemail. "Marvin, I know you stole my damn money. I want it all back now!"

Janice lit a cigarette and tried to calm her nerves. She started up her truck, drove down Interstate 50 and ended up in the lobby of the Sheraton Hotel. As soon as she got there, she redialed Marvin's number and ordered a vodka and cranberry juice. Again, Janice's call went to Marvin's voice mail. "Damn, he's not taking my calls."

The bartender placed Janice's drink in front of her. While she decided what to do next, she took a big gulp. "My message light is on." Janice listened to her message—"*Janice, this is Marvin. I understand. In a couple of days, that's Thursday, I'll send AJ to pick up my clothes. I'll get everything and you will be rid of me forever. Janice, I'm really sorry about everything. I will always love you and hope one day you'll forgive me. Bye."*

"Today is Thursday. I'll call AJ. He'll know where that lying, thieving bastard is hiding."

"Hello," AJ answered.

"AJ, this is Janice. Where is he?"

AJ was silent.

"AJ, don't play games with me. I know you know where he is. Tell me dammit!"

"Janice, Marvin is dead."

76

Desiree

"That son of a bitch won't get away with this! I'll make sure Paul and that gold digging tramp Janice Perry suffer for taking away my millions. I'll give her ambiance all right. From now on, everything she touches will magically turn into dust. That will teach her not to mess with somebody else's husband, especially mine. Paul is my husband!"

When Desiree heard a knock at her door, she stopped her ranting and yelled, "Who in the hell is knocking at my door? Who is it?"

"Your favorite person in the world," a man shouted from the other side of the door.

"Give me a damn break.

Desiree swung open the door.

"Not now Brent."

"Diva, I could hear you out in the hallway. When are you going to get a real house? As much damn time as you spend in this hotel, you'd think you owned it. Did hubby put you out again?"

"What do you want Brent?"

"Diva, I came to tell you all bets are off. When you sent me back over to the Radisson, I got my ass kicked by your drunken hubby."

Desiree laughed.

Brent rubbed his jaw. "Oh, you think that's funny, huh? After I told that young Eric Estrada looking dude that helped you framed me to arrest Davis, he knocked me out. He can have this one, but the next time, his ass is mine."

Desiree's eyes lit up. "Roberto was there?"

"Who? I don't know his damn name. All I know I better not see either one of them on the street again."

Desiree walked over to the window. She smiled as she thought Roberto was the only one that treated her like a lady. While Desiree daydreamed about Roberto, she didn't hear Brent yell, "Diva Devil!"

"Why are you yelling?"

"Look, I'm through. I just came over to see you living in poverty and to tell you in person."

"Brent Darling, don't give up so easily. Didn't you like little Miss Janice?"

"She's cool, but no woman is worth me getting my ass kicked twice, especially in the same night."

"If you want any more money, you have to find a way to get me back with Paul and the only way that can happen is if *we* keep the two of them apart. Although, after I visited him in his office the other day, I'm sure the road is now quite rocky."

Desiree gave Brent a wicked smile. "I may not need you after all."

"Whatever Diva. By the way, how is our daughter?"

"Still not speaking to me."

"She just needs a little more time."

"Look at you sounding like a concerned daddy."

"Believe it or not Diva, I am concerned. If you hadn't got on the stand and lied the way you did, I wouldn't have pulled that card. I didn't want to hurt the girl. She has enough to deal with just being your daughter."

Desiree rolled her eyes. "Brent, I have things to do. If you don't mind, let the door hit you from behind."

"Gladly, I have to meet an old friend anyway."

Desiree decided to call Cynthia. She hadn't seen or talk to her since Brent's trial.

"Cynthia Darling, this is mother."

"Hello Mother, what do you want?"

"I want my baby back. We need to talk and get through this. Your father misses you terribly."

"Which one?"

"Cynthia, please. Paul is miserable without you in his life. I tell you what, come to dinner with us. He's been down lately and I know seeing you will make him feel better."

"Why do you care how he feels?"

"I know I've done a lot of bad things and believe me, if I could take them all back, I would. I still love your father, I mean Paul and I just want to try and make things right. Will you come to dinner tonight?"

Cynthia didn't answer.

"Please, please, with a cherry on top?" Desiree begged.

Cynthia giggled.

"I'll take that as a yes. Let's meet at the Sheraton Hotel, say six o'clock?"

"Okay Mother."

"Fabulous darling. I'll see you at six."

Desiree got off of the phone, jumped up and clapped her hands. "Damn, its three o'clock. Now, all I have to do is get Paul to come."

Desiree dialed Paul office.

"Davis Graphics," Vivian answered.

"Vivian, is Paul in?"

Vivian whispered into the phone, "I heard what happened the other day. He told me if I as much breathe anything to you that I would be fired. I can't lose my job Desiree. Besides, the way things are looking, you won't have the money you already owe me."

"Oh, Vivian, just shut up and put Paul on the phone."

"I'm sorry Desiree, but I can't do that."

"Just tell him it's about Cynthia."

"Hold on."

A few minutes later Vivian came back to the phone.

"He'll talk to you."

"What is it Desiree?"

"Paul Darling, I have great news. Cynthia has agreed to have dinner with us tonight. She's anxious to talk to us both."

"How is she?"

"She sounds wonderful. Will you come?"

"When and where?"

"Tonight at six o'clock sharp, here at the Sheraton Hotel, the same one you and I made mad passionate love at not so long ago."

"I'll be there."

When she heard the dial tone, Desiree rolled her eyes at the phone. "Well damn, that was rude." She jumped to her feet and sang, "Tonight, I'm having dinner with my family."

Desiree spent the next two hours getting ready for her family reunion. She wanted everything to be perfect. She missed her daughter and hoped that tonight would put things right again.

Desiree threw all of her clothes on the bed. Her phone rang. "Who could be calling me now?" She looked at her caller ID and smiled. "Oh, it's Cynthia again. Hello darling."

"Mother, I was thinking. Since we're having a family reunion, I would like to have my real father there too."

Desiree was silent.

"Mother, did you hear me?

"Cynthia Darling, I don't think, I mean, I know that wouldn't be a good idea. Paul would kill him. I don't understand why you would want him there anyway."

"According to you, he is my father. Daddy knows that now. So, what's the problem?"

Again, Desiree was silent.

"If my real father can't come, I won't come either."

"Cynthia, listen to me. I'm telling you, it's a bad idea. Let's try this at a later date when things have simmered down."

"Like I said Mother, if he doesn't come, I won't come."

"All right, I will see what I can do."

Desiree hung up the phone and called Brent. "That girl is going to get me killed."

"Diva, I'm busy," Brent answered.

"Brent, wait. I need a favor."

"So soon, I just left you. If you wanted some of my good loving, you should have just taken it like you always do."

"Not that fool. I just spoke to Cynthia and she has finally agreed to have dinner with us."

"See, I told you she'd come around."

Desiree took a deep breath before she hit Brent with her favor. "She wants you to come to dinner too."

"Me, why me?"

"I guess she wants to get to know you."

"Who will be at this dinner?"

"Cynthia, her husband, me, and Paul," Desiree quickly said.

"Hell no! Me sitting down at the dinner table breaking bread with Davis? You have got to be kidding. We wouldn't even get through the pleasantries without that man trying to kill me. Is she crazy? Are you crazy for agreeing to it?"

"Please Brent—I need to see my baby."

"Does Davis know I'm going to be there?"

"Yes, he wasn't thrilled about it, but because that's what Cynthia wants, he agreed."

"I don't know Diva. That doesn't sound like Davis to me. You better not be setting me up again."

Desiree crossed her fingers and closed her eyes. "Will you come?"

"You better be glad that I'm downstairs right now meeting with my buddy. If it wasn't for that, my answer would be a definite hell no. I must be a glutton for punishment. Okay Diva. I'll think about it."

"Good enough. Stay there til six o'clock. When you see us, just come over. Bye."

Desiree called Cynthia.

"Cynthia Darling, everything is all set. Just as you requested, both of your fathers will be there."

"Good, I'll see you all at six o'clock. Bye Mother."

Desiree hung up the phone and fell back on the bed. She was no longer looking forward to her family reunion. She knew as soon as Paul sees Brent that he was going to go off. "If I told Paul Brent was coming, he wouldn't show. I'll just keep that information to myself and hope for the best."

At 5:55, Desiree was downstairs and eagerly waited for her family. The hostess walked up and cheerfully asked, "Hello Ma'am how many will be dining with you this evening?"

Desiree looked around. "Unfortunately, four more. They should be here any minute now."

"Would you like to be seated now?" The greeter asked.

"No, I'll wait for them."

Minutes later, Cynthia and Brian arrived. Desiree cried as she held Cynthia in her arms. "Cynthia Darling, how I've missed you. Don't you look beautiful? You're glowing."

Desiree hugged Brian and kissed him on his cheek. Again, she hugged Cynthia. "I can't believe you're finally here. I've missed you so much."

"I've missed you too Mother."

"How about me," Paul said as he walked up behind them.

"Hi Daddy."

"Come here Baby Girl."

Paul took Cynthia in his arms and hugged her tightly.

"How have you been?

"I've been good."

"You look great, almost like you have a glow."

Cynthia laughed. She looked at her mother and asked, "Is my . . . ?"

"Cynthia darling, let's all sit down."

Once everyone was seated, Desiree leaned over and whispered into Cynthia's ear, "He'll be a little late."

The server came over to take their drink order. The entire family laughed, talked and caught up. Desiree thought so far, so good.

Cynthia looked at Desiree and asked, "Mother, is he coming?"

"Yes."

Desiree saw Paul raise an eyebrow.

"Daddy, I have some wonderful news, but I want to tell everyone at once."

"We're all here, aren't we?"

"Not everyone," Cynthia said.

"Who else are we . . . ?"

Paul stopped talking when he saw Brent approaching their table. Desiree looked at Brent swiftly turn left and walked over to the bar. She took a drink of her Martini and looked at Paul. His eyes were on Brent. Desiree also looked over at Brent at the bar with a woman whose back was turned.

"Daddy, is everything all right?" Cynthia asked.

"Yeah Baby Girl. I'm fine. I just need to go to the bathroom. I'll be right back."

"I'm so glad you're here Cynthia. I'll be right back too," Desiree said.

Desiree followed Paul to the bar and stood to the right of the bar beside a heavy-set man. When she saw Brent put his arm around Janice, her mouth fell open.

Paul also saw Brent put his arm around a woman, but he couldn't see who it was. When Janice turned around to also go to the bathroom, she looked up into Paul's face.

Under her breath, Desiree said, "Dammit, that bitch is going to ruin my family reunion."

"Brent, I thought I told you to stay away from her," Paul loudly said.

"Paul, what are you doing here?" Janice asked.

Brent pointed to the table where Cynthia and Brian were sitting. "He's having dinner with his family over there. Where's your wife Davis?"

Paul looked across the bar at Desiree and Janice followed his gaze. Janice said nothing.

Brent stood directly in front of Paul. "Look Davis, I don't want any trouble with you tonight. Desiree said you would be civil if I joined you."

Under her breath, Desiree said, "Here go the fireworks. Bartender, give me a Martini now!"

"Join me? You stay the hell away from Janice and my family. Janice, what are you doing here with this con artist?"

Still, Janice didn't say a word. She just looked from Paul to Brent and then squint her eyes when she saw Desiree put her Martini glass in the air. Janice pointed to the table where Cynthia and Brian were now eyeing them.

"The same damn thing you're doing with your happy family over there. Leave Paul. I've had a rough day and I'm in no mood."

"Davis, you heard the lady. Leave. It seems that you lose all of your women to me. First it was your hot tail wife over there, my lovely daughter and now the beautiful Janice." Brent put his arm around Janice. "I'll take real good care of her." Janice jerked away just in time before Paul hit Brent across his jaw.

"Paul, what the hell is the matter with you?"

"Sweetheart, you don't know what this man is capable of."

"Don't sweetheart me. He's a potential client, that's all!"

"All of your potential clients hug you Janice?"

"He was just consoling me. Marvin died today!" Janice stooped down to help up Brent. "Just go back to your family and leave me the hell alone."

Desiree saw the devastated look on Paul's face. On her way back to her table, she overhead Brent tell Paul he was going to make him pay if it's the last thing he did. Under her breath, Desiree said, "Not if I get to him first."

When Paul got back to his table, Cynthia and Brian were getting ready to leave.

"Daddy, I asked him here. What's wrong with you?"

"You did what?"

"I don't want any part of this family and neither does my child."

"Cynthia, I'm tired of your spoiled attitude. Since birth, I've taken care of you and if you want that low life as a father, so be it. From now on, make sure he supports you. As of this moment, consider yourself no longer a Davis and the Davis money train is officially over!"

Paul walked away.

"Paul, you don't mean that. Come back. Cynthia Darling, Brian, wait. Please, don't leave. Please stay."

Desiree threw her hands in the air and caught a glimpse of Janice and Brent at the bar. Desiree was on her way to confront Janice when Brent caught her before Janice saw her.

"Hold up Diva."

"Let me go Brent. I'm going to tear every hair out of her damn head for spoiling my family reunion."

"Diva, Janice didn't do anything. I told you, once Davis sees me—he would try to kill me. You wanted them apart and it looks like they are."

Desiree looked at Janice with her head hung down. "Who is that with her?"

"That's my buddy Dave. She knows him too."

"She better be glad you stopped me. I'll let her ass grieve for now, but the next time, you won't be able to stop me."

77

Janice

The next morning, Janice awoke and hoped everything that happened yesterday were just scenes from a bad dream.

Chester handed Janice her coffee. "Here, drink this. How are you feeling?"

"Thanks Chester. I feel like my head is about to fall off."

"Girl, when you showed up on my doorstep this morning, you were in pretty bad shape. I'm surprised you made it here safely. You really need to stop that drinking and driving."

"Yeah, yeah."

"I mean it Janice. You weren't making a lot of sense. Did you say Marvin was dead?"

"Yes."

"How did he die?

"All I know is what AJ told me. When I found out he . . ." Janice dropped her head and shook it from side to side.

"When you found out what?"

Janice wanted to tell Chester Marvin stole $370,000 of her money, but decided now wasn't a good time.

"Nothing. I was looking for Marvin, so I called AJ and that's when he told me he was dead. I went to the hospital to meet AJ and to talk to the doctors. The doctors said by the time Marvin got to the hospital, he was already dead, but they continued their efforts to revive him. Chester, they wouldn't even let me see him."

"Did AJ or the doctors say what happened?

"The doctors said it was a heart attack. AJ told me Marvin was at his house and he wasn't feeling well. He called 911 and when the paramedics came, they worked on him and took him to the hospital. Chester, I feel awful. It's all my fault."

"What are you talking about?"

"If I hadn't told you to change the locks, he would have been home and still alive."

"Janice, you couldn't have known this would happen."

Janice put her hand up in a stop motion.

"Janice, listen to me. This is not your fault. You couldn't save him any more than you could have saved Lainey."

Chester got up and walked over to the window. "Janice, I called Ma, Jasmine and Reginald. They should be here shortly."

"Okay. Chester, my open house is in a few days. Maybe I should just cancel it."

"No Janice. You've worked too hard on that. I know it's going to be difficult to have a funeral one day and an open house two days later, but you're strong. You can do this. I will help you. We will all help you."

As Janice thought about Marvin's unexpected death and the time she found Lainey's body, she took both of her hands and covered her face. "I need to call Dee."

"I already called her. She said she would come over after her appointment."

"I can't believe Marvin is really gone. Two days ago, he left me a message telling me he was going to pick up all of his clothes. That was the same day he died."

Chester hugged his sister. "I want to help you Sis, but I don't know what else I can do. I feel bad myself. The last encounter I had with Marvin, I punched him out."

Janice looked up at Chester. "What?"

"Never mind. That must be Ma and them."

Chester got up to answer his door. Beatrice, Reginald and Jasmine walked in Chester's tiny one bedroom apartment. Beatrice immediately hugged her daughter. "Janice, I'm so sorry. This is just terrible. What happened?"

"The doctors think he had a heart attack."

Beatrice shook her head. He's so young. Where were you when this happened?"

"I was at Ambiance. AJ called me. Marvin was with him when it happened."

Beatrice sat down on the black leather sofa and closed her eyes. "It's just too close to Lainey."

"I know Ma."

Jasmine sat down beside Janice. "Mommy, are you all right?"

"I will be sweetie."

Reginald hugged his mother. "I'm sorry Ma. Is there anything I can do?"

"No Son, but having you all here helps.

Janice's phone rang. She looked at the caller ID and saw that it was Paul. "Excuse me, I have to take this." Janice went into Chester's bedroom.

"Hello Paul."

"Honey, I'm so sorry about Marvin."

"Thank you."

"I'm also sorry about last night."

"It's okay. Things happen."

"Baby, I'm here for you. If you need anything, just call me."

"Thank you for calling. Take care Paul."

Paul let out a huge sigh. "You too Janice."

Janice went back into the living room with her family and sat down next to her mother. Beatrice put her hand on Janice's hand. "I guess we need to make arrangements."

"Yeah, I suppose so. I'll just go to the same place we went to for Lainey and get it over with."

Beatrice looked at her daughter. "Janice, I'm concerned about you. I know you're still coping with Lainey's death and with Marvin's happening so close, I think you should come and stay with me."

"No, Ma. I'm going home."

"Do you think that's wise?"

"I'll be fine Ma."

"Mommy, you can stay with me."

"Thank you sweetie, but I'll be fine at home. As a matter of fact, I need to go home and take a shower. Then, I will go make arrangements."

"Mommy, do you want me to drive you home?"

"Sure."

Janice looked at her mother looking back at her with concern in her eyes. "Ma, I'll be right back and then, we can go to the funeral home."

Beatrice looked around the room at Chester and Reginald. "Take your time Janice. We'll be here when you get back."

Jasmine drove her mother home to shower and change clothes. While Janice changed her clothes, she drank three glasses of wine.

An hour later, Janice and Jasmine were back at Chester's. Shortly thereafter, they all left for Jenkins Funeral Home. Janice made each arrangement as if she was a robot. Unlike when they made arrangements for Lainey, Janice showed no emotion and shared not one tear. The entire process took less than one hour. Marvin's funeral was set for the following Wednesday just two days before Ambiance's open house.

Janice noticed her family watched her every move. She felt at any moment, they were waiting for her to fall to pieces. Janice thought if they only knew what Marvin did to her, they wouldn't look so worried.

"Everything is done. Now, I have to get back to the office and finish working on some last many details for my open house."

"Surely you aren't going to work today. You are acting like it's just another day. Your husband just died. For goodness sake Janice, what's wrong with you?" Beatrice shook her head.

"Ma, it is another day and life goes on. My husband is gone and will never come back. What do you want me to do, sit home, cry my eyes out, and lose my business?" Janice thought right now, she was so mad that crying is the last thing she wanted to do. If Marvin wasn't dead already, she would kill him for stealing $370,000 from her account. Now that he's dead, she probably won't ever get her money back.

"No, of course not. I'm just worried about you Janice, that's all. I'm just worried about you."

"I know you are Ma, but I'm fine."

"Promise me that you'll take it easy and if you need anything that you will call one of us."

"I promise."

Janice left her family at Chester's house and drove to Ambiance. Antoine was there diligently working on the open house.

"Hey Antoine."

"Miss Perry, what are you doing here?"

"The same as you. I'm getting ready for the open house."

"I'm sorry to hear about your husband. These came for you."

Antoine brought in two bouquets of flowers. "The pretty roses and one white rose are from Mr. Davis and these Daisies are from that swelled up guy."

Janice half-heartedly smiled. "Thank you Antoine."

She read Paul's card first. "*I gotcha. Love Always, Paul.*"

Second, she read Brent's card. "*In deepest sympathy. If you need a shoulder to lean on, I'm here for you, Brent.*"

Janice put the cards away and tried to focus on the task at hand. The more she tried to focus on work, the less productive she became. Janice dialed AJ's number.

"Hello," AJ answered.

"AJ, this is Janice. I just want to let you know that I made arrangements for Marvin and the funeral will be held on Wednesday at the Jenkins Funeral Home. The death notice should be in the newspaper tomorrow."

"Janice, did you mention anything in the paper about Marvin's son and daughter?"

"Excuse me? I just found out he had a son, but I definitely didn't know about a daughter."

AJ quickly apologized. "I thought Marvin told you he has a daughter in Texas by his first wife."

"I also didn't know he was married before. I guess there's a lot I didn't know about Marvin. AJ let me ask you something. Marvin stole a large sum of money from me. Would you know anything about it?"

AJ hesitated before he said, "No, he never mentioned it to me."

"Would you tell me if he did?"

AJ's voice squeaked when he said, "Sure I would."

"Sure you would. I'll see you on Wednesday."

Janice hung up the phone and sat back in her brown leather chair. "Funerals have a way of bringing out the skeletons people have hidden in their closets. I wonder how many of Marvin's girlfriends, fiancées, ex-wives and other unknown children will show up at the funeral crying all over his body."

Janice got up from her desk and walked outside to smoke a cigarette. She looked up at the huge Ambiance sign. "Oh Lainey, I'm so sorry. I know you left me that money for me to do something good with it. I know Marvin has done many things, but I never thought he would steal from me. The money will find its way back to me. You'll see. With or without the money, I promise you, I will not lose Ambiance and I will make you proud of me."

78

Paul

Once again, Paul was at work and desperately tried to concentrate on business. His mind drifted back to last night's fiasco and the look Janice gave him right before she told him to leave her alone. Paul wondered if Janice received the flowers he sent her and how she was handling Marvin's death. As much as he wanted to hear her voice, at the moment, the best thing he could do was to give her space and hope that she would soon reach out to him.

Still unable to concentrate on any of his work, Paul shuffled papers back and forth on his desk. He laid his head back on his chair and closed his eyes. The first thing that popped in his mind was Brent's taunt, "Seems you lose all of your women to me."

Paul pushed back his chair, stood up and walked over to the window. "Brent being anywhere near Janice or Cynthia makes my blood boil. I could care less about him and Desiree, but Cynthia and Janice—never. Potential client my ass. All Brent wants to do is use and abuse Janice just like he does anyone he comes in contact with. I can't let that happen."

Paul went back to his desk and dialed Jarrod.

"Long time," Jarrod answered.

"Jarrod, my man, how's it going?"

"I can't complain. What can I do for you?"

"Glad you asked. Have you been driving Janice anywhere?"

"Just to a couple of places. She doesn't use me that often."

"I need your help with something. Between you and me, I'm worried about her. I need you to be my eyes and ears."

"If she won't use me, I don't know how."

"Yeah, that is going to be a problem. Let me worry about that. You just go over to Ambiance and camp out there."

"If that's what you want."

"Yes, that is what I want and Jarrod, I'll be the one paying you. I'm sure you will be more than pleased with the salary."

"Now you're talking. I'm on my way."

Paul smiled. "On second thought Jarrod, drop past my office before you go there. I just thought of how I'll get her to use you more."

"I'll be right there."

Out of nowhere, Paul felt energized and full of focus. He stuck his head out of his office. "Vivian, as soon as Jarrod arrives, send him in."

"Yes, Mr. Davis."

"Also, send two dozen long-stemmed red roses and one white rose over to Janice Perry at Ambiance. She's having an open house on Friday. Make sure they get there by Thursday. Don't forget, I'm giving you plenty of time."

"Is that your way of telling me I'm forgetful Mr. Davis?"

"I know you're a top notch assistant. It's so I won't forget."

"Oh."

Paul thought if the roses didn't arrive, that would tell him Vivian was still leaking information to Desiree and he would surely fire her.

When Jarrod walked in, Paul was looking out of the window.

"Looks like someone is in deep thought."

"Have a seat Jarrod."

Paul closed his door and joined Jarrod at his conference table. "Like I said over the phone, I'm worried about Janice and I need you to be my eyes and ears."

"I got that. What is it that you're looking for?"

"Nothing."

"Why are you spying on the woman?"

"I'm not spying on Janice. I'm just trying to protect her."

"Spying. Okay, who are you trying to protect her from?"

"From this guy." Paul handed Jarrod a picture of Brent.

Jarrod took the picture and looked at it closely. "He looks like Popeye."

Paul laughed. "He's bad news and I just want you to keep an eye on her to make sure she's safe."

"Is he trying to hurt her or something?"

"I wouldn't put it past him, but he plays a lot of mind games. This man uses and abuses everyone. I just don't want her hurt in any way."

"I got it."

Paul went to his desk and took out an envelope. "Now here is what will guarantee that Janice will use your services."

Jarrod took the envelope. "May I sir?"

"Be my guest."

Jarrod placed the piece of paper back into the envelope and smiled. "This should do it."

Paul handed Jarrod another envelope. Jarrod's eyes widened when he saw his advance payment for his services.

"Thank you."

"Jarrod, the thanks is all mines. I really appreciate this."

Satisfied with his plan to keep Janice safe, Paul concentrated on the many papers on his desk.

79

Janice

The first thing Jarrod saw when he pulled in front of Ambiance was Janice standing on the sidewalk smoking a Virginia Slims Menthol. "Those things are going to kill you."

"Hey Jarrod, what are you doing here?"

"Hey Janice, I've come bearing gifts."

Jarrod handed Janice the envelope Paul gave him. Janice threw away her cigarette and took the envelope. When she opened it, she looked at Jarrod and said, "A coupon."

Chauffer Janice Coupon

This coupon entitles you to three months of Chauffer Service with you in the Passenger's seat where you will be safely and comfortably driven to wherever you want to go.

Restriction—Must be fully enjoyed.

"I take it this is from Paul."

Jarrod hunched his shoulders. "Who else?"

"I tell you what Jarrod—I will use your services on one condition."

Jarrod smiled at Janice as he waited for her condition.

"While you are chauffeuring me around, you do not go back and tell Paul everything you see and hear. Do we have a deal?"

Jarrod laughed. "You and Paul think alike. "It's a deal."

"Great! You can start by taking me to Paul's office."

"Your chariot waits."

Jarrod opened the door for Janice and she slid into the back seat of the limo. She called Antoine to let him know she was leaving and to lock up if she was not back before he left.

Janice and Jarrod talked and laughed all the way to Paul's office. She liked Jarrod and Jarrod liked her. They both had a sense of humor, they both understood Paul had his own way of doing things and they both agreed that Paul had a good heart.

Jarrod pulled right in front of Paul's building.

"I'll only be about 15 minutes. I just want to thank him and show him that I'm using you."

"Using me?"

"You know what I mean."

As soon as Janice walked into Paul's office, she could feel the coldness coming from Vivian's stare.

"May I help you?" Vivian asked.

"No you cannot," Janice said as she walked right passed Vivian into Paul's office.

Vivian yelled, "You can't do that. Come back here!"

Janice opened Paul's door with Vivian behind her heel. She closed the door in Vivian's face and locked the door. Paul was on the phone and smiled at Janice when he saw her lock his door. Janice went over to Paul and turned his swivel chair towards her. As he tried to continue his phone conversation, Janice kissed him on his forehead, his left cheek, his right cheek, his lips, and then his neck, and rubbed his shoulders down to his waist. She could tell Paul found it hard to compose himself on the phone.

Paul chuckled. Janice smiled at him, took his pen out of his hand and wrote on his pad, "Thank you for my gift. Just know that Jarrod will not be your ears and eyes, just my chauffer. You're still in my heart."

Before she left, she kissed Paul on his cheek, and left him with a gigantic smile on his face.

By the time Janice made it downstairs, Paul was right behind her. Janice got into the limo and Paul followed suit. Both Janice and Paul laughed. Paul put his arms around Janice. "Jarrod, take us for a very, very long ride."

"Yes sir." Jarrod smiled.

For two hours, Jarrod drove Janice and Paul around Interstate 495 while they sat in the backseat and talked about everything. When Jarrod got two blocks from Paul's office, Janice stared at Paul. "How do you know Brent?"

"I could ask you the same?"

"I met him through an old friend of mine. He was interested in customer service training for his businesses."

"Customer service, huh? I know him through Desiree. The guy is bad news."

"You've told me. Don't you trust that I'm capable of handling myself?"

"As long as you have me, I'll always protect you."

"At the moment, I don't need protecting."

"What do you need Janice?"

"I need you to tell me the truth more than you lie. I need to know that you have my back instead of just having me on my back."

Paul looked into Janice's eyes. "I gotcha."

"Do you got me, got me?"

"I gotcha."

"Davis Building," Jarrod yelled out.

"I guess this is my stop," Paul said.

Before Paul got out, he kissed Janice long and passionately. He shook Jarrod's hand and headed into his building.

Jarrod looked at Janice in the backseat. Janice laid her head back on the seat and closed her eyes. What seemed like 10 minutes to Janice was 45 minutes and she was back in front of Ambiance.

"Ambiance Building," Jarrod yelled out.

"Mmm, thank you Jarrod. I won't need you tomorrow because I have a funeral to go to, but I will need you bright and early on Friday morning. So, be at my house at eight o'clock sharp. Here is my address."

"I'll be there Miss Perry."

"Bye Jarrod. I think I like being chauffeured."

"I guess you do. See you on Friday."

Janice walked into her office and plopped down in her chair. Most of the work day was gone and so was Antoine. She looked at the invoices he left for her to sign. Money dwindled fast and the money Marvin stole from her placed Janice in a delicate financial situation. As Janice signed the invoices and checks, she prayed that her open house will be a success and that none of Marvin's women show up to the funeral and make a scene.

Janice cleaned off her desk and grabbed her purse. On her drive home, at the last minute, she decided to stop by Paul's office to see if he wanted to have dinner.

Janice was in the lobby waiting for the elevator. To make sure her hair was in place, she looked at herself in her mirror. Janice was about to apply more lipstick when someone yanked her on the shoulder.

"I told you once and I'm not going to tell you again. Stay the hell away from my husband."

Janice turned around and looked at Desiree dressed in a long sequined gold gown with diamonds around her neck, on her ears and in her hair.

"I would appreciate it if you didn't put your hands on me. Isn't he almost your ex-husband?" Janice asked.

"Is that what he told you? Please, we've been married so long that Paul fails to remember that we try to stay apart, but we just end of getting right back together again. We just had a lover's quarrel, but it's over now. You're not the first little skank that has tried to come between us."

"Desiree, is it? I'm not a skank and I think I would like to hear it from Paul."

Janice walked away from Desiree and got on the elevator. Just as the doors were about to closed, Desiree stuck her arm between the doors. Once on the elevator, she pushed the stop button.

"Maybe, I didn't make myself clear. Paul and I are married and we are going to stay married. I will kill him before I let him leave me and anyone else that tries to come in between us. If I find out you were anywhere near him, I'll just have to use this."

Desiree reached into her purse and pulled out a 25 caliber Beretta and pointed it right at Janice's head.

Janice screamed, "You're crazy! When I tell Paul, he will have you locked up and put away."

Desiree waved the gun in Janice's face.

"You don't want to do that. If he ever tries to put me in jail, I'll just have to kill him and it will be your fault."

Desiree pushed the elevator to on again. "So, man stealer, are you going up or down?"

Janice briefly closed her eyes and pushed the button to the lobby."

"Excellent choice."

When Janice stepped off the elevator, she turned around to face Desiree. "One day, you will get exactly what you deserve."

"Oh darling, I'm going to get what I deserve right now, and that's a six-foot piece of pure chocolate by the name of Paul Davis. Run along dear. I'm sure you have some seminars or something to put on."

Desiree laughed in Janice's face and closed the elevator door.

Janice ran to her truck and looked over her shoulder. "I have to find a way to warn Paul, but he might do something that will probably get us both killed."

Not sure what to do next, Janice lit a cigarette and looked up at Paul's window. Janice's phone rang. She looked at the caller ID. *It's Paul.* "Paul!"

"No darling, it's Paul's wife. Are you still here? Do I need to give you another reminder to stay away from my husband? Remember, I got my eye on you. Wherever you go, I'll be there. Paul and I are busy, now skedaddle!"

Desiree slammed the phone down in Janice's ear. Janice started her engine and sped out of the parking lot.

80

Desiree

"Desiree, get the hell out!" Paul yelled.

"Not until I talk some sense into you about our daughter. Paul, you can't cut her off now. She's having our grandchild."

"I'm not her father, remember? Cynthia has made it perfectly clear that she doesn't want to be a Davis."

"Oh, darling, that's just hormones talking."

"I don't give a damn. She gets no more money from me and neither do you. So, if that's all you've come here for, I'm busy."

Desiree didn't budge. Paul picked up the phone to make a call. *He's calling that bitch.* With her hands on her hips, Desiree stood by the door and stared at Paul while he dialed the number.

"Why are you still here?"

"Are you calling that slut?"

"That's none of your damn business."

"You know she's seeing Brent."

Paul slammed down the phone. "No, she's not."

"Okay, believe what you want. I know for a fact she is."

"I'm not going to tell you again, get the hell out of here before I throw you in jail for getting on my nerves among other things."

Desiree walked back to Paul's desk. "Do you think I want to do the things I do? You make me do them."

Paul's eyebrows went up and laughed. "Woman, you are acting crazy. I can't make you do anything. If I could, we would still be married."

"We are still married and you and I will never get a divorce."

"Now, I know you're crazy."

"You go right ahead and keep pushing me Paul and I will just have to show you how crazy I can be."

"Desiree, I told you, I don't have time for this. Now either you go on your own or I'll have security throw you out."

"No need, I'm leaving. Just remember, I don't take too kindly to threats."

"Okay, I'll make you a promise then. I promise you that I'll personally see to it that you spend the rest of your life in a jail cell with your baby daddy for stealing from me and killing my brother."

Desiree leaned over Paul's desk and looked him directly in his eyes.

"I'll make you a promise too darling. The day I spend in jail will be the day that slut joins her husband and not mine."

"Are you threatening Janice?"

"No, I'm just making you a promise darling."

"Desiree, stay the hell away from her. Do you hear me?"

"Oh, settle down. I'm not going to kill her or anything, I'm just going to make her life a living hell that she wished she was dead!"

Desiree turned on her heels and walked out of Paul's office.

Paul yelled, "Desiree, Desiree!"

81

Janice

It was four o'clock in the morning and Janice was still awake. She wanted to return Paul's call, but decided to take heed to Desiree's very convincing threats. Janice tried to tell herself that it was all part of a very bad, alcohol induced dream only she hadn't gone to sleep yet. She looked over at the black suit hanging on her door. As much as she didn't want to believe it, Desiree's threats were as real as Marvin's funeral that was to begin in just a few hours.

Janice was not looking forward to another funeral. At first, she felt like she was burying Lainey all over again. Her emotions were all over the place until she remembered that it was the day she would bury Marvin and watch him take her $370,000 with him to his grave. Apart of Janice felt it was some type of payback for changing the locks and forcing him out of his home. The other part of her felt sad about the way things ended and hurt that Marvin thought so little of her that he stole from her like she was just a pawn in one of his many presentation scams.

Janice climbed into bed and hoped to at least fall asleep before the sun came up. When she closed her eyes, all she could see was Desiree shooting Paul, Lainey's body on her sofa, and Marvin lying in a casket.

For the time being, Janice gave up on sleep and opened her eyes. She stared up into the ceiling and allowed her thoughts to freely run through her mind. She thought about whether Marvin's harem would show up at the funeral, whether one or all would make a scene in front of her family and lastly, she thought about whether she could go through yet another funeral and come out with all of her faculties in tact.

Janice propped herself up in bed and turned on her TV. Two hours later, she finally drifted off to sleep only to wake up in three hours to the buzzing sound of her alarm.

Slowly, she dragged herself out of bed and went downstairs to make a pot of coffee. While she waited for the coffee to perk, she walked over to Marvin's room and stood in the doorway. Janice looked around at all of Marvin's belongings and remembered his message that AJ would pick them up on Thursday, the day he died.

Janice folded her arms as if she suddenly felt a chill. She went back into the kitchen and poured herself a cup of coffee with a splash of vodka. She looked down into her cup and then up at the clock on her wall. She rubbed her forehead and said, "My family will be here in one hour. This will give me the courage I need."

Before Janice went back upstairs, she put two more splashes of vodka into her cup and carried the bottle of vodka with her.

An hour later, Janice was dressed in black from head to toe and felt no pain. Minus the fact that at ten o'clock in the morning, she was already half drunk, she was fully ready to get through the funeral and face any chaos the day would bring.

Janice's door bell rang. She went to the door and flung it open to the concerned faces of Beatrice and Chester. "Right on time, come on in."

Beatrice immediately hugged her daughter. "How are you holding up dear?"

"I'm fine Ma."

"Hey Sis," Chester said.

"Hey yourself."

Beatrice saw dishes in Janice's sink and began to put them into the dishwasher.

"Ma, I'll do them later."

"Honey, I don't mind. Don't you worry about a thing. While we're at the funeral, Travis's crew will be here setting up the food for the repast."

Janice totally forgot about the repast. She hunched her shoulders and said, "I didn't plan for a repast because I wanted everything over and done with. I'm going to get some coffee. Would anyone like some?"

Chester frowned, walked over to Janice and whispered into her ear, "It looks like you've had enough coffee royales for all of us. Are you sure you're okay?"

"I'm fine. Sit down and take a load off."

Again, Janice's doorbell rang. This time, it was Reginald and Jasmine. After Janice hugged both of her children, she sat down next to Chester, drank her spiked coffee and watched everyone examine her as if she was under a microscope. "The car should be here shortly."

Everyone just nodded.

"Reggie, how's the investment business?" Chester asked.

"It's good. I can't complain."

"Well, I guess you'll be getting married soon and have someone to help you spend all of that money you're making."

"That's possible." Reginald laughed.

Janice smiled and turned her head to look at her son. "Are you trying to tell us something Reginald?"

"Ma, I was going to wait for another time to tell you, but yes, I have asked Layla to marry me."

Chester looked at Reginald and smiled. "Well nephew, what did she say?"

"Oh, she said yes."

Janice jumped to her feet and almost spilled her coffee. "That's wonderful! I'm so happy for you. Although I wasn't going to let her know it, as soon as I met her, I knew she was the one for you. I'll call Layla later. I have the perfect place for your wedding reception." Janice had Reginald's wedding planned in 10 minutes flat.

Chester shook Reginald's hand. For just a few minutes, Reginald's joyous news took the glumness out of the house.

"Mommy, the Family Car is outside," Jasmine yelled.

"Okay family, let's go."

Except for the gospel music that played on the radio, the ride to the funeral home was long and silent. The entire ride, Janice looked out of the window through her dark shades and thought about nothing in particular. Reginald and Jasmine checked their text messages while Beatrice and Chester stared at Janice.

The car pulled up to the funeral home and everyone quickly got out. Janice walked into the funeral home past all of the people she knew and some she didn't know. For several minutes, she stood in front of the casket and just stared down at Marvin until she saw a line begin to form behind her.

Janice sat down in the front row in between Chester and Beatrice. One by one people came up to pay their last respects to Marvin. Although Janice wasn't surprised, there were more women than there were men. She didn't recognize any of them except for Linda and her son. Through dark shades, Janice watched Linda pick up her son so he could kiss Marvin and then she did the same.

Linda turned around and walked up to Janice. "The least you could did was include MJ in the obituary. You knew Marvin was his daddy."

Beatrice stared at Linda and her son. Janice said nothing and continued to look straight ahead. Linda raised her voice. "I'm talking to you Mrs. Perry."

"This is not the time," Chester said as he stood up.

"This is exactly the time! I guess you're happy now that my son don't got no father. You never could stand the fact that Marvin was with me more than he was with you. You probably killed his ass anyway."

Chester stood an inch from Linda's face. "Like I said, this is not the time. Get out now before I throw you and your son out."

Linda rolled her eyes at Chester. "I'll go so Mrs. Perry can continue grief."

"You do that." Under his breath Chester said, "With your non-talking self."

Janice could feel her mother's shocked stare burn a hole in the side of her face. She continued to look straight ahead and said nothing.

Chester sat back down and put his arm around Janice. "Are you okay Sis?"

Janice just nodded. Behind the dark shades, no one could see that most of the time, Janice had her eyes closed. She felt the effects of the vodka and counted from one to whatever to block out everything and everyone around her.

AJ and five other pall bearers picked up the casket and walked out of the funeral home. Janice followed behind the casket and again, looked straight ahead. As she walked past the many people, Janice thought everyone felt sorry for her after they witnessed Linda's display of "you killed my baby daddy."

The car pulled into the graveyard. Like a robot, Janice got out and sat down in the chair. After 20 minutes, Marvin was finally laid to rest. Janice let out a huge sigh of relief that the funeral was finally over. On the drive to her house, Janice closed her eyes and thought if only she could skip the repast.

She looked at all of her family and not much of Marvin's family in every square feet of her house. She couldn't wait until she was alone again.

"Hey Sis, how are you holding up?" Chester asked.

"I'm fine."

"Yeah, I can see how fine you are. Any more fine and you'll be flat on your face. Go eat something."

"I'm not hungry."

"I'm going to fix you a plate anyway and you're going to eat it."

Janice ignored Chester and walked to the other side of the room to where Dee stood.

"Hey girl, how are you holding up?"

Janice thought if one more person asks her that question, she would fall out on the floor and give them what they want.

"I'm good."

"What do you say we go run over Linda and her son?"

Janice laughed. Dee got a little closer so no one could hear their conversation. "I can't believe that chicken head had the nerve to come up in the funeral home and make a scene like that. I tell you, that Marvin sure knows how to pick them. No offense Janice."

"None taken."

"Let's take a walk outside."

"Okay, I need to smoke anyway."

"Hey Janice, who is that?"

"Who?" Janice turned around.

"My future husband."

Janice looked at the young man that got out of a black SUV. "It's so many people here. I don't know. I just assumed most of them are Marvin's friends or just people that knew him."

The young man walked over to Janice and Dee. "Hello Janice, I'm very sorry for your loss. My name is Roberto Goode. You hired me as security for your open house."

"Oh, yeah, that's right."

"I just wanted to pay my respects."

"How nice of you Roberto. Thank you. This is my friend, Dee Phillips."

"It's very nice to meet you Roberto," Dee said as she looked Roberto up and down in places she shouldn't have looked.

Janice knew exactly what her friend was thinking and smiled at her.

"Roberto, there is plenty of food and drinks in the house. Please help yourself."

"Thank you, I will and I will also see you on Friday."

"I'll see you Friday too Roberto," Dee yelled.

Roberto turned around, smiled at Dee and said, "I look forward to it."

Dee laughed and looked at Janice. "Keep a date open, that's my next husband."

"You said that about Brent."

"Girl please, Brent was too busy looking up in your face. I called him once and he brushed me off. That man is interested in you. Are you seeing him?"

"No, but I did run into him at the hotel the other night while Paul was there with his family."

Dee's mouth flew open.

"Brent and Paul got into a fist fight."

"See, I told you that bastard was a married, married man and he had the nerve to be at the funeral."

"Paul was at the funeral?"

"Yeah, you didn't see him? He was in the back looking all handsome and married. All he did was stare at you."

"Was he there when Linda was acting like a fool?"

"Yeah, I saw him shake his head and look over at you."

"Dee, it's not like that."

"Janice, let me break it down for you."

"Not today Dee."

"Okay, but we will have this conversation later."

Janice let out a deep breath. "I'm sure we will. Let's go back inside."

Hours later, Janice was left with plenty of food and plenty of quietness. She changed into her pajamas and went downstairs into the family room. With a drink in one hand and a cigarette in the other, Janice sat down on the sofa. Again, she thought about how her life quickly changed. "I'm no longer in a marriage I don't want. I'm now a widow and my dead husband left me almost broke with plenty of reminders of his countless infidelities. That Linda acted like a pure fool at the funeral accusing me of killing Marvin and taking away her son's father. At least I don't have that baby mama drama anymore. Unlike Linda, the other fiancée seemed to have class and just viewed Marvin's body and left. I wonder why AJ and Marvin's sister didn't come back to the house. Dee said Paul was there. For the life of me, I don't remember seeing him at the funeral. I guess he was there to support me. Maybe, I should call him. No, I can't call him."

All of a sudden, Janice felt alone. Marvin was gone and she couldn't risk Paul's safety by continuing to see him. Janice took a huge gulp of her vodka and lit another cigarette. She could feel her strength dwindling, but knew she had to stay strong and find a way to get through her tribulations. Her open house was in two days and she had to get it together and keep it together.

Janice put out her cigarette and dumped the rest of her drink down the drain. She then got down on her knees and prayed to God that He gives her triple strength and keeps her, her family and Paul safe, happy and healthy.

82

Desiree

"Brent, why haven't you returned any of my calls?"

"Diva, do you know what time it is?"

"Yeah, it's almost noon. What are you still doing in bed?"

"I've had a rough couple of days. What do you want?"

"I want to know how our plan is going. It's time to put some pressure on that home wrecking bitch."

"Diva, not now, the woman just lost her husband."

"Now is the perfect time. She's vulnerable, not to mention she is now free and clear to be with Paul. No, now is the perfect time to strike. Do you remember all of those reservations we made?"

"What about them?"

"I want you to cancel them one by one."

"Diva, you do realize she can keep the deposits."

For a brief moment, Desiree was quiet. "She can have the measly $10,000, but the most important thing is she will lose five times that amount. There is no way she'll be able to replace six months of reservations just like that."

"Leave the woman alone. She's not seeing Paul anymore. Unlike you, Janice really seems like a nice, decent person."

"Don't tell me you're falling for her too."

"Diva, all I'm saying is that it looks like you have succeeded in splitting them up. Go find somebody else to torment like a new employer. You know your money is getting low." Brent laughed.

"I haven't worked in all of these years and I don't plan on starting now."

"Well, some of us poor souls have to work for a living. Why do you need to mess with her business anyway?"

"Because I want to. I want her to have nothing, not my husband, not her business, not you, nothing."

"Me? What do I have to do with this? Diva, do you still love me? Ah, isn't that sweet. Diva still loves me. Come on over here Diva Devil and show me how much you love ole Brent."

Desiree was tempted but fought against it. "Brent, don't flatter yourself."

"Your loss. Since you got me up, I think I will go do a little shopping."

"Shopping? What are you going to buy me?"

"Why would I buy you anything? You won't even take what I want to give you because you're still stuck on stupid in love with Drunk Davis."

"I don't love Paul and I don't love you."

"Who do you love Diva?"

"I love me, my daughter and my money. Paul has financially cut off Cynthia and I have to find a way to make it up to her and get my millions back."

"I see you're still on that lost cause. How do you propose getting back your millions? By ruining that sweet woman's business?"

"Sweet woman! You are falling for that tramp! She doesn't want you. She only has eyes for Paul."

"We'll see about that."

Desiree was spitting bullets when she heard yet another one of her men had fallen for Janice.

"Brent, get your head out of the clouds and stick to our plan."

"That's your plan Diva. I have my own plans and they don't include sabotaging Janice's business or hurting one hair on her pretty head. That woman has potential. She'll be worth millions before you know it and I plan to be right by her side whereas you will be worth . . . How should I put this? You will be worth $2 just as you were when I met you, except you will be an old $2 Ho."

"You ungrateful son of a bitch!"

Brent hung up on Desiree. She dialed Brent's number again, but he didn't pick up the phone. Desiree threw her phone down and screamed, "I don't need you. I don't need any of you! I'll just show up tomorrow at her open house and do it my damn self. Brent Foster, if it's the last thing I do, I'll make you and that little tramp pay and I do mean dearly."

Desiree searched through her luggage and garment bags for something glamorous to wear to Janice's open house. She pulled out everything. "Damn, this won't do and I can't go to the house. My credit cards are almost maxed out and my savings is down to $200,000. Well, I guess this call for an emergency shopping spree."

Desiree showered, put on her shopping gear and headed out to the boutiques to find the perfect killer outfit. She went from shop to shop until she completed her ensemble. On her way out, she came across a baby store. Desiree looked at all of the cute tiny outfits, furniture and trinkets for babies. "My grandchild must have the finest of everything."

By the time Desiree left the store, she purchased over $10,000 worth of baby clothes, furniture, books—you name it, and Desiree bought it. She left the shop with 10 bags and paid the delivery guy an extra $100 if he delivered the rest of the items to Cynthia's house within the hour.

Desiree loaded her packages into her car and drove to Cynthia's house. She was very hopeful that her surprise of baby gifts would bring her closer towards making a mends. When she pulled into Cynthia's driveway, she saw Cynthia's car. "Good, she's home."

Desiree ran to the door loaded down with all of her goodies for her unborn grandchild. Both anxious and nervous, she rang the doorbell. After a few minutes went by with no answer, Desiree rang the doorbell a second time. Still, there was no answer. Desiree's excitement was turned into disappointment. When Desiree was about to leave, Cynthia swung open the door. "Mother, what are you doing here?"

Desiree frowned when she saw Cynthia dressed in her bathrobe and hair uncombed. "Cynthia Darling, I've come to see you. Have you been crying?"

"No, I just got up."

Desiree looked around Cynthia's house and noticed the dirty dishes in the sink, clothes thrown around the floor, and uneaten food on the stove and counter. "Cynthia, what's going on here?"

"Nothing."

"Something is definitely wrong. I know what will cheer you up. Look Cynthia, I have some lovely things for the baby. Look at all of the stuff I've bought."

Desiree laid out all of her purchases on the table for Cynthia to see. Cynthia barely looked at them and walked to the refrigerator to get a soda. "Do you want anything?" Cynthia asked.

"No. Cynthia Darling, do you like them? There's more. The truck should be here shortly with the rest of the things."

Without looking at the baby items or Desiree, Cynthia said, "That's nice Mother. If you don't mind, I would like to go back to bed."

"As a matter of fact, I do mind. Your house is a mess and so are you. I've just brought you gifts for your baby worth thousands of dollars and that's all you have to say. What is the matter with you?"

Cynthia threw her soda against the wall. "Money, money, money! Is that all you people think about? I don't want your damn money. I don't want Daddy's money and I don't want these stupid baby gifts. Just get the hell out of here!"

"Don't you talk to me like that. I am still your mother."

"Don't remind me. You make me sick. You've lied to me my entire life and took away the only father I've ever known and now I've lost . . ."

"You've lost what?"

"Nothing, just go!"

"I'm not going anywhere until you tell me what's going on."

Cynthia grabbed the baby clothes from the table, opened the door and slung them into the front yard. "Get out. Take this stuff with you and don't ever come back. As far as I am concerned, I don't have a mother and thanks to you, I don't have a father. You will never get anywhere near my child. Now, just go!"

Desiree began to cry. She picked up the clothes from the yard and left. As she backed out of the driveway in high speed, she almost ran into the delivery man with the rest of the baby items. Desiree stopped and got out of her car. "Just take everything back to the store. I'll be by later to get a refund."

The delivery man looked puzzled.

"I just lost my grandchild."

"I'm sorry to hear that Ma'am. I'll take them back."

Desiree dialed Paul.

"Davis Graphics," Vivian answered.

"Vivian, put Paul on the phone."

"Desiree, he told me not to put through any of your calls."

"Vivian, you stupid fool! Put Paul on the damn phone now!"

"But I can't."

"If you don't put him on the phone, I'll come down there and pull out every strand of hair you have and tell him everything you've done. Now, do it!"

Vivian put through Desiree's call and hung up before Paul answered. "Paul Davis."

"Paul, something is wrong with Cynthia.

Paul was quiet.

"Do you hear me? Something is wrong with our daughter."

"Your daughter has made it perfectly clear that I'm not her father."

"For one moment, will you stop feeling sorry for your ass and listen to me. I just came from her house and it's in shambles. She looked like hell. I think she and Brian are having problems. I'm really worried about her."

"Then, I suggest you call Brent."

"You can't mean that. Paul, Paul."

When Desiree realized Paul hung up on her, she yelled, "I swear if anything happens to Cynthia, I will kill you Paul. I will kill you!"

Desiree flung herself over her steering wheel. She could feel herself losing control as well as losing everything and everyone she once held dear to her heart. She needed someone to comfort her just until she found her way back to more stable ground. Desiree thought about calling Brent, but changed her mind. She wiped her tears away and dialed Roberto.

"Hello," Roberto answered.

"Roberto Darling, how are you?"

"I'm good. What do you want Desiree?"

"I want you. I need to see you."

"You want to see me or do you want to use me? Desiree, I loved you, but you didn't want my love. I've moved on now. I suggest you do the same. Have a good life." Roberto hung up on Desiree.

Again, the tears flowed down her cheeks. Desiree's world was crumbling down all around her with no signs of stopping. Desiree couldn't remember the last time or if any time that she felt this way. All she knew was she didn't like the feeling of being alone and out of control. With no one else she could think of to call, Desiree put her car in gear and drove back to the hotel.

Once inside her room, she threw her packages and purse on the bed. For a few moments, she stared at the gun that slid out of her purse. She picked up the gun and aimed it at the wall and imagined she was getting rid of everyone who got in the way of her happiness. Slowly, Desiree lowered the gun and placed it back into her purse. "I need a nap. Maybe when I wake up, things will be clearer."

Desiree laid across the bed and mumbled, "There is one thing I'm definitely clear about. Tonight at the open house, that bitch will get the surprise of her life."

83

Paul

Paul yelled, "Vivian!"

Nervously, Vivian answered, "Yes Mr. Davis" and ran into his office.

"Didn't I tell you not to put through any of Desiree's calls?"

"Yes, but she said it was an emergency about Cynthia. I thought you would want to take the call."

"You thought wrong. The next time you don't follow my instructions, you will find yourself out of a job. Do you understand me?"

Vivian hung her head down and said, a meek "Yes sir."

Paul picked up his contract on his desk and glanced at it. Without looking up at Vivian, he asked, "Now, did you send the flowers to Janice Perry?"

"Yes sir."

"When did they arrive?"

"I told them they had to be there yesterday."

"Call her office and confirm that she received them.

Vivian was still standing in front of Paul's desk. "Why are you still here?"

In tears, Vivian ran to her desk.

After she confirmed Janice's receipt of her flowers, Vivian slowly walked back into Paul's office. "Mr. Davis."

"What is it Vivian?"

"The flowers were delivered yesterday."

Paul didn't answer and continued to work. Vivian turned around and walked back to her desk. Paul threw his pen down on his desk, walked over to his window and looked out into his parking lot. "Janice should have called me by now. She could at least call to say thank you for coming to the funeral or for the flowers or call just because she wants to hear my voice. I'm tired of waiting for her to reach out to me and I can't stand not knowing how she's doing. I need to warn her about Desiree's threats."

Paul dialed Janice's office.

"Thank you for calling Ambiance, Antoine speaking, how may I help you?"

Paul shook his head at Antoine practically singing out his words. "Is Janice in?"

"Who may I say is calling Miss Perry?"

"Paul Davis."

"Just a moment Mr. Davis, I'll see if she wants to talk to you. I mean, I'll see if she's available."

"Hello Paul," Janice answered.

"Hey baby, I hadn't heard from you. I was getting worried."

"I'm sorry. I've been meaning to call you. Thank you for the flowers."

"You're welcome. How are you doing?"

"I'm hanging in there. Dee told me you were at the funeral. Thank you for coming."

"Baby, I was there to support you. I guess you didn't see me with those dark shades you were wearing."

"Yeah, I guess not."

Paul noticed Janice's voice lacked its normal cheerfulness and decided to change the subject to something more pleasant. "Are you excited about your open house tonight?"

"Yes, I am. I'm just a little tired."

"That's understandable. Sweetheart, where in the world did you get your singing assistant?"

"Leave Antoine alone. He's a very good assistant." Janice laughed.

"Baby, he needs to be more professional and put some base in his voice."

"Like you sound in the morning?"

"Yeah, like I sound in the morning you woke up in my arms. I wish you could wake up in my arms every morning."

"Yeah, just like that."

Paul let out a long sigh. "Well, I know you're busy, so I won't hold you up any longer. I'll see you tonight."

"Paul, I'll understand if you can't make it."

"Why wouldn't I make it?"

"With Marvin death, I thought we shouldn't see each other right now." Paul rubbed his head and said nothing.

"Paul, are you still there?"

"Yes, I'm still here. If that's what you want, but I will be at your open house tonight. After that, I will give you the space you need. Is that okay Miss Perry?"

"That's fine Mr. Davis."

"Goodbye Janice."

"Goodbye Paul."

Paul hung up the phone and put his head in both of his hands. Just as Dante walked in, Paul yelled, "Damn."

"Should I come back at another time?" Dante asked.

"Boy, don't you know how to knock?"

Dante went back out and knocked on the door.

"Dante, what do you want?"

"I wanted to tell you that Janice sent me an invitation to her open house. Kim and I are going. Are you going?"

"Yeah, I'll be there."

Dante sat down in the chair in front of Paul's desk.

"What's eating you? I thought you would be all excited that your Wow Woman is having her big night."

"I am."

"You don't sound like it."

"Dante close the door. When is the last time you've seen or talked to your sister?"

"I talked to her about two weeks ago. Why?"

"Desiree saw her today. She said Cynthia looked like hell and her house was in shambles. Desiree seems to think Cynthia and Brian are having problems. Would you know anything about that?"

"No, Cynthia didn't mention anything to me."

"What did you two talk about?"

"She was just talking about how happy she is and her baby. She thinks it's a boy, nothing out of the ordinary."

"Did she say anything about me?"

"Just that you disowned her and cut her off financially."

"Did she tell you why?" Paul smiled.

"She said you got mad because she wanted to share her news about the baby with her other father and you punched him out." Dante smiled. "Is that true?"

"Something like that. I'm just trying to protect the people that I love and it seems that every time I turn around, someone is out to get Cynthia and Janice."

Dante had a puzzled look on his face. "Who's out to get Janice?"

"Nobody, Desiree came in here the other day like a mad woman and threatened to kill me and Janice."

"Do you believe her?" Dante asked.

"Son, she had this crazed look in her eyes. I don't know what to believe." "Did you warn Janice?"

"I was, but she told me she needed space so I didn't say anything. I have Jarrod keeping a close eye on her. He will protect her, but I think Desiree was just running off at the mouth. What do you think?"

"You know how I feel about Desiree. The woman is capable of anything and everything."

"I'm no good here. I think I'm going over to the condo and lie down until Janice's open house."

"Okay Dad."

"Hey Dante, give your sister a call and see what's going on with her."

"All right Dad."

"I'll see you tonight."

Paul threw some papers into his briefcase, grabbed his jacket and left his office. "Vivian, I'm leaving for the day. If you need me, you know how to reach me."

"Yes sir."

"Vivian, I'm sorry for yelling at you earlier."

Vivian just nodded and continued to type her letter.

Paul walked to his condo and hoped the fresh air will clear his mind. On his way there, he called Jarrod. "Jarrod, my man. How is everything going?"

"I can't complain."

"How is driving Miss Janice?"

Jarrod laughed. "Pretty good. Three months have gone by rather quickly."

"Any plans to stay on?"

"She hasn't asked me yet, but you know once you get a taste of ole Jarrod chauffeuring you around, there's no going back to the steering wheel."

Paul laughed. "I'm counting on it. Are you going to be at the open house tonight?"

"Yeah, I'm going to take her home in a few minutes and come back to get her at six o'clock."

"Good, I need you to keep a close eye on her."

"Don't tell me you want me to spy on her again. You know she's on to you."

"No, it's nothing like that. I just need you to make sure no one hurts her."

"Who would want to hurt Janice? Is she in any kind of danger?"

"Yes, no . . . I'm not sure, but just in case, I need you to keep a closer eye on her and make sure she's never alone."

"I'll do my best."

Paul raised his voice. "Jarrod, I need you to do better than that."

"This sounds serious."

"Jarrod, I think her life may be in danger."

"Does Janice know?"

"No, and I don't want her to know either. If this whole thing turns out to be Desiree just venting, then we would have worried Janice for nothing."

"Desiree is trying to hurt Janice?"

"Yeah, she made some threats the other day that has me concerned."

"If it came from Desiree, I'd be worried. No offense, but that woman isn't wrapped too tight."

"None taken. I'll see you tonight."

Paul walked in his condo, threw his brief case down on the sofa, and headed straight to his bar. Between thinking about Cynthia, Janice and Desiree, his head was about to explode. Paul kicked off his shoes, turned on his Jazz, laid on his bed and hoped the smooth sounds and the warm effects of the vodka will ease some of the stress before he headed out to Janice's open house.

84

Janice

"Hey Miss Perry, are you ready for your open house?"

"Antoine, are you ready for the open house?"

"Yes, I guess so."

Janice looked at the rim of Antoine's brightly colored underwear that showed above his tight fitting pants and thought about how she was going to address it.

"Antoine, tonight, I need you on your best behavior and dressed in a suit that fits."

Antoine sucked his teeth.

"Don't suck your teeth at me."

"Sorry Miss Perry."

"We have to be very professional. *We* are the faces of Ambiance."

Antoine spoke with a heavy base in his voice. "I understand. Tonight, I'll even talk like this."

Janice laughed. "You'll be fine. I need you back here no later than 6:45. Now get out of here and rest up. We have a big night ahead of us."

Jarrod stuck his head in Janice's door. "Get a move on lady. Your chariot waits."

"Hey Jarrod, have a seat. I need to talk to you about something."

"What's on your mind?"

"Well, as you know, my three-month coupon is up."

"Already? Time does fly when you're being chauffeured around by the finest."

"Anyway, within that time, you have become very valuable to me, not to mention a good friend." Janice looked up towards the ceiling. "For some reason, I have grown accustomed to being chauffeured around by the finest."

"Jarrod said, "Go on."

"Although I would only need you a few days out of the week, I really want you to stay on and be apart of Ambiance."

Janice handed Jarrod a slip of paper. "I know the amount is probably not as large as the amount Paul paid you, but keep in mind that I will not be using you as much."

"You shouldn't be using me at all."

"Jarrod, just look at the figure."

"Janice, how much is not as much?"

"I foresee using your services about four days out of the week."

Jarrod looked at the figure and smiled. "I like you too girl. You know I'll stay on and if you need to use me more, we can work out something."

"Great. Now please drive me home."

"Then get your cheap butt up and come on."

"Cheap? You call $500 cheap?"

"You didn't see what Paul paid me?"

"Whatever Jarrod. Paul paid you for other services, like spying."

"Get in the car woman." Jarrod laughed.

Janice got in the limo and thought what if Desiree showed up tonight and tried to ruin her big night or hurt Paul. "Jarrod, do you know Bernard, Paul's chauffer?"

"Yeah, we're buddies. Why do you ask?"

"Can you do me a favor?"

"What, you want to hire him for the other three days?"

"No, nothing like that. Can you ask Bernard to keep a closer eye on Paul when he's with him? You know . . . make sure he's all right."

Jarrod looked in his rear view mirror at Janice. "Is Paul in some kind of danger?"

"He might be. I don't want to alarm him. I don't want you to tell him anything that I'm about to tell you. Okay?"

"Okay, lay it on me."

"After you drove us around that day, I came back to Paul's office to see if he wanted to have dinner with me. Desiree was in the lobby. We got on the elevator together and she pulled a gun on me."

"She did what?"

"You heard me. She pulled a gun on me. She went on and on about she and Paul were going to stay married and she would kill him before she let him leave her. She then said if she finds out I was anywhere near him, she would just have to use her gun. I told her she was crazy and Paul will see to it that she was locked up and put away."

"What did she say?"

"She told me if Paul ever tried to put her in jail that she would kill him and it would be my fault. After that, I got in my truck and drove home as fast as I could. Ever since that happened, I just stayed away from Paul. Today, I finally spoke to him and just told him I needed space. It's killing me, but I don't want to get the man killed."

"Damn, that woman is crazy. Janice, don't you worry about anything tonight except your open house. When I come back to pick you up, I want you to look beautiful and come out without a care in the world. I'll talk to Bernard and I'll see you at six o'clock sharp."

"Thanks Jarrod. You're a good friend."

As soon as Janice opened her door, she kicked off her shoes, poured herself a glass of wine, turned on her Jazz and waited for the smooth sounds to soothe her aching head. Janice looked at the clock. She had four hours to relax before her open house. She laid her head back on the sofa and talked to her dead sister. "Lainey, tonight is the night. It's going to be a success and I know you'll be there."

Janice planned to relax, but she spent the last two hours on the phone talking to her family, friends and associates about her open house. "Where did the time go?"

Janice hopped into the shower, came out refreshed and ready for her big night. Wrapped up in towel, she sat down on the side of her bed. Out of the blue, she felt as if her stomach was tied into knots. "What if something goes wrong? What if nobody shows? It has to be a success."

Janice lit a cigarette and tried to calm her nerves. "I need my Mama."

"Hi Ma."

"Hi Janice. Are you getting ready for your big night?"

"Yeah, are you still coming?"

"Yes, I am. Chester is picking me up."

"Good."

"Janice tonight is going to be a success. They will all love you as I do. Then, you'll make all of this money and leave your poor old mother behind. All I say is don't forget where you came from."

As Janice listened to her mother's reassuring words, she felt better. "I won't. I'll just take you with me."

"No, I think I'll just stay here."

"Hey Ma, have you gotten that housekeeper and chef yet?"

Beatrice let out a hearty laugh. "You know, today, I was just thinking about that."

"Why don't you? You know you're a millionaire now."

"Sometimes I forget I have that money. I haven't spent a dime of it yet."

"Well, maybe it's time you do. How about next week, we put an ad in the paper?"

"Oh, Janice, that's so much. Besides, the house isn't that big."

"Hey, we can always get you a bigger house. I'm serious Ma. Think about it."

"I will. Now you go get ready and I will see you at the Variance."

"At the what? You mean Ambiance." Janice laughed.

"That's what I said."

"See you later Ma."

After Janice talked to her mother, she felt much better. "Now, it's time to get beautiful."

Janice put on her sexy undergarments, sat down at her makeup table and carefully applied her makeup. To give her hair more body, she put in a few more curls. Next, she put on her long dangling earrings and slipped on her black evening dress with sequins around the cleavage. Janice then stepped into her black peek-a-boo toe patent leather pumps and looked carefully at herself in the mirror. "Very nice, if I say so myself."

Janice changed her purse and looked around to make sure she didn't forget anything. "I almost forgot the most important thing."

Janice sprayed on Knowing and said, "Now, I'm done."

Janice walked down the stairs and sang, "I feel pretty." When she got to the bottom of the stairs, she saw Jarrod pull into the driveway. Janice closed her eyes, said a quick prayer, grabbed her jacket, and stepped out the door.

Jarrod held open the car door for Janice and whistled. "Girl, you clean up nice."

"Thank you kindly sir."

"Here, I got you something." Jarrod handed Janice a shiny red gift bag.

"What did you get me? Janice smiled as she looked into the bag and saw a bottle of Moet.

"Oh, thank you Jarrod. We'll keep it to toast after the open house."

"Are you nervous Janice?"

"Just a little."

"You'll be an instant hit. Just be yourself and everyone will love you just as we do."

"Ah Jarrod, I love you too. Hey, did you do that favor for me?"

"Janice, all you need to be thinking about is your open house. The answer to your question is yes, I spoke to Bernard and he's going to keep his eyes open and protect your Paul."

"Great."

Satisfied with Jarrod's answer, Janice sat back in her seat and enjoyed the ride.

"Here we are Miss Instant Success. In 30 minutes, this parking lot will be full," Jarrod said.

Janice got out and kissed Jarrod on the cheek before she opened the doors to Ambiance. She stood in the lobby and looked around at all of the decorations. The Jazz band she hired already set up. The people from Elaine's were cooking and some put up tables while others put on linens.

"Mommy, you're here."

"Jasmine, what are you doing here so early?"

"I thought you could use a hand."

"Aren't you sweet and yes, I can. Is Antoine here yet?"

"He's in the back. He's funny."

"I know. What does he have on?"

In his deep voice, Antoine said, "I have on a black pin-striped suit. How do you like me now?"

Janice laughed and hugged Antoine. "You look fiercely handsome."

"Thank you Miss Perry and you look like you're ready to win the hearts of everyone who walk through that door."

"Thank you. Let's go back to my office. I have a few things to go over. Here is the guest list. Antoine, make sure you check off their names and most importantly, do not let anyone in who is not on this list unless of course you know them."

Janice thought Antoine looked a little nervous. She remembered whenever Antoine ran into confrontations, he got flustered. Janice hoped tonight wouldn't be the same way, but was glad that Jasmine decided to come early.

"This place can only hold so many people. Is security here yet?" Janice asked.

"Yeah, all of the handsome men in blue are here."

"Settle down Antoine. You too Jasmine. I believe Dee has her eye on one of them."

"Dee needs to sit her old butt down." Antoine turned his head.

"Hey, we're the same age."

Antoine and Jasmine laughed. "What do you want me to do Mommy?"

While Antoine's head was turned, Janice winked at Jasmine. "You can keep Antoine company at the door."

"Okay Mommy." Jasmine smiled.

Janice's hands were sweaty and the knots in her stomach returned. She grabbed a napkin and smiled as she saw Roberto walk towards her. "Hi Roberto. How are you?"

"I'm fine. Are you ready for tonight?"

"As ready as I'm going to get."

"Janice, is your friend going to be here tonight?"

"You mean Dee?"

Roberto shook his head.

"She'll be here." Janice smiled.

"Can you tell her I said, Hello?"

Janice saw Dee walk towards them. "You can tell her yourself."

As soon as Dee walked up, she said, a very friendly "Hello Roberto."

"Hi Dee. You look very nice."

"Thank you and you look very strong and blue."

Roberto cleared his throat and smiled. "I'll see you ladies later. Good luck Janice."

Janice looked at Dee and laughed. "Strong and blue, what was that?"

"Girl, he caught me off guard."

"Lucky for you, he likes you and didn't notice that clever comment you made. Go sit at the reserved table. Ma, Chester and the rest of the family will be sitting there."

"Good luck Janice."

"Thank you Dee."

At 7:15, people trickled into Ambiance. At 7:30, people covered almost every inch of the ballroom. Janice looked at Antoine and wondered if he could handle it, but surprisingly, he did very well. Jasmine was the perfect hostess. She welcomed guests, gave them literature about Ambiance and stayed close to Antoine.

Janice stood in the back of the ballroom out of sight in a corner and watched Antoine handle the people that stood in line. She smiled when she saw Paul handsomely dressed in a khaki colored suit.

"Paul Davis."

"Oh, you're Mr. Davis."

"And, you're Antoine. Very nice to meet you Antoine. That's a nice suit you're wearing. It goes with the deep voice."

"Thank you Mr. Davis."

"Chester Scott."

Jasmine gave Chester a little shove. "Oh, Chester get in here."

"Jasmine, what are you doing at the front door?"

"I'm helping out Mommy."

Chester mocked Jasmine. "I'm helping out Mommy. Girl, you know you still sound like you're four years old, calling your mother Mommy."

"She likes it. Hi Grandma. Do you like my work?"

"Hi baby, did you do all of this?" Beatrice asked.

"Yep."

Beatrice looked around and almost cried when she saw how beautiful everything looked. "It's beautiful Jasmine. Where's your mother?"

"Here I am," Janice said as she hugged Beatrice and walked her to the reserved table.

At 8:15, Ambiance was full. People drank, mingled, smiled and had a good time. Janice looked at Jarrod walk up to Jasmine and Antoine.

"Hey you two, how's it going?" Jarrod asked.

Jasmine said, "Hey Jarrod. It's going great. Do you see all of the people here?"

"Yeah, the parking lot is full. Well, you two carry on. I'm going to get a drink."

Jasmine waved her finger at Jarrod. "Oh, no. Don't you be drinking and driving my Mommy around."

"Girl, one drink won't stop me from driving your *Mommy* home safely. If I get drunk, I'll give you the keys and you can drive her home."

"I don't think so. I plan to get my drink on as soon as I leave this door."

"Then who will drive you home?" Jarrod smiled.

"You." Jasmine laughed.

At 8:30, the music was lowered and Janice was about to make her debut. Per her mother's instructions, Jasmine closed the doors to the ballroom.

Janice forgot her notes and was on her way to her office when she heard Antoine say, "I'm sorry, your name is not on the list."

Janice peeked around the tree and saw Antoine's nose turned up. She started to go over to help him, but when she saw Desiree dressed in a silk, off white pants suit with diamonds sparkling around her ears, neck and on her silk hat stand in front of Antoine with her finger in his face, she decided to look for Roberto. When she saw that Jasmine already walked over and stood beside Antoine, she said, "Good."

"Ms. Davis, like I said, your name is not on the list and I can't let you in."

"Look darling, it's Mrs. Davis and I have 12 reservations in this place and you damn well better let me in."

"We thank you, but I still can't let you in."

"I want to speak to the owner Janice Perry. Tell her to get her ass out here right now and let me in."

Janice took a drink of her wine. "Damn, Paul's in there. I wonder if she has her gun. Where is Roberto?"

For a brief moment, Antoine appeared flustered and lost the base in his voice. "Miss Perry is not available."

"That solves that problem, I'll just go in."

With his slim body, Antoine blocked Desiree's entrance.

"Move, you little punk."

Antoine continued to block Desiree's entrance. "You need to get on out here with all that silk and satin on making me hot."

Janice couldn't help but to laugh at Antoine's comment. She too thought Desiree had on too much of everything. Janice was about to go find Roberto when she saw Jasmine, who also tried to hold back her laugh, raise her hand and got Roberto's attention.

Roberto saw Desiree and ran over to Antoine. "Well, well, what do we have here? Is there a problem Antoine?"

"Yes Officer. This woman is not on the list and I can't let her in."

Roberto looked at Desiree. "Do you hear that Desiree? Your name is not on the list."

"She's my guest. Brent Foster, I know I'm on the list."

Antoine checked the list. "Okay then."

Janice hurried down the left side of the ballroom. When she got to the edge of the stairs that led to the stage, she looked at Roberto place his hand on his gun and Jasmine escort Desiree on Brent's arm to their seats.

Janice walked out in her black evening dress with a smile as bright as the lights off of the chandeliers. "Hello, is everyone having a good time? For those of you who don't know me, I am Janice Perry. Welcome to Ambiance, the place where the ambiance says Wow!"

Everyone in the hall jumped to their feet and wildly clapped. Janice looked at all of the people in her hall there to support her and the butterflies flew away. She smiled and said, "Wow, I'm so glad you all could make it."

Janice continued her speech about customer service and the other services available at Ambiance. She ended her speech with "There's plenty of food and drinks. Enjoy yourselves and I hope Ambiance will be your first choice for all of your special occasions and *Remember What Your Mamas Taught You* will be your number one resource for your customer service needs. Thank you so much for coming."

Janice walked off of the stage and into the audience where everyone smiled and clapped. The music resumed and people began to mingle again.

Every few steps, Janice was stopped by a different person who was either interested in her book or booking a date for Ambiance. Unable to handle the volume alone, Janice called for her assistants, Jasmine and Antoine.

Finally, Janice made her way back to her family's table. The first person she saw was Paul sitting with her family. She smiled, wrinkled up her nose and thought how in the world did he end up at her family's table.

As soon as Paul saw Janice, he stood up and hugged her tightly. "Sweetheart, you were wonderful."

Janice saw Brent and Desiree across the way and instantly froze in Paul's arms. She hurriedly broke away and turned to her family. "Everyone, this is Paul Davis. Paul, this is my family."

Dee gave Paul a smirk while Beatrice smiled at Paul and her daughter.

"Hey Sis, you weren't half bad."

"Thank you Chester."

Reginald stood up with his lady friend beside him. "Ma, I want you to meet Layla."

"Hi Mrs. Perry, I've heard so much about you."

"Layla, it's very nice to meet you again. Reginald acts like this is the first time we've met." Janice hugged her future daughter-in-law.

Reginald said, "It's the first time I've introduced her."

Janice smiled at her son hugging his new fiancée and gave him the thumbs up behind Layla's back. "Well family, I must mingle."

Janice quickly moved through the crowd and away from Paul. She turned around and saw Paul talking to her mother. Without them seeing her, Janice stood close enough to hear what they said to each other.

"It was a pleasure meeting you all. Janice is going to be a real success." Beatrice smiled and said, "Thank you. Paul is it?"

"Yes Ma'am."

"I'm sure I will see you again."

Paul chuckled and again, said, "Yes Ma'am."

Janice smiled and looked at Paul leave out the double doors. She slid out the door and called his name. "Paul."

Paul stopped and looked at Janice. "Thanks for coming." She smiled and blew him a kiss.

"Anytime Pretty Lady."

A few minutes later, Janice saw Desiree walk out. She ran outside on the steps and yelled, "Paul."

Again, Paul stopped and so did Desiree. Janice looked at Desiree and then at Paul. "Nothing, have a good night."

Paul got into his limo and closed the door. Desiree gave Janice a cold look and pointed her finger at her. Janice went back inside and headed straight to the bar and stood beside Jarrod.

"Is everything okay Janice?"

"Hey Jarrod. Yeah, it is now. I can't believe that damn woman was here. She just followed Paul and I ran out there to warn him. She had the nerve to point her finger at me like it was a gun. I swear that woman is crazy. I'm getting scared for me and Paul."

"Don't worry, you're safe with me. Trouble at three o'clock."

"Well, aren't you an overnight success."

"Hi Brent, how are you?"

"I'm excellent."

"Brent, this is a friend of mine, Jarrod."

"What's up?"

"Hey, where's Desiree?" Jarrod asked.

"She went home. She had a headache."

"Probably because she wasn't supposed to be here in the first damn place," Jarrod mumbled.

"What did you say?" Brent asked.

"Nothing."

Brent turned to Janice. "I just wanted to congratulate you and show my support. Let's get together next week. I have some clients who may be interested in holding their events here."

"Okay, just call me."

Brent looked at Jarrod and then to Janice. "You two enjoy the rest of your evening."

"Thank you Brent."

Janice took a generous sip of her wine and looked at Jarrod. "It's ten o'clock. People should be leaving soon and then we can have our Champaign toast."

"You bet. I'll see you in a few."

Janice mingled some more, drank some more wine until the crowd was down to 10. She flopped down at the table and looked at Dee and Roberto laugh and talk. "Hey Dee, the man is still working."

Roberto smiled and said, "I am working."

"For whom?"

Again, Roberto smiled and turned his attention back to Dee. Antoine and Jasmine came over to the table and also flopped down. "Mommy, I'm tired. Is this what it feels like to run a hall? I have blisters on my feet."

Antoine said, "Mine too."

Janice smiled at Antoine. "You can talk normal now."

"No, I can't Miss Perry. I've been talking so much that now, I'm hoarse."

Janice laughed so hard she almost fell out of her chair. "Antoine sweetie, can you please go to my office and get the Champaign?"

"No need Miss Perry. It's already at the bar chilling and ready to be consumed."

"Aren't you just the greatest assistant?"

Antoine came back to the table with the Champaign and several glasses. Jasmine put her glass out in front of her. "Fill us up Antoine, except for Jarrod. He has to drive Mommy."

"Girl, get out of here with that."

Janice smiled at her extended family and raised her glass.

"Dee, Roberto, Jarrod, Antoine, Jasmine, here's to a . . ." When Paul walked through the door, Janice stopped. She smiled and gave him a glass. "Let's try this again. I couldn't have done this without any of you, your love and support. I especially thank my top notch, base speaking, and classy dressing assistant Antoine who has worked his butt off for several weeks and tonight is no different. To my daughter whose impeccable taste along with her enormous design skills brought Ambiance to life and to Lainey, without her, none of this would be possible."

Janice slightly tilted her head to one side and smiled at Paul. "Thank you. I thank all of you. Okay everybody, raise your glasses. To Ambiance!"

85

Paul

"Hey Dad, are you busy?"

"Yeah, but you can come in. What do you need Son?"

"I just have some proofs for Janice. I thought you might want to personally deliver them to her and get her approval."

"No, you can messenger them over."

"What's going on with you two?"

"Nothing. That's the problem. Since the open house, I really haven't seen too much of her and that's been what, three month ago. She said she needed space, so I'm giving it to her."

"Is that why you have suddenly become the jet setter and taking all of my business trips?"

Paul looked at Dante and smiled.

"Maybe Janice is just busy trying to get her business off the ground. I heard the open house was a success."

Paul leaned back in his chair. "That's right, you didn't make it."

"No, I had to take care of an emergency and by the time I was done, it was too late."

"What was the emergency?"

"I'll tell you about it later."

"Hmm. Yeah, it was a success. You wouldn't believe who showed up?"

Dante asked, "Who?"

"Desiree and Brent."

"You're kidding."

"I kid you not. I thought they were going to start trouble. Thankfully, they were both cool. Janice did her thing and had the crowd eating out of her hands."

"Did she have you eating out of her hands too?"

Paul shook his head at Dante. "We still talk, but I miss spending quality time with her. To tell you the truth, I'm getting a little starved for attention. At my age, I've been thinking about dating again." Paul smiled.

"When did you come up with that bright idea?"

"When my divorce became final, I rushed over to tell Janice the good news and saw her having lunch with that no good Brent. She says he's just a client, but I don't know. My track record with women hasn't been that good. Most of them seem sneaky and I don't know who to trust. It's like they start out like Janice, all sweet and innocent and end up like Desiree, sour and evil."

"Have you seen old step mommy dearest lately?"

"Come to think of it, I haven't seen Desiree since the open house. I thought once the divorce was final that I would hear from her, but not a peep. When the judge told her after all of the stuff she'd done that she'd better take that $1.7 million and the mansion or she would give her 1.7 years in the big house on the hill, I thought Desiree would kill me right there in the courtroom."

"Maybe she took a long vacation somewhere." Dante laughed.

"The estate is hers now, but she hasn't even been there. All of the staff left. Sarah said she'd rather live on the streets than to work for Desiree. I guess the others felt the same way."

"So Dad, getting back to dating. Are you sure you want to date? It's different than you probably remember."

"I'm not sure about anything. I just know that maybe I need to take some time before I rush into another marriage and have it end up like my first. I really love Janice, but is she my Wow Woman?"

"You know she is. I think you're just horny."

"I think you're right, but I still want to make sure." Paul laughed.

"Okay Dad. Go on out there and tell me how it is? Me personally, I'm out of the dating scene."

"You and Kim?"

"Yeah, I think I'm going to pop the question."

"Kim is a good girl. Is she still going to work here after you get married?"

"Yeah."

"Bad idea, plus there's a nepotism policy. You can't supervise your wife here or at home. Already, you have a lot to learn."

Dante smiled. "Like you when it comes to dating?"

Paul stood up and walked to the window. "While I was in Texas, I went on my first date. Her name was Sandra. I've known her for some time, but I never looked at her in that way. We went out to dinner and I had a nice time. She's a very nice person. I'd see her again."

"Very nice person, but no Janice."

"No, she wasn't Janice and I'm not looking for another Janice."

Paul's phone rang. "Don't go anywhere Dante. Yes Vivian."

"Mr. Davis, there's a Carolyn on the line."

"I'll take it. Hello Carolyn."

"Hi Paul, I hope your day is filled up with thoughts of me."

"No, but my nights could be. Are you free for dinner?"

Dante frowned at his father.

Carolyn said, "Yes, I am. They say a way to a man's heart is through his stomach. I think it's time I show you my skills."

"I think you're right. Does seven o'clock work for you?"

"Sounds great. Paul, I know you have my address. I'm glad to see you're finally going to use it.

Paul hung up the phone and smiled.

"Who was that?"

Paul looked at Dante with a sheepish grin on his face. "Not that it's any of your business that was Carolyn, my date for tonight."

"I'll take these over to Janice. Can you call her and let her know I'm on my way."

"Yeah, okay, I know what you're trying to do."

Paul picked up the phone and dialed Janice's office.

"Thank you for calling Ambiance, Antoine speaking, how may I help you?"

Paul almost laughed out loud. He hadn't heard Antoine sing his greeting in a while. "Antoine, how are you? This is Paul Davis."

"Hello Mr. Davis."

"Is Janice in?"

"No, she's not in today." Antoine whispered into the phone. "She's been a little crabby lately. Maybe you can put a smile on her face."

"I'll do my best Antoine. Dante is on his way over there to get her approval on some proofs.

"Well, I guess she'll be in tomorrow."

"Hey Antoine, don't tell her I called."

Antoine let out a tired sigh. "It's your world Mr. Davis."

"Not quite Antoine."

Paul hung up the phone and wondered if Janice was all right. "I should call her at home. Good morning baby. Are you eating your toast and applesauce?"

"Not yet."

"I tell you Janice, I don't know how you make any money sleeping half the day away and lounging around the other half. See, a savvy businessman like me, gets up when money gets up. All successful people know in order to make money—you have to get up before the sun comes up and work until the sun goes down. That's how you get it done Baby."

"I guess I learn something new from you every time I talk to you Paul. I guess your sleepy eyed, toast and applesauce-eating baby wouldn't know what to do without you giving her such powerful and insightful advice. For your information, I made $286,000 in the last three months and the royalties from my book brought me $12,500 just last night, all while I laid my pretty head on my pillow. So you see baby, I work smarter not harder like a very handsome man who shall remain nameless that I haven't seen much of lately."

Paul took a moment to digest all of what Janice said and realized Janice was very business savvy and very crabby. "Baby, I'm impressed. I now have a new found respect for toast and applesauce."

"You should try it sometimes. Maybe then, you'll have time for other things besides work."

"Look Janice, you were the one who wanted space and now that I'm giving it to you, you don't want it? Make up your mind."

"Paul, I needed space because . . ."

"Because what Janice?"

"You're right Paul and I still need space. I'll talk to you later."

Janice hung up on Paul. Before he hung up the phone, he looked at it and said, "See, that's exactly why I'm dating again. Damn fickle woman."

Paul spent the rest of the day diligently working. At five o'clock, he left the office and went to his condo to shower and change for his date with Carolyn. He looked in the mirror to check out his casual attire. "I look good enough to eat. Okay Carolyn, let's see if your food is the same."

Paul grabbed a bottle of Chardonnay and headed out the door. Thirty minutes later, he was at Carolyn's house and rang the doorbell.

"Right on time. Come on in," Carolyn said.

Paul kissed her on the cheek and handed her the bottle of wine. He walked into the three-level townhouse, stood in the middle of the floor and looked around at the unopened newspapers on the floor, clothes on the furniture, shoes in the hallway, mail coming down the stairs and a sink full of dirty dishes.

"Carolyn, you did know I was coming?"

"Paul, you're so funny. Just move that stuff out of the way and take a seat."

Paul moved a pile of clothes to the other side of the sofa. As soon as he sat down, a black cat with a white stripe under his neck jumped in his lap. Paul immediately jumped up. "You have a cat?"

"Yes, this is my baby, Terrible Blow. I call him that because he has a wicked paw punch." Carolyn picked up the cat and kissed it in its mouth.

"Carolyn, I'm allergic to cats." Paul pretended to sneeze. "I can't stay here."

"Don't be silly. I'll just put him out."

Again, Paul pretended to sneeze until he was half way out the door. "It's too late. I've already come in contact with him. I'm sorry. Maybe we can reschedule. I'll call you later."

Paul got into his Bentley and miraculously stopped sneezing. "Carolyn, you need to clean up your house first before you call yourself cooking for me. Damn cat running around jumping up on the counter. No thank you, I'll eat out."

Paul drove around and tried to decide where he wanted to go for dinner. He turned off of Interstate 495 south and ended up at McCormick and Schmick's. He walked in, sat at the bar, and ordered a glass of Chardonnay. Under his breath, he said, "I should have kept the bottle I had."

A young woman that was well endowed in all of the right places stared at Paul from across the bar. Paul smiled and looked away. When the bartender gave him his Chardonnay, he said, "It's already paid for by the pretty woman over there."

Paul smiled, raised his wine glass and said, "Thank you."

A few minutes later, the woman came over and sat down beside him. "Hello, my name is Kathy."

"Hello Kathy, my name is Paul. Thanks again for the wine."

"You are so very welcome."

Again, Paul smiled at Kathy, and thought very nice indeed.

"Kathy, have you had dinner yet?"

"As a matter of fact, I haven't."

"Would you like to join me?"

"Sure."

Paul got the bartender's attention. "We need a table. We're going to carry our drinks with us."

86

Janice

Since the open house, Janice worked non-stop to make her business a success. She had several seminars lined up, both in and out of town, she sold thousands of copies of her book, and Ambiance was reserved for the remainder of the year. She even recouped the majority of the money Marvin stole from her. Ambiance was everything Janice wanted it to be and more.

Constantly, Janice ensured Ambiance's success, which took up the majority of her time. The rest of her time, she spent writing her first romance novel. Occasionally, she took a break and did nothing but think of Paul. She missed him terribly, but reminded herself that staying away from him was for the best. As long as Janice stayed away from Paul, Desiree stayed away from her and the threats on their lives were null and void. For the most part, Janice was happy, but something was going on inside her that even she didn't realize.

At four o'clock in the afternoon, Janice was still in her bathrobe. She went to the kitchen to get a cranberry juice. "I guess I should call Antoine to see how the day went."

"Thank you for calling Ambiance, Antoine speaking, how may I help you?"

"Hey Antoine."

"Hey Miss Perry. Are you feeling better?"

"I'll survive. How did everything go today?"

"Well, I'm afraid not so good. I was just about to call you. I've been taking cancellations all day long."

"How many cancellations?"

Antoine slowly said, "Twelve."

Uncharacteristic for Janice, she let out a loud four letter word.

Antoine was quiet.

"Antoine, did they say why?"

"Just that they changed their mind."

"That's strange. Did you tell them they would forfeit their deposits?"

"Yes, but it didn't seem to bother them."

"Why didn't you call me earlier?"

"Miss Perry, you've been so crabby and today you're sick and I didn't want to bother you."

"Crabby, I am not crabby. Something like this, you should have contacted me right away. I could have called them to talk them out of canceling."

Antoine sucked his teeth. Under his breath he said, "I told you that you were crabby."

"What did you say Antoine?"

"Nothing. I'm sorry. I'll see you tomorrow Miss Perry."

"I am not finish talking to you. Did you call Brent Foster to cancel our dinner meeting?"

"Oh, I forgot."

"Damn Antoine."

"It's been busy Miss Perry."

"Never mind, I'll call him myself. Don't forget to set the alarm before you leave."

Janice hung up on Antoine and let out a scream. "Damn, I don't feel like going out to dinner tonight." Janice's phone rang. "Now who's calling? Hello!"

"Hey girl, what are you doing at home and why are you yelling?"

"I'm not working today."

"I know, I called Antoine and he told me you were ill. What's wrong?"

"Nothing, I just need a break."

"Good, because I have something I want to tell you. Can I stop by?"

Janice closed her eyes. She didn't want any company, but decided to let Dee come over anyway. "Okay, I'll be here."

Janice sat on the sofa, drank her cranberry juice and thought about Paul. "Now, he's eager for space."

Janice opened her door. "Hey Dee, you must have been down the street."

"Sure was. What's wrong with you?"

"I told you nothing, just a little tired."

"Too tired to put on some clothes I see."

"Do you want anything to drink?"

"A bottle of water would be good."

Janice walked to the refrigerator to get Dee her water and sat down on the sofa. "So, what is this big news?"

"Roberto and I have been seeing each other. I really like him. He's sweet, strong, kind and a great kisser. He likes to do things and he's intelligent too. He asked me to go away with him this weekend. When I come back, I'm booking September 24ᵗʰ for my wedding day."

"Well, I'm sure that date is free and any other date you want."

"What are you talking about?"

"Antoine just told me I had 12 cancellations today."

"Damn, 12 is a lot."

"I know. Anyway, I'm happy to hear about you and Roberto. He seems like a really nice guy. I hope it works out for you two."

"Thanks Janice. Are you all right? You seem a bit off."

Janice got up and paced the floor. "Dee, during these last three months, do you think Paul even thought of me?"

Dee rolled her eyes. "Is that what's bothering you?

"It's not bothering me. I just asked your opinion. If you don't want to answer me, don't."

"Excuse me Miss Crabby."

"I am not crabby. Antoine said the same thing."

"It's no wonder if you're biting his head off like you're doing me. No offense Janice, I know you always want to see the good in people and you believe Paul is your gift from God, but let's look at the facts. Shall we?

1. You haven't been with too many men. I don't mean to talk about the dead, but you didn't even know Marvin had a fiancée, another fiancée and a son. You were with him two years before you got married and almost another year after you got married and you still never suspected his lying ass."

Janice was quiet.

"Well, I'll just move on.

2. You've only known Paul for what, about six months and already you're madly in love and believe he feels the same way too.

3.   You only have his cell phone number and his office number.

4.   You've never been to his home.

"I have been to his home."

"No Janice, you've been to his bachelor pad condo. I mean the place he lays his fine ass head down on his pillow the majority of his nights. Do you think a man with the kind of money Paul has lives in a condo? Janice, you really don't see anything wrong with this picture?"

Janice didn't answer.

"Okay, you don't want to talk then I'll talk. Janice, I'm sorry, but you really need to hear this.

5. You told me that lately, you've only been able to reach Paul at work and very seldom at night. That's because wifey has put her foot down. He's spending the nights with his wife. Come on Janice. With your own eyes, you saw Paul having dinner with his family. Hell, his wife even told you they were never getting a divorce. His divorce still isn't final because there is *no* divorce. The answer to your question is hell no, in the last three months, he has not been thinking about you."

Janice looked at her watch. "I told him I needed space."

"Do you suddenly have some place to go?"

"Antoine forgot to cancel a dinner meeting with Brent."

"Are you going?"

"No, I'm not going."

"Girl, go out to dinner with Brent. Hell, start dating again and stop waiting around for a married man that is going to stay married. Janice, there's no future in a married man."

Janice said nothing and just stared ahead.

Dee snapped her fingers. "Janice, wake up. You didn't meet your Wow Man. You met an upside down Wow Man—MOM."

"What's a MOM?"

"A man on a mission for new pu—. Do I have to spell it out for you?"

Janice lowered her head and squeezed the top of her nose with her two fingers and laughed.

Dee stood up. "I need something stronger than this water and so do you. Do you have any wine?"

"Yeah, over there."

Dee poured each of them a glass of wine. She drank one glass and poured another. "How do you feel now Miss Janice?"

"Dee, I feel like you're crazy. I know things look bad, but things are not always what they appear to be. All men are not dogs and all men are not just out for sex. If that's the case, why did you continue to look for a man? Is Roberto that way?"

Dee was quiet.

"I hear both women and men say the same thing that they want a good man or a good woman and it's hard to find one. It's not hard. There are plenty of good women and good men in the world."

Dee shook her head and said, "No."

"Really, there are. Think about it for a moment. You and I have met plenty of good men, well you have anyway, but for some reason, we just didn't want them. You know what I think most people really mean when they say that?"

"What?"

"I think most people are saying they want the woman or man they desire to be good."

Dee smiled and shook her head in agreement. Janice took a sip of her wine before she continued. "Counselor Dee, common sense tells me that all of the facts that you've presented are 100% correct, but there's something so different about Paul. I feel him in my heart and soul like no other."

"Can you feel in your brain that he's lying to you?"

"Yes, I can. Although he may lie about things, I know it's mostly to protect my feelings and of course, him avoiding conflict. I don't feel or believe that lying is his way of life. You know, someone that lie the majority of the time. That's the way Marvin was. With Paul, I can always feel when he's down. Most of the time, I can predict what he's going to say before he says it. I know he has a good heart, I know he loves me and I know I love him. I just believe he's the man God sent me. He's my Wow Man."

Dee looked up in the ceiling and rolled her eyes.

"Dee, I know you can't understand it, and I don't expect you to."

"You're right, I don't understand why you're holding on to something that will never happen.

"Where men are concerned, I know you think I'm not very bright, but believe me, Janice Perry is a very smart cookie. Because I smile a lot and I don't curst out people or scold them on everything I do not like, most people, including you, misconstrue that as being stupid or gullible. I'm not saying my Wow Man doesn't come with its share of problems. Just because someone may be perfect for you doesn't mean the relationship will be perfect."

"I don't think you're stupid or gullible where men are concerned."

"I know you do, but that's okay Dee. I also know that you find it difficult to be happy for me when you aren't happy."

"What is that supposed to mean?"

"It means that you won't be happy for me unless you are already happy for yourself."

"I'm happy now so that doesn't make any sense. You want me to be happy for you stewing over a married man? Janice, I'll say it again, wake up, the damn man is married with a capital M."

Janice put up both of her hands. "Paul just has some issues that he needs to straighten out. One day, you'll be happy for Paul and me—you'll see."

"Well, I don't see it today. Janice, carry your ass out to dinner with Brent. As a matter of fact, go to dinner with Tom, Dick, Harry, Wayne, Todd, Rod, anybody but Paul."

"Okay Dee, you're right. From now on, I'll be a Ho."

Dee almost choked on her wine as both she and Janice laughed.

"See, there's hope for you after all."

"Whatever Dee."

"Just go call Brent. How is he doing anyway with his fine self?"

"Still tall, dark, handsome with money, and muscles."

"He did look good at your open house, but now, I only have eyes for Roberto. Seriously Janice, go out with Brent and forget about what's his name. Enjoy yourself tonight and tomorrow. Get yourself back to work before you won't have a business to go back to. Who knows, this could be the first of many dates to follow."

"It's not a date. It's a business meeting."

"Whatever, it has to start somewhere. Well Janice, this has been fun, but I have to go and so do you. I'll talk to you tomorrow."

"Thanks for the unsolicited advice.

"Anytime."

Janice looked at her watch. It was 5:30. She thought if she hurried, she could still make the meeting with Brent, but first, she had to make a call.

"Thank you for calling Ambiance, Antoine speaking, how may I help you?"

"Antoine, I'm sorry I yelled at you earlier."

"It's okay Miss Perry."

"What are you still doing there?"

"I was just wrapping up some things."

"Go home. Don't worry about the cancellations. Everything will work itself out. I'll be in the office tomorrow."

"Okay Miss Perry."

At 6:30, Janice was dressed and on her way to meet Brent. She walked into McCormick and Schmick's and immediately looked around for Brent, but he hadn't arrived yet. Janice sat at the bar and ordered a glass of Chardonnay. As she waited for her wine, she continued to look around the restaurant. Her eyes widened when she saw Paul at a table laughing and having dinner with a voluptuous young woman. When the bartender gave Janice her wine, she took two big gulps before she looked at Paul and the woman again. Tears began to swell up in Janice's eyes. She took two more gulps of her wine and laid her money on the counter. She was about to leave when Brent walked in.

"Hello Janice. You weren't leaving, were you?"

"No, I thought I forgot something in my car, but I have it."

A staff member of the restaurant walked up to Janice and Brent. "Are you ready to be seated?"

Brent said, "Yes we are."

"Follow me please."

Janice and Brent walked right past Paul and Kathy's table. At first, Paul was so busy laughing that he didn't see them, but as soon as he saw Janice and Brent sit just a few tables away, Paul's laugh abruptly stopped. For several minutes, Janice and Paul's eyes locked until the server stood in front of Janice and finally broke their ice-cold stares.

Janice did everything she could not to look in Paul's direction again. When she did, she saw Paul kiss the woman before they both stood up. On his way out, Paul looked back at Janice and gave her a salute. Janice continued to stare at Paul and the woman until they were out of sight.

Brent smiled. "Janice, Janice, are you okay?"

"I'm sorry Brent. What did you say?"

Again, Brent smiled. "I just asked you if you're ready to order."

"No, I need a little more time." Janice picked up the menu and covered most of her face.

"I should be thanking Davis."

"Why do you say that?"

"He just made a huge mistake."

"What?"

"He left the door open just wide enough for me to slide right on in and take his place."

87

Paul

The next morning Paul was in his office bright and early doing everything he could to keep his mind off seeing Janice and Brent together on a date at the restaurant. "She needs space all right. You can't trust no damn body."

"You can trust me Dad. I take it your date didn't go so well."

"Dammit Dante, I'm not going to tell you again about knocking."

Dante went back out and knocked.

"I don't have time for your games today."

"Dad, calm down. You must have really had a bad night. I told you dating wasn't like it used to be."

"My dates were fine."

"Dates?"

"Well, one was fine anyway."

"Well, if it was so fine, why are you so cheery?"

"I was having a good time and of all the damn restaurants in the world, who walks in?"

"Let me guess, Janice."

"Not just Janice, it was Janice and that no good Brent. I could have killed him and slung her little ass out the door."

Dante laughed. "Brent and Janice were at the restaurant? No wonder you're in a foul mood."

"Talking about space. Now I see why she wanted space. Son, I told you. Women are sneaky. Hold up on proposing to Kim. She'll turn out to be just like Desiree and Janice."

"Wait a minute Dad. Kim is a good woman like Janice is a good woman. I won't even say anything about step mommy dearest. She's in a non-class all by herself. I think you and Janice need to talk. It seems like you both have some kind of miscommunication going on. I felt the energy between you two. It's powerful. Anyone who's around you can feel it too. I just can't see Janice with Brent at least not the way you're thinking."

"Well, I can and I did. He had this smug look on his face like he had something on me. Man, I wanted to punch his lights out so bad, but the young lady I was with didn't deserve my drama."

"What young lady?"

"Kathy, I met her at the restaurant. She was nice enough and had everything in the right places, but not a damn thing between the ears. I knew if I went home with her, she would have no problem giving it up."

"Give what up?"

"Son, get back to work."

"She was no Janice, huh?"

"I told you I wasn't looking for another Janice."

"Yet the very person you weren't looking for, you found."

Paul covered his face.

"Okay Dad, I'll leave you alone about Janice. Since I have you here, I need to talk to you about Cynthia."

"I definitely don't want to hear anything about Cynthia right now."

"Come on. She's still your daughter."

Paul uncovered his face. "I know, go on."

"On the night of Janice's open house, remember I told you I had an emergency?"

"Yeah."

"Cynthia was the emergency. She called me crying and screaming that she didn't want to live anymore and she didn't want the baby. When I got there, the house was a mess and she was an even bigger mess. I called a cleaning service. Kim and I stayed with her all that night."

Paul looked down in his lap and shook his head.

"Dad, Brian left her for another woman and that woman is pregnant too."

Paul just sat there quietly and looked at the papers in front of him. In a low voice he said, "I know."

"How do you know?"

"I know everything about my children. For months, Brian ran up Cynthia's credit cards, got $100 to $500 cash advances a day. He even got Cynthia to write him some very healthy checks from one of her bank accounts that she never touches. That's when I knew something was up. I didn't want to believe he was just using her for her money, but evidence suggested otherwise. I froze her accounts and made sure he heard me telling her that I was cutting her off financially. After that, I knew he would leave her. I went to his job and tried to beat every dollar out of him that he swindled from her. He was still trying to tell me how much he loved Cynthia and he wanted to be a good father to their baby."

"Dad, maybe he does."

"If he does, he can love her from afar. I told him if he ever steps foot back into that house again, he would have me to deal with."

"What was he doing with all of the money?"

"Giving it to his other baby mama. How is your sister doing now?"

"She seems to be handling things and paying her bills."

"I'm paying her bills."

"I knew you wouldn't cut your baby girl off." Dante smiled.

"I did, just not totally. She may say I'm not her father, but she will always be my baby girl."

"She'll come around, you'll see. Dad, one more thing."

"Now what?"

"Janice still hasn't given me her approval. I need them today."

"Give them to me. I need to see her anyway. Maybe I can talk some damn sense into her about that good for nothing, no count boyfriend of hers."

"He's not her boyfriend Dad, you'll see."

"Dante, why don't you see if you can get some work done instead of gazing in Kim's face all day long and worrying the hell out of me? Give me the proofs."

Dante smiled and handed Paul the proofs. Paul grabbed them. "I'll be back in a couple of hours."

"Tell Janice I said hello."

Paul ignored Dante and left his office.

As Paul pulled up to Ambiance, Brent pulled out of the parking lot. "Look at that scheming bastard."

Paul parked, grabbed the proofs and went into Ambiance.

"Hello Mr. Davis, may I help . . . ?"

Without a word, Paul brushed past Antoine, went right into Janice's office and threw the proofs on her desk. "Janice, here are your proofs. We need your approval by today."

Janice turned around, but never looked up from her pad. "I'll call Dante later."

"Janice, what the hell are you doing with Brent?"

"I told you, he's a client."

"You go to dinner with all of your clients?"

"I will go to dinner with whomever I want to, just like you."

"That woman didn't mean anything to me?"

"I know, just like I don't mean anything to you."

"You know I love you, but Brent, he could care less about you. He's just using you and you can't seem to see past his muscles and his fake sweet talking."

"Are you calling me stupid and gullible?"

"No, I'm just saying you're making a big mistake dealing with Brent. You're sweet and nice. He's ruthless. You can't handle a man like Brent."

"Now, you're calling me weak. How in the hell do you know what kind of man Brent is?"

"Trust me, I know."

"Trust you Paul, a man with a wife and a girlfriend who still wants me to be his chick on the side. You have some damn nerve. You can have a wife, a girlfriend and do what you want, but I'm supposed to believe in you and wait patiently until you summon me to your bachelor pad. I don't think so. You just want your cake and eat it too."

Paul frowned and said, "My bachelor pad. Janice, if that was the case, how do you think I've managed to be with you for months?"

"You were just a lying, cheating bastard."

"Oh, I'm a lying, cheating bastard. Sweetheart, you have it all wrong. Brent is the lying, cheating bastard and a murderer."

"A murderer? Paul, I've heard enough. You don't want me and you don't want anyone else to have to me either. Well, that's too damn bad. I like Brent and I'm going to keep on seeing him and anyone else I choose to date. You are not my husband. My husband is six feet under and your wife is over there in your mansion no doubt waiting for you. So why don't you just leave me alone and go home to your crazy wife."

"For your information, no one is waiting for me and I am well aware that I am not your husband. Seems to me, I don't qualify. In order to be your husband, one has to be a liar and a cheater and then you love them to death. If you hadn't been so stupid looking up in the clouds when your husband was alive lying to you and cheating on you, maybe you would have put his ass out and got with a good man. Marvin had to die before you moved on. Now, you're making the same mistake hooking up with Brent, but you can spot a liar and cheater."

Janice threw her pad down on her desk and swung her door wide open. "I have seven words for you Paul Davis. Get the fuck out of my office!" Janice held the door open for Paul to leave.

Paul was shocked. This was the first time he'd heard Janice use such vulgar language. He snatched the door from Janice's hand and slammed it shut. "I hope using that type of language did something for you, because it didn't do a whole hell of a lot for me. Now, if you're finished, sit your pretty ass down and listen to what I have to say." Paul pointed to her sofa.

"No thank you, I would rather stand."

"Janice, sit down."

Unwillingly, Janice did as she was told. Paul went over to sit on the sofa next to her. "As I was saying, Brent is not capable of loving anyone but himself and his physique. You ask me how I knew Brent. Well, I'll tell you. While Brent was in prison, he and Desiree were married. She married me for my money. Once he got out, they plotted and scammed me out of millions." Paul lowered his head. "They even lied to me about Cynthia."

"What about Cynthia?"

"After all of these years, the daughter I've known to be mine is really Brent's. I also think they killed my brother. Janice, he's a dangerous con artist."

Janice stood up. "I don't know what to believe."

Paul also stood up. "Janice, I've loved you from the moment I laid eyes on you and probably always will. All I'm trying to do is protect you from being made a fool of."

Janice gave Paul a long, hateful stare as she once again walked toward the door and opened it. "I promise you this Mr. Davis, I will be very careful not to let anybody and I mean anybody make a fool out of me again. Is that good enough for you?"

Paul was angry all over again. He thought he just poured his heart out to Janice and she's still bent on not paying any attention to his warning about Brent. "Okay Janice, stay stuck on stupid. You're on your own. I'm through."

"Good. Tell Dante he can go ahead with the proofs."

"You didn't even look at them."

"I looked at them this morning. Dante dropped them off yesterday."

Paul stormed out of Janice's office and almost knocked over Jarrod when he walked through the lobby to the front doors.

"Hey, where's the fire?" Jarrod asked.

Paul held up both of his arms. "Man, I'm through."

"Wait a minute Paul. What happened?"

"Jarrod, she's on her own. I don't give a damn if Brent uses her until he can't use her no more."

Paul got into his Bentley and sped out of the parking lot. On his drive back to his office, he thought about the argument he and Janice had which was their first and only argument since they've been together. "Damn, Janice has another side to her. Since she's been hanging around with that no good Brent, she has turned into a hard ass. Standing up to me like she was Betty Bad Ass and telling me I got seven words for you."

Paul counted the words to see if it was seven and laughed. "It's seven all right. That no good Brent has tarnished my sweet Janice. That's okay, he can have you for now, but what God wants to bring together, not even a scheming Popeye and a tri-polar ex-wife can stop. Don't worry Janice, I gotcha. I'll keep my baby safe." Paul laughed. "I just have to do it from afar. I swear that is one woman I'll go to jail for. Well, at least for a day or two. Hell, I can't do anybody any good in jail." Again, Paul laughed. "Now, she got me talking to myself. I got to give Jarrod a call to tell him to continue on as planned. He can keep his eyes on Janice while I keep my eyes on Desiree and Brent's crazy asses. That's all right Janice Baby, I got three words for you. "I love you."

88

Janice

"Paul almost ran me over getting out of here. Janice, what in the world happened?"

"Jarrod, I don't want to talk about it. We are through and for one, I couldn't be happier. In here trying to stake claim while he's still married to his crazy ass wife."

Jarrod's phone rang. While Janice continued her ranting, in a low voice, Jarrod answered Paul's call and looked back at Janice. "As hot as a firecracker. You two really need to stop all of this mess."

Janice heard Jarrod. "Are you talking to Paul? You better not be talking to him. I don't want to hear his damn name."

"Janice, Janice, calm down."

"Don't tell me to calm down. Damn man coming in here, talking to me any kind of way. And now, here you go."

Jarrod whispered into the phone, "This is your fault, I'll call you back."

"You'll call who back. You don't have to call him back. You can get out of my office too."

"Hey, I just want to take you out to lunch before I take you to the airport, that's all."

Janice covered her face. "I'm sorry Jarrod. I can't let Paul get to me. I have to bring my triple A game to New York. He just makes me sick." Janice let out huge sigh.

"Let's go eat and forget about him for the moment." Jarrod smiled.

"I'd like to forget about him all together."

"Janice, you don't mean that."

"Yes, I do."

"I'll get that for you." Jarrod reached for Janice's luggage.

"I can manage on my own Jarrod. I'm not stupid and I'm not weak either."

"Excuse me."

Janice didn't get one foot inside the limo before her phone rang. She looked at her caller ID and it was Antoine. "Didn't I just leave there?"

"I know, but you told me to let you know as soon as it happens again."

"When what happen again?"

"Another cancellation. Hold on Miss Perry."

A few minutes later, Antoine returned to the line. Janice didn't wait for Antoine to tell her what she already knew. "That was another cancellation, wasn't it?"

"I'm sorry Miss Perry."

Janice closed her eyes. "Antoine, just put the files on my desk. I'll deal with it when I get back."

"Okay, you have a safe trip."

Janice hung up the phone and shoved it in her purse.

Jarrod asked, "Bad news?"

"This is the 14th cancellation I've received in the last few days. I don't understand it."

"Everything will work out Janice, you'll see."

When Janice and Jarrod arrived at the restaurant, the first thing she did was order a vodka and cranberry juice. In a concerned voice, Jarrod said, "I haven't seen you drink one of those in a while."

"I haven't felt this way in a while."

Throughout lunch, Jarrod purposely stayed away from any conversation about Paul. He mostly talked about his wife Audrey, her shopping habits, his children, and told his usual non-funny jokes that surprisingly had Janice laughing at all of them. Janice talked about how cheap Jarrod was when it came to spending money on things Audrey wanted and jokingly advised him if he didn't stop, his wife would find tall, dark and handsome with money. Since Janice was now calm and seemed to have forgotten about the rash of cancellations and just how mad she was with Paul, Jarrod disagreed but kept it to himself.

At the end of lunch, a skinny young server with a badly needed trim laid the check on the table. Jarrod was the first to reach for it, but ultimately, Janice was the one who picked it up. "This is my treat Jarrod. It is the least I can do for you putting up with me."

"No Janice, I was taking you to lunch."

"No Jarrod, I have it."

"Have it your way Miss Perry."

"I will."

Janice gave the server her credit card. When the server returned, Janice signed the bill and although the server messed up their order a couple of times, she wrote in a generous 20% tip. Within minutes, the server brought back a receipt with $2.06 placed inside the restaurant check holder.

Janice looked at the receipt. *This is someone else's change.* "Excuse me, this isn't mine." Janice tried to hand the $2.06 back to the server, but the young woman wouldn't take it back. She whispered in Janice's ear, "I don't make much money, but evidently, you need it more than I do. Keep your $2 tip. I don't want it." The server then stood up straight and walked away.

Janice's mouth flew wide open. She couldn't believe what the young woman said to her. Janice looked at Jarrod. "I didn't give her a $2 tip. I didn't even pay with cash. This is somebody else's receipt and change."

Again, Janice called out to the server and tried again to convince the woman she made a mistake. From across the restaurant, the young woman rolled her eyes at Janice and continued to wait on the other customer.

Something came over Janice. She stood up and yelled across the restaurant, "Fuck you! I told you it wasn't mine."

The server, as well as the entire restaurant became quiet and all eyes were on Janice.

"Janice," Jarrod yelled out, but she didn't pay him any attention. "I wrote the book on customer service. I tell people how to tip. You shouldn't work in any establishment where people are involved. I want to speak to the manager now!"

The police officer two tables away looked as if he should do something, but decided not to budge.

Janice took the $2 that didn't belong to her and searched for the manager. Jarrod followed her. Janice told him what happened and how the server rudely and cruelly insulted her. The manager offered Janice an insincere padded apology. Janice turned on her heels and vowed never to return to that restaurant again.

Jarrod looked at Janice through his rear view mirror. "Damn, you really let her have it. I've never seen you this way. You were carrying on so bad that the police officer didn't know whether to put the cuffs on you or get out of the line of fire."

Janice laughed on the outside, but on the inside, she didn't see anything that was funny. She felt bad for cursing at the server and felt even worst for allowing a teenager to take her to a place where she would be cursing and carrying on like that in public. Janice realized there must be something deeper that caused her to react that way.

"Is everything okay Janice?"

"I'm fine Jarrod."

"Liar."

Janice smiled.

Jarrod continued to drive and put in one of Janice's favorite Jazz CDs. Janice was in the backseat and pretended to look over her notes, but mostly, she gazed out of the window. Her mind was unusually heavy with all kinds of thoughts, current fears and potential fears about her personal life and her business life. Janice's mind was filled with thoughts of she and Paul's argument, Marvin stealing from her and his unexpected death, finding Lainey's body, and her business accounts that dropped off like flies.

She closed her eyes. If her business kept going in the direction it was headed, she would have to cut back on Jarrod and Antoine's hours. They have become like family to her. She couldn't let either one of them down. Mostly, she couldn't let Lainey down.

Janice wished for a Wow moment to take her out of her funk. She knew she had to get it together fast and find a way to clear her mind of everything that was not about New York.

When Janice saw the airport, she sighed deeply. Jarrod got her luggage out of the trunk and placed it on the sidewalk. "Are you sure you're up to this trip?"

"Thanks for your concern, but I'm fine. Now go."

"Have a good trip Janice."

Janice stayed on the sidewalk until Jarrod drove away. She lit a cigarette and looked at her phone. She saw there were five calls from Antoine. "Now what?"

Janice listened to all five of Antoine's frantic messages that told her the New York seminar had been cancelled and how they apologized that she didn't get their previous message, but promised to reschedule at a later date. Because she was already numb, the news didn't seem to bother Janice.

For the next thirty minutes, she stood in the same spot, smoked one cigarette after the other and watched the many people run to get to their flights. After she smoked her last cigarette, Janice decided it was time she went home. She didn't want to face Jarrod so she hailed a cab. When the cab driver pulled up in front of her house, a feeling of sadness loomed around her. Janice paid the cab driver and went into her house.

Once inside, she kicked off her shoes and went directly to the vodka bottle she placed in her bottom cabinet. Janice poured herself a huge vodka and cranberry juice and sat at the kitchen table. Without warning, tears that were stifled for months finally poured out of Janice like water running from a faucet. She rocked backward and then forward. With no fear that once she started, she wouldn't be able to stop, Janice cried for Lainey, cried for Marvin, and cried to release all of her pent up frustrations. After 45 minutes, the feeling of tremendous weight that was once on her shoulders disappeared and the heaviness in her heart became lighter.

Janice got up from the table and took her vodka and cranberry juice with her. She stood in the middle of her living room floor and looked around in every corner and listened for the slightest movement of life besides her own. The reality of being alone surrounded Janice like quicksand. Again, tears began to pour. "Paul is now out of my life and as much as I hate to admit it, I miss the good part of Marvin. Most of all, I miss my sister and friend, Lainey."

Janice dried her tears and lifted her glass into the air. "I may be all alone right now, but I'm going to be all right. I got to be all right."

89

Desiree

"Diva Darling, I thought you fell off the face of the earth."

"I bet you'd like that, wouldn't you Brent?"

"Not at all. My life wouldn't be complete without the madness of my Diva Devil around to remind me of the good old days. So tell me, what has my beautiful, scheming ex-wife been up to these last six months?"

"Oh, you know a little shopping, a little sabotaging and planning three murders."

"Who are you planning to murder, me, myself and I?" Brent laughed.

"You're partly right."

"Diva, stop joking. Don't tell me you're still begrudging me for the little incident in court. I'm really sorry about that. I never wanted to hurt our daughter, but you gave me no choice. You tried to put me away for life and you know my muscles don't look good in stripes."

"Brent, the only thing you're sorry about is that the money dried up."

"Didn't I return to you $500,000 of your money?"

"Yeah, you did."

"See, that should have showed you how sorry I was. You know I don't disperse money. I accumulate money, especially yours. Come on Diva, let bygones be bygones. Put all of that stuff behind you. I know I have."

"I'm not putting a damn thing behind me. For six months, I've done nothing but tried to get my family back and show them how sorry I am. Do they care? Noooo. I've put this damn monster up for sale, but all the offers are below my asking price. I only have $10,268. 24 in . . ."

Desiree was at the end of her rope and had no faith that her future would be anything other than what she saw at the moment.

"Diva, are you still here?"

"Yeah, I was just thinking."

"What were you thinking about? Forgiving your sweet, handsome, loving ex-husband?"

"No, forgiveness is for the weak."

"There's something different about you Diva, but I can't put my finger on it. I'm not weak and I've forgiven you."

"That will be the day."

"I really have. A lot has happened in the last six months."

"What?"

"For one thing, I've changed."

"You, please. Brent, you will always be that cold hearted, manipulative, double-crossing, selfish, money grubbing pompous ass."

"Diva, you're wrong. I'm a new man."

"Since when?"

"Since you've been gone out of my life. Without the drama, it gave me a chance to really look at my life and figure out what I want for my future. Diva, my life was full of lies, schemes, hatred, and emptiness. I was on a path of loneliness and destruction. If I didn't stop, eventually I'd end up right back in jail. I finally realized what my life was missing."

Desiree was beginning to get bored with Brent's conversation. "Okay Brent, what was your life missing?"

Brent said, "Love."

"Love?"

"Yes, love. Years ago, I loved you with all of my heart and when you married Paul and took away my child, I vowed never to love anyone ever again. I became this cold, bitter, angry robot that was only out for revenge. I didn't give a damn about anybody except myself."

"And now?"

"Now, I'm different. I care about you Diva and I care about our daughter. I want to try and make things right. Do you think we can start over?"

Desiree smiled and said nothing.

"Diva, I want us to get along and try to repair all of the damage we've done to Cynthia and to each other. I want us to have a life full of love and one we can be proud of."

Desiree imagined a different future, one with Brent and Cynthia instead of Paul and Cynthia. "I want that too Brent."

"I'm glad you feel that way. I know Janice will be happy to hear that too."

"Janice, what the hell does that little tramp have to do with anything?"

"Settle down Diva. Since Janice's husband died and you broke up her and Paul, she had no one. After you sabotaged her business almost into ruins, I just stepped in and gave her a shoulder to lean on and helped her keep her business afloat.

"What the hell did you do that for?"

"Because she's a good person and didn't deserve it. She didn't break up your marriage. You did it with all of your lies and schemes."

"I didn't do it alone."

"I know. I was partly to blame and I'm sorry. Taking it out on Janice won't help anything. Besides, I can't have you hurt my future wife."

Desiree saw stars, darts, bullets and anything else that could shoot and kill. "I didn't break them up to have her end up in your arms. You mean to tell me while I was gone—you've been cuddling up with that bitch?"

"I wouldn't say we've been cuddling, but I will say I'm in love. I almost forgot, she's written a new book and I helped her. We make a great team. Diva, I plan to pop the question to her right before her book signing."

"Brent, you son of a bitch. You haven't changed. You've just traded one money train for another. You don't love her, you're just using her just like you used me and I'm going to put a stop to all of this shit once and for all. You are crazy, if you, Paul and Janice think for one minute that you can all live happily ever after while my life is in ruins. The three of you have caused me nothing but pain and heartache. I for one will never forgive you, Paul or that Janice Bitch. All of you bastards are going to pay for everything you've ever done to me. So go and be happy with little Miss Janice. You better enjoy your new life while you can, because you never know when it's all about to end."

Desiree hung up on Brent. "That son of bitch thinks he can just discard me after all of the years I've spent loving him and scheming for him. And Paul, he has taken everything away from me, my money, my properties and my daughter. That Janice, the little goodie two-shoes tramp that keeps winning the hearts of all my men, but I'll be damned if you get Brent. He's mine and always will be. He's the father of my daughter and the only man I have ever loved."

Desiree ran to her purse and took out her gun. *It's time I make things right*. She poured herself a drink and called her daughter. "Cynthia Darling, we need to talk."

"Mother, there's nothing to talk about."

"Look, you little spoiled brat. For months, I've let you disrespect me and today, it all stops. You're almost ready to pop and whether you realize it or not, you need your mother. That good for nothing Brian is out of your life and you are all alone. What are you going to do when the baby comes?"

"I'll manage. Brian will be a good father."

"Brian? Don't tell me you've let him back into your life."

"Mother, it's none of your business what I do."

"Cynthia, he's no good for you—the two timing little punk. I'll take care of him."

"Don't bother, Daddy already handled it."

"Paul, what has he done?"

"He took care of things."

"So, you can forgive him and not forgive your own mother?"

"Daddy was just a victim. He never lied to me, but you did."

"I'm coming over. We have to settle things between us before the baby comes. I'm on my way."

Desiree hung up the phone and paced back and forth. "Paul has turned her against me. It wasn't enough that he stripped me of everything else. He had to take my daughter away too. Well, he's not going to get away with it."

Desiree took one last sip of her drink and threw the glass against the wall. "I need something stronger than alcohol."

Desiree went into her drawer and pulled out a tiny packet of cocaine. "That's more like it." She grabbed her purse, started out the door and turned back around. Desiree picked up her gun and shoved it back into her purse. "I can't leave without my good friend. By the end of tonight, things will be just as they should be and I will finally be at peace."

90

Paul

Desiree yelled, "You back stabbing, low life son of a bitch! How could you turn my own daughter against me?"

"Woman, what the hell are you talking about?"

"I'm talking about you telling Cynthia all of those lies about me. I just came from her house and she told me what you said."

"Desiree, I only told her the truth."

"She didn't have to know all of that. It was none of her damn business."

"She asked. Did you want me to lie to her?"

"What do you think?"

"You've done enough lying for the whole world. The girl deserved to know what kind of mother she has and what kind of man her sperm donor is."

"Don't act like you're anybody's saint. For years, I've put up with your drinking, your selfishness, your controlling ways and your cheating."

"I've never cheated on you."

"Ha! You claim you met Janice after we were separated, but that's a lie. It was too soon. Nobody falls in love that fast. I know you were seeing the tramp while we were together."

"Think whatever you want. Who cares anyway?"

"I do. You, Brent and that bitch think you can do whatever you want to do to me. She was the reason why we're divorced."

Paul laughed. "Don't blame Janice. You did all of that yourself. She's a good person and just came into my life at the wrong time."

"Good person my ass. She's so good that now she's planning to marry Brent. That Ho will sleep with anybody and that's who *you* allowed to break up our marriage. You men are just stupid."

"Desiree, I don't know what kind of drugs you're snorting, but there is no way Janice is marrying Brent."

"You're right, she's not because I'm going to kill the bitch."

After Desiree abruptly hung up, Paul looked at his phone. "That woman has lost her damn mind. She can't be serious, can she? No, she and Brent must be up to their old tricks again."

Paul walked outside along the edge of the water and looked out at the waves that rolled in and hit the banks. He thought about the last time he saw Janice was six months ago when she threw him out of her office. For the four months that he was at the Paulster, not one time did Janice call. The idea of Janice and Brent getting married was ridiculous. It can't be true. Paul was sure Jarrod would have told him if Brent and Janice were getting close enough to get married.

Paul dialed Janice's office.

"Thank you for calling Ambiance, this is Antoine speaking. How may I help you?"

"Antoine my man, this is Mr. Davis."

"Oh, hi Mr. Davis, I've haven't heard your voice in a while."

"Yeah, I know. I've been out of town. How are things?"

"Slow and chilly."

"What do you mean?"

"Mr. Davis, business is not good at all."

"I thought after the open house, everything was booked."

"Oh, it was, but one by one, cancellations kept coming in and then there was nothing."

"What has Janice been doing?"

"Miss Perry has been working from home mostly. She did manage to finish her book."

"Good for her." Paul smiled.

"Miss Perry is having a book signing party tonight. You should come."

"She probably wouldn't want to see me, but thanks for the invite Antoine. By the way, where is she now?"

"I think she went to lunch with that old muscle bound guy."

Paul closed his eyes.

"Mr. Davis, he's not right for her. I like you much better."

"Thank you. Has Brent been around much?"

"Oh, he's always sniffing around here. He acts like he owns the place."

Paul balled up his fist. "Don't tell Janice I called."

"Why not Mr. Davis?"

"I want to surprise her at her book signing tonight."

"Marvelous, I know she would want you to be here. Okay, mums the word. See you tonight Mr. Davis."

"See you tonight Antoine."

Paul continued to walk along the beach and thought about all of the times he and Janice shared. "I still love that woman. I wonder why she never called me. Could it be because of Brent?" Paul shook his head. "If that's who she wants, so be it. To hell with her. I've survived this long without her. I sure don't need her now."

Paul's phone rang. "Hey Dante, the Banks' account is a done deal. They should be coming by the office at five o'clock to sign the contract. Just tell them I had an emergency and won't be able to make it, but to go ahead and sign. I will talk to them tomorrow."

"Dad, I didn't call you about the Banks' account. Your crazy ex-wife was just here high as a kite waving around a gun and yelling she was coming to kill you."

Paul's eyes opened wide.

"She kept going on about you and Janice and you turning Cynthia against her. I told her you weren't here and she said I was lying. She then walked out to Vivian and pointed the gun at her. She said Vivian even turned against her. She also said Vivian helped her with all of the bogus contracts she used to steal from you. Dad, that's not all."

"What?"

"Desiree said she was on her way to kill Janice."

"Are you sure?"

"Yeah Dad. At first, I didn't take her seriously. I thought she was just carrying on as she always does, but if you had seen how crazed she looked when she came into your office swinging around that gun, you would have no doubt that she was serious."

Paul rubbed his head. "I have to get back. Who is that yelling in the background? What's going on there?"

"Hold on."

Dante came back to the phone. "Dad, there's someone here who insist on speaking to you. I'm going to put him on speaker phone."

"Davis, this is Brent Foster."

"I know who you are. What the hell are you doing in my office causing a bunch of disturbance?"

"Sorry about that. Your gatekeeper wouldn't let me in and I had to use a little muscle."

"What is it?"

"Davis, I know you don't like me."

"That's an understatement if I ever heard one."

"I've come to warn you about Desiree."

"What about Desiree?"

"She's on the warpath. When I told her I was going to ask Janice to marry me, I think I set her off.

Paul took the phone away from his ear and swung it in the air.

"Davis, are you still here?"

"You don't love Janice. You don't love anybody but yourself. Why are you destroying her life? You'll have her just as crazy as Desiree. If you care anything about Janice, you'll leave her alone."

"Davis, you're wrong. I know I've done a lot of rotten things in my time and believe me, I'm sorry for all of them. I love Janice. If she'll have me, I do plan to marry her and I don't give a damn if you or anybody else don't like it. I came to warn you that Desiree is out to kill you, so watch out. Oh, she threatened to kill Janice too, but I'll take care of her. Davis, that's all I came to say."

Brent left the office. Paul was in total silence.

"Dad, are you still here?"

"Yeah. That smug bastard. He's no good Dante, especially no good for Janice."

"You still love her, don't you?"

"Yes, I do. I don't care if she doesn't want me. I can't let anything happen to her. I'm coming home. Son, I'll call you when I get there."

"See you soon Dad."

Paul dialed Jarrod. Before the call connected, he said, "I can't believe this is happening. I can't let anything happen to Janice. Jarrod."

"Hey Paul."

"Don't hey me. Why didn't you tell me that no good Brent was sniffing around Janice?"

"Man, I wanted to, but I also promised Janice that I wouldn't tell you about anything that was going on with her. I've been looking after her.

Every chance Brent gets, he's around her, but I see him as just helping her with Ambiance. I don't see anything going on between them. To me, she still smiles, but she doesn't seem all that happy."

"Look Jarrod, I've just received two calls, one from Brent and the other from Desiree. It seems Desiree is on the warpath. She has threatened to kill Janice."

"Damn! I knew I shouldn't have let her drive today."

"Jarrod, listen to me. I need you to find her now and when you do, don't let her out of your sight for a minute. Do you hear me?"

"Yes sir, I hear you. I think she's with Brent now."

"No, she's not. I just spoke to him. I'm on my way back home, but I won't be able to get there until tonight. Jarrod, please find her before Desiree do."

"I will Paul, you can count on it."

91

Janice

"Hello Ma'am, can I get you anything while you wait?" the server asked.

"Yes, I'll have a glass of Chardonnay please."

Janice looked around Mo's Seafood and waited for her date to arrive.

"Here you go Ma'am."

"Thank you." Under her breath, Janice said, "I wish people would stop calling me Ma'am every five minutes. I feel old enough as it is."

She sipped her wine and glanced at her watch. Her date was already 15 minutes late. "I have a lot to do before tonight. I don't have time to wait around for him." Janice's phone rang. *That must be him now.* She looked at her caller ID, saw that it was Jarrod and pushed it to go directly to her voicemail.

Janice took another sip of her wine and watched the middle-aged couple at the next table gaze into each other's eyes whenever the other one spoke. "How in the hell did I end up alone and dating again at 47? He's 30 minutes late. Why should this one be any different than the last seven bad dates I had?" She shook her head and thought about her Wow Man, a man that was not perfect, but was perfect for her. "I know you're out there somewhere and one day you'll find me." Janice giggled. "A girl can dream."

"Ma'am, are you ready to order?" the server asked.

"I guess I've been stood up. Yes, I'm ready. I'll have a broiled crab cake sandwich. That's it. Thank you."

"Coming right up."

Janice looked at her watch. "I better check in with Antoine."

"Thank you for calling Ambiance. Antoine speaking, how may I help you?"

"Hey Antoine?"

"Hey Miss Perry, where are you?"

"I'm at lunch. What's going on?"

"Well, Jarrod is looking for you. Mr. Foster is looking for you, your mother called, some other lady called, but she wouldn't leave her name, and Mr . . . . , never mind."

"Mr. Who?"

"Nobody. Oh yeah, Officer Goode wants you to call him too."

"Wow that was a lot of calls. How is everything else going?"

"Fine, everything is all set for tonight. Oh, I almost forgot. The UPS man left you a package. I put it in the middle of your desk."

"Okay, after I finish my lunch, I'm going to stop past my house and hang out there until tonight. You can leave at two o'clock, but be back no later than . . ."

"I know, 6:45. Just like the open house."

"That's right." Janice smiled.

"Are you excited Miss Perry?"

"Yes, I am. This is my first novel and I can't wait for people to read it."

"I've read it. It's fabulous."

"Thank you Antoine. Let's hope everyone else thinks so too. Okay, my crab cake is here. Call me if you need me."

"I'll see you later."

Janice ate her crab cake and thought maybe she expected too much from the guys she dated. No one person had all of the attributes she was looking for. "I can't expect other people to be like . . ."

Janice dropped her fork and let out a deep breath. What she figured out on paper was what she already knew in her heart. Paul was her Wow Man and although for months, she tried to deny it, she still loved him.

Janice quickly finished her lunch. After she paid the check, she walked past date number eight, smiled and went out the door. Janice jumped into her BMW and drove home with her top down and played her favorite CD. She felt good again and looked forward to her big night.

Twenty minutes later, Janice pulled into her driveway. Sitting in front of her door was a vase with two dozen long-stemmed red roses and one white rose. Janice heard her house phone ring. "Beautiful, I'll get you when I come back."

By the time she reached the phone, it stopped ringing and the doorbell rang. She opened up the door and was shocked to see Brent with the two dozen roses in his hand.

"Brent, what are you doing here?"

"I'm sorry I didn't call first, but I had to see you."

"Okay, come on in."

"Here, I got these for you."

"Thank you." Janice smiled and put the roses on the kitchen table.

"Janice, I want to talk to you about something."

"Sounds serious."

"It is."

"I'm all ears."

Janice sat down at the kitchen table and waited for Brent to tell her what was so important that he had to come by without calling. Brent looked at the roses and quickly looked away. "Can we go into the living room?"

"Okay."

Janice showed Brent to the family room. "Comfortable Brent?"

"Yes, this is much better."

Brent sat down on the sofa beside Janice and took her hand into his. Janice stared at Brent and wondered what it was he wanted to tell her.

"Janice, we've been spending a lot of time together. We've laughed, talked, ate together, did seminars together, danced and I think we have something between us that can really be special. You're a wonderful woman. I know I haven't been the best person in the world, but being around you make me want to be a better man."

Janice smiled. *Why is he telling me this?*

Brent rubbed his forehead and was about to speak when Janice's doorbell rang. Janice stood up. "Oh, I'm sorry Brent. I'll be right back."

Brent frowned.

"I won't be long."

Janice walked to the door and opened it to a young man with a gigantic smile. "I have a letter for Janice Perry. Is that you Ma'am?"

"Yes, I'm Janice Perry."

"Please sign here. Here you go. Have a nice day Ma'am."

On her way back to the family room, Janice opened the envelope and started to read the letter. She sat down on the sofa and said, "Sorry Brent, go ahead," and continued to read her letter.

"Janice, I love you. I thought I would never feel this way again about a woman, but you're different."

Brent was on one knee and reached into his pocket and pulled out a ring.

"Janice, will you marry me?"

"Wow! I can't believe it. I knew it would find its way back to me."

Janice looked at Brent and saw the ring he held in his hand and her mouth dropped to the floor. She fanned herself with the $300,000 certified check AJ sent her. Wow! Again, the doorbell rang. Janice smiled. "It's like grand central station here. Brent, I'm sorry."

"Janice!"

"I'll be right back. I promise." Janice laughed.

Again, Janice opened the door. Jarrod stood in the doorway with his finger pointed towards her. "Why haven't you returned my calls? I've been calling and calling."

"Jarrod shut up and come on in."

Jarrod followed Janice into the family room. "What the hell is he doing here?"

"It seems Brent was just proposing to me."

Jarrod's eyes got huge.

Brent stood up and reached for Janice's hand. "Well Janice, what do you say? Will you marry me?"

Janice looked at Jarrod and then back at Brent. "I guess I say yes."

Jarrod threw up his hands and yelled, "Ah, hell no!"

Brent hugged Janice and placed the two-carat diamond ring on her finger. Janice walked Brent to the door. He took her hand. "Baby Doll, I'll pick you up for the book signing at six o'clock."

"No, I'm driving her there," Jarrod said.

"Okay then, I guess I won't be picking you up. I'll see you at the book signing."

Brent gave Janice a peck on the lips. Jarrod turned his head and under his breath, cursed several times.

Janice smiled at Jarrod's reaction. "Bye Brent."

She closed the door and looked at her new diamond. Jarrod shook his head. "Woman, have you lost your damn mind?"

"Jarrod, I know what I'm doing."

"Do you? That man is a con artist. He's no good for you. You don't love him. You love Paul and you know you do."

Janice walked towards the roses and took out the white rose. "I haven't talked to Paul in months."

"Janice, Paul still loves you. I know he does."

"Well, *Paul* is not here and he didn't ask me to marry him—Brent did. I said yes and you are just going to have to get used to it."

"Janice, you're making a big mistake."

"Jarrod, trust me. I know what I'm doing. What are you doing here so early anyway?"

"I was in the neighborhood and wanted to see how you were doing?"

"Ooookay. I won't be ready to leave for another four hours yet."

"I have a terrible headache. I didn't get much sleep last night. Do you mind if I stay here and take a nap?"

"Sure, you can use the guest room."

Janice walked out of the room.

Jarrod shouted, "Where are you going?"

Janice wrinkled up her nose. "Uh, upstairs and wherever I want to go in my own house."

"I'll be right down here."

"Okay Jarrod. If you need anything, just yell."

Janice took her envelope and went upstairs. Jarrod heard a car stop on the street in front of Janice's house. He ran to the window and put his hand on his gun that was in his pocket. The car slowly moved, made an illegal U turn and parked directly across from Janice's house. Jarrod looked to see who was in the car. Under his breath he said, "Damn," and quickly dialed Roberto.

"Goode, I need you to come over to Janice's house right away. Desiree is sitting out front."

"I'll be right there."

In 10 minutes, Roberto pulled up behind Desiree. As soon as Desiree saw the police car, she sped away. Jarrod ran outside. "That woman is crazy. Tonight at the book signing, I know I'll have to keep my eye out for her. I'm afraid she's going to hurt Janice."

Roberto wrote down Desiree's tag number on his pad. "Not on my watch Jarrod. Don't worry about a thing. You just don't let Janice out of your sight between now and the book signing and I will take it from there."

Jarrod wiped the sweat from his forehead. "Man, this is stressful." Roberto laughed. "Does Janice know what's going on?"

"No, I haven't told her."

"I guess it's best she doesn't know. Is Paul here yet?"

"No, he's in South Carolina."

"I talked to him about an hour ago. He said he was on his way here."

"Good, maybe he can talk some sense into Janice."

Robert looked puzzled. "What's going on?"

"Brent just asked Janice to marry him and she said yes."

"Man, you must have heard wrong."

"Roberto, I was right here. The woman said yes."

"Well, it looks like I better look out for Brent too because when Paul finds that out, he'll be trying to kill him." Roberto laughed.

Jarrod laughed. "Roberto, I have much respect for your profession, but I think I'll stick to being a chauffer. It's definitely less stressful."

Roberto patted Jarrod on his shoulder. "All right man, I'll see you later."

When Jarrod went back into the house, Janice was already downstairs. "Was that Roberto?"

"Yeah, he was just checking to see what time he should be at Ambiance tonight."

The doorbell rang and Jarrod ran to door and yelled, "I'll get it." He looked at Janice and slowly opened it to the smiling face of Beatrice. Jarrod let out a huge sigh. "Come on in Miss Beatrice."

"Hello Jarrod. Are you Janice's butler now too?"

"No Ma'am. I'm just trying to make her day easier." Jarrod smiled.

"Ma, he's driving me crazy today. Come on in. What brings you by?"

Beatrice smiled and looked at the beautiful roses. "Well, I've come to wish you good luck tonight and to tell you I've read your book. I love it and I know its going to be a best seller—I just know it."

"Thanks Ma. Aren't you coming tonight?"

"No, I can't make it."

"Why not? Are you getting spoiled over there in your new house with your housekeeper and personal chef waiting on you hand and foot?"

Beatrice laughed. "It is nice Janice. I don't have to do a thing, but ask and I receive. My friend and I are going to Las Vegas. That's why I can't make it."

Janice laughed at her mother enjoying her well overdue luxuries. "Are you eloping?"

"Not to my knowledge."

"Okay, you enjoy your trip and be safe."

"I will and you have a wonderful night Janice."

Jarrod ran over to the door. "I'll get it for you Miss Beatrice."

"Thank you Jarrod. You take good care of my Janice."

"I plan to Ma'am."

Janice stood at the bottom of the stairs and looked at Jarrod. "If it's all right with you, I am going upstairs."

"Yes, go. This damn place is like a revolving door. Do you always have this much company?"

"No, I really don't. I guess today is just one of those days. I'll see you in about two hours."

Janice went upstairs and sat down on her bed. She looked at the $300,000 check and held it up in the air. "Wow, see Lainey, I told you it would find its way back to me. It's short $70,000, but at least AJ found it in his heart to return to me the majority of what his brother stole."

Janice laid her head down on her pillow and looked up into the ceiling. She glanced at the ring that was on her finger. "Hmm, Brent has pretty good taste. Not the one I would have picked out, but nonetheless, a very nice ring. I need a nap."

Janice set her alarm to wake up in an hour, but she couldn't sleep. The whole time she thought about her book signing, the miraculous check she received, her sudden engagement to Brent, and how bright her future looked.

"Well, it's time I get gorgeous," Janice said as she jumped out of bed and into the shower.

Thirty minutes later, she was refreshed and on top of the world. "Tonight will be a night that I will never forget and I'm going to look good remembering it all."

Janice put on her makeup, jewelry, her red one armless dress, and her red strapless sandals. "Tonight, I am the lady in red." She sprayed on Knowing, grabbed her purse and walked downstairs.

At the bottom of the stairs was Jarrod with a huge smile on his face.

"Look at Miss Hot Tamale. Girl, you look like you're ready to set them on fire."

"I am." Janice smiled.

"Well, let's not keep them waiting. Your limo waits."

"Limo, I still like the sound of that. Jarrod, hold up for a moment. I just want to tell you I appreciate everything you've done for me. I think of you as my friend. I hope you know that."

"I do."

"I love you Jarrod."

"I love you too girl. Now, let's go."

Almost the entire ride, Janice was on the phone. When Jarrod got to Ambiance, he pulled up so close to the door that if he moved over a few inches, he would be right on the steps. Jarrod got out, stood by Janice's door and wouldn't let her out until he was certain Desiree was nowhere in sight. When he finally opened the door, Janice just stared at him. "For a moment, I thought you weren't going to let me out."

"Sorry about that. My mind was elsewhere. Hurry up and go in."

"Jarrod, remind me to give you some time off."

Jarrod looked to his left and then to his right. "Yeah, I could use it."

Janice walked into Ambiance and smiled at her approaching Assistant. "Hello Antoine. Don't you look nice?"

"So do you Miss Janice. You are really saying something in that red dress."

"Thank you. Is Jasmine here yet?"

"Yeah, she's in your office."

"Great."

Janice and Antoine walked back to her office. "Jasmine, will you please get out of my chair?"

"Hi Mommy. Don't you look like you're about to steal somebody's man."

"Now, here you go. You look nice yourself. Pretty and pink."

"Mommy, what's that on your finger? Did Mr. Davis ask you to marry him?"

Antoine looked at Janice.

"No, Mr. Foster did."

Jasmine looked at Antoine and frowned. "That muscle bound guy that looks like Popeye?"

"Yes, that's him."

Again, Jasmine looked at Antoine. "Oh, what do you want us to do Mommy?"

"Jasmine, I take it you're not happy with my engagement."

"I'm okay with it. I just want you to be happy. Congratulations Mommy."

"Yeah, congratulations Miss Perry."

Janice sat down and looked through some of the papers on her desk.

"Tonight, you two don't have to man the door—people will just come and go. That way, you all can enjoy yourselves. If I run low on books, I'll just need for you to bring out more."

"That's all? All right, we can get our drink on tonight Antoine."

Janice gave her daughter the mother's eye. "Jasmine, don't you and Antoine get drunk and act like fools out there."

"Mommy, I can't believe you said that."

Janice didn't hear what Jasmine said because she was reading the letter Antoine placed on her desk earlier. She looked at her ring and smiled. "Antoine, is Roberto here yet?"

"Yes Miss Perry. I saw him in the ballroom."

"Great, I need to speak to him. People should be coming in now. You two enjoy yourselves, but not too much."

In unison, Jasmine and Antoine both said, "We will."

Janice left her office in search of Roberto. She found him at the door with two other officers. "Hey Roberto."

"Hey Janice."

"I heard you were by my house today."

"Uh, yeah, I was in the neighborhood."

Janice handed him an envelope. "Is Dee on her way?"

"Yeah, she should be here in an hour. When I left, she was putting on her makeup."

"I'm really glad you two found each other."

"So am I. We're happy and we plan to make it official."

Janice put both of her hands over her mouth. "Roberto, did you?"

"No, not yet, but I'm going to."

Roberto pulled out a ring from his pocket. "Do you think she will like this?"

"I don't think—I know she'll love it."

Roberto pointed to the ring on Janice's finger. "As much as you love your ring?"

"No, she'll love hers more. "I'm so happy for you two." Janice hugged Roberto.

"Thanks, I know you'll be happy too."

Janice nodded.

Roberto held up the envelope. "Let me go take care of this."

People began to fill up the ballroom. Janice placed her new book in the showcase cabinet in the lobby across from her first book. Posters of her new book were hung all throughout Ambiance. A table on the side opposite from the food table was set up for Janice to sign her books for a two-hour period.

Chester tapped Janice on her shoulder. "Hey Sis."

"Chester, you made it."

"I wouldn't have missed it for the world. Man, it's a lot of people in here. Looks like another success."

Janice looked around the ballroom. "I know, isn't it great?"

"I'm proud of you Big Sis."

"Thank you Little Brother."

"I always thought you had your head in the clouds. It's good that you can make money off of it by putting it down on paper."

"Thank you, I think." Janice laughed.

"I'm just kidding. I finished reading your book last night. It was really good." Chester looked around the beautifully decorated, packed ballroom and nodded. "Lainey would be proud too."

A tear slid down Janice's cheek. "You think so?"

Chester hugged his sister and said, "I know so."

Brent walked up and looked at Janice in the arms of a man unknown to him. "There you are."

Janice turned around and wiped her eyes. "Hi Brent, I want you to meet my little brother, Chester. Chester, this is Brent."

Brent cleared his throat. "Pleased to meet you."

He put his arms around Janice's shoulder and whispered into her ear, "Did you tell him yet?"

"Not yet, later."

Chester looked puzzled and asked Janice, "Tell me what?"

Janice moved away from Brent's hold. In Chester's ear, she said, "I'll tell you later."

Janice heard her author friend begin to speak and made her way to the front of the ballroom.

"This is a powerful, eye opening, faith and thought provoking dramatic love novel that I know you all can't wait to get your hands on. Without further delay, it is my pleasure to introduce to you my friend and the next best selling author, Janice Perry. For the next two hours, she will personally autograph your book. So, line up and get them while they last."

For the next two hours, Janice sat at the decorated table and talked, laughed, and signed two hundred copies of her first novel. It was like a dream come true. Janice beamed with joy. As Jazz played throughout the ballroom, some people mingled, some ate, and others talked and laughed while the rest waited patiently in line to have their books signed.

Janice signed so many books that her hands began to cramp. Jasmine placed a glass of Chardonnay in front of her mother. "Here Mommy. I thought you could use this."

"Thank you sweetie. My throat was getting a little dry."

Jasmine pulled up a chair and sat beside her mother. "How much longer?"

"Five more minutes and then I can get my drink on."

Jasmine laughed at her mother doing one of her old dance moves in her chair.

"It turned out really nice, didn't it Mommy?"

"I couldn't be happier."

Janice looked around the room at all of the people. The book signing was everything she wanted it to be yet something was missing. Jarrod whispered into Janice's ear, "What's the sour look all about?"

"What sour look?" Janice smiled.

"The look on your face that said he didn't come."

"Jarrod, don't you have someone else to harass."

"Nope."

Janice stood up.

"Where are you going?"

"Jarrod, I am going over to the bar. When I get there, I am going to get another drink and celebrate. Is that okay with you?"

"Yeah, but I can get it for you."

"You know, you have been hovering over me all day. What is with you? No, I've been sitting here for two straight hours. I need to stretch my legs."

"Yes Boss Lady."

Jarrod kept his eyes on Janice. When she got half way to the bar, he waved to Roberto to let him know she was coming his way.

After being stopped several times by people congratulating her, Janice finally made it to the bar. She took a quick sip of her wine and tried to make her way through the crowd to where Dee stood, but an old colleague stopped her in front of the double doors in the back of the ballroom.

"Janice, your book is outstanding."

"Thank you Mr. Thomas."

Mr. Thomas put his arms around Janice's shoulder. "Everyone, please gather around for a well deserving toast. Raise your glasses to Janice Perry, our next . . ."

Out of nowhere, someone shot a gun. Brent flew across the room and knocked Janice and Mr. Thomas to the floor. People ran, screamed and looked for cover. A loud scream from the far corner overpowered everyone else's screams. "No! No! Not my baby."

Desiree slowly came into full view with the gun pointed directly at Paul. Shocked, that his very pregnant daughter was shot in the chest and lying in a pool of blood on the floor, Paul stood frozen.

"Looked what you've made be do," Desiree yelled.

Paul slowly turned around.

Tears streamed down Desiree's face. "Oh my God, what have I done? My baby. I'm sorry Cynthia. Hang on, please hang on. You're going to be all right. My grandson is going to be all right too. I just have to take care of something and I'll get you to the hospital. Oh no, no."

Desiree yelled when Paul kneeled down beside Cynthia. "Stand up. Don't you touch her."

Paul stood back up.

"This is all your fault. I didn't mean to shoot my baby. I was trying to shoot that bitch. Janice, get out here right now. You have until I count to three or Paul goes next."

Janice tried to get up, but Brent held her tightly down on the floor.

Desiree briefly looked around the room for Janice. When she didn't see her, her eyes once again rested on Paul. "You took everything away from me. You took my houses, my family, my money, and now you've taken my baby away from me. You are just like your brother, always meddling in my damn life. I killed him and now I'm going to kill you!"

Desiree was about to pull the trigger when Roberto shot her two times in the chest. Desiree fell to floor and died instantly.

Janice stood up and was shocked to see what happened. She didn't even know Paul, Desiree or his daughter was there. With tears in her eyes, Janice looked at Paul on his knees holding his daughter. She listened to him as he talked to Cynthia. "Baby Girl, what were you doing here?"

Cynthia could barely speak. "To warn you about Mother. Daddy, take care of my baby."

"No Baby Girl, you just hold on. Everything will be fine and you will take care of your own baby."

Cynthia gave Paul a weak smile. "I'm still your baby girl?"

"Always."

Cynthia whispered, "I'm sorry Daddy. I love you," and closed her eyes.

Paul yelled, "Cynthia, Cynthia," but she didn't answer.

The paramedics rushed in and Paul yelled at them. "Take her, take her now. This can't be happening. Not my baby girl and my grandchild. God, do you hate me that much to do this to me again? You took Chester when you should have taken me. Please don't take them. This time, take me. Take me!"

With tears in his eyes, Paul stood up and looked over at Brent holding Desiree in his arms.

Brent was on his knees. He rocked Desiree back and forth and cried out, "Diva, what did you do that for? You shot our daughter. You stupid, stupid woman. I was just doing this for us. It's always been you and me. Why didn't you just let me handle it? Did you really think I could love anyone but you? Oh Diva. What am I going to do without you?"

Janice turned around and looked at Paul with tears in his eyes and still unable to move. She ran over to Paul and hugged him around the waist and Paul held on to her tightly. He kissed her on top of her head and asked, "Are you all right Janice?"

"I will be."

"Thank God you're all right. I just walked in the door about five minutes before the shot went off. I didn't even know Cynthia was here until Brent pushed you out of the way and I saw her lying on the floor. She was standing behind you Janice."

Janice began to cry. "That bullet was meant for me?"

"Yes, I know. When I heard what Desiree was up to, I tried to get here earlier, but my plane was delayed."

"You knew?"

"Yeah, I have to go to the hospital."

"I'll go with you."

Brent stood in front of Paul and Janice and looked at the two in each other's arms. "Janice, you're my fiancée now and you're not going anywhere."

Roberto stepped in front of Brent. "And neither are you. Brent Foster, you're under arrest."

"Hey man, I had nothing to do with this. This was all Desiree."

"Oh, I know." Roberto handcuffed Brent.

"Then why are you arresting me?"

"Other than me loathing you, I'm arresting you for 10 counts of tax evasion, 20 counts of fraud and five counts of severe arrearages on your child support payments. For years, it seems that five very angry women have been looking for you. Shame on you for not taking care of your five kids."

"Brent, is this true?"

Brent looked at Janice and laughed. "What can I say? I love women and the women love me."

"Let's go lover." Roberto tightened Brent's handcuffs.

"Ouch!" I'm going to sue you and the whole damn police department. I'm suing you too Janice for breach of promise. Davis, you haven't heard the last of me.

In tears, Jasmine ran over to her mother and held her tightly. "Mommy, are you all right?"

Antoine, Dee, Chester, Jarrod, Dante, and Kim also ran up and huddled around Paul and Janice.

With tears in his eyes, Dante immediately hugged his father. "Dad, Cynthia . . ."

"I know Son."

"Are you all right?" Dante asked.

"I'm okay, but I have to get to the hospital."

Paul let go of Dante and looked at the crowd that stared at him and Janice. "We are both all right, but we have to get to the hospital."

Paul took Janice by the hand.

Jarrod wiped his forehead. "Come on, I'll drive you."

Janice and Paul got into the limo. Paul kept his arms tightly wrapped around Janice. He looked at the ring on her finger and asked, "You were engaged to Brent?"

Janice held up her finger. "This old thing? It was the only way to keep you safe."

"Me safe? I thought I was keeping you safe."

Jarrod yelled out. "Yeah, and for the last six months, it was a hard job trying to keep her stubborn butt safe while she was out chasing June Bug and them."

Janice waved her hand at Jarrod. "Paul, do you remember the day Jarrod took us for a ride?"

Paul said, "Yes."

"Later, I went back to your office and Desiree caught me in the lobby. She threatened me with a gun. She told me to leave you alone or she would kill you and me."

"Janice, why didn't you tell me?"

Janice looked down in her lap and shook her head. "Many times, I wanted to tell you, but you would have put her in jail."

"You damn right I would have put her ass in jail."

"I know. That's why I couldn't tell you. She said if you ever tried to put her in jail that she would kill you and it would be my fault. I couldn't let that happen. So, I stayed away from you and decided if I looked like I was involved with Brent, maybe she would leave us both alone. I didn't know that she was in love with him." Janice cried.

Paul pulled Janice closer to him. "I know you didn't. Those two had a long history together."

Janice wiped her eyes and nodded. "Do you think that's why she wanted to kill me tonight?"

"I think that was part of it. For months, Desiree tried to get back what she lost and when she couldn't, I guess she just snapped. You were another person she thought took something away from her."

Paul let out a deep breath and laid his head back on the seat. "I can't believe you went through all of this alone and for me. You are one strong and brave lady. I had no idea all of this was going on. When you stayed away and didn't return any of my calls, I just assumed you didn't love me."

"Paul, I've never stopped loving you. Do you remember the day you came to my office and told me I was stupid for dealing with Brent?"

Paul chuckled. "Sorry about that."

"Well, I ran a background check on him and found out all of that stuff. Then, I called Roberto."

"So, you were the one that got him arrested?"

"I knew Brent was just after what he thought I had. He had money of his own, cars, houses, businesses, and hid it all from everyone, including his five baby mamas. Let's just say the kids will have an early Christmas this year."

Paul laughed. "You are something else. I'm glad you were on my side."

"Paul, I was never with Brent, not like that. I was shocked when he showed up at my door with your roses in hand and a ring ready to propose to me. I had to say yes to make sure he came tonight so Roberto could arrest him."

Again, Jarrod yelled out, "When she said yes, I was ready to kill her."

"Shut up Jarrod," Janice said.

"Baby, how did you know the roses were from me?"

"You send me the same two dozen roses and one white rose for every occasion."

"I guess I do. I have to remember to change that. Brent must have thought what I've always known that your business and your book were going to be a big success."

Paul took Brent's ring off of Janice's finger and tossed it to Jarrod. He hugged Janice even tighter and said, "Wow, I love you Janice. You are indeed my Wow Woman."

"I love you too. And you Paul are indeed my Wow Man."

Jarrod looked in his rear view mirror and smiled at Janice and Paul's long awaited kiss. "Ah, and you two are indeed my Wow People."

Both Janice and Paul said, "Shut up Jarrod."

When Jarrod pulled the limo in front of the hospital emergency room, under his breath he said, "Damn shame that innocent girl and her baby have to pay the price for her crazy mother's rage."

Janice let out a deep breath. She couldn't help but wonder what heartache they would soon face on the inside. She squeezed Paul's hand and looked at him. "I gotcha."

Paul kissed her on the cheek and said, "And, I got you."

Again, Jarrod looked in the rear view mirror. "I'm so happy to see both of you finally together again and unharmed. I'll say a prayer for Cynthia and her baby."

"Thanks Jarrod," Paul said.

Janice and Paul got out of the limo and walked through the emergency room doors. Janice held on to Paul's hand and silently said a prayer for Cynthia, her baby, Paul, and herself.

92

One Year Later

One year later, without a cloud in sight, the sun shined brightly in the sky. Janice turned to her daughter. "Natalie, I have dreamed about this day for so long, I can hardly believe it's finally here."

"Ma, you look beautiful."

"Thank you and so do you. I'm so happy you and the girls are with me today. Are Kayla and Taylor ready?"

Natalie looked at her very energetic daughters. "As ready as they're going to get. I'm trying to keep them both calm and clean, which is hard to do with white, white, and more white. They keep stomping on the A in the circle."

"They'll be fine. We only have 20 more minutes to go."

Jasmine waited patiently until Natalie and her mother finished talking.

Mommy, you look all right."

"All right?"

"I'm just kidding. You look beautiful Mommy."

"Thank you. You don't look so bad yourself."

"Mommy, you know I look good."

"You know you look beautiful sweetie."

Jasmine looked in the mirror and admired her dress. "That's more like it."

Janice shook her head at her baby girl. "Jasmine, are people starting to arrive?

"Yeah, the place is packed."

Janice looked around the room and asked, "Where is Layla?"

"I'm right here," Layla said as she entered the room.

Janice stood up and smiled. "Look at you. You look almost as beautiful as I do."

Layla laughed. "Has anyone seen Reginald?"

Janice said, "I believe he's with Jarrod."

"He is definitely not with Jarrod, because I'm right here."

Janice smiled at her dear friend.

Jarrod walked over to Janice and gave her a big bear hug. "I hope this will be the last time I chauffer your stubborn butt around."

"Oh Jarrod, you will always be my personal chauffer."

"No thank you. I've had enough of you and that. These days, I just sit behind the desk and in the backseat. I have to tell you, running a chauffer business is an entirely different ballgame, but I do love it."

"I'm glad you're enjoying your career of leisure."

"Janice, how do you like it in South Carolina?"

"We love it there. Natalie and the girls are close by."

"Word on the street says Ambiance II is a hit."

"Isn't it something? We just opened six months ago. We mostly work from home, but it's located just a few hundred feet from the house. Natalie had two of her concerts there and they were both sold out."

"That's nice. Natalie and Jasmine are like day and night. I go over to Ambiance about two days out of the week. Kim and Antoine are doing a great job. I don't see Jasmine there at all."

"Okay Jarrod, you know I got my design business. I'm there when they need me." Jasmine tapped Jarrod on his head.

"Girl, go somewhere."

Jarrod waved his hand at Audrey as she came towards him. "Janice, you remember my wife?"

"Of course I do. Hello Audrey."

"Hi Janice. Thanks for inviting me."

"You are very welcome. I know Jarrod is working today, but I hoped my invitation gave you a reason to spend some of old tightwad's money."

Audrey laughed. "Lately, my sweetie has been spending a lot of money and he has been spending it on me."

Audrey extended her left hand towards Janice and wiggled her fingers. "Isn't it gorgeous?"

Janice almost choked when she saw it was the two-carat diamond ring Brent gave her a year ago. She briefly looked away and tried not to laugh as she said, "It's beautiful Audrey. Your Jarrod is a real big spender."

With one of his hands, Jarrod covered his face. Audrey smiled with joy and said, "Thanks again Janice. I guess the next time I see you, you'll be walking down the aisle."

"That's right." Janice smiled.

Jarrod walked behind Audrey to the door and tried to hold back his laugh. "Honey, get us a seat. I'll be right out."

When Jarrod closed the door and turned around, he laughed so hard, he couldn't stop. Janice placed her hands on her hips and shook her finger. "Jarrod, don't tell me you gave that ring to your wife and pretended that you bought it."

"I sure did. Did you want it back?" Jarrod wiped his eyes.

"No." Janice laughed.

"All right then. It didn't make much sense to let a perfectly good ring go to waste."

"Brent could have used that ring to help with his child support payments."

"I doubt it. Audrey took it to the jewelers to get it sized and while she was there, she got it appraised because she was sure I spent too much. Your two-carat diamond ring turned out to be a fake like Brent."

"You're kidding."

"Nope, the jeweler said it was a very nice Cubic Zirconia."

"What did Audrey say?" Janice laughed.

"Nothing. She loved it as if it was the real thing."

"Jarrod, you are one lucky man."

"I know. I'll see you later."

"Hey girl," Dee said as she walked through the many people around Janice.

"Dee, it's about time you got in here."

"My man didn't want to let me go."

"How is Roberto?"

"He's wonderful. Dee showed Janice her two-carat round diamond ring. He's out there with the guys. Hey Janice, since we couldn't have September 24th as our wedding day, can we have a date next month?"

"Will you be ready by then?"

"Girl, just give us a date and we'll be ready."

Janice laughed. "I'll have to check Ambiance's calendar. You know Kim and Dante are getting married next month too, but we'll squeeze you and Roberto in somewhere."

For a moment, Dee just stared at Janice. "Girl, you look absolutely beautiful and you're even glowing. I'm so happy for you. I'm so happy for you and Paul."

Janice hugged her best friend. "I told you one day you would be happy for us."

"Yeah, you did and I thought you were crazy too."

Dee laughed. "Where is your Wow Man?"

"I think he's with Dante, going over DAP's business."

"Davis and Perry. You did good Janice. Dee looked around at the other ladies in the room. "You all are so pretty. Natalie, girl, come over here. I haven't seen you in a month of Sundays. How is your singing career going?"

"Great, I have a concert next week."

"How do you like it in South Carolina?"

Natalie looked over at her mother. "I love it now."

Dee smiled and stood up. "Okay Janice, I'll see you in a bit. It looks like you have a line waiting for you."

Beatrice and Chester walked in. Beatrice beamed with joy as she hugged her daughter, her granddaughters and her great granddaughters. "You all are so beautiful."

Janice turned around to look at her mother. "Thank you Ma."

Jasmine and Natalie said, "Thank you Grandma."

Chester smiled at all of the women in the room. "Yeah, all of them are beautiful except for old Janice."

"Whatever Chester."

"Hey Big Sis." Chester hugged Janice. "I hate to admit it, but you do look beautiful. It seems the good life has been agreeing with you."

"Seems like something is agreeing with you. How do you like working with Dante over at DAP Graphics?"

"Love it. Dante fired that nosey Vivian and we hired two new assistants—young, nice looking and hardworking young ladies."

"Good to hear."

"Janice, are you ready for this?"

"I've been ready for a long time."

Travis, Alicia and Little Travis walked in. Travis hugged his aunt and said, "Hey Auntie, you remember Alicia, don't you?"

"Yes, hi Alicia. How are you?"

"I'll be fine if I can keep Little Travis from taking the flowers out of the baskets," Alicia said.

Chester laughed. "Maybe he wants to be a flower girl."

Travis pretended to punch Chester. Janice tried not to laugh at her little brother, but couldn't help herself. "Chester, you have no sense at all."

"The ladies don't think so."

"Well, I've seen the ladies you go out with and that don't say much."

"Janice, because this is your dream day, I will let you have that one."

Chester turned his back to Janice and faced Travis. "When are you and Alicia going to make that move?"

Travis looked at Alicia running after Little Travis. "Soon, I've been so busy with Elaine's, Alicia and Little Travis barely sees me. Auntie has been keeping me really busy."

Janice tried to speak to Travis, but Chester stood in her view. "Move Chester. Travis, I wish your mother was here to see you, a big time chef owning the famous Elaine's Restaurant. She would be so proud of you."

Janice reached down to stop Little Travis from taking another flower out of the basket, but missed him. "I know she would be one of those grandmothers that wouldn't let anyone get near little Travis. I miss her and I wish . . ."

A tear slid down Janice's cheek.

"Me too Auntie, but Ma is with us today. I can feel her watching down on all of us."

Victoria, Katrina and Kristina walked in. "Janice, I'm so glad you invited us," Victoria said.

"Of course I would invite you and the girls. I'm so happy you all came."

"How do you like living at the Paulster."

"We love it. It's beautiful and plenty of room for us. Oh, I almost forgot, Sarah told me to tell you hi."

"When you get back, tell her I have a new recipe for her."

Victoria looked around the room. "Oh, everybody looks so pretty and you look like the answer to Paul's prayers. If Chester were here, he would be so proud that Paul finally found true happiness."

"Thank you Victoria. This is my brother Chester."

Victoria smiled and put both of her hands on Chester's face. "My Chester was a good man and I'm sure you too are a good man."

Janice smiled at her little brother. "He tries to be."

The wedding planner yelled, "If you are not a part of the wedding party, I need for you to please leave now and take your seats."

Janice looked around at everyone. "I guess it's show time. With tears of joy in her eyes, she looked back at the wedding party. Janice had never seen a more beautiful sight than the people she loved all standing in line beautifully and handsomely dressed as they happily waited for their cue to walk down the aisle.

The four bridesmaids wore a long and straight sleeveless v-neck dress with a black silk base covered with sequins that sparkled under the dim lights. The maid of honor wore a long and straight one-arm dress also with a black silk base covered with sequins. Each bridesmaid and the maid of honor wore a pair of slim, single strand long diamond earrings, black strapless patent leather sandals and carried a bouquet of deep red roses.

Each of the four groomsmen wore a black Tuxedo. The best man also wore a black Tuxedo that was slightly different from the groomsmen. All wore a black bowtie around the necks of their crisp white shirts held together at the wrist with platinum cufflinks. Each groomsman wore a single red rose on their lapels while the best man wore a single white rose on his lapel.

The two flower girls both resembled a miniature bride, each wearing a no sleeve white sequined ball dress with pearls in their ears and baby's breaths placed throughout their curls. The two ring bearers were as handsome as their fathers and looked like mini groomsmen that were totally unaware of their role in the wedding.

The music began to play and it was time for the mother and father of the bride to walk down the aisle. Next, it was time for the mother and father of the groom to walk down the aisle. Janice and Paul proudly walked out arm in arm followed by Jasmine and Antoine, Natalie and Brandon, Kim and Dante, Alicia and Travis and the maid of honor, Justine Turner who was a beautiful model. Paul, Jr., who just turned one year old, flew down the aisle like a little bullet, ran right to Paul and would not budge. Little Travis who was a year older than Paul, Jr., held on to his pillow, walked down the aisle like a pro and stood next to his father. Kayla and Taylor slowly made their way down the aisle and giggled as they threw what little flowers they had left.

The music stopped and after a few moments, then resumed. All of the guests stood up and watched the beautiful bride, Layla as she made her way down the aisle in her white sequined, straight fitting gown with one arm holding tightly to her father and the other holding her bouquet of deep red roses with two white roses in the middle. Layla had tears in her eyes as she looked straight ahead and saw no one but Reginald who looked as handsome as ever in his black Tuxedo, crisp white shirt and white bowtie. Reginald nervously stood beside his best man, Chester. When Layla reached Reginald, both smiled at each other and the crowd sat down.

Janice sat in the front row and smiled. Every minute, she dabbed her eyes dry as she looked at her oldest son and her soon to be daughter-in-law. Janice thought about how blessed Layla and Reginald are to have found each other and the glorious and not so glorious moments of life that were ahead for them. As Natalie and Brandon sang, "You're the One for Me," a song by Smokey Robinson and Josh Stone, Janice and Paul looked at one another.

Janice thought about how blessed she and Paul are to have found each other at a time in their lives when most people would have thought it was too late in life to start over again. Janice also thought about the loss of her sister, the journey of woe after woe she and Paul went through and to finally get to a place where she is still sane, still loved by Paul and together sharing this wonderful moment with him and all of their family and friends. Janice closed her eyes and under her breath said, "Wow, thank you God. I have finally found true happiness."

Janice remembered what Paul told her just last night. "He was blessed that he and Janice found each other, especially when he resisted starting over and gave up on a life of happiness. Losing his brother, losing his daughter twice, the journey of woe after woe he and Janice went through and to finally get to a place where he is still sane, still loved by Janice and given the opportunity to put all of his love for Cynthia into Paul, Jr., he was thankful and sure that God didn't hate him, but always loved him.

Janice looked at Paul whisper into Paul, Jr.'s ear. "Wow, this is our family. Thank you God. Just as Chester said, I have finally found true happiness."

Again, Janice had tears in her eyes as she listened to Paul and looked at her grown and handsome son on the alter marrying the woman of his dreams just as she married the man of her dreams. Janice smiled at Paul, Jr. who looked more and more like Cynthia every day. She smiled at Paul who looked as handsome as the day she met him. She then looked at the wedding party who was now all her family except for the maid of honor who was Layla's best friend.

Again, Paul whispered in Paul Jr.'s ear, "See Paul, Reginald is marrying the woman of his dreams just like I married the woman of my dreams."

Janice smiled at Paul and Paul, Jr.

Paul looked at the entire wedding party from left to right and chuckled when the beautiful model Justine winked at him. He smiled at Janice and their eyes locked.

Paul put his right arm around Janice and gently squeezed her shoulder. With Paul, Jr. in one arm and Janice in the other, Paul whispered into Janice's ear, "At times, the grass may look greener on the other side, but when my heart found Wow, it went through woe after woe just to get to the one and only side to be with you Mrs. Davis.

THE END